The Woodhead Diaries

Dave Cherry

Copyright © 2014 Dave Cherry
07766920159
All rights reserved.

ISBN-13:
978-1497581517
ISBN-10:
1497581516
The Woodhead Diaries
'The Tunnel of Hell'

©davecherry 07766920159

The Woodhead Diaries
By Dave Cherry

This book is a work of fiction. Names, characters, businesses, organizations, places, events, and incidents either are the product of the author's imagination or are used fictitiously. Any resemblance to actual persons, living or dead, events, or locales is entirely coincidental.

ACKNOWLEDGEMENTS

This book would not have been possible without the support and encouragement of my wife Sandra.

Words cannot express my gratitude to her, especially while we were on holiday and she was very ill.

Special thanks are due to Anne Grange from Wild Rosemary Writing Services for her professional advice and assistance in polishing this manuscript. Being a simple Barnsley lad who never understood punctuation and grammar, she has brought the story to life.

Special thanks are also due to Geoff Briggs, the Core Project Manager of Writing Yorkshire, which develops writers from Yorkshire. Geoff pointed me in the direction of Anne.

I would like to express my deepest gratitude to my son Simon in New Zealand, who explained the rudiments of Three Card Brag, and rewrote the card game chapter.

Many thanks to my niece Holly Jones who resembles Sergeant Susan Priestley, and posed for the wonderful cover photographs, taken by my old friend John Timmis. Also my niece, Chloe Mann, deserves a special mention for her logo design.

I would also like to refer to the readers an excellent reference book, 'The Railway Navvies' by Terry Coleman, which gave me the idea for this novel.

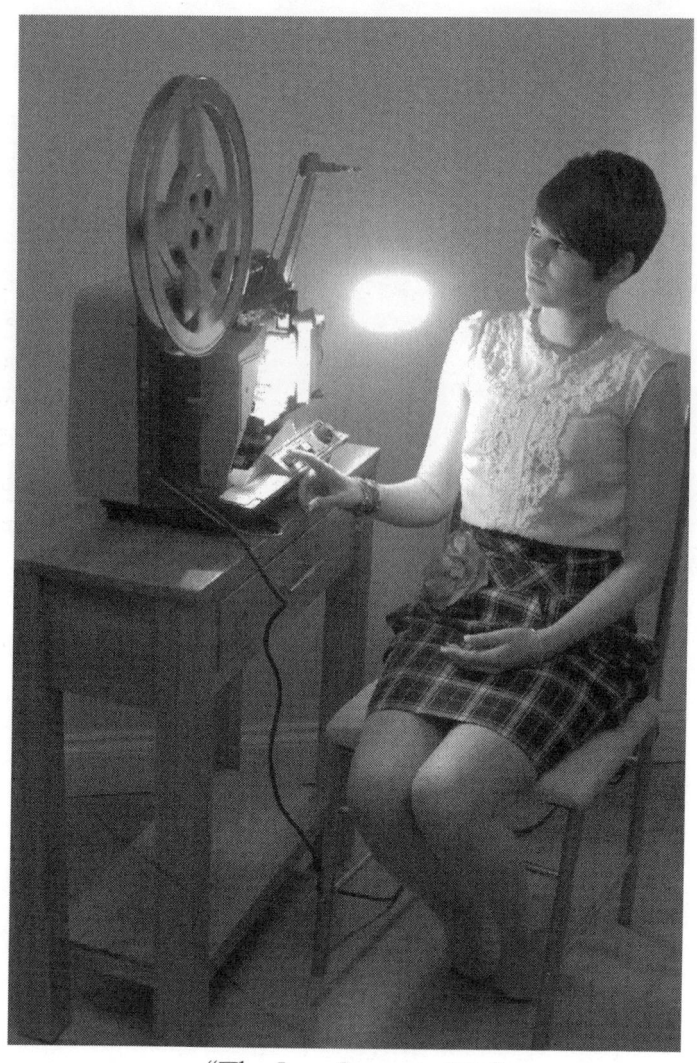

"The Lass Starts to Dig"

THE WOODHEAD DIARIES
PART ONE

SKELETONS IN THE SHAFT

'You will not apply my precept,' he said, shaking his head. 'How often have I said to you that when you have eliminated the impossible, whatever remains, *however improbable*, must be the truth? We know that he did not come through the door, the window, or the chimney. We also know that he could not have been concealed in the room, as there is no concealment possible. When, then, did he come?'

Sir Arthur Conan Doyle, *The Sign of Four* (Sherlock Holmes), 1890.

Foreword

Woodhead is a desolate place on the summit of the Pennine moors, commonly known as the "backbone of England". It is now a small hamlet of about two hundred and fifty people, on a narrow peninsula of Cheshire, which reaches out eastward through Lancashire and Derbyshire, into Yorkshire.

The remains of the railway and the tunnels that were bored into the Pennine rock can still be seen from the busy A628 Trans Pennine road. No one today can ever imagine the death and suffering caused when the tunnels were driven.

The story of Woodhead is the most degraded adventure, filled with stories of heroism, savagery, magnificent profits, and devout hypocrisy.

The great Railway engineer George Stephenson said 'the tunnels would be impossible to build and he would eat the first locomotive to go through the tunnel.'

At its highest point, the moor above Woodhead is 1,500 feet above sea level. It is halfway between Sheffield and Manchester and, although hazardous, it was considered that digging tunnels through the moor was the easiest way to build a railway line to link the two cities.

There have been three railway tunnels through Woodhead. The first one was a single track, taking from 1839 to 1845 to dig. A second was driven alongside the first track between 1847 and 1852. The third was built for a double electric line, completed in 1954. The first tunnel was three miles and thirteen yards long.

The Sheffield, Ashton-under Lyne and Manchester Railway Company was formed in 1835 and an Act of Parliament was passed in 1837 to authorize it. The original estimated cost of £60,000 spiralled to over £200,000 before completion.

The navigators or 'navvies' who constructed the tunnels were from the labouring classes. Predominately Irish, but many were from England and Scotland as well.

At its peak, some 1,500 men were constructing the tunnel. They took to building primitive huts, which held ten to fourteen lodgers. Some of the men brought their wives or mistresses with them, who were called 'tally-women'. These women looked after the huts.

The workers were paid every nine weeks. They lived in appalling conditions in shanty towns, in the most inhospitable place in England.

The casualty and death rate among the navvies was horrific. No accurate figures can be found for fatalities but soon the desolate moorland churches were busy with funerals. Accidents, cholera, and disease accounted for many of the Woodhead deaths. The House of Commons Select Committee of 1846 investigated the deaths, and wretched lives of the navvies, but chose to ignore the evidence.

The first tunnel was driven by sinking five shafts. Each of these was five hundred feet deep, and ten feet in diameter. The main tunnel was driven from the base of the shafts. It was fifteen feet high, and eighteen feet across.

The remoteness of the place caused great difficulties. The tunnel was nine miles distant from both Glossop, on the western side, and Penistone on the eastern side. Provisions had to be lugged up the steep hills, to the navvy camps around the five shafts.

Little wonder then that Henry Pomfret, a surgeon, who was paid by the navvies from their wages, described the camps to be in a 'brutish state and the set of people were thoroughly depraved, degraded, reckless, drunken, and dissolute'.

The Victorian Establishment had been shaken to its foundations by the Huskar Coal Mine tragedy of 1838. Twenty six children had been drowned in the Silkstone Common Colliery, just ten miles from the Woodhead Tunnel. The 1842 Mines and Collieries Royal Commission resulted in the banning of woman and child labour from working underground.

However, all this made little difference to the Woodhead railway directors. They were oblivious to the conditions at their sites, and were driven by the illusions of profit and avarice.

Prologue
January 1953

Winston Spencer Churchill doffed his Havana cigar, and put on his tortoiseshell-rimmed glasses.

'Chief Inspector Columbine and Sergeant Priestley,' he said, glancing at his notes to check if he had got his visitors' names correct. He peered over his glasses, pointed to the bound report, and continued. 'This is the most fascinating thing I have ever read. Agatha Christie, or indeed Conan Doyle, are not anywhere in this league. You have a copy, I take it, David?' He glanced at his Home Secretary, Sir David Maxwell Fyfe, who nodded.

The indomitable war leader was back in government. And he'd been presented with a very unusual problem by these police officers from the West Riding of Yorkshire, who were now sitting opposite his desk in the Prime Minister's private office at Number Ten Downing Street.

'Did you know that this physician, Harold Thompson, saw my father Lord Randolph just before he died?' He shook his massive head solemnly.

'This could rock the whole Establishment. This news could be rather embarrassing for our new Queen.' The Prime Minister spoke his thoughts aloud.

He sat in deep thought for a whole minute, as his three visitors waited patiently for him to continue.

'I need to deliberate further on these difficult matters,' Churchill said. 'I must say, Sergeant,' he smiled at the young, pretty Yorkshire girl. 'You have given me plenty to think about.

'I can see that I will have to contact my old friend, and indeed adversary, Mr Éamon de Valera, the Taoiseach of the Irish Republic, for his views.'

He cleared his throat. 'Time is of the essence,' he concluded. 'We certainly do not want this out in the press. The Home Secretary here will contact you with further details. Come back in two days. I bid you both good day.'

CHAPTER ONE
July 1952
The Tunneller

Peter Woodcock had his mind elsewhere. He was thinking about his army days. He had fought at the Battle of *El Alemein* in 1942. They had just been talking about it at snap time. He had served in the Eighth army, in the war, and he had driven a tank in the desert.

He had been one of Montgomery's 'Desert Rats'. He recalled the heat and the stifling conditions inside the tank. Ten years later, it was just the opposite here in this cold, wet tunnel. He was working as a tunnel driver with the civil engineering company Balfour Beatty, constructing the new Woodhead Tunnel.

Peter had been demobbed after the war, and he had returned to his home town of Barnsley, in the West Riding of Yorkshire. Like most of the male population there, he had worked in the collieries, but chasing more money for his wife and family, he had come to Woodhead for the superior civil engineering wages.

A shaft, sixteen feet in diameter, had been driven down four hundred and sixty seven feet from the Pennine Moors, and now they were fanning out, making the tunnel. They had advanced over five hundred yards eastward, using modern machines to get the dirt and rubble out.

The shaft work had been slow and laborious. It had been dug by hand, just like the old shafts driven in 1840, one hundred and twelve years previously. They could make some progress now they were using mechanised equipment, Peter thought. They might earn some bonus.

The air borers had driven into the Pennine rock, and then the dirt had been blasted out by shot firing. Pete was operating a rail-mounted compressed air bucket, which tipped the muck into mine cars. His twin brother Dave was at his side, giving hand signals that told him where to empty the bucket.

It's a funny old world, thought Pete. In the desert, he'd thought that the Germans had been defeated. He had also been in Germany at the end of the war, and had seen some of the concentration camps. He would never forget that.

The irony was in front of him. The *Eicoff* shovel he was using was bloody German, and it had a lot of German writing on the pneumatic control levers.

In his experience, '*Achtung*' seemed to be the most common word in German. It was written on this machine. The same word had been used at the Bergen-Belsen, a concentration camp which they had liberated in 1945.

It also said: '*Diese Maschine Funktioniert Besser in Den Trockenen Bedingungen.*' What a joke, thought Pete: '*This Machine Works Better in Dry Conditions.*'

There are no dry conditions here, he thought wryly. Water was a big problem. They had to keep stopping work, to pump it out. He dismissed it from his mind and carried on tipping the muck into the mine cars.

Pete knew they were driving near one of the old Victorian shafts that had been filled in over a hundred years ago. One of the surveyors had warned him that it was just a couple of yards to the right of the heading. Today, they were doing well. They had been filling out a good two hours.

Dave held up his hand for him to stop. Pete halted the machine. As the dust began to clear, he looked to where Dave was pointing. On the right-hand side of the tunnel, they could clearly see the bottom of an old Victorian air shaft. It had been filled in, but a large boulder and some old railway sleepers were wedged a few feet from the bottom. The men shone their cap lamps into the cavity.

Pete was thinking that somebody must have made an almighty cock-up of the survey calculations, when his brother interrupted his contemplations.

'There are some old rags there – something's gleaming!' Dave exclaimed.

He grabbed a boring drill bit and managed to poke it into the cavity to turn the rags over.

'Bloody hell, it's a skeleton,' he shouted. 'The gleaming. It's a ring on one of the fingers. Stop the job! Get on the phone to the surface. We've got a body here.'

CHAPTER TWO
The Female Copper

'So children, have you got any questions?' CID Sergeant Susan Priestley asked the three hundred children sitting in front of her. She was at Penistone Springvale Primary School.

The 16mm cine film had just finished, and the noisy *Bell and Howell* projector clattered to an end. The distorted soundtrack concluded, and the single fifteen-inch loudspeaker, housed in a wooden case, fell silent.

The CID Sergeant and Detective Inspector Andrew Monroe had just shown a film on Road Courtesy. She knew what was coming next. The children had remained quiet while the twenty minute film was being shown in the school hall but she knew that they now were bored out of their minds.

Susan Priestley was a rare breed. She was a Sergeant in the West Riding Police. Not many women were promoted in this predominantly male profession, but she fitted in well with her colleagues.

Sergeant Priestley was an asset to the police. Her lively personality dispelled the old *Mr Plod* vision of the English bobby. Tall and attractive, she wore her dark ebony hair clipped in a pony-tail.

She came over as a friendly, down to earth Yorkshire girl who would help anybody. She felt at home with the public and her senior officers alike. Her warm smile and brown eyes were her biggest assets when people met her for the first time. Her slender, trim frame was a result of her physical fitness. In her spare time, she enjoyed rambling on the moors, for the fresh-air and the time it gave her to think.

Things were very quiet on the crime scene and she had been given the task of showing the film and promoting road safety to schools in the area. The silence after the noisy film show was now deafening. A police technician broke the peace as he started to rewind the film spool.

Susan stood in front of the projector screen dressed in plain clothes that made her look the part, with her tweed skirt below her knees and a crisp short-sleeved blouse.

'Come on children, don't you want to ask the Sergeant any questions about road safety?' The headmistress addressed the assembly, trying to help. 'What about you, Billy?' She bent down to a nine year old boy, sitting cross-legged on the front row. 'You normally have a lot to say.'

The boy stared at the headmistress, rather perplexed, then at the Sergeant.

'I'd rather watch Laurel and Hardy,' he said. The school hall exploded into laughter.

The Sergeant seized the moment and began her talk on road safety. She was a very eloquent speaker, and was at home in this environment. Having been brought up as an only child, she was as yet unmarried, but she loved being with children.

Out of the corner of her eye, she noticed a member of the school staff enter the hall and approach DI Monroe. She was in full flow with her talk on road safety when the DI came up to her.

'We have to go,' he whispered. 'A skeleton has been discovered in an old shaft at Dunford Bridge. Finish off here Sergeant. I've informed the headmistress, and she'll give our apologies. Fred will see to all the gear.' He motioned to the police technician to pack up the film equipment.

The headmistress took over. The two police officers left as the children were still applauding them. This was a big change from the everyday robberies and domestic disputes they usually had to deal with.

The unmarked police car was soon speeding across the moors. Susan was at the wheel, with the CID Inspector in the passenger seat.

Detective Inspector Andrew Monroe was thirty eight, and had come up through the ranks as a beat bobby in the nearby village of Dodworth. He was happily married with two teenage boys, and although some of his colleagues had raised their eyebrows, he saw nothing unusual in his working relationship with his young female colleague.

Susan was good company, with a quick brain and sharp detective skills. Monroe had been the first officer to recognise her knack for seeing clues that other people had missed, and he had helped her to attain her recent promotion, recommending her to the police board.

There was something else that Monroe had noticed about her. She was very good at crosswords. She could complete the *Daily Mail* crossword in ten minutes.

Susan had a natural detective's brain. She was fascinated by crime books. While her school friends were reading *The Girl's Own Paper*, she would be deep in the mysteries of an Agatha Christie novel. At the age of ten, she had read *The Thirty Nine Steps* by John Buchan, but her favourite detective was Sherlock Holmes.

Her father had taken her to the cinema to see *The Adventures of Sherlock Holmes* in 1939, when she was twelve, and since then she could not get enough of *whodunits*. She had read all the Arthur Conan Doyle novels and noted how small clues became important in crime work. She was also very well read in English Literature and was familiar with all the classics.

She had passed the entrance exam for Barnsley Girls' High School, and had excelled, despite her working class, council house background. Susan had always wanted to go to university, but her mother could not afford to send her. Her options had been narrow, but she had applied to the Police, passed all the examinations, and now found herself in the CID.

Her uncle, her mother's brother, had lent a helping hand. He was a Chief Inspector with the London Metropolitan Police. He had become famous in his dealings with the Cable Street riots in 1936. He had used his influence by obtaining Susan an opening in the Police.

Susan was thinking about how Sherlock Holmes would tackle this skeleton find when her thoughts were disturbed by DI Monroe.

'This is different,' he said to Susan. 'A change from road safety.'

'It sure is, Sir.' She checked her mirrors and overtook the Holmfirth bus, a single decker, struggling up the hillside towards the remote hamlet of Dunford Bridge.

Monroe waited while she passed the bus. 'The forensic pathologist should be on site already. Have you ever been in a tunnel, Sergeant?'

'Yes, Sir. We went down the Barnsley Main pit on a school visit,' she replied.

When they reached the construction site, the Balfour Beatty manager was waiting for them. He gave them both protective work wear for their journey underground. The manager showed Susan to a site cabin that served as a ladies lavatory. She quickly donned the off-white overalls and put on a miner's helmet.

The manager then led them to a company Land Rover. They set off across the moor to the shaft, a mile away, on a narrow dirt road.

The manager warned Susan. 'I am afraid it's not very lady-like going down in the kibble.' He indicated to the big bucket, which descended the shaft. 'The pathologist has beaten you to it. He's already down there. He came by train from Sheffield.'

Susan just nodded and shrugged her shoulders.

'All in a day's work, Sir.' She answered the manager with a smile.

As they descended the five hundred foot shaft in the kibble, the sunlight of the lovely July day gave way to the darkness of the shaft. She shuddered, thinking about her father. He had been killed at the Old Carlton mine when she was just fifteen. She would never forget her mother's screams when the knock on her door came, in the early hours of that morning in 1942. She was now twenty five, but she still missed her Dad.

They got out of the bucket at the shaft bottom. Susan soon became the centre of attention. It was almost as if the workers had never seen a woman before, judging from the surprised looks on their faces.

'Watch your Ps and Qs and all the other letters as well. We have a lady present,' the manager shouted, warning the men to watch their language. Susan was unperturbed. She was used to being a woman in a man's world.

They walked from the kibble and were soon at the site of the old shaft. Monroe immediately took charge of the situation, his experienced eye assessing every visible detail.

'Right, this is a crime scene,' he addressed the manager. 'We are going to need better lighting. Is it safe to go in there?' He pointed to the cavity.

'We're trying to shore up the cavity for your people to get into,' the manager quickly answered him. 'There's tons of rock up there. It's a miracle how it has held up after all these years – and I can't believe how dry it is.'

Ned Lawson was the forensic pathologist. He had arrived at the tunnel half an hour before the police. He kneeled next to the void. The Woodcock brothers were next to him, trying to make the cavity safe. Lawson's camera was flashing away, taking pictures of the scene. Their cap lamps shone into the void, and the bones of the skeleton were clearly visible. Lawson acknowledged the two detectives and shook their hands.

'A bit of luck and I should be able to crawl in there soon,' the pathologist said. Susan admired Lawson's eagerness to investigate the skeleton. Grey-haired and pot-bellied, she wondered if he was capable of crawling into the tight space. Susan wasn't sure she would want to be alone in a confined space with a Victorian skeleton.

'Have you a telephone down here which connects to the outside world?' Monroe asked the manager. 'I need to speak to the station.'

The manager nodded and took Monroe back to the shaft bottom. Susan started taking notes.

'Hey yup, Sue. What are you doing here?' Dave Woodcock asked, emerging from the cavity, a curious grin on his dust-covered face.

'I've come to see what you've found,' Susan answered, and shook his hand.

The two brothers were from her village. The mining communities were very close-knit and everybody knew everybody.

'How's your Mam, Sue?' Pete Woodcock asked, as his brother knocked in a wedge to hold the timber prop.

'She's fine, Pete. She still goes to the bingo,' she told him. It felt odd, chatting to the Woodcock brothers all this way underground, as they shored up the roof of the old shaft bottom. But apart from the skeleton, it was all in a day's work for them.

Susan wanted to know more about the tunnel.

'What was this shaft for, Pete?' she asked, coming straight to the point.

'They constructed five shafts down to the old railway tunnels, which are just a few yards from here,' Pete started to explain. 'They sunk shafts first, like we've done. They then dug out the tunnel from the bottom of the shafts. Three of them were filled in when the tunnels were completed. They used rubble from the tunnel and all kinds of rubbish from the camp. These old sleepers were chucked down the shaft first,' Pete paused to blow his nose. 'After the body, of course.'

Lawson started to inch into the void.

'You must be careful in there,' Pete warned him. 'It's only a temporary job. We're going to fix some arc lights up so you can see better.'

The Woodcock brothers left to fetch the lights. Monroe returned. He and Susan waited in a tense silence, as Lawson explored.

'Can we get the remains out, Ned?' Monroe asked the forensic pathologist. 'The skeleton may give us some clues.'

'Andy!' Lawson exclaimed from the cavity. 'This is big stuff. There are two skeletons in here. The other is a small child.' He paused. '...and what's this?'

He continued his work, taking more photographs of the bodies in situ. Susan held her breath, fascinated.

'The clothing is remarkably well preserved. There's a gold watch and chain fastened to the child's waistcoat.

There's also a piece of paper – inside the larger skeleton's mouth.'

The pathologist passed the piece of paper to Susan. It was furred with dust, stained brown with dried blood. Overcome with curiosity, the Sergeant carefully blew off the dust, and read out the words:

"O Conscience! Into what abyss of fears
And horrors hast thou driven me;
Out of which I find no way,
From deep to deeper plunged!"

CHAPTER THREE
The Pathologist

Ned Lawson had spent two days examining the two skeletons in the Sheffield forensic pathology laboratory. He'd been a pathologist for over thirty years, but had never seen anything quite so intriguing as this before.

He hadn't been surprised that the story had leaked out to the press. Journalists had descended on the tunnel site, and the news had even been carried on the BBC wireless news. Everybody was talking about it, and Lawson held the key to the mystery.

The morning copy of the *Sheffield Telegraph* lay on a nearby table. The headlines shouted:

'100 YEAR OLD MURDERS' and **'THE SHAFT SKELETONS'**

It was the new topic of conversation on the local streets and a temporary diversion from the Malayan war, along with continuing interest in the young Queen Elizabeth.

The two Barnsley detectives arrived in the laboratory to find Lawson noting his finds at a large stainless steel table. The bones of the two skeletons were neatly displayed.

Andrew Monroe inspected them with interest, folding his jacket over his arm.

'We can see there is no rigor mortis,' he laughed. 'Come on, Ned. All the world is wanting to know how they died.'

'What can you tell us?' Susan asked. Her notebook was opened at the ready.

'It is a woman, in her early twenties,' the pathologist started. 'And the child is male and roughly two years old.' Ned paused.

'What was the cause of death, Ned?' the Detective Inspector asked. 'Were they thrown down the shaft?'

The pathologist shook his head. 'No, Andy. It was not as we first thought. There are no broken bones, so they cannot have been thrown down the shaft. The bodies were placed there.' Ned had their interest.

He pointed to the skull of the woman with a scalpel. 'There's something interesting about her. The teeth have been disjointed by a wound.'

'Was that the cause of death, then?' Susan asked.

'It's an ante mortem confession, Sergeant,' the pathologist answered.

'In layman's terms please, Ned?' Monroe asked him, impatiently drumming his fingers on the table.

'That wound was done preceding death. It's a much earlier injury. It must have disfigured her face. It was most probably a knife wound.' Ned explained, jabbing the scalpel towards the skeleton's mouth, as if it was a weapon. Susan winced involuntarily.

'So what was the cause of death, Ned?' Monroe asked.

'Oh that's easy.' The pathologist pointed to the lacerations on the hyoid bone on the woman and child's skeleton. 'Their throats were cut.'

'Oh, right.' Susan took the news in. This is serious stuff, she thought. 'What else can you tell us?'

'Not much more, I'm afraid,' Lawson said. 'The rest is conjecture. Nothing certain.'

'Well, we've got something, anyway.' Monroe said, putting his suit jacket back on. 'We're all seeing the Big Chief this afternoon, and he's looking for some answers.'

CHAPTER FOUR
The Chief Inspector

The Chief Inspector of the West Riding Police Force, Christopher Columbine, stared out of his office window, overlooking the industrial city of Wakefield.

On his table lay the *Times*, opened on page three, with an article on Malaya. Further down the page was a piece on the tunnel skeletons. A creature of habit, Columbine had removed the crossword page. It was folded in two with the puzzle partly filled in. He had his mind on other matters.

Columbine walked with a limp. A German bullet from Ypres, in 1917, constantly reminded him of his army days. Following his recuperation from the army, he'd enlisted in the Police Force in 1919 at the age of twenty three.

He had risen through the ranks and had been Chief Inspector since 1946. He had receding brown hair with vivid blue eyes and appeared quite handsome for a man in his mid-fifties. Despite his limp, he was a keen golfer. His trophies were proudly displayed all around his office.

Today, he was very worried. The skeletons in the tunnel had caused such a stir. They may have been there for a hundred years, but now the grisly discovery had captured the public imagination, and people were expecting answers.

His visitors knocked and entered. He motioned for them to sit around the polished conference table.

'Any news from your son, Sir?' Monroe glanced at the Times. Columbine's son was serving in Malaya.

'It is a bad business, this war, DI Monroe,' replied Columbine. 'At least in our wars, we knew who we were fighting. He's well, at least. We heard from him the other day.'

Monroe nodded. All the ranks referred to the Chief as Christopher Columbus, but Andrew Monroe had a lot of respect for him and knew him well. *Better the devil you know*, he thought.

Chief Inspector Columbine, Detective Inspector Andrew Monroe, Sergeant Susan Priestley, and the pathologist Ned Lawson were all trying to make some sense of the macabre finds.

'Sergeant,' Columbine opened the meeting. 'What was that writing on the parchment? Is it from the Bible?'

Susan produced her notebook and read out the words:

"O Conscience! Into what abyss of fears

And horrors hast thou driven me;

Out of which I find no way,

From deep to deeper plunged!"

'No. It's not the Bible, Sir. It's John Milton. *Paradise Lost* 1, Book 10, verse 842 to 844.'

Susan paused while they digested her information. The men looked suitably impressed.

'What is the abyss of fears? Does it mean the shaft?' Monroe asked. They all look puzzled. He continued. 'Where was the paper found, Ned? And what do the clothes tell us?' he asked the pathologist.

'I suspect the paper had been put in the mouth of the woman,' Lawson explained. 'Her clothes were just rags, of very poor quality, and conflict with the expensive ring. The baby boy was a bit different, Andy. The waistcoat looks very expensive. It had this on it.'

He showed them a clothes label, embroidered with:

Benjamin Hyam, St Marys Gate, Manchester.

'The watch and chain were fastened to the waistcoat,' the pathologist explained.

Columbine shook his head. 'Rags, and riches, together with a John Milton rhyme. It just doesn't make sense.'

'Any more clues, anybody?' Columbine looked at the three of them.

'The paper is interesting, Sir,' said Susan. She had their attention. 'It's very expensive. I have been speaking to the British Museum. I described it to them and they think it's actually vellum – fine parchment made from calf skin. Important documents were made from this material – which explains why it's so well preserved. There's a wax seal on the other side, so the parchment may have originally been an envelope.'

'The writing style is rather nice, Susan. Is it Gothic?' Monroe commented.

'I showed it to the *Barnsley Chronicle* printers' explained Susan, as she checked her notes. 'They recognised it immediately. It's nineteenth century German.'

Columbine nodded pensively. 'What about the ring, and gold watch, Susan?' he asked, addressing her by her Christian name as he warmed to her.

'The ring is a very expensive gold wedding ring,' Susan explained. 'It has a distinctive hallmark. It's a kind of crest, and it's very unusual. It has a Latin inscription: "*Amor est vitae essential*". I'm having trouble identifying it. I've sent it to Scotland Yard. They have an expert on crests down there. I'm taking the watch to a jeweller in Sheffield later today.'

'Andy,' Columbine turned to the detective. 'What do you reckon?'

Monroe spoke without reference to any notes. 'Well, Sir, with your permission, I'm putting Susan on the case. We need her to dig a bit more. Let's start with what we know. The bodies have got to be from the 1840s. Ned has told us that the skeletons are a woman in her twenties, and a two-year-old child.' He looked at Susan. 'John Milton, *Paradise Lost*, you say?' Susan nodded at him.

Columbine himself nodded. 'I have no problem with Susan staying with this case,' he said. 'I want her to delve into the history books, to find out when the first tunnel was filled in. Check our police archives as well. Chase up the railway company, The Great Central. In particular, what was a young woman, and a baby, doing out there, in the middle of nowhere?'

He paused and stared at the unfinished crossword. This set his mind in motion as he turned to Monroe. 'What have you let out to the press with regards to the note and the gold watch?'

'The press knows nothing about them,' Monroe answered. 'The Woodcock brothers don't even know. They were busy putting up the lights, when they were passed to us. They saw the ring of course, but the press has not mentioned it.' He waited until the Chief responded.

Columbine lit his pipe.

'Let me know about any more developments, as soon as you get them.' He turned to Susan to finish. 'Pardon the pun, but do some digging about the tunnel. Research into what happened in the 1840s may answer our questions.'

Susan nodded. She pointed to the crossword. 'You may want to try five across, Sir. The clue is: *Across the table from*. Try *face to face*.'

The Chief Inspector puffed at his pipe and nodded his head thoughtfully.

CHAPTER FIVE
The Lass Starts to Dig

The next day, CID Sergeant Susan Priestley visited the offices of *The Manchester Guardian*, to study the archive sections of the 1840s archive editions.

Unexpectedly, she felt out of her depth with the bound volumes of old newspapers and she wasn't sure how to load the Microfiche reels into the large metal reading device.

'Hey, I saw you at Woodhead yesterday. You're with the Police.' A young man approached her. 'I was there reporting the body finds. It's very interesting. I'm keen on nineteenth century history. I studied it at university.'

He reached out his hand and she shook it.

'I'm Roger Thompson, by the way.' He smiled warmly.

'CID Sergeant Priestley,' Susan replied. She sighed. 'Have you any clues for me, Mr Thompson? I really don't know what I am looking for.'

'You want to be looking in the 1839 to 1850 sections - but I can tell you there's not much there. I've checked it all before. I have a special interest in the Woodhead tunnel,' the reporter told her.

Susan's brown eyes opened wide. Roger had caught her attention. She waited until he continued. He sat down at the desk with the Microfiche reader and motioned for her to sit next to him.

'This may interest you,' he said.

Roger quickly found a reel of tape and loaded it into the reader. He started to turn the wheel. She studied him as he searched the archives. He was roughly her age and she immediately liked what she saw.

He did not fit the caricature of a reporter in a grubby raincoat. Quite the opposite, he wore a smart striped shirt and a tie which sported the latest Windsor knot. His smile revealed a lovely set of teeth that reminded Susan of a toothpaste advert she had seen in a magazine. His thick, carrot-coloured hair was immaculately parted and tamed with Brylcreem. She hadn't come across many men like Roger in Barnsley.

Roger wore square-framed glasses which suited his face. He took them off to view the Microfiche, and she was amazed by the transformation. His blue eyes had been hidden behind the spectacles.

He turned to her, his eyes open wide. 'Gotcha. I knew I would find it!' he grinned. 'It's the March 7th, 1846 edition,' he said. 'And it's very critical of the Woodhead tunnel contractors.'

'*The contractors, being exposed to fierce competition, are tempted to adopt the cheapest methods of working, without any close reference to the danger to which the men will be exposed,*' Roger read from the archive. His voice had a slight trace of a Mancunian accent. '*Life is recklessly sacrificed: needless misery is inflicted; innocent women and children are unnecessarily rendered widows and orphans.*'

Roger turned the wheel to another article.

'Life was very cheap in those days,' the reporter commented. 'But look at this as well. This is from the March 11th 1846 edition – just four days later.'

He gave Susan the chance to view the grainy newspaper report on the film.

It was a mock wedding ceremony, and a navvy, and his woman, jumped over a broomstick, whereupon they were put to bed, while the wedding party caroused in the same room. A large body of people such as this could not be allowed to live in a state of such fearful savagery, without inflicting serious mischief, upon society.

Susan read, taking notes.

'So on one hand, the paper was criticising the railway company, but on the other hand it was castigating the morals of the workers,' she commented.

'That's right,' Roger answered. He turned, and looked at her seriously. 'There might only be snippets here, but I have some big news for you. The Irish government has recently released some important diaries after one hundred years under the censorship rule.'

'Diaries?' Susan asked.

'An Irish MP, Robert O'Neill – the Earl of Wexford, was at Woodhead. He kept an account of his stay there.'

'What was an MP doing in the middle of that hellhole?' Susan was curious.

'He served on two Royal Commissions. The first one investigated the use of child labour in the Coal Mines. Queen Victoria took a personal interest in the Huskar disaster. A few years afterwards, the Queen asked him to lead another Commission – into the high death toll at Woodhead,' Roger explained.

'Why was his diary censored for a hundred years?' Susan asked, deeply intrigued by this young man who took such an interest in history.

'Well,' Roger continued. 'Ireland was part of the British Crown then. From my research, apparently the Prince Consort's brother was implicated in some sort of scandal.'

'Prince Albert's brother?' she asked.

'That's him,' Roger replied. 'He was at Woodhead with the Earl.'

Five days later, Susan was back in Chief Columbine's office, with DI Monroe and Ned Lawson. She was presenting the report of her findings. She read from her notes:

'I visited the offices of the Great Central Railway in Manchester to inspect their records. The tunnel at Woodhead was dug out by mostly Irish labourers called navigators, or 'navvies' for short. They were a pretty lawless breed, who travelled the land in search of work. They built all the railways, and canals, and other large construction projects of the Victorian era. The railway over the moors needed hundreds of these navvies, and they lived in shanty towns. Dunford Bridge was one of these shanty towns, with Woodhead at the other end of the tunnel.

Conditions were unsanitary in the extreme. There was a major outbreak of cholera in 1842. Their graves are unmarked in the local churchyards. Some are in mass graves like the small chapel of St James, on the Woodhead side of the tunnel. Likewise, the churches around Penistone have a lot of graves. There are no official figures. Some sources state that hundreds of people lost their lives to disease and accidents.

Some of the men brought their women with them. They were called tally women.'

Susan pointed to the copies she had made of the articles that Roger had found for her in the *Manchester Guardian*.

'There were also a series of strikes and lockouts on the railway,' she continued. 'I visited our old Cases and Archives office in Sheffield. The archives of the 1840s were in old boxes, and had not been opened for years. It seems the navvies were a pretty lawless lot in those days. The Irish and Scottish workers caused a lot of trouble. Drunkenness and licentious behaviour was common in the railway districts. Prostitution and fighting were rife. I concentrated on cases of missing women and children.'

She paused. She had the rapt attention of her colleagues.

'Get ready for a shock. There may be many more bodies.'

CHAPTER SIX
The Game is Afoot

'How many bodies?' the Chief Inspector gasped. 'And where are they? In the same shaft?'

'There were five shafts in total, Sir,' Susan answered. 'The contractors have only reached one of them. That's the Number One shaft. I'm still researching the police files, and I'm following a lead which came from the *Manchester Guardian*.'

'Sounds promising,' Columbine commented. 'You've been working hard.'

'I was at the newspaper researching their archives, and I spoke to a reporter,' Susan continued. 'His name is Roger Thompson. He's very interesting and knowledgeable, and he's an expert on nineteenth century Social History. We may be able to get hold of some vital information.

It seems an Irish MP called Robert O'Neill – the Earl of Wexford – stayed in the area on a Royal Commission. The Commission had been set up to investigate the deaths on the railway. Hundreds were killed, and a lot of people went missing – though of course, not as many records were kept in those days. Previously, O'Neill had been on the Coal Mines Commission in 1842, investigating the use of female and child labour in the mines.'

'Was that linked to the Huskar disaster, at Silkstone Common, when all the children were drowned, Sergeant?' Monroe asked.

Susan nodded. 'Yes, sir, that was just before this tunnel was dug. The Huskar was in 1838. The reporter, Thompson, is convinced that the diaries hold the key that will unlock our inquiries.

O'Neill's account has been the subject of censorship under the hundred year rule. It has only just come into the public domain. Unfortunately, since the partition of the six Northern Counties in 1922, the documentation is kept in Dublin Castle.'

'Dublin Castle? Why there?' The Chief looked surprised.

'There is some Royal connection, I understand.' Susan had his full attention.

'Queen Victoria's reign? I was bottom of the class in History,' Columbine joked.

'That's right, Sir. It seems that her husband's brother is mentioned in the diaries,' Susan said.

'Prince Albert?' he frowned. 'So you think that's where this censorship thing comes in? The plot thickens.'

The Police officers went quiet as they pondered the implications of this news. Monroe broke the silence.

'Susan. Have you any more information about the ring, the waistcoat, and the gold watch?'

'The man from Scotland Yard contacted me this morning,' she replied. 'It is definitely a Swiss ring with a very obscure crest on it. Apparently rich individuals invented their own crests. The Latin inscription *Amor est vitae essentia* means *Love is the essence of life*. The watch is priceless and was made by an eighteenth century jeweller. Abraham-Louise Breguet.'

She handled the watch carefully, showing it to the investigating team. 'It was made to order for a gentleman. Look – it has the letters SC, on the back of the case. The jeweller has cleaned it. Miraculously, it still works. He has told me it is the most beautiful watch that he has ever seen.'

Susan checked her notes. 'As for the child's waistcoat, I used records from the *Manchester Guardian*. Benjamin Hyam's shop was on St Marys Gate, Manchester. It moved to another location in 1847. I found adverts in the newspaper that confirmed this. So we can assume that the waistcoat was purchased before then.'

Chief Columbine thanked Susan for her report, and he turned to Chief Detective Monroe 'Well Andy, what do you reckon?'

'I have made notes, Sir, and here are the main points. I have listed them for you.' Monroe read his notes, his voice slow and thoughtful.

1: The words on the parchment were obviously written by an educated person. Knowing the literacy standards of the time, could it have been perhaps a clergyman or school teacher?

2: The words from Milton give the impression that someone wanted revenge.

3: The woman wore poor clothing and she had a previous knife wound. It is most probable that she was lower class.

4: The puzzling thing is the expensive wedding ring on her finger.

5: Likewise, the child is interesting. He was also dressed in rags, apart from the expensive waistcoat and the priceless watch and chain he wore.

6: Who gave them these items? The engraving of the ring, the watch and chain, and the expensive waistcoat, brings into play someone with aristocratic breeding.

7: The motive of the crime cannot be theft. If so, the ring on the woman's finger and the gold watch on the child's waistcoat would have been taken.

8: The bodies were not thrown down the shaft. They were placed at its bottom before it was filled in. It was sealed at the bottom. *The murderer must have known this before he did the dirty deed.*

9: How did the murderer get the bodies into the tunnel to put them at the shaft bottom?

10: Was it a workman?

11: It seems strange that the woman's family did not raise the alarm when she and her child went missing.'

Chief Inspector Columbine was silent as he contemplated the situation. He looked sharply at Susan.

'Pack your bags, Sergeant. You're going to Dublin. I will get permission for you to look at the diaries.'

Columbine puffed his pipe. 'I will quote English Literature as well. It is from Shakespeare's HENRY V: 'THE GAME IS AFOOT'. I believe Sherlock Holmes said it also, Sergeant. Was it *The Hound of Baskervilles?*' he asked, joking with Susan.

'No. *The Adventures of Sherlock Holmes*, Sir.' The Sergeant got the last word in with a smile, secretly thrilled that she had been given the chance to continue her investigations in Dublin Castle.

CHAPTER SEVEN
May 1842
The Blacksmith's Lad

Walter Rainsford was shoeing a horse outside his father's blacksmith shop. A customer was waiting for the horse inside the Smithy and he was deep in conversation with his father. It was raining and there was nothing unusual about that. It rained every day. That was a fact of life on the Pennine Range, known as 'the backbone of England'.

Young Walter had been told this ever since he was born. More like 'The pisspot of England' as he had heard it described by one of his Uncles.

Walter Rainsford lived in Thurlstone, close to the small town of Penistone. Who had called it Penistone? What a name, he thought. Who would call a town after a man's genitalia? Penistone! Did somebody really make a stone penis?

'Walter. Watch what tha doing with that horse!' His father disturbed his daydreams. 'Mr Beechcroft is waiting to get them supplies to the Dunford Bridge tunnel.'

He turned to the customer, who was relighting his pipe from the forge with a taper.

'What do you reckon, Jim? How's the tunnel going?'

Jim Beechcroft was a haulier, taking supplies to the worksite some four miles away. His horse had lost a shoe. Jim stared into the fire, as if in a trance, before he answered.

'Well I don't rightly know. I have heard it's a bad to do there. There's already a lot been killed,' he slowly answered in his Yorkshire dialect.

'It's worse than the coal pits, they say. That's why all the Irish navvies have come for the work. The colliers will not have the tunnel work. Since the Huskar disaster, the pit men have got better wages, and nearly all of them have joined the union.'

Walter pricked up his ears on hearing the word Huskar. He had known a lot of children who had been killed there, four years previously, in 1838.

Twenty six children had been killed, and the feeling of grief still hung over the area.

The children were buried in the Silkstone churchyard.

An Act of God. That's what they said it was. The Silkstone church headstone read: 'On that eventful day the Lord sent forth his Thunder, Lightning, Hail and Rain'.

But Walter knew what had really happened. The air door was on the wrong way round. It could not be opened. The children were drowned as they were swept against the door by the flood water. The mine owners had got away with murder.

Walter kept his thoughts to himself. You never knew who was listening. Tensions were high in these parts, and there were a lot of company informers. His father had always told him to choose his words very carefully.

It was May 1842, and Penistone was on the verge of becoming a boom town. The once sleepy Yorkshire village, on the eastern side of the Pennine range, was going to have a new railway driven through the middle of it. The aim was to connect Yorkshire with Lancashire, from Sheffield to Manchester.

The railway would then branch off to tap into the mighty Yorkshire coalfield. This would take coal to the west side of the country, to feed the colossal mills and factories of Victorian England.

CHAPTER EIGHT
The Railway Engineers

Charles Blacker Vignoles was on his way to Dunford Bridge on horseback in the pouring rain. He had come from Penistone, on the old trail overlooking the valley where the railway was being built. Vignoles was the chief engineer of the project, and he was feeling very despondent.

He was now forty seven years old. An Irishman by birth, he had lost his parents at an early age, and he had been brought up by his grandfather.

Originally a military man, Vignoles had come through the Napoleonic wars under the great Duke of Wellington. He had started as a surveyor for the railways in 1825, when they were a new and exciting invention.

He now found himself in a very inhospitable place trying to construct a very inhospitable railway tunnel.

George Stephenson, the pioneer of the new railways, had said that the tunnel would be impossible to build. Vignoles thought about Stephenson as he slowly passed through Thurlstone. What did he know? He had fallen out with Stephenson years ago on an earlier project, the Liverpool to Manchester railway.

Vignoles was a very difficult man who had an Irish temper. He did not suffer fools gladly, and he was used to getting his own way. He was a bully. Although he was an excellent railway engineer, he did not know how to deal with people, and his attitude to man-management was atrocious.

Vastly overweight, he was now a very heavy drinker and his red cheeks were extremely prominent on this cold, wet morning.

Travelling with Vignoles was his subordinate, Richard Ward. Ward was a Yorkshireman, from Sheffield, and Vignoles hated everything about him. He was twenty six and he came from the new middle classes that had emerged in post-Napoleonic Britain.

Ward was stockily built with very short mousy hair and a friendly face. A compassionate man, he was diametrically opposite to Vignoles.

Vignoles and Ward were lodging in a Penistone inn, The White Hart, while the construction work was being carried out. They had not spoken one word since leaving the inn. Vignoles would dearly love to thrash this Yorkshire spy.

He was convinced that Ward was the eyes and ears of Lord Wharncliffe, the Chairman of the railway, and had been running to him with information. He remembered his army days and the soldiers' unofficial code. The army had their own special way of dealing with dissident, wayward soldiers.

Vignoles was in a foul mood. Lord Wharncliffe had instructed him to report on the many problems at the railway. Wharncliffe had originally appointed Vignoles after Stephenson had turned him down.

Things were not going well. To appease the shareholders, Wharncliffe had called an extraordinary meeting. He had sent Ward to accompany Vignoles on a fact-finding mission.

To make matters worse that morning, Vignoles had just learnt that there had been two more deaths in the tunnel.

Richard Ward had indeed been appointed by Lord Wharncliffe. He despised everything that Vignoles and his kind stood for. They were part of the pompous, arrogant, landowning classes, who were army trained, and ignorant.

Vignoles was now about a mile from Dunford Bridge. Instead of going along the newly-constructed railway bed, he had chosen the old trail. This was the old packhorse trail from Yorkshire to Lancashire.

The railway was sorely needed, as the trail was very precarious, with notorious hairpin bends and steep drops into the valley below. His horse's hooves slipped on the muddy, rain-drenched surface.

He wanted to surprise the workers. He needed someone to blame and someone to vent his rage upon.

Vignoles was awoken from his reverie by a woman's shrill screams. In front of them, a cart was blocking the trail. A small company was gathered around it, including a woman and a Catholic priest. On the cart were two bodies. Vignoles recognised the local blacksmith and his son, who were working on the cart. One of his railway managers was kneeling at the side of them.

It was obvious what had happened. The cart was jacked up on some stones, and the blacksmith was making a temporary repair to the axle. The woman was screaming, partly in Gaelic, about God and the Virgin Mary.

Vignoles could well have done without this disruption on this cold wet morning.

CHAPTER NINE
The Blacksmith is Wanted

Earlier that morning, Walter Rainsford had been stoking the forge fire for his dad, when a man had come rushing into the blacksmith shop, breathless from galloping on horseback.

Walter knew who he was. He was a railway man and he was in a state of vexation.

'Mr Rainsford, pardon my intrusion.' The man addressed his father. 'But you are wanted on the Dunford Road. One of the carts has a broken axle, and you are to attend as soon as your duties permit.'

Walter knew what his father was thinking. They had been doing a lot of work for the railway, but the method of payment was erratic, and sometimes his father was waiting months for his bills to be paid. His father pondered the situation before answering the rider.

'Where are your own blacksmiths? Why do they not attend?'

'Sir,' answered the man. 'They have all left the site, except two. One is busy in the tunnel, and the other is sick with the runs. The trail is blocked by the cart which was taking two bodies to the mortuary at Carlecotes. They were killed on the night shift.'

The blacksmith turned to the fire.

'I am instructed by Mr Meredith to say that you will be paid in cash on completion of the job, Mr Rainsford.'

Rainsford nodded, and turned to his son.

'Walter, get some tools ready, we're going for a walk.'

Within minutes, he and his son were following the rider to the place of the accident.

CHAPTER TEN
The Site Foreman

Vignoles dismounted from his horse in an ungainly fashion. As he neared the stricken cart, he saw that the blacksmith was struggling with the broken axle. Rainsford's intention was obviously to temporarily fix the axle, to get the cart moving and repair it properly at his forge. But it looked like a slow, painstaking job and Vignoles didn't have time for this delay.

The trail was blocked on either side by a steep incline. It could not have happened in a worse place. Wind and rain were now battering the valley, and the woman, in her tattered, rain-drenched shawl was screaming loudly.

Vignoles could stand it no longer.

'Push the damn cart over the side, so that we can pass!' he shouted at the blacksmith.

The blacksmith heard Vignoles and stopped what he was doing. He looked at Peter Meredith, one of the railway managers, for instructions.

Meredith knew all too well who this man was.

'Mr Vignoles, with respect, we have two corpses on the cart,' he explained. 'We cannot do that. We have a priest here who is accompanying us to the morgue and, as you can see, the lady is in distress.'

'And you are, Sir?' Vignoles interrupted the manager.

'I am Peter Meredith, a site foreman on this section, Sir.' He pointed down into the valley. 'My men are down there excavating the new track.'

'Well, Mr Meredith, I will instruct you again. Get that cart off this trail, and go back to your section. Do the work that we are paying you to do.' Vignoles shouted at the man.

Meredith and Walter, the blacksmith's lad, had put a lever under the axle, and it took all their strength to hold the slippery, wet wood.

'Sir. I am holding up the axle so that he can put the wheel back on it.' Meredith tried to object.

'Do as I say, damn you!' screamed Vignoles. He withdrew his horse whip and lashed out at Meredith. Blood spurted from the manager's face as the whip cut him.

He screamed and lost his grip on the lever, throwing Walter to the ground. The cart dropped, causing the bodies on the cart to fall off and roll down the ravine.

A macabre sight followed. A severed head rolled from one of the bodies. The navvy had been decapitated when the dynamite had blown back. The head finally came to rest in the stream at the bottom of the gully.

'Náire ar tú Béarla dúnmharfóir!' The woman screamed at Vignoles in Gaelic Irish. Being of Irish descent, Vignoles understood most of what the woman was screaming at him.

Calling him an English murderer only made him angrier. The site foreman, disgusted at what Vignoles had done, came to the woman's aid.

'Have you no shame?' Meredith cried. This only served to inflame Vignoles more. He unleashed his whip, and lashed Meredith again. He fell to the ground with blood now pouring from his face.

He turned to the woman, and whipped her across her face.

'Get off this site, Meredith, and you, trollop - go back to the witches that spawned you!' Vignoles shouted at the unfortunate pair.

The woman screamed even louder. Vignoles dismounted and squeezed past the cart. He set off down to the tunnel entrance on foot. His face was now bright red with his exertions.

'Follow me after you have seen to the horses.' He shouted to Ward, as he slid downhill on the muddy, rocky surface.

Richard Ward had remained silent until now. He dismounted his horse.

'Are you hurt, son?' he asked. Walter shook his head.

'Get the cart going, and take it back to your forge to do your repairs properly.' Ward told the blacksmith. 'We'll send some men to assist you. Take care of our horses. Use them as necessary'.

Ward bent down to the unfortunate Meredith. He was holding his head, still bleeding from the whiplash. He told Meredith to go to the site surgeon for medical assistance as soon as possible, and to write an account of everything that had just happened.

The Catholic priest was trying to calm the woman.

'I'll need a report from you as well, Father,' Ward said. 'I apologise for this unfortunate incident.'

Ward set off on foot to find the work gang for assistance.

Within an hour, the cart was mobile, and reloaded with its grisly cargo. It set off to Carlecotes to unload the bodies, and then to the forge, where the repairs would be more easily carried out.

Richard Ward now had all he needed. He was appalled at the incident. He had the statements, and the ammunition he needed for Lord Wharncliffe.

CHAPTER ELEVEN
The Surveyor

Richard Ward finally reached the tunnel workings an hour behind Vignoles.

His twenty five years had not been without incident. From an industrial family who were involved in the steel industry, he had been educated in Sheffield. He had not followed his family line of work, but had instead taken a keen interest in the new railway construction boom that was sweeping the land, and had worked hard to become the head surveyor on such a major project as the Woodhead railway tunnel.

Ward was part of the new liberal class, and he did not agree with slave-labour policies. They just caused discontent amongst the workers. He hated the way that Vignoles ran his workforce and was keen to introduce more progressive working practices.

As he neared the tunnel, he took in the sight. The shanty town on the hill did not look too bad from afar. But the closer he got, the worse it became. The stench was appalling. There was no proper sewage system, and human excrement was everywhere. The town was segregated from the working areas by a small fence.

He passed the company shop, at the foot of the incline that led to the navvy's huts. The navvies were forced to buy goods from this shop, mostly by credit. This method of payment was called 'truck' and at the tommy or tally shop, the prices were sometimes fourfold the normal prices. As the nearest shop was four miles away, the navvies were compelled to buy from it.

The company paid the wages every nine weeks, so the workers were always in lieu of wages. The navvies used tickets to obtain food from the shop. The bills were settled every month. It was a totally unfair system.

Ward caught up with Vignoles near the portals of the tunnel. He did not take much finding as he could hear him shouting from the makeshift office.

Vignoles was now berating two company officials who simply dared not answer him back. But Ward didn't have much sympathy for these men: Wellington Purdon, the manager of the eastern site and Henry Nicholson, the western site official.

Vignoles, Purdon and Nicholson must be the three most hated men in England, thought Ward. They were nothing short of arrogant bullies.

The deaths were mounting up, and Ward wondered if they would ever be brought to account.

Vignoles turned around and glared at Richard Ward.

'Mr Ward, you will accompany me on a visit to the accident scene,' he barked.

He stormed out of the flimsy wooden building, which shook under his footsteps.

CHAPTER TWELVE
The Lord

Colonel James Archibald Stuart-Wortley-Mackenzie was the first Baron of Wharncliffe. He was the former Lord Privvy Seal, and he was sixty three years old.

Like Vignoles, he was not a happy man. He was in overall charge of the railway, and the latest fatalities had brought him to Dunford Bridge that morning.

Wharncliffe had travelled from Wortley, some twelve miles away, where he held his country seat and parliamentary constituency. These latest deaths were the last straw.

In his appearance, he typified the landed gentry, wearing riding breeches with a calf-length frock coat and the customary top hat. He was suffering from ill health and had been forced from his sick bed.

He had received the news in the morning, and he had immediately set off to Dunford Bridge on horseback. He was an hour behind Vignoles and Ward.

As he passed the cart, the blacksmith had managed to replace the wheel, and the work gang had replaced the bodies and covered them respectfully with a cloth.

Wharncliffe was shocked to find the foreman Meredith bleeding profusely from what looked like lash marks to his face, but refusing to leave the cart until it was ready to continue its journey.

Wharncliffe learned the truth of the incident from Meredith, whom he liked and trusted. He brought Meredith to the tunnel site to see the surgeon, Henry Pomfret.

Pomfret was a short, stubby man, and a highly respected doctor, who had dedicated himself to helping the navvies.

They paid him directly from their meagre wages. Therefore the surgeon was independent, and operated at no cost to the Railway Company.

Wharncliffe had given Pomfret permission to use the company's premises. The Number One shaft boiler house was used as a makeshift casualty room, as it was the warmest place on the site. As Meredith was being bandaged, he and Pomfret told Wharncliffe about the two deaths. The Lord became incandescent with rage and fury.

'I'd guessed it was that. Bloody stemming – again.' Wharncliffe clenched his teeth. 'I instructed Vignoles and Purdon to stop stemming with iron, and to use copper.'

There had been many casualties caused by the stemming rams. The rams packed the gunpowder into the holes to blast the rock. Iron rams caused the danger. They caught the rock, causing sparks, which then ignited the powder.

The deaths in the night had severed the head of one of the poor wretches, and had blasted the other poor soul into extinction.

CHAPTER THIRTEEN
Recall the Calls

Vignoles, Purdon and Ward returned from the tunnel after two hours, in silence. As they passed the boiler house, Vignoles spotted Meredith. His face was bandaged and he was sitting outside the makeshift infirmary.

'I instructed you, Meredith, to leave the site. What are you doing here?' Vignoles screamed at him.

Before Meredith could answer, Lord Wharncliffe came out of the boiler house.

'If anybody is leaving this site, Mr Vignoles, it will be you,' he said, his voice calm. 'You as well, Mr Purdon.'

Vignoles had not been expecting Wharncliffe.

'My lord, I did not know that you were visiting here today,' he stammered. 'You should have sent word that you were coming.'

Wharncliffe was in no mood for Vignoles' fawning.

'I am telling you, Mr Vignoles, and you Mr Purdon, that I am at the end of my bloody tether with these deaths. You are in serious trouble with the shareholders. You are not paying the calls.' Wharncliffe spoke his mind.

Vignoles was surprised at the ferocity of the attack from Wharncliffe. He was aware that he had an audience and he did not want to be made into a public spectacle.

'If we may have a word in private Sir? Perhaps I can explain,' he said, trying to placate Wharncliffe.

Lord Wharncliffe mounted his horse, a stern expression masking the grimace of pain that crossed his face.

'You can give your explanations to the shareholders at the extraordinary meeting that I have called next week.'

He turned to Ward.

'I shall require a report on the fatalities and today's unfortunate proceedings. The meeting will require a full account of what has occurred.'

Ward touched his hat as an acknowledgement, as the Lord rode off, back to Wortley.

Vignoles knew that he was finished. He had taken out £80,000 of shares in the company. It was a princely sum. He should have listened to his wife and cashed them in when the shares were high.

Now they were worthless, and the shareholders were calling in the money. He would be bankrupt. The shareholders were after his blood. He had been publicly humiliated, in front of his own workers.

CHAPTER FOURTEEN
The Union Lad

William Birkenshaw crouched down in the tunnel, and waited for the dynamite shot to detonate. This was the only time that the men rested. His clothes were sodden and his long blond hair dripped with water and sweat.

It was not much better than the coal pits. He had never got used to these conditions, but at least it was a job. He took a gulp of his water from his bottle, and drifted back in his memories. He was thinking about the Huskar, four years before, and that terrible day.

William or "Billy Birk", as everyone called him, was *persona non grata* from working in the coal industry. As a union man, he had helped to form the fledgling miners' union.

Billy was now eighteen but he had only been fourteen that Sunday, at the Huskar. He was one of the lucky ones who had escaped when the water had rushed into the mine. So many children had died. It hurt him to even think about it. He still had nightmares about that day. So many of his friends had gone, and the carnage had been terrible.

The dynamite shot went off with a resounding blast. The air was thick with dust. The ventilation in the tunnel was useless. It stank of men, horses, and dynamite fumes. The tunnel started to come alive.

'Come on Billy Birk, it's clear.' The Irish foreman, Wellington Purdon, shouted in the thick dialect that Billy hated. 'Get your shovels. There's muck to be moved.' Purdon barked his order.

Billy hated the way that the Irish spoke. He detested everything about them. He was English and the Irish blamed the English for everything.

Mostly they blamed the English for driving them off their lands and the absentee landlords who left them with starvation wages while prime beef and grain was exported to England for the tables of the gentry. Billy was sick of hearing about it.

He could not understand how primitive the Irish were. Hardly any of them could read and write, and most of them lived like animals.

They were all Catholics, and he despised them all. He was a Protestant, but he did not attend church very much. The Huskar burial at Silkstone Church was the last time he had been to one. As well as the Irish, there were Scottish navvies in the tunnel. They were Presbyterian. They hated both the Irish and the English. Everybody hated everybody.

Billy remembered the union man who had spoken to the coal miners at a large meeting in Barnsley. 'United we stand. Divided we fall' were the words.

Well, they were certainly divided here at Woodhead. The company just did as they pleased with them. They applied the principle that while their men were arguing amongst themselves, they were not arguing with the company.

Purdon! What an excuse for a man, he thought. He was a company man, who would stand for the "egg under his cap": easily led and easily fooled. Billy bit his tongue. He had to. He had to earn a living somewhere, and he was reduced to working in these atrocious conditions. Also, it was nine weeks before he got paid.

Billy was fortunate in one respect. He could go home to his parents' house, every night, which was just four miles away, at Thurlstone. He was well educated and his tall, strong body could keep pace with any other worker. But Billy was a thinking lad and he could see the cruelty all around him.

He had seen the conditions that the navvies lived in. It was not fit for dogs, he thought, never mind the Irish. It stunk of shit everywhere. There were no proper drains. The constant rain and excrement poured into a running sewer, where the rats thrived.

Billy was used to working with Yorkshiremen, in the coal mines, and he had difficulty having conversations with these people. The only good thing was that they were all in it together. However, in his opinion, they should stand together as well.

He had seen the bodies of the two men. They were brought out of the workings when he was going to work at five thirty that morning. The navvies doffed their caps in reverence, but nobody dared to say anything.

The managers – Charles Vignoles, Wellington Purdon and Henry Nicholson, thought Billy, were nothing short of murderers. He guessed what had killed the men. Stemming! The company would not give them copper stemmers. Copper stemmers lost too much time, and cost too much money, they were told. The navvies were gradually being killed and maimed by the iron stemmers, which sparked the gunpowder when they were rammed into the holes.

Billy had recognised Vignoles and his party as they passed him on their way to the scene of the deaths. He kept his thoughts to himself, but he knew the inquiry would be just another cover up. Billy was still thinking of that fateful day at the Huskar as he returned to the tunnel face.

Wading in over a foot of filthy water, he picked up his shovel and started shifting the massive pile of rocks that had been loosened from the dynamite blast.

CHAPTER FIFTEEN
The Limerick Lad

Three days after the accident, "Mick Mac" was working ten yards from Billy Birk. He was feeling terrible.

He had been sick now for two days. Michael McNamara was his full name but "Mick Mac" was his nickname. He was fifteen and from Limerick, in Ireland. He had left home only a week before, with his two older brothers, Seamus and Patrick, for the promise of a job in England.

Mick Mac had been excited and hopeful as he'd waited in the two hundred yard queue for the recruiting agent in Limerick. It had taken him all day to get through the recruitment process. He'd had to answer all sorts of questions about his past health; if he was in any trade union, or had any political affiliations.

He had signed papers which asked for the names of his dependents, and religious denominations. His big brother Patrick had helped him to fill in the forms, and he had left his parents to start his working life.

They set off for Dublin in the horse and cart that the railway company had sent for them. His father's last words stuck in his memory: 'Never trust the English, young Mick. Burn everything English, except their coal.'

It had taken two days to travel from Limerick to Dublin and they slept in makeshift tents that the company had sent. They had caught the Dublin to Liverpool ferry, along with about a hundred other young lads, at the North Wall Docks. At Liverpool, they were herded into open-topped railway trucks, bound for Manchester.

That night, they reached Dunford Bridge after a two-hour walk across the Pennines. This was the eastern portal of the tunnel and it seemed like hell to Mick. By the time they reached the site, it was dark and he could hear the noises of men and horses, and the constant drumming of steam engines.

His brother Seamus had promised to meet one of his cousins, Daniel, who had been at the site for a month.

'Limerick boys, welcome to the pride of the English Empire. The Hotel Woodhead!' shouted a voice he recognised, among a small crowd awaiting the new arrivals.

It was his cousin Daniel. He shook hands with the three McNamara boys and motioned them to follow him up the steep hillside, to the shanty camp.

'Danny boy, what is this shithole you have brought us to?' Seamus asked him.

Daniel just laughed as he led them through the filth and deprivation of the shanty town. He took them through a crude doorway into a box-like stone building. It was built of loose stones and mud. The roof was thatched with ling, a type of moorland heather.

Mick had been told that he was going to be working on the new railway, and he'd naively expected something better than this hovel, far worse than tenant farmers' conditions back in Limerick.

A woman was sitting by the peat fire in the corner. She was mending an old shirt. The smoke in the hut was trying to escape up a pipe, which was meant to serve as a chimney. The fire gave off a poisonous, combustive reek, which combined with the smell of drying clothes and tallow candles.

'Meet my tally-woman, Mary Maloney. She will feed you and wash your clothes. A very honest Cork woman.'

Mary turned around to meet the newcomers with a slight smile. Mick detected the sadness in the woman's eyes, and wondered what she was doing there.

His more streetwise brothers knew who she was. She was Danny's woman, and she was one of the camp followers who trailed the navvies around the work sites.

'Find a bed and get some sleep,' Danny told them. Mick was so tired that he was asleep as soon as his head fell on the damp straw.

He awoke to the 'Dunford Buzzer', the deafening noise of the steam whistle that blew for five minutes every morning at four forty every morning, to rouse the workers. It could be heard at Penistone, nine miles away.

His brother Patrick shook him awake.

'Come on young Mick Mack, welcome to the real world.' Mick was tired, but he dragged himself up and followed his brothers outside, into the main yard.

Outside, the dawn was breaking. Mick had never seen anything like it. The slums of Limerick were like palaces, compared with this sight. On the hills above Dunford Bridge were all kinds of buildings that made up the shanty town. It was home for the labouring classes who lived in the makeshift town.

The stench was awful: a mixture of sewage, filthy clothes and bodies, and smoke from the endless peat fires. Rubbish and putrid food had been thrown everywhere. It was a giant rubbish dump.

A big Irishman addressed all the new recruits. At his side was a small well-dressed man, wearing a top hat, whom Mick took to be the boss. The Irishman took all their names, and issued them with picks and shovels.

'These have to be paid for out of your wages,' he said.

Mick Mack was a navvy now.

CHAPTER SIXTEEN
The Cork Girl

In May 1842, Mary Maloney was seventeen.

When she was born, her mother already had thirteen children. She entered service as a young girl, but things had gone wrong and she had ended up in the Cork Magdalene laundry workhouse. The cruelty of that place had forced her to run away.

She had been a prostitute for the past two years. She had been a very pretty girl with long dark hair and a thin but very pleasing body, but a drunken Englishman had slashed her face and raped her when she was just fourteen.

This had disfigured her lips in a grotesque way. It was only when she smiled that the deformity vanished. In the cruel Ireland of 1842, there was nothing much to smile about, so Mary took to wrapping her shawl over her scar.

She left Cork and was soon plying her trade in the notorious Monto district of Dublin. There she had met Danny McNamara and became his woman. Together, they were happy and she stopped selling her body to other men.

Hoping to start a new life, Danny had signed up with the railway company and she had come along with him on the ferry to Liverpool. She followed him across to Woodhead, where she became his tally woman.

She looked after the fire and cooked and cleaned for him and twelve other navvies.

In 1842, Dunford Bridge had more than three hundred of these tally women. They were part of the Victorian underclass that followed the navvies from place to place.

Mary's education had been basic, but she was very familiar with the ways of the world. Like most of the women who had been brought up in Ireland, she knew her

Catholic Catechism. She regularly attended the makeshift Catholic Church at Dunford Bridge on Sundays.

Danny had told her that his Limerick cousins were coming. The sleeping conditions would be more cramped, but the increased income from their wages would be more than welcome. She loved Danny and would remain faithful to him whatever happened.

Mary considered herself fortunate. Some of the other men would lend their tally-women out for a gallon of beer. Other women were sold for as little as four pence. She knew that many of them suffered from the French pox.

The hut was very basic and it was full of the navvy's clothes. They hung on a makeshift clothesline where they were drying. The problem was that they never got fully dry. The stench of them filled the air, mixed with sweat and foul odours from the unwashed navvies. Still, she did her best in the awful environment.

Some of the navvies were at work while the others tried to sleep in the hut. It could be worse, she thought. At least she was with Danny, the man she loved.

CHAPTER SEVENTEEN
The Coming of the Plague

Mick Mac had only been at Woodhead for a week, but he had already started feeling ill, with the runs and sickness. Mary Maloney had tried to help him. She suggested that he ought to see the surgeon, Henry Pomfret, but Danny just shrugged.

'You'll be all day waiting to see Pomfret. There's a queue a mile long, all the time. They die, in that queue, waiting to see Doctor Death.' He laughed at his own joke.

Mary glared at her man.

'Your brother is very ill. There is a lot of this sickness. I was speaking to Elizabeth, from the next hut. She reckons it is the plague. The Black Death'

'Stop your cackling, woman. He's just sick, that's all. It's this beer. He can't take it.' Danny drained his mug of the foul home-made brew.

Mick had convinced himself that his cousin was right. He forced himself to go to work, but he was very sick.

He was standing close to Billy Birk when the illness overtook him. He stopped shovelling, and slowly rose to his feet, but he started to vomit violently. He staggered over to Billy Birk and collapsed. Billy was shocked as the young Irish lad tumbled into his arms.

'Mr Purdon!' he shouted to the foreman. 'Man down here.'

Purdon took one look at Mick, and motioned to Billy.

'Get him out to the Surgeon.' He turned back to the gang of men, who were anxiously looking on. 'Back to work!' he shouted.

CHAPTER EIGHTEEN
The Surgeons

Henry Pomfret was from Hollingworth, which was six miles from the Manchester end of the tunnel. He was a very popular man with the navvies and they had voted for him to tend to their welfare. He was paid by voluntary contributions from the navvies, which were docked out of their pay.

Working with his young assistant Harold Thompson, Pomfret visited the camps every day, in all weathers and all hours, but he was simply appalled at the conditions. He treated the men for broken limbs and any other sicknesses and maladies.

His makeshift surgery in the boiler house close to Number One shaft was where the sick men were put, as it was the warmest place on the windswept moors. It was a primitive infirmary and he had his work cut out in this infernal place.

He had almost finished bandaging a young man whose arm had been badly burned in the stemming accident on the nightshift a few days ago. Pomfret was used to the long queue of people waiting stoically for medical attention. Still, it was sunny and warm this morning. At least they didn't have to wait in the rain today.

The noise in the boiler house was deafening and it was full of smoke that came from the coal fire. A noisy twenty-five horsepower pump was housed in the boiler house. It constantly pumped water from the tunnel.

Smashed-up limbs caused by rock falls kept him busy. Most of the navvies had chronic coughs, caused by the perpetual damp and constant inhaling of the dense gunpowder smoke.

Henry Pomfret and Harold Thompson kept very efficient records of their patients at the Woodhead "slaughterhouse", as the navvies called it. They thought it would be invaluable for later reference.

Already, Pomfret had calculated that more than half of the men and women he'd treated suffered from syphilis. Nothing surprised him about this place anymore.

Drunkenness, and chronic sleep deprivation were rife among the navvies. Many of the night workers drank all day, when they should have been sleeping, and the infrequent pay days were followed by days of heavy drinking and rowdiness.

The surgeons treated everything from accidental injuries to syphilis. Pomfret was appalled at the antics of the workforce. As an ex-army surgeon, he had been at Waterloo in 1815, and he had seen some sights there. However, nothing compared to this human abattoir.

Pomfret had left the army and set up his practice in Hollingworth. He'd expected a sleepy, rural setting, with not much to do. How wrong he was. The start of the railway here in 1839 had brought hundreds of migrant workers with all kinds of ailments, who had descended on the country villages like a plague.

A commotion from the waiting crowd disturbed him, and Pomfret came to the door to see what was happening.

It was Billy Birk, carrying Mick Mac out of the tunnel. The strong Yorkshire lad brought the unfortunate Irishman straight past the waiting queue, into the boiler house.

Pomfret glanced at the sick youth, and he immediately guessed what he was suffering from. The fishy diarrhoea odour from the patient and his constant vomiting were giveaway clues.

Cholera!

Billy carefully laid Mick Mac down onto a makeshift bed.

'What is it, Mr Pomfret? Is it contagious?'

'Birkenshaw. Get back to your work!' A loud Irish voice boomed, louder than the noisy pump engine. Wellington Purdon had followed them out of the tunnel.

Billy chose to ignore the hated voice. Instead, he knelt down at the side of the sick Irishman. The poor lad had only been here a few days and he certainly did not deserve this.

Pomfret examined the sick young man.

'This is the third case in two days and I suspect it's cholera. God only knows how many more cases we shall have in this death-ridden place.'

'It is nothing of the sort,' Purdon quickly answered. 'It's caused by the liquor they brew. They put everything into their homemade distilleries.'

Purdon indicated in the direction of the navvies' huts. 'You are scaring my workers, Pomfret.'

He turned to Billy. 'Birkenshaw, I have instructed you to get back to your work.'

Billy ignored his request.

'There is something in them tunnels that's causing this pestilence, Mr Purdon.' He said out loud what the workers had been superstitiously whispering for the past few days. 'It's a place of death.'

'Birkenshaw, you've had your warning!' Purdon shouted. He kicked Billy, knocking him to the floor. The young man landed on some bottles belonging to Pomfret, which broke on impact.

Billy sprawled on the floor. Blood welled from his arm where he had been deeply impaled by a shard of glass. His eyes widened with shock.

'That's quite enough, Purdon!' Pomfret stood and faced the foreman, red with rage. 'You and your butchers. Have you no compassion at all?'

'Keep out of this, Pomfret. Do the work that you are paid to do,' Purdon sneered, asserting his authority. 'Any more, and I will have you thrown off this site.'

Purdon turned to Billy. 'You, Birkenshaw, are finished. You are a militant Yorkshire bastard. We've heard of your dealings with the unions. They finished you in the coal pits. You and your kind want putting down.' He kicked Billy in the ribs.

Billy rose to his feet, and glowered at Purdon. He had stirred up some bad memories from his past. Then he lost control of his emotions.

He swung at Purdon and caught him square on the face with a right hook that knocked him into a pile of coal.

Purdon bled profusely from a broken nose. His screams could be heard above the noisy boiler.

CHAPTER NINETEEN
Black Death

Purdon had got what was coming to him. He had totally misjudged the situation. The crowd of waiting patients, who were normally very placid, became hostile.

'This plague – is it catching? Are we all going to die, Doctor?' One tally-woman asked, voicing everyone's fears.

'You people must get back in the line and wait your turn.' The hapless surgeon tried to calm the situation.

This did nothing to placate the woman. She rushed out of the boiler house, screeching.

'The plague! It's the Black Death. We are all going to die. I am taking my man. We are off!'

She ran into the navvy camp, sending the whole place into a panic. The word spread like wildfire. Soon all the workers were out of the tunnels and shafts.

Purdon retired to the site office with the rest of the managers, and contemplated the situation. He would now have to send for Vignoles and Wharncliffe, with this news.

He knew Vignoles was already in enough trouble with the company. It had only been a few days since the incident on the trail with the two bodies. But Purdon was more wary of Wharncliffe.

The navvies gathered outside the boiler house, where Surgeon Pomfret was still dealing with the sick. He had tended to Billy Birk's cuts and bruises, and he was trying to answer the questions from the workforce.

He was in a difficult situation. Although he had great sympathy with the plight of these poor wretches, he did not want to be blamed for causing a walk-out.

'Are we all to die, Doctor? What are we to do?' The crowd bombarded him with questions.

Some families were already moving, with their meagre belongings piled on their backs. Soon there would be a mass exodus.

He decided to politely ignore them.

'I will come and talk to you in a couple of days, when I have spoken to the directors,' he said. He knew that he would have to address the shareholders with a report.

Billy Birk stood in the infirmary, bandaged but unbowed. He had stood his ground with the devil incarnate Purdon. He was the hero of the day with the other navvies.

The McNamara family gathered around their brother Mick. He was in a terrible state.

Mary Maloney caressed his forehead gently, but Mick was very pale, and he looked close to death.

'This Yorkshire lad, Billy Birk, should not be sacked.' Danny was the first to speak. 'I will walk as well, if they finish him. He has stood up to those murdering bastards. They care not if we all die. All they care about is their tunnel being built. If it's not the stemming fuses, it's this pestilence, that's killing us one by one. What do you say, Billy Boy?'

Danny wrapped his arm around Billy.

Billy didn't have many options left. He had been dismissed from his job, but he had made many friends by his actions this day. He rose to his feet. The crowd silenced and the only sound was the steam pump. It was the first time that Billy had ever spoken in public.

'Friends and workmates, there is something seriously wrong here. I worked in the pits over there.' He pointed eastwards. 'I was in the Huskar pit when twenty six bairns were drowned. It was the same there. An Act of God, they said it was. An Act of God! It was nowt to do with the air doors that were on the wrong way. They got away with murder. The murderers are still walking free today.'

Billy paused and looked around the large crowd which had gathered in the boiler house. They sensed there was something new about him; something heroic.

'Well, it's up to you. We either let this lot get away with murder here, or we do something. What can we do? I hear you thinking. You either do nought or we fight them like we did in the coal pits. I will tell you what we did there. We all joined the union to fight those murdering bastards. We pressed for changes to the working practices and challenged the bully boy managers like that Purdon.' He gestured in the direction of the manager's office.

'They are naught but coffin fillers,' one navvy shouted. The crowd clapped loudly. Billy was winning them over with his heart-felt speech.

'But what can we do except go back home, Billy? If we leave on our own steam, we won't get paid. What choices have we got? Danny asked.

'When is this shareholders meeting?' Billy asked the surgeon.

'Tomorrow, in Manchester,' Pomfret answered.

'Right, and that's where we are going, too. To Manchester – to see the great high and mighty Baron, Lord Wharncliffe!' Billy shouted. 'Anybody coming with me?'

'Yes, Billy Boy we're all going with you!' The crowd shouted.

CHAPTER TWENTY
The Army Cometh

The villages on the eastern side of Manchester were awoken early by the sound of marching. It was not an army of soldiers. It was an army of navvies.

A rag-tag array of workers from Woodhead descended on the city, along with navvies from other sites. At the head of the march was Billy, with Danny McNamara and his brothers, and the foreman Peter Meredith, whom Vignoles had dismissed.

They had marched the twelve or so miles from the tunnel. They were in good heart, notwithstanding their problems. At least they were all in it together, thought Billy.

The unfortunate brother, Mick Mack, was now in the care of Danny's woman, Mary Maloney, in their hut. Mary knelt by him constantly, and gave him a little port wine, as Surgeon Pomfret had instructed. He was in the hands of God, and she prayed to all the saints in heaven that she knew, to save him.

Surgeon Pomfret had also been summoned to the meeting, but he had set off long before the navvies. He was expecting trouble.

As the navvies drew closer to the city, their numbers started to swell. The horrific events of 1819 were still fresh in the minds of the working class people of Manchester. On that fateful day, a crowd of 60,000 people, including women and children, had gathered in St Peters Square to complain against poverty and to demand democracy. Eighteen protesters had been killed when the Riot Act had been read. The Hussars had bayoneted the crowd.

Billy was treated like a Pharaoh, in front of his troops, but he was now becoming nervous. What would they do when they got into the city?

The night before, the foreman, Peter Meredith, an educated man, had written their grievances down. His face was still marked from Vignoles' whiplash.

Billy had become quite friendly with Meredith, and they had spoken at great length into the night about what they would do in Manchester.

They had both decided to see what happened when they arrived in the city. The crowd was now some two or three thousand strong. Fate soon played its hand.

As they marched on London Road, Billy and Peter realised their worst fears were being confirmed.

A cavalry unit had been sent to confront them and it was blocking the road.

CHAPTER TWENTY ONE
The Cavalry Captain

Captain Hugh Gregory, of the Manchester and Salford Yeomanry, had been placed in a most uncompromising situation that morning. He had been summoned by the local magistrates, and been issued with Riot Act orders from them.

Gregory was forty five, and a veteran of the wars against France. He had carried out his duty against a foreign enemy. However, he was unhappy with this war against his own English people. He had been at Waterloo in 1815 and had been a Cheshire Hussar in 1819 at the St Peters Square massacre.

His family were from Oldham and were part of the new industrial classes. He clearly recalled that day, thirteen years ago, and he was convinced it had been wrong to attack the crowd.

There was still understandable resentment about what had happened. The massacre had been nicknamed *Peterloo*, after the Waterloo battle. His family were in the textile business and he had taken the advice of his father, who owned mills in Oldham. His father had hundreds of workers but had avoided trouble from the Luddites. These were a group of protesting workmen who destroyed labour saving machinery.

Gregory's father worked on the principle that a happy workforce was a good workforce. To avoid agitation from the emerging trade unions, he spoke with his workers on a regular basis regarding their issues, in a conciliatory manner.

The magistrates had issued him with orders as he lined his troops up on the main London Road. As he awaited the approaching navvy army, his mind flashed back to the fateful day in 1819.

Gregory remembered the charge, and the bodies lying everywhere. Many of the Hussars had boasted about the carnage afterwards, but Gregory had been convinced that it was wrong. He remembered the Inquiry, and all the lies and mistruths that were told by the military.

Since then, he'd rapidly risen through the ranks in peace time England. Gregory was happily married to a local Oldham girl, with three grown up children. He'd put the horrors of war behind him.

But now, his ears were still ringing with the words of the pompous magistrate. He had been summoned to see him earlier that morning. The magistrate's offices overlooked St Peters Square. His words were: 'Captain, we are instructing you to maintain the peace of the city'.

He'd waved two pamphlets at the Captain. One was the 1838 Act, *Keeping the Peace Near Public Works*. The other was titled *The Seditious Meetings Act* of 1819.

'We do not want this rabble in our City. Do you understand?' the magistrate had said to him.

Captain Gregory waited while the navvy army came closer. He dismounted from his horse. He instructed the Yeomanry to stand down.

'Captain. Call us to arms. Let us put flight to these subversives!' A young, hot-headed Lieutenant shouted.

Gregory glared at him.

'Lieutenant, I have issued orders for you to stand down. Any more disobedience and you will be on a charge.' The Lieutenant gave him a sullen look.

'Yes Sir,' he was forced to answer.

The navvy army approached the Hussars. Meredith was the first to challenge Gregory.

'Captain. Will you let us through to the offices of the railway company, to deliver our letter of grievance?'

The Captain was impressed by this man. Although his attire was rough, he spoke with an educated voice.

'It seems that you know military rank, Sir?' the Captain asked Meredith.

'I do indeed, Captain. I held the line at Hougoumont, as a gunnery Sergeant.' Meredith referred to the battle of Waterloo.

'Well, ex-gunnery Sergeant,' said the Captain. 'I will deal with you and see what sense prevails.' Gregory decided to appeal to Meredith's military background. 'If you will order your men to hold off, as I have ordered my men to stand down, I then will escort you and your leader to deliver your letter to the railway company. What say you?'

Billy heard the Captain, and addressed the navvies who were now deathly quiet.

'The officer has suggested that we see Lord Wharncliffe in person.'

'It's a trick, Billy. They will arrest you!' The navvies started shouting.

The Captain held up his arms. 'I will assure you that no harm will come to these two men.' He addressed the crowd. 'If you will not allow them to come with me, I have here the Riot Act orders, and you know what will happen if they are read out.' He glanced at the waiting Cavalry, and the army of navvies shrank back from their agitated stance.

'We do not want bloodshed,' Meredith proclaimed. 'I suggest that you give us a chance to see Lord Wharncliffe.'

This seemed to placate the crowd. The Captain and his Lieutenant accompanied Meredith and Birkinshaw to the railway offices, leaving the soldiers and the railway workers facing each other in an uneasy truce.

CHAPTER TWENTY TWO
The Shareholders' Meeting

Charles Vignoles' hands shook at he lit his cigar. He was waiting his turn to speak at the shareholders' meeting. The minutes from the last meeting were being read, but the minds of every shareholder were on today's meeting. The boardroom of the Sheffield, Ashton-Under-Lyne and Manchester Railway offices in Manchester was packed with shareholders, waiting for answers.

Vignoles puffed on his cigar. He was a desperate man. Things were not going well for him. Rising costs and financial difficulties were on the agenda today. There were a lot of problems with the railway. He did not know how to answer these people with their demanding questions.

He could hear the noise of the crowd shouting and chanting outside. They were after blood. It might be his blood. He could do nothing right, either by the shareholders, or the workforce. The fifty six local bigwigs, led by Lord Wharncliffe, were after a return on their investment. Vignoles' face was now bright red as he feared the worst.

Charles felt miserable. He was not used to speaking in public. To make matters worse, they were mostly uneducated northerners. They had no idea what it was like out there at Woodhead. They were all entrepreneurs, textile people, who had invested money and wanted a quick return.

The railway had been under construction for nearly two years. In desperation, the shareholders were forcing the company to bring in another railway engineer, Joseph Locke. Vignoles didn't like Locke. He was from the new breed of railway engineers, who got things done quickly.

He had a name for making fast returns on capital. Locke sat opposite Vignoles, who shifted uncomfortably in his chair. It was time for Vignoles to face the music.

Samuel Jewson, the chairman, moved progress to the matters in hand. He was a successful businessman from Manchester. *Another bloody Jew that likes to hear his own voice, and is full of his own importance*, thought Vignoles.

The meeting had been in session for ten minutes. Jewson turned to Vignoles.

'I call upon Mr Vignoles to give his monthly report. I will remind the meeting to please give order, and please, no interruptions like the last few meetings.'

Vignoles got to his feet, but he was very apprehensive. He shuffled his papers. His mind was swirling. He had not slept for two days. He had been staying in a Manchester hotel and he had been drinking heavily.

His Irish eyes were bleary. Vignoles hated this place and he had completely underestimated this job. He had first come here three years ago, in the middle of summer, to survey the railway. In hindsight, he had not considered enough the harsh moorland climate and the logistics of getting supplies to the isolated place.

He had been involved in railways for fifteen years. However, his overbearing attitude had upset many people, including the great George Stevenson. At times like this, he wished he was back with his wife, Mary, in Hampshire, leading a quiet life.

Lord Wharncliffe was in charge of the overall project and he had appointed Vignoles to construct the tunnel. He was in the meeting, but he had remained silent so far.

'Come on, we don't have all day. We have other business to attend to.' A Yorkshire voice disturbed the smoke filled room.

'I have spent the last two weeks visiting the site, and have my report here.' Vignoles swept his hand across the papers. He spoke in an educated voice, with no trace of his Irish upbringing. His military background, however, betrayed his contempt for his audience. 'I take cognisance of the shareholders' concerns but I would remind the gentlemen of the terrain, and climate of the sites.'

'We know all about that. Get to the point. Explain why you are asking for more money!' A heckler shouted.

'Let Mr Vignoles carry on.' The chairman interceded. Jewson nodded to Vignoles.

'The eastern drive in the tunnel is causing great concern.' Vignoles said. 'We have trouble holding the roof falls in drivage two, from shaft number two.'

'What about your magic steam boring machine? You told us it was the eighth wonder of the world. It's been parked up now for a year, rusting away in the tunnel.' A raw Lancashire voice boomed out.

Vignoles tried to continue.

'The steam borer is still in the experimental stage. It's not designed to hold up the roof. It is a drilling machine' said Vignoles.

'We gave you four thousand pounds for it, and now it's sitting idle. We heard it was useless.' The Lancashire shareholder had clearly been doing his homework.

One of the major shareholders now rose to his feet. The shareholders fell silent.

'Mr Vignoles, we are most concerned about the events of last week. It seems you are now whipping the workforce into submission, while more of your people are getting killed by what we are lead to believe are unsafe working practices.'

The shareholder gestured towards the doors and the noise outside.

'Why has your workforce come here? Why are they not at work? We want to know why they have downed their tools.'

Vignoles found it difficult to keep his temper with these ignorant business men. The meeting was becoming rowdy. Samuel Jewson banged his gavel on the table, but with little avail.

'If you will allow me to answer...' Vignoles shouted above the noise.

The major shareholder rose to his feet again.

'What about the calls that you have reneged on? You owe us a great deal of money.' He delivered the coup de grace.

The room went deathly quiet. This was the lynchpin of their animosity towards Vignoles, and the question that he had been dreading. Vignoles, his face now ashen, hesitated, but events from outside took over.

CHAPTER TWENTY THREE
Bad News

The surgeon, Henry Pomfret entered the room with an envelope. He marched straight up to Lord Wharncliffe, who had sat impassively through the meeting until now. Wharncliffe opened the envelope. His face drained of colour as he read its contents.

He rose to his feet, and broke his silence.

'Gentlemen.'

Wharncliffe did not need the gavel. The room was silent already.

'Cholera has been confirmed at Dunford Bridge. We have had nine dead and twenty seriously ill. Many more cases are to be confirmed.'

He paused, and the shareholders listened to the murmurs of the large crowd assembled outside. 'The navvies have deserted the site. We know they want answers.'

All eyes were on the chairman, Samuel Jewson. He seemed to be gripped, as if he was in a trance. He roused himself.

'We all recognise the good doctor, Surgeon Pomfret,' Jewson said, breaking the deadlock. 'I ask him to address the meeting.'

Pomfret took to the stand confidently.

'Gentlemen. As you know, I am one of the surgeons at the tunnel. I will give you extracts of the daily records that I have been keeping.' He spoke eloquently.

He opened his journal.

'I am most certain that the sickness is Cholera.' He paused as the shareholders gasped. 'This sickness is relatively new to these shores, but I have seen the symptoms myself before, in Spain, at Televera, and in Portugal, when I was with the Duke's army.' Pomfret referred to the Duke of Wellington.

The shareholders wanted to ask questions, but the chairman banged his gavel.

'Through the chair, gentlemen. Let us wait to hear what the good doctor has to say.'

He motioned to Pomfret to continue.

'We have had now six deaths at Dunford Bridge and three at Woodhead. I am afraid to say that another twenty are very sick, with the same symptoms. The disease is difficult to treat. I find that regular meals, and a little port wine, seems to ward off the disease.'

Pomfret was interrupted by a man in the second row. He was waving the *Manchester Guardian*.

'Surgeon, it says here' he said. 'And I quote from the paper – that the disease is caused by drink, gross imprudence, and intemperance.'

'That is ridiculous speculation, and is not proven.' Pomfret answered the man. 'I have carried out my own diagnosis, and in my opinion, it is the water that these people drink at the sites. That is the source of the disease. They are exposed to gunpowder reek and they are drinking from the foul water in the tunnel. The water supply in the navvy camp is mixed with sewage. That is where the cholera comes from. It is highly contaminated. Their daily diet does not help. The medical symptoms are identical to what we witnessed in Spain.' Pomfret stared at the assembled bigwigs.

'The symptoms of the disease are vomiting, cramp, collapse, shrivelling of the fingers, sinking of the eyes and diarrhoea.'

He addressed Lord Wharncliffe.

'If I may continue with the recent events, my Lord, those poor wretches outside are treated worse than animals.' Pomfret stared as Vignoles and Purdon. 'Neither the Foreman Meredith, and the navvy Birkenshaw deserved the treatment they received at the hands of these men.'

He then turned to address the other shareholders.

'I suggest to you good people, that some sort of contrition and redress of their grievances might possibly build your precious tunnel a little bit faster, with far fewer deaths.'

Vignoles had listened to the surgeon, but did not agree with him. Now Pomfret's comments and criticism about the navvies' treatment were being levelled at him.

'Sir, we pay you to tend to the health of our workers.' Vignoles interrupted. 'You are not here to pontificate, or to be judgemental as to their grievances. You are not party to these matters.'

Lord Wharncliffe had waited for this moment to confront Vignoles. He could hear the sound of the navvies outside and he had a lot of respect for the surgeon.

Wharncliffe rose to his feet and signalled to the chairman.

'Mr Vignoles. We have asked the good doctor to explain this pestilence. You will retract your remarks. I will make transparent to the shareholders that the company does not pay the surgeon. He is paid by the navvies themselves at some three halfpence a day each, if I recall.' He glanced at Richard Ward, who nodded to confirm the fact.

Wharncliffe needed to blame somebody and to deflect any wrongdoing on his part. He continued to vent his wrath, playing to the shareholders.

'If my information is correct,' he paused, and stared fiercely at the two managers. 'Mr Vignoles and Mr Purdon are to blame for the men's grievances. There is still the matter of your calls to discuss. But first, we will let the doctor finish.'

Wharncliffe turned to Pomfret.

'I will ask the question that is on everyone's lips. Is this pestilence contagious?'

'In my opinion, my Lord. No. It is not directly contagious.'

Before Pomfret could continue, the doors of the room opened, and two officers of the Yeomanry entered the room. Pomfret, Wharncliffe and Vignoles recognised their ranks from their military days: a Captain and Lieutenant. They were accompanied by the dismissed foreman, Meredith, and the insurgent navvy, Birkenshaw.

CHAPTER TWENTY FOUR
The Captain Takes Command

The Captain, resplendent in his blue and white uniform, strode to the front of the meeting.

'Gentlemen, pardon my intrusion,' he started. 'I am Captain Hugh Gregory, of the Manchester and Salford Yeomanry. I have these two gentlemen with me.'

He ushered the two navvies towards the front of the room.

'As you are probably aware, we have a serious situation outside. The riot act instructions have just been issued to me by the City magistrates. I will categorically tell you that I will not be the one who will have blood on my hands. It will be on your hands if the crowd has not been dispersed in an orderly fashion.'

The shareholders began to mutter.

'I have promised the crowd that you will listen to them. If you do not hear them out, then I shall not be responsible for the consequences. I was at the 1819 massacre, and I am sure that you do not want a repetition of that.'

The room was hushed into silence as Peter Meredith and Billy Birkenshaw made their way to the platform. As they passed Vignoles and Purdon, the two managers rose to their feet in protest.

'These are the two men that have been dismissed. This man for gross misconduct!' Vignoles shouted, pointing at Meredith. 'And this man physically attacked Mr Purdon!'

Captain Gregory took an instant dislike to these two railway engineers. He decided to take matters in his own hands.

'Which of you gentlemen is Baron Wharncliffe?' he asked.

'I am he, Captain. What do you require?' Wharncliffe said.

'My Lord,' Gregory continued. 'I require you to hear these two gentlemen out with their grievances. There are thousands out there and they are getting restless. I wish to avoid bloodshed at all costs.'

'Right you two,' Wharncliffe barked. 'State your business before these shareholders.' He motioned for the navvies to speak.

'I must object, my Lord.' Vignoles interjected. 'These men have been dismissed.'

The Captain stepped in and turned to his fellow officer.

'Lieutenant,' he ordered. He pointed at Vignoles. 'If this man – or his companion – opens his mouth, arrest him, under the Riot Act conditions.'

Vignoles knew very well that this was no idle threat. He decided to keep his own counsel. Purdon however, knew little of military matters and stood up.

'But this man...!' he started to protest.

The Captain nodded to his Lieutenant. He grabbed Purdon by his shoulders. The Lieutenant then frogmarched him unceremoniously out of the room. Purdon loudly protested his innocence.

'Ex-Gunnery Sergeant,' the Captain announced. He motioned for Meredith to begin speaking.

Meredith now took the chair. In an educated voice he began.

'Gentlemen, I have here a summary of our grievances. They summarise as follows.'

He read:

'1: This plague. What is being done about it?

2: *The deaths and accidents caused by using the wrong stemming fuses.*
3: *We need more assistance with our housing and welfare.*
4: *The bullying of the managers.*
5: *The exorbitant prices in the Tommy shops.*
6: *The nine week wait to get our wages paid and...*'

Wharncliffe had heard enough. He put up his hand.

'Enough, Meredith. I have heard enough.' He felt like his dirty linen was being washed in public, in front of his shareholders. 'I promise you that I will conduct a full inquiry. In return, will you, and the rest of the navvies, return to your place of work?'

Wharncliffe turned to the Captain and the navvies.

'I require a few minutes, Captain Gregory. You two men also – in private, please. Surgeon Pomfret, I need to speak with you as well.'

Wharncliffe took command.

'I move we adjourn this meeting for a week, to take stock of the situation. Same time, and venue, next week.'

The gavel came down, and the chairman declared the meeting adjourned. There was plenty for the shareholders to think about, not least the return on their capital. Events were overtaking them.

Charles Vignoles was reprieved for now, but Wharncliffe gripped his arm.

'It would seem logical to appraise the situation, Mr Vignoles. I would appreciate a report on the morrow – and Mr Vignoles,' he paused. 'If the blame points anywhere for these happenings, I will venture to say that the axe will fall somewhere. I can assure you that it will not be on my head. Follow me to the camp. I need to appraise the situation for myself.'

CHAPTER TWENTY FIVE
Compromise

Lord Wharncliffe ushered the four men into a side room.

He immediately started to speak. He turned to Gregory.

'I served at Waterloo. I witnessed *Peterloo* as well and a most unsavoury incident it was. All it served to do was to infuriate, and politicise, the masses.'

He looked at the Captain and then at the two navvies.

'What will it take to send the men back to work?'

'My Lord. Remember, we have been sacked.' Billy now spoke.

'I will sack Vignoles before you two!' Wharncliffe thundered. 'If I give you my promise to consider your complaints and deal with this plague outbreak, what say you?'

Wharncliffe was in a difficult position. If blood was going to be spilt today, he would be culpable. The newspapers, especially the *Manchester Guardian*, were baying for somebody to blame. The railway had brought shame – and the plague, to the good city of Manchester.

'You're not going to get a better deal than that. Let us disperse the crowd peacefully.' Captain Gregory addressed the two navvy leaders.

Meredith looked at Billy and nodded. He turned to the doctor.

'Surgeon Pomfret. This plague. Is it contagious? What can we do about it?'

'I told the shareholders that in my opinion it is not contagious,' Pomfret answered. 'I suspect it is caused by the drinking water. We need fresh water for the men to drink.'

The five of them marched outside. The crowd was gathered anxiously. The murmurings died away as they saw their two leaders and their doctor emerge from the railway offices.

At the back of the crowd, the soldiers of the Yeomanry were stood down, awaiting orders from their Captain.

Meredith addressed the throng.

'We have been given assurances from Lord Wharncliffe that he will consider our grievances. To avoid any bloodshed, we would ask you to clear the streets, and return to your workplace.'

An Irish voice boomed from the crowd.

'What about the plague? We have seen carts of coffins on the Woodhead road.'

The crowd started to shout.

Billy raised the palms of his hands to calm the crowd and they quietened down.

'Lord Wharncliffe is coming back with us to assess the situation.' Billy's powerful voice carried over the noise of the navvies.

At this, the crowd began to disperse.

'You have done well, Gunnery Sergeant,' the relieved Captain Gregory said to Meredith. 'I wish you well in your enterprise. However, I have the feeling that we shall meet again in the near future. The situation is volatile'.

With that, he marched over to the Cavalry men and issued the order for a return to barracks.

CHAPTER TWENTY SIX
The Pestilence Bites

The ragtag army started to return eastwards, towards the tunnel. They felt that the message had been hammered home to their superiors. Some of them sang their familiar navvy songs.

Wharncliffe, and his surveyor Ward, went on ahead on horseback. At Hollingworth, they overtook a cart full of empty coffins that were bound for the tunnel.

Wharncliffe said nothing, but he shook his head. As they approached the western end of the tunnel, they saw the remnants of the navvies who had remained in the camps, packing their meagre belongings to escape the plague. They were carrying anything they could. It was a pitiful sight to see. Ward kept his thoughts to himself. He wondered where the navvies were going to. They had come here to find work. Now they were being driven away by a terrible sickness.

The lower end of humanity was being driven along by industrial progress, avarice, and sickness.

Surgeon Pomfret was not far behind Wharncliffe. He too saw the fleeing navvies as he was approaching the camp. He tried speaking to the poor wretches, trying to convince them that the disease was not contagious. They would not believe him and continued on their way.

Wharncliffe and Ward rode up the trail to the tunnel entrance.

'Where is everybody?' Wharncliffe finally broke the silence. The site was deserted 'Where are all the foremen and overseers? Have they all left, or are they all dead as well? What a rabble they are.'

Pomfret had now reached the site, and he went to assess the situation at Dunford Bridge. He soon found the McNamaras' hut, where Mary Maloney was still comforting the sick Michael. His eyes were now sunken and his fingers were shrivelling. After an initial examination, the Surgeon turned to Mary.

'You must feed him regular meals and make him drink the port.'

'He is in the hands of the Lord, Doctor,' she answered. 'Can somebody read the scriptures to him?' All Pomfret could do was pat her head.

Wharncliffe and Ward were now standing in the doorway of the hut. Ward was taken aback at Mary. Even though she was shabbily dressed, she looked very pretty as she was tending to the poor navvy. Apart from his dealings with these people at work, he really did not know much about them. He had heard the stories of men trading their women to other men for a gallon of ale. His middle class background, and his own circle of friends, was a world away from these poor people's lives.

Billy Birk, Meredith, and the two McNamara brothers, now pushed their way into the hut. Ignoring the managers, the eldest brother, Danny, went straight to his youngest brother's side. He started to whisper to him.

'We must leave these people alone,' Pomfret quietly said to Wharncliffe, retreating outside.

The remnants of the navvy army were now descending on the camp, but the sight of the coffins had made up their minds. The stench of death hanging over the place was overbearing. Most navvies soon packed their meagre belongings to leave the plague-infested hell.

By nightfall, there were only around a hundred people left in the camps. Billy set off back to his mother's house in Thurlstone. He had a lot to think about.

At least he was still in work and he was alive. *What a life*, he thought, as he left the tunnel of death.

CHAPTER TWENTY SEVEN
July 1842
The Irish Earl

Robert O'Neill, the nineteenth Earl of Wexford, listened to the debate intently. It was July 1842 and the Coal Mines Act was being discussed in the Houses of Parliament.

At twenty nine, he was a rising star in politics. He was known as forward thinking, and progressive in the House of Commons. A favourite of the former Prime Minister Arthur Wellesley, the famed Duke of Wellington, he had spent some two years on the matters in hand. He had been involved with the Royal Commission looking into child and female labour in the coal mines. It was now being debated.

Lord Ashley-Cooper, the 7th Earl of Shaftesbury, was speaking to a full house. Shaftesbury had headed the commission. He was being constantly harangued by the Members of Parliament who were under the pay and influence of the mine owners.

The loss of children's lives, at the Huskar mine in Yorkshire in 1838, had sparked off the Commission.

O'Neill vividly remembered the day in 1840 when the young Queen Victoria had summoned him to Buckingham Palace. There had been public outrage at the treatment of children in the mines. The Queen had ordered an inquiry. She was demanding answers to the issue of child labour.

The Queen had met O'Neill and Lord Ashley-Cooper in a large room. At first, O'Neill had been rather overawed at the pomp and circumstance of the occasion. This soon changed as the Queen started to speak. She was obviously distressed at these events in her kingdom and she was demanding a change.

The young Queen sat with her new husband, Prince Albert, at her side as she addressed her visitors. The room resonated with her prophetic words.

'Gentlemen, I am not prepared to keep listening to stories of barbaric cruelty to these children. They are my subjects, and my children. It is unthinkable that young girls and boys should be exposed to these practices. The Huskar mine disaster was a tragedy but it should have simply never happened. These ruthless mine owners make money out of cheap labour. We abolished slavery in the colonies – yet the conditions these children labour under are no better. We shall not rest until the Commission has done its work. We require a conclusion to this matter. Women and children need removing from the coal pits.' The Queen's voice was calm, but determined.

'Gentlemen, I have taken the liberty of permitting my younger brother, Frederick, to accompany you on your mission,' the Prince Consort said, in his thick German accent.

Lord Ashley rose as if to question the Prince.

'Our instructions to him are quite clear,' Albert continued. He looked at his young wife, who nodded. 'He is not to interfere. It is purely an advisory role. We think it gives more credence to the Royal Commission.'

'It will be a good way to teach him how our people live. It may occupy his mind as well,' the Queen continued. 'He may need guidance, Lord Ashley. He is not used to our ways. You are to report to me if he steps out of line. Is that clear?'

'I will let the Earl of Wexford attend to the Duke.' Lord Ashley smiled at O'Neill.

The Queen looked at the Earl. She seemed to like what she saw. She slowly nodded as she appraised his blue eyes and nut-brown hair and moustache. He was tall and elegantly dressed in a tight-fitted calf-length frock coat with a single breasted waistcoat. His linen shirt was turned down and he wore a wide cravat.

'My Lord, you are single, are you not?' She addressed O'Neill. She had obviously done her homework on him.

'I am, Your Majesty,' O'Neill quickly answered.

She obviously thought that the Irishman would be a prize catch for some lady in her realm. The Earl was indeed single.

Sadly, he had lost both his parents five years earlier. The doctors had told him that it was consumption. O'Neill had left his dwindling Irish estate in the hands of a landlord, to take up his seat in Parliament.

The once lovely house on the Hook Peninsular in the County of Wexford, was now crumbling. Times were very hard, even for the ruling classes in Ireland. He had been forced to sell parts of the estate to generate income after his parents' deaths.

'Splendid.' Queen Victoria nodded. 'You will take good care of the Duke in our Northern realm. Albert – you will send for him as soon as possible.'

Sitting in Parliament, O'Neill remembered the Queen's prophetic words two years previously. She must have known that there would be trouble with the Duke.

The Commission's work had been very thorough but it had been made very difficult by the establishment of the day. Working practices that many people thought were normal were cruel and inhuman.

CHAPTER TWENTY EIGHT
1840
The Old Bear

O'Neill had been sent to the North of England. His destination was Yorkshire, where a big proportion of the coal mines were situated.

His first posting had been the town of Barnsley, in the West Riding of Yorkshire, close to the Huskar mine.

O'Neill had a full complement of secretaries who had been trained in the new Pitman's Shorthand. The verbal comments were to be recorded verbatim. The report would use the word-for-word transcripts of the miner's statements: the unvarnished truth.

The Earl of Wexford was an Irish Catholic and he had been a Whig MP since he was twenty. The law had previously not permitted Catholics into the all-Anglican British Parliament. However, Robert Peel and the Duke of Wellington had much sympathy with the Irish Catholics. In an unprecedented move, Catholics had been allowed back into Parliament in 1829.

This move had successfully prevented an Irish uprising, but there was still a lot of antipathy against them. The Westminster establishment did not like change. O'Neill endured the generations of hate that had developed ever since the Tudor monarchs and Oliver Cromwell's days.

On his arrival in Barnsley in June 1840, the young Earl was given rooms near the centre of the town, in a hostelry called The Old Bear in Shambles Street.

Daniel Defoe had not called it Black Barnsley for nothing, thought the young MP, as he set about his new role with vigour. The stone buildings were covered in soot from coal fires. There were collieries everywhere. Some large, and some with just a few men working them. It was boom time here. There was coal everywhere, and it was in urgent demand, to feed the Industrial Revolution.

He had been told that he would have some twenty five commissioners working under him. His task was to visit the collieries to investigate the practice of child labour. Lord Ashley had warned him of the unscrupulous mine owners, whose only desire was making fast money. They did not welcome change and would stop at nothing to derail the commission.

O'Neill decided he would visit the place that had started this investigation. He would go to the Huskar mine. The next morning, he took five commissioners with him to the village of Silkstone. He needed to get a feel of the place where the accident had occurred, just under two years previously, in July 1838.

It was five miles out of Barnsley. The commissioners left their horses at the Red Lion inn, where the inquiry had been held into the recent disaster. In Silkstone, some of the coal seams outcropped at the surface. The seam that was named after the village was top-quality coal.

First, O'Neill visited the All Saints Church to look at the large headstone commemorating the twenty six children who had died in the mine. A torrential downpour had flooded into the pit and it had trapped the children who were trying to escape.

A woman was putting some flowers on the mass grave and to O'Neill, it was quite touching. He read the writing on the headstone and it struck him as odd. *An Act of a God*, the message gave out.

He slowly read the words: '*On that eventful day the Lord sent forth his Thunder, Lightning, Hail and Rain carrying devastation before them and by a sudden irruption of water into the coal pits of RC Clarke esq. twenty six human beings whose names are recorded here were suddenly summoned to appear before their maker.'*

He had read the findings of the inquiry but it seemed grossly hypocritical that God, whether he was a Catholic or Protestant, would want to kill little children.

O'Neill was rather puzzled by another thing he had read in the inquiry findings. Why had the ventilation door not opened when the children were trying to escape the deluge of water? They were trapped against it. There was no mention of the door being stuck. *Could it be an attempt by the mine owners to deflect the blame*, he wondered?

'My Elizabeth is in there...' The women's voice interrupted his thoughts. 'Eleven, she was'. The woman's Yorkshire dialect was rapid, and difficult for the Irish Earl to follow. 'Aye, and my James. He was sixteen. Hurriers they were,' she continued.

O'Neill nodded compassionately at the woman. 'A terrible business,' he said.

'I was with them, on that day.' A young lad appeared and stared solemnly at the Earl. He had been standing on the other side of the tall monument. The boy had long blond hair and he was dressed in rough working clothes.

'I have told Mrs Clarkson what really happened,' the young lad said. He put his arm on the shoulder of the grieving woman.

O'Neill motioned to one of his men to take notes.

'Would you give us a statement? We are part of the Royal Commission. What is your name?' he asked the boy.

'Billy Birk. Tha's going to be late for thi shift. Watch what thar saying!' A gruff voice shouted across the quiet churchyard before the boy could answer. It was a burly man, also dressed in working attire but with a bowler hat perched on his head. He was obviously somebody in authority.

CHAPTER TWENTY NINE
The Fox

On hearing the man's voice, the woman left the headstone and hurried off down to the village. It was obvious to see her antipathy towards him.

The young lad doffed his cap.

'Aye, Mr Fox. I am away,' he said, in a tone that did not seem very sincere.

The stranger barrelled up to the Commissioners.

'Might I ask why you fine gentlemen are upsetting these good people?' he asked, in a belligerent Yorkshire voice.

'I am the Earl of Wexford,' O'Neill answered. 'I am in charge of the Royal Commission concerning the coal mines in these parts. My task is to interview as many people as I deem necessary to ascertain the facts. You are, Sir?' O'Neill faced the man.

The man was taken aback at the Earl's educated Irish voice, but he meant to stamp his authority.

'I am Ebenezer Fox, the Colliery Overseer, at the Huskar and Moorend Collieries.' He glanced at the smoke from the nearby Colliery chimney. 'Any interviews will go through me. You will not speak to these people without me being present.'

'Mr Fox –' O'Neill was used to dealing with bullies educated, or uneducated. 'I am giving you fair warning. If you prevent these officers carrying out their lawful business or prejudice any witnesses, I will have you arrested for obstructing the Royal inquiry.'

O'Neill nodded to one of his secretaries. 'Mr Fulwood. Note my warning to Mr Fox.'

Fulwood dutifully started to write in his ledger.

Fox had met his match. He was seething, muttering under his breath as he marched out of the churchyard.

O'Neill and his party set off towards the colliery. The miners on their way to work kept their heads down. The Irish Earl knew these workers were ruled by fear, and that the mine owners would try everything to block the Commission's work. Word was already spreading about their visit.

CHAPTER THIRTY
The Mine Owner

Robert Cauldwell Clarke looked out of the window of Noblethorpe Hall. His wife, Sarah Anne, sat opposite him at the breakfast table. He ate in a moody silence.

'Who was that, Robert?' His wife broke the atmosphere. She had heard a commotion at the door earlier, and knew there had been a visitor.

'Ebenezer Fox,' he said. 'The Moorend overseer. The Royal Commission is here.'

'So soon?' she replied. 'What are you going to do about them?'

'Fox is warning the workers that if they talk to these people, they will be dismissed,' he snapped.

'That is rather strong, Robert, is it not? You cannot silence them all. Can you?'

Sarah was far more benevolent than her husband. She had lessened the blow of the recent Huskar tragedy by providing the funds for the headstone that was erected in the churchyard. She had also visited the mothers of the bereaved children. She was a mother as well. But she did not stand in the way of her husband's business.

'I have told Fox to get the children out of the mine by the Silkstone drift, as soon as possible. I do not want these Commissioners to see anything untoward.'

Clarke wanted to keep the children away from these prying people. He had told Fox to keep them on surface work, while the Commissioners were around.

'I am on my way to the Moorend pit now, to meet these Royal Commissioners.' He gritted his teeth as he spoke, and put on his top hat. This was a sign of his authority. He was a small man but he more than compensated for his stature with his domineering character.

His horse had already been saddled by one of his many servants. As he rode up to the mine, he passed more of his workers. They were pulling the coal tubs up an incline.

All the workers doffed their caps, and some even ventured to say 'Good Morning, Mr Clarke.'

He was the King of his own domain. The workers were all afraid of him.

In half an hour, Clarke was at the colliery. He soon spotted O'Neill and his party speaking to some of his surface workers. He rode straight up to them and vented his anger at the strangers.

'You people are on my property. You have no business here. You are to leave this instant.'

O'Neill guessed who he was.

'Mr Clarke, I presume?' He offered his hand for Clarke to shake.

Clarke ignored his handshake and spoke to Fox, the overseer.

'Mr Fox. Escort these people off my property. Take them to the colliery gates. They have no business here.' he ordered.

'Pardon my impertinence –' O'Neill interrupted. 'It is the Queen's business that we do here today. I will warn you, Mr Clarke, not to interrupt our work or I shall hold you in contempt. I could have you arrested.'

Clarke was red-faced, incandescent with rage and fury.

'How dare you tell me what I can, or cannot do? These are my people. You are on my land. You have no right to interfere with my business.'

'If these are your people, as you maintain, it follows you should take more care of their welfare,' the Earl berated him. 'Perhaps you enjoy digging mass graves for children. It is transparent that the only people you keep in employment are the coffin makers and the undertakers.'

Clarke had heard enough. With his right hand, he pulled his rifle from the scabbard strapped to his saddle. He pointed it at the Irishman.

'Mr Clarke. I would suggest that you put down that rifle.' A voice boomed from the entrance of the colliery. An imposing policeman stood at the gates.

Mr Clarke dropped his aim, so the rifle was pointing harmlessly at the ground.

CHAPTER THIRTY ONE
The Police Sergeant

'Sergeant Stead. It is no business of yours. These men are trespassing on my land and I want them removing.' Clarke commanded.

'Can you state your business on Mr Clarke's property?' Sergeant Stead asked the Earl. The Sergeant had heard of the Commissioners visit, and had anticipated some trouble with the mine owners. It was his duty to keep the peace on his territory.

O'Neill handed the Sergeant an official letter of introduction.

'I am the Earl of Wexford,' he explained. 'I must apologise most profusely. I should have seen you before I came here. I wanted to see this place for myself.'

The Sergeant glanced at the documents. 'It seems to me that both parties have got off on the wrong foot, so to speak.'

The mine owner had reluctantly put his rifle away.

'Mr Clarke,' the Sergeant said. 'You are bound by law to let these Commissioners carry out their duties. They are on the Queen's business.'

'What exactly do you want here?' The Sergeant turned to O'Neill.

'We need to question witnesses about child labour in the mines. We have to record them verbatim, for the records. I need to start work as soon as possible.' the Earl said.

The Sergeant nodded. 'Well it seems to me, Mr Clarke, that you have no choice in the matter. Might I suggest that you find these gentlemen a place where they can conduct their business?'

Clarke stormed off and left Fox to attend to the commissioners' needs. Fox took the party to a shed at the side of the blacksmith's shop. It was a shoddy place to work, thought O'Neill, but it was under cover, with a few rough chairs and a desk, of sorts. At least it gave him an insight into the workers' conditions.

O'Neill stopped the scowling overseer before he could leave the shed.

'Mr Fox. I shall be interviewing some of your workers. I need to speak with the children who work underground. May we start with you?'

CHAPTER THIRTY TWO
Who is the Fox?

This was something that Fox was dreading.

'Since the accident we do not deploy children underground,' he told O'Neill. He sensed there would be a lot more awkward questions to answer. One of the secretaries was ready with his quill.

O'Neill pursed his lips, but remained silent.

At the coroner's inquest the previous year, Fox had escaped justice by a quirk of fate. The deaths of the children had been caused by water rushing into the mine. The children had tried to escape by going up a ventilation drift. Unfortunately, an air door had been put on the wrong way, trapping the children. This had contributed to the large death toll. Who had put the door on the wrong way round? This question had never been asked at the inquest.

It was in fact Fox who had instructed the door to be turned around. He had done it to prevent the workers from going that way out of the pit. He had suspected some of the children had been sneaking out early up the ventilation drift.

However, the subject of the door had never arisen. The mine management had sighed with relief at the verdict of 'accidental death'. Of course, everybody knew who had done it, but nobody dared to come out and say it. They all feared losing their jobs at the mine. Fox ruled with an iron fist.

Sarah Anne Clarke had paid for the funerals of the children, and for the headstone in the churchyard. This had taken the pressure off her husband but now these commissioners were stirring up memories.

Since the accident, the mine had been boycotted by some miners, who had gone to different collieries. But the harsh conditions and low pay made ideal recruiting grounds for the new trade unions. Already there had been a series of strikes and lockouts in the booming coalfield.

The mine owners were getting organised too, and any trouble-makers were blacklisted. Some miners had been forced to leave the area for Lancashire or South Wales.

O'Neill left Fox with one of his men. He was burning with anger, but he told himself that it really did not matter what Fox said. If there was any ambiguity with his statement, he would be recalled later. The Earl wondered whom he should talk to next.

He was suddenly distracted by one of his men, who had been inspecting the mine buildings.

'My Lord,' the commissioner whispered. 'There is a boy who wishes to speak with you. He is over by the mine shaft.'

At the head of the shaft, a young boy beckoned him into a dark corner of a noisy engine room. He recognised the lad from the churchyard.

'They call me Billy Birk, Sir,' the lad said. O'Neill strained to hear him over the machines. 'Fox is a liar. I was in the pit that day and saw what happened. It was Fox, who had the door turned round. He killed those bairns.'

O'Neill nodded, unsurprised. It was obvious that the pit owners had something to hide.

'Summat else, Sir. He has brought us kids arta pit today. He didn't want you to see owt.'

'Will you give us a statement?' O'Neill asked.

'I dare not. Fox has told us not to speak with you.' The boy was shaking, and pale under the grime of coal dust. It had obviously taken a lot of courage to speak to O'Neill in secret.

'I will have to go. Fox's spies are everywhere.' The boy crawled into a small hole that led outside, and he was gone.

CHAPTER THIRTY THREE
The Public House

The next night, O'Neill was in his room in the Barnsley inn. He had plenty to think about. In Ireland, he had been brought up to be wary of the English.

Even though he was part of the landowning classes, he had seen how the Irish were treated. The economic conditions were killing the Irish economy, and people were dying. They were leaving in droves for America to find a new life, but thousands of Irishmen were coming here to England to work as the industrial revolution gathered pace.

A new life? He pondered. The English did not treat their own people properly; never mind the foreigners who were coming from Ireland.

He shook off his thoughts as he went downstairs to order his meal.

The Old Bear was like many Victorian public houses. The landlady was a stern middle-aged Yorkshire woman in a starched apron; a widow, who kept a clean, rather austere establishment, mostly for visitors who came here on business connected to the coal trade or the new railway.

O'Neill ate alone in the parlour. As he finished his meal, a gentleman with deep-set eyes and a determined expression entered the room.

'May I join you, Sir?' he asked, in an educated voice with a hint of a Yorkshire accent. 'You look as if you need company. They are wary of strangers in these parts.'

O'Neill motioned the stranger to a seat opposite him.

'I am Joseph Locke, a railway engineer.' The stranger introduced himself. 'You are the Earl of Wexford, are you not? There are no secrets around these parts.'

O'Neill laughed, and shook his hand. He also knew of Locke.

'You are local, Mr Locke?' O'Neill already knew the answer.

'Yes, my house is nearby,' Locke replied. 'Can I recharge your glass?'

The two of them spoke for over two hours on political matters, and the great earthworks that Locke was involved with on the moors. They found they had a lot in common and were roughly the same age.

In particular, O'Neill had an interest in the Irish navvies that Locke employed in their hundreds.

The landlady suddenly entered the parlour, interrupting their conversation. She was flushed and distressed.

'Pardon me, gentlemen. There is a policeman here. He wants to speak to the Earl. He has a young lad with him – in a bad way.'

Before O'Neill could answer, a policeman entered the room. He was half-carrying, half dragging an injured youth. The boy's face was cut and bleeding, and his eye was bruised and puffed up. But the Earl immediately recognised his blond hair, which was now matted with blood.

The policeman was Sergeant Stead. He gently lowered the lad onto a bench.

'Billy, what's wrong? Have you been injured in the pit?' O'Neill asked.

The boy's mouth was swollen and he had difficulty opening his mouth.

CHAPTER THIRTY FOUR
The Two Bully Brothers

Ebenezer Fox was still seething at the way the cocky Irishman had spoken to him. The Commissioners had now left the pit head, and he was alone in his office.

It had been a bad day. The tonnage was well down. The removal of child labour had caused a backlog at the coal faces. The coal could not be trammed out of the pit as quickly now the children had been brought out of the mine. The coal cutters had to be redeployed to carry out the children's work.

He was trying to add up the production figures for Clarke. He knew the mine owner would be very angry, and would vent his wrath on him. He was disturbed by a knock on his door. A man entered. It was his brother Joshua. He was a colliery foreman, and one of his snitches. The Fox brothers knew everything that happened at the mine.

'Young Billy Birk, brother Ebenezer. He has been seen with the Commissioners.' Joshua broke the news. 'He was gone over half an hour from his workplace,' he exaggerated.

Fox threw his papers on the floor. 'Get him here now. I want to see him.' He had to take out his frustration on somebody.

Soon afterwards, Joshua Fox brought Billy into the office.

'Birkenshaw, I expressly told you not to talk to the Commissioners. The foreman tells me that you were with them for half an hour. What have you told them?' The overseer laid straight into him.

Billy read the situation in an instant. He was determined to stay quiet.

'Birkenshaw, I am asking you a question. What have you said to them?' Fox demanded.

Billy kept silent. It only made his interrogators angrier.

'Answer me!' Ebenezer Fox screamed in Billy's face.

His brother Joshua was intent on using the situation to impress his brother. He went one step further. He swung out at Billy, hitting him hard across his face. Billy barely flinched.

'You will answer the question, Birkenshaw? What did you say to the Commissioners?'

Billy was bleeding from his eyelid and fighting back smarting tears, but he was not prepared to let these two bullies see him weak.

'You have been seen at union meetings, in Barnsley as well.' Joshua shouted. He hit Billy again.

'Joshua. Just a moment.' Ebenezer Fox put his hand out to stop a third blow. It was one thing to shout at the lad but to physically attack him was a step too far, even in the cruel world of the mines. He would have difficulty explaining this to Clarke. And the commissioners would surely hear of this. There was only one option left.

'Birkenshaw. Mr Clarke has kept you in employment since the accident out of kindness, and this is how you repay us?'

Fox knew that this was a lie. The boy had been kept on because he knew too much about the children's deaths. Billy knew all about the air door and the cover up in the inquiry. In keeping him close, they would be able to control him. But now there was no alternative. He would have to sack Billy.

'You are finished, Birkenshaw. You will leave this site now.'

CHAPTER THIRTY FIVE
Billy Hits Back

Joshua Fox escorted Billy from the office. Blood poured from Billy's eyelid. He made a pitiful sight to the workers who had heard the disturbance and were gathered outside.

The foreman could not resist showing off in front of the workers.

'And don't come back, Birkenshaw,' he shouted. 'The wrong ones got killed that day. It should have been thee behind that door.' He shoved Billy in the back.

On hearing these words, Billy snapped. Since the accident, he had kept his mouth shut, but now he was free. He hated these two with a vengeance. He was a fit lad and could hold his own in any street fight.

Billy spun round and cracked the foreman a right hook. Joshua Fox fell backwards onto a pile of pit props. His overseer brother was now out of his office. Before Ebenezer Fox could react, Billy hit him with another right hook, knocking out several teeth. A second blow hit him between the eyes. The overseer was down and out.

The crowd of workers cheered. They had never seen anything like this. Billy had certainly made his mark. The two most hated men in the area were both reeling with pain in the muddy yard.

Before the men could come to their senses, Billy left the pit and started walking to his mother's home five miles away in Thurlstone.

His parents were shocked when they saw him. Billy's mother bathed his swollen eyelid.

'Tha will have to come and work with me, Billy Boy, in the shop', Billy's father said, smoking his pipe. 'We've worried ever since that accident. I am not happy with thee going down that pit.'

Billy heard him but he did not want to work in his father's butcher's shop. He wanted a more adventurous life.

'So what does tha intend doing now, Billy?' his father asked, exhaling a cloud of smoke.

'I need to see the Commissioners again, Dad. They need to know about this, and aye, I will go and see the union in town' Billy was determined he would see this through.

The next morning he set off for Barnsley.

CHAPTER THIRTY SIX
The Mine Owner's Wife

Robert Cauldwell Clarke's rage knew no boundaries.

He had summoned the two Fox brothers to his house. He could hardly believe what he was hearing. The whole area was buzzing with the news of what had happened the day before and he did not know what to do next.

Normally he kept his wife, Sarah Anne, out of his business, but in a situation like this, he needed her advice. She had guided him through the Huskar disaster. Her humanity had taken the pressure off the accusations that he was an uncaring mine owner.

He had asked her to be present at this unsavoury meeting as a voice of reason.

The two brothers stood in front of them both, with their caps in their hands. They presented a sorry state. Both of them had missing teeth, cuts, bruises, and black eyes where Billy had hit them.

The mine owner listened to their version of events while he tried to keep his temper.

'It seems that you have met your match with this young chap Birkenshaw.' His wife spoke first. She did not have much time for these two bullies. As a God-Fearing pillar of the community, Sarah opposed violence.

Clarke clenched his teeth.

'I cannot believe what you have done. Do you not realise the danger that you have put us in? Birkenshaw knows too much. We need him back on our side. You were stupid to sack him.' He paused for a moment. 'I should really sack the both of you.'

The two brothers looked at him sorrowfully.

'Can you not understand the implications of sacking Birkenshaw? If I dismiss the two of you, the workers would see it as Billy Birk being in the right, and you idiots being in the wrong.'

'You need to get Birkenshaw back here so that we can deal with him,' Sarah said. 'If he goes to the Union, or to that Commission, it could be the ruin of us. In my opinion, that is the only option. Robert, send these men away while we ponder on it.'

Clarke appreciated her wise counsel. He nodded.

'Go back to your work while I consider what to do with you.' He ordered the Fox brothers. They left the house in a dejected state.

CHAPTER THIRTY SEVEN
Dirty Deeds in Dog Lane

Billy decided to see the Miners Union in Barnsley. He hoped that they could help him. He had been to a few meetings in town, and he knew that they had an office on Shambles Street. He needed a job. He could always help his father in his butcher's shop, but he was desperate to stand on his own two feet.

The Union Office was in a dingy yard, and when he knocked on the door, no one answered. There was a notice pinned the door saying it would be open the following day. Billy would have to wait.

He set off towards the market square to see if anyone else would take him on. But he had no luck among the farmers. Billy didn't blame them. He was no picture with his bruised, puffed-up eye.

At dusk, Billy walked up the steps of a narrow alley called Dog Lane. It was lit only by a faint glow from a gas lamp on the main street. But Billy knew the lane well.

He had not gone far when two men blocked his way.

He recognised them from their silhouettes as the Fox Brothers.

Joshua Fox held a short curved knife in his hand.

'Billy Birk. Come here to tell tha tale, ez tha?' he hissed through his teeth. 'When we've done with thee, tha will never speak again. I'm going to cut that tongue out'

He lunged for Billy.

Sidestepping the first move, Billy lashed out at Joshua. But Ebenezer Fox hit Billy with an iron bar. Billy fell to the ground and the man hit him again. The last thing Billy heard before he passed out was the sharp blast of a Police whistle.

CHAPTER THIRTY EIGHT
Rescue

Sergeant Irving Stead was on Shambles Street when he heard the disturbance. He saw the shadows of two men attacking someone. He immediately blew his whistle and ran down the narrow lane. But before he reached the scene of the attack, the two men fled.

Stead recognised both assailants. He decided to let them go. He would deal with them later. He knelt over the prone body of Billy. He was breathing raggedly, gradually returning to consciousness.

'You'll be alright, lad,' Stead reassured him.

The policeman saw the glint of a blade on the cobbles. He wrapped it in his handkerchief and pocketed it as evidence against the suspects.

In a matter of minutes, the area was alive with curious people, roused by Stead's blast on his whistle. His police constables arrived, out of breath.

'The Fox brothers are behind this. They ran down the steps.' Stead instructed his subordinates. 'Arrest them. They will probably be on the Penistone Road by now.'

The Sergeant decided the best thing would be to take the boy to the Old Bear, which was close by. He knew the Earl of Wexford was staying there, and may be able to help. The Sergeant's police training told him that the attack was somehow connected with the Royal Commission.

Stead and a local man carried Billy to the public house. Billy was only fifteen, but he was a tall, strapping lad. Stead had heard about the incident at the pit the previous day. Billy had been able to handle himself, but the consequences had been serious.

On the bench in the parlour of the Old Bear, Billy was trying to answer the Earl's question about his injuries. He looked confused.

'He was attacked in Dog Lane, my Lord, by the two Fox brothers. I saw it with my own eyes.' Stead answered. 'I have detached my officers to apprehend the two men for attempted murder. They tried to stab Billy.'

He showed O'Neill the knife.

'Good God.' The Earl exclaimed. 'Perhaps it was our fault. We should have dealt more carefully with those villains at the mine.'

Billy tried to speak again, trying to sit up.

'Mi mam. Mi mam – she'll be worried,' he mumbled. Stead heard him.

'Don't worry yourself, Billy Boy. My men will inform her. You're safe now.'

'Have you a room for the lad?' O'Neill asked the landlady. 'Put him on my bill, of course.'

She nodded, and hurried away to prepare a room. She returned with a bowl of warm water and cloths to clean and bind Billy's wounds, which she did briskly, yet tenderly.

'You were brave, lad, to stand up to those Fox brothers,' she said. 'But it was lucky the Sergeant came along before they could do their worst.'

Billy tried to smile.

'I will arrange for my surgeon to attend you,' Locke told him. 'A capital fellow – name of Pomfret. Works wonders with the railway navvies.'

'Will you gentlemen carry Billy to his room?' the landlady asked. 'It's rest he wants.'

Once Billy had been made comfortable in a clean bed, O'Neill, Locke, and the Sergeant returned to the parlour to discuss the matter.

'Have you time for a drink Sergeant? Is it permitted?' O'Neill asked Stead.

'Well I won't tell, if you don't,' replied Stead. 'Just a tot of whisky, if you please Sir.'

O'Neill turned to Locke. 'It's a sad affair, this. Is there much trouble on your railway earthworks?'

'Not much, my Lord, but our work is newer than the coal mining. We have a lot of Irish workers, and begging the present company,' he raised a sly grin, 'it is either liquor, or sectarian matters that we have problems with. We have Scottish, and English Presbyterians who cannot get on with the Irish Catholics.'

'Like Mr Locke here, I am local, sir.' Stead added. 'I know the people very well. But the boom in industry has brought a lot of new people here to work. Some of them are lawless. The crime rate is rising. And people don't trust the mine owners – especially after the disaster.'

'It must be difficult to keep law and order around here,' O Neil sympathised.

The Sergeant nodded.

'You'll have a difficult task with this Commission, my Lord,' Stead told him, drinking his whisky. 'These mine owners look after their own. They think their power is absolute. But this attack on Billy Birkenshaw is attempted murder. I intend to interview Mr Clarke to see if he is implicated in this business.'

The Sergeant turned to leave.

'I had better return to the Station. My constables should have arrested the Fox brothers by now.'

'It has been an eventful evening.' Locke said. 'I too, must be away. You will keep in touch, my Lord, I hope. I feel our paths will cross again.'

Locke put on his top hat.

'Just one last thing,' he said, before he left. 'I suspect that this lad will be blackballed in the pits. That is the way of these mine owners. Here's my calling card. I will offer Billy a job. He lives at Thurlstone does he not? It is not far from my new tunnel, at Dunford Bridge.'

O'Neill finished his drink alone, and thought about the day's events.

'I must record all these happenings,' he mused to himself. 'I will start a diary. I will start writing tonight and carry on every night until we have completed the task. That is what I must do.'

CHAPTER THIRTY NINE
July 1952
The Fair City

It was a lovely sunny evening in Dublin. After her evening meal in the hotel, Susan explored the city. She didn't look like an English "bobby". She would have passed for a tourist in her pale yellow summer dress and smart handbag.

The journey had been tiring, but it was exhilarating to be in such a big city. She found herself walking down the wide boulevard of O'Connell Street, until she reached the magnificently wide bridge which spanned the Liffey, looking towards Nelson's Pillar. The streets were still bustling with people and buses.

That morning, she had caught the Manchester train from Barnsley and travelled through the old Woodhead tunnel to the Manchester London Road station. The train had stopped at Dunford Bridge before it entered the tunnel. She could see the site cabins where the new tunnel was being driven. She thought about the skeletons. It was her responsibility to unravel the mystery surrounding them. As her dimly-lit compartment rumbled through the tunnel, she shivered in her summer clothes. It took the train twelve minutes to pass under the desolate moors, but it had taken the Victorian navvies over thirteen years of back-breaking work and danger to build both tunnels.

This tunnel was hiding the truth, she thought. She had researched it as much as she could. She had visited Pennine churchyards with graves that told of cholera epidemics and accidents. They only told part of the story. She hoped she could find the answers in Dublin.

From Manchester, she had caught the Irish Mail to Holyhead, and from there, to Dublin, on the steam package.

At the ferry port, a friendly taxi driver had taken her to the Shelbourne Hotel, on St Stephen's Green, near Grafton Street. It had an ornate ironwork canopy and revolving doors. She couldn't believe that the West Riding Constabulary had booked her into somewhere so grand. The taxi driver had been very curious, but she had told him that she was on holiday in Ireland.

Before she had left Yorkshire, Susan had signed the Official Secrets Act. The politics of the Irish situation were very sensitive. After years of Republican turmoil, the Royal connections in O'Neill's diaries could be inflammatory.

Chief Inspector Columbine had warned her not to tell anyone where she was going. Not even her mother knew her whereabouts. She was bound by the Official Secrets remit.

'Be careful, Susan,' her mother had said. 'Promise you'll write to me when you get the chance.'

'I'm not sure I can, mam. You'll see the post mark.' It was so frustrating – and a little lonely, to be here and not able to tell anyone what she was doing.

Early the next morning, she met a local policewoman in the hotel lobby, as arranged.

'I'm Garda Eileen O'Rourke,' she introduced herself. She wore a smart navy uniform.

Susan was pleased to find that the Irish Police officer was around her own age, slightly plump with curly blonde hair.

'I am to stay with you, Sergeant,' Garda O'Rourke told her, in her thick Dublin accent. 'I have a car outside.'

They were at Dublin Castle in a few minutes. While she was driving, Eileen gave Susan a potted history of the Castle. She had done her own research, but she felt it would be rude to interrupt the Garda officer, who was chatting away.

'It's more of a tourist attraction now, really. President O'Kelly was inaugurated here last month. But some parts are top secret – especially the archives. It's quite exciting.'

'What we can't understand in England is why these documents have been locked up for over a hundred years.' Susan asked. 'Somebody must have wanted to keep them secret.'

The Irish Garda shrugged her shoulders.

'You've got a real mystery. I envy you.' She laughed. 'But looking after you makes a change from arresting drunks, and raiding pubs that stay open too late.'

CHAPTER FORTY
The Forgotten Past

Dublin Castle was very imposing, a mixture of Georgian and Medieval architecture set around a large courtyard.

Susan wondered what stories these walls could tell. The castle had seen centuries of turbulence, risings, civil war, and the birth of the Irish Free State.

The two policewomen were ushered into an office where a very business-like woman introduced herself as the Archives Director, Jean Flanagan.

She studied both the policewomen's identity cards intently, and then produced the paperwork that had been sent from England.

'I have been briefed by the West Riding Constabulary,' she explained to Susan. 'It appears that we have some information relating to the bodies that have been found in your railway tunnel.'

'The diaries of the Earl of Wexford,' Susan said, smiling.

Jean Flanagan passed a contract to Susan.

'The Irish Free State Official Secrets Act. Sign here, please,' she said.

Susan read the document quickly, signed it and slid it back across the desk.

The Archives Director took them through a maze of doors and corridors, into a long room in the deepest recesses of the Castle. There were many rows of bookcases and mobile aisle shelving. The archives were accessed by turning a device that looked like a car's steering wheel, attached to the end of each row.

Jean Flanagan checked her index.

'Here we are,' she said. She found the location of the diaries. Flanagan turned the wheel at the end of the row, and found what she was looking for: a small pile of box files stored just above head height. They were each labelled:

Robert O'Neill - The Earl of Wexford
Diaries: 1840-1846

Flanagan stood on a small round stool. She lifted the heavy boxes down to the two policewomen and they carried them into a small office.

The Archives Director then gave them cotton gloves, to protect the valuable documents in the boxes.

Flanagan carefully pulled the large, leather-bound books out of the box files.

'You've signed the Official Secrets Acts, so you know what is expected of you. Do not take these books away from here. Drinking and eating are not allowed in the archive section. I shall return at one o'clock,' she addressed Susan.

Susan slowly opened the first volume. The book was in beautiful condition, filled with exquisite copperplate handwriting in the formal, bygone language of the Victorians. She started to read.

The first entry was Tuesday 16th June 1840. She checked her notes. It was two years after the Huskar disaster. The Earl mentioned the public house that he was staying in on the first page: The Old Bear, in Shambles Street, in the Yorkshire town of Barnsley.

'Wow' she muttered. The Irish Garda had wandered off to explore the archive, and Susan was alone in the office.

'I know the White Bear pub, but not The Old Bear', she muttered. 'But mum said that there used to be five pubs on Shambles Street with the name Bear in them.'

The Earl gave his account of his visit to the Huskar mine, and the events leading up to Billy Birkenshaw being attacked on Dog Lane.

Susan became absorbed by the diary. She was absolutely besotted by O'Neill's account. She knew the places that the Earl described. She felt as if she was transported in a time machine into the past.

O'Neill finished off his first diary entry:

I am very grateful to my new friend, Joseph Locke, for offering the boy, Billy Birkenshaw employment on his railway. I feel I am to blame for the lad's predicament, for if I had not pressed him to give a statement, he would not have been attacked. Sergeant Stead has promised he will arrest his assailants for attempted murder.

Susan started taking notes. The name Billy Birkenshaw seemed important. She felt sure the name would crop up again. Susan was also intrigued by the mention of the railway engineer, Joseph Locke. 'They named a park after him,' she murmured.

The Office Keeper, Jean Flanagan, dutifully returned at one o'clock and had to virtually prise Susan away from the books.

'Sergeant' she joked. 'They have been here for over a hundred years. I am sure that half an hour away from them will not make any difference.'

After tea and sandwiches, Susan carried on with her research. For the rest of the summer of 1840, O'Neill and his Commissioners were hard at work interviewing the mine workers, finding more evidence of female and child labour. Susan made notes in shorthand.

Garda Eileen O'Rourke looked up from her magazine and watched Susan intently.

'What are you looking for now, Sergeant?' Eileen asked.

'I'm trying to find if the Police apprehended the two men that attacked the boy, Billy Birkenshaw,' Susan answered.

CHAPTER FORTY ONE
A Beacon of Light

It took Susan another half an hour to find the information she was looking for. She read more diary entries.

The Irish Lord had visited a lot of Coal Mines. The pits, and place names, had a familiar ring to them: The Oaks Colliery, Swaithe Main, the Darley, and the Mount Osborne were all mentioned.

Suddenly she found it. Friday 19th June 1840. It read:

The Good Sergeant Stead has paid me a visit. He told me that the two felons had been arrested at Penistone. Joshua and Ebenezer Fox are now awaiting trial at the Leeds Assizes.

The young lad William Birkenshaw has almost recovered from his ordeal, thanks to Locke's surgeon. I am thinking of paying another visit to the Mine Owner, Robert Clarke, at the Moorend and Huskar Mines. There are discrepancies in his Colliery statements. I will take Birkenshaw with me to see how Clarke receives him.

Susan turned to the next entry, dated Monday 22nd June 1840. She smiled at O'Neill's comments:

I have yet to find on God's Earth people like these Mine Owners. The Good Lord must have kept the mould that created them, and cast them again in the same image. They appear all the same, and indeed they have a law unto themselves. I broached the matter of Billy Birkenshaw, with Clarke, and he said the matter was closed. He has resolved not to employ him again. He did not want the boy on his property and threatened to set his dogs on him if he trespassed.

I mentioned the two felons, the Fox brothers. He was of the opinion that it was no concern of his, and declined comment.

The Railway Engineer, Mr Locke, has meanwhile told Birkenshaw that he is to report to the Dunford Bridge tunnel, to start work, when he is fit enough. He will be under his fellow Engineer, Charles Vignoles, and under the auspices of Lord Wharncliffe, whom I am well acquainted with.

Susan continued to study the diaries from Tuesday to Friday of that week, almost getting used to the opulence of the Shelbourne Hotel.

She was thoroughly absorbed in the diaries. Their Yorkshire setting made her feel less homesick. Garda Eileen O'Rourke was chatty and welcoming, and after the first day, left Susan to work uninterrupted.

Every day, at four o'clock, Susan telephoned Chief Inspector Columbine, as he had instructed her, with her updates. By Friday, she had reached September of 1840 in O'Neill's diary.

The Irish Lord had been very busy inspecting mines in a wide radius of the county. The inspections seem to have almost reached their conclusion. Susan was puzzled. If the Royal Commission was nearing its end, why did O'Neill's diaries carry on until 1846?

An entry from Friday September 11th 1840 caught her interest. It was hidden at the end of a long account on a Yorkshire Colliery. It read:

I have received a letter with the Royal seal.

Susan found the letter tucked into the back of the first volume. It had the Buckingham Palace heading on it and it was hand-written by Queen Victoria. She slowly read the words:

Dear Lord Wexford,

You are to expect a visit from the Prince Consort's brother, Frederick. He is to travel to the Masbrough Railway Station at Rotherham, and then by carriage to Barnsley. You should expect his arrival on Monday September 14th 1840. We entrust him to your good guidance and counsel.

Susan then turned back to the diary:

It would appear that the Duke is being sent to us in an advisory capacity. We are already being treated with suspicion by these Northern Mine Owners. I fear that this German aristocrat will not be received with any further trust.

At last, Susan had found something intriguing in the Commission's work. Why would a German Duke be sent to the Yorkshire Coalface by the Queen herself?

At three o'clock that afternoon, Garda O'Rourke came down to the vaults to find her. 'Sergeant, your Chief Constable has telephoned us. You are to ring him immediately.'

Susan rang Columbine from the Archive Keeper's Office.

'Ah, Susan,' he said. 'You'd better put your archive work on hold. The workers have found another body in the tunnel.'

'Shall I come back to Yorkshire?'

'Tomorrow, if you can. We need your quick thinking.'

Susan would have to shelve the mystery of the German Duke.

CHAPTER FORTY TWO
More Discoveries

By July 1952, the new Woodhead tunnel was well advanced. The new Eastern bore was now roughly half a mile in from the Dunford Bridge end of the tunnel.

Mechanised machines were ripping into the Pennine strata, but one age-old element always held them up. It was water. Everything was wet, and the electric pumps were working constantly to keep the water levels down.

The workmen drilled through the strata with large air-borers. The rock was then ignited and blown out. The *Eicoff* mechanical shovels emptied the rock to advance the roadways.

To combat the water problem, Balfour Beatty, the company constructing the new tunnel, had decided to open up an old connecting passage which had linked the 1845 tunnels. If the water could be pumped into the old tunnel's drainage system, it would run down a gulley at the side of the tracks.

The connecting tunnel had been sealed in 1845, to prevent the foul combustion from the old steam locomotives short-circuiting and choking the tunnels. The passage was roughly twenty five yards long. It had been sealed by large building blocks. The old plans from 1845 revealed that they were only twenty yards from the old slit.

A new tunnel was driven to connect into the old passage. The engineers fully expected it to be full of foul air and water. Surprisingly, it was dry. The engineers shone their lights into a space that had been sealed for a hundred years. The hard rock had sealed it and had kept it waterproof.

'What's that over yonder?' a young Liverpool lad wondered. He flashed his light to a shape lying in the old tunnel. 'It looks like some old sacks.'

Once the safety tests were completed, it was declared safe to enter the old passage. The young Scouser was first in. He curiously investigated the hessian sack.

'Bloody Hell!' he shouted. 'There's a skeleton in here!'

The alarm was raised. Within three hours, Chief Inspector Columbine, Detective Inspector Andrew Monroe, and the pathologist Ned Lawson were examining the scene.

Like the first body, there was a piece of parchment inside its mouth, inscribed with:

"Good night, sweet friend
Thy love ne'er alter, till thy sweet life end."

CHAPTER FORTY THREE
Deja Vu

It was Monday morning. Susan and her police colleagues entered the pathology laboratory in Sheffield. They met Ned Lawson and gathered around the new skeleton.

'Déjà vu,' Chief Inspector Columbine whistled, as they gathered around the new skeleton. 'Here we are again. Well, Ned. What have you got for us this time?'

'Female, without any shadow of a doubt,' the pathologist said. 'In her mid-twenties. Cause of death – a stomach wound caused by a sharp object.'

'But take a look,' he said, pointing to her remains. 'Her right leg had been amputated at the thigh, and this,' he touched a piece of rotten wood, 'was her wooden leg.'

The Chief Inspector turned to Susan.

'Sergeant, the paper. Is it the same parchment as the last time? And what about the wording? Is it Milton again?'

Susan had been examining the inscription and had discovered something strange.

'No Sir. This time it's Shakespeare. A *Midsummer Night's Dream*, Act 2, Scene 3,' she answered. 'But when I was comparing them, I discovered that they were written on the same piece of expensive parchment, which had been torn in half. This half joins up exactly with the manuscript from the first two bodies. And the writing is in the same German script.'

Columbine pondered, staring at the skeleton, as if he was expecting it to tell him the answer.

'I am trying to get my head around all this,' he said. 'This time, the skeleton was in a sealed passage. How did it get there? Obviously someone must have taken the body there in the sack. It must have been a workman. It's all very strange, and why the Shakespeare and Milton verses? Someone very educated must have written them. How many of the navvies would be able to read and write in those days? Let alone quote English Literature.'

He looked at his two subordinates.

'Have you got any ideas, Andy? Susan, what about the Irish diaries?'

Susan produced her notes.

'Well, sir. I believe there are more clues in the diaries. I've reached 1840 - there are pages and pages about the Royal Commission's investigation of child labour in the mines. It's a microscopic insight into the time - a living historical document,' Susan sighed. 'But so far, I'm perplexed. Why were they banned from public view? There must be something in there to help us.'

'We need you to find some clues,' Columbine said.

'It's fascinating stuff, but there are four more volumes to wade through,' Susan explained. 'It may take some time. But I have found out that the Earl of Wexford was well acquainted with the railway engineer, Joseph Locke. He was in charge of the construction of the tunnel from 1842, until 1845, when it opened.'

Columbine nodded.

'Susan, you had better return to Dublin. As I say, it's a long shot, but we're relying on the diaries to help us.'

'Andy,' Columbine addressed DI Monroe. 'I know the news is out.'

He held up Lawson's copy of the *Sheffield Telegraph*. On the front page was the bold headline:

ANOTHER BODY FOUND IN THE TUNNEL

'But I don't want any more details about the case leaking to the press,' the Chief Inspector explained. 'The public are getting over-excited, and we have serious work to do. Nothing about the verses on the parchment, or Susan's research in Dublin. Do you understand?'

Monroe nodded.

CHAPTER FORTY FOUR
1840
The Royal (Loose) Cannon

Monday September 14th 1840 had been a hot day, and for Robert O'Neill, it had been very tiring.

He had been visiting a coal mine called Mottram Wood. His secretaries had interviewed the colliers for evidence of children, and females, working underground.

Pressure from the mine owner had got through to the families. He had threatened them with eviction from their rented cottages if they divulged the truth to the Commissioners.

He returned to the Old Bear Inn at seven o'clock, as the light was beginning to fade. The landlady handed him a note, written in spiky German script.

It read:

My Lord Wexford

I command you to meet me at the Royal Hotel on your return. Frederick, Duke of the Duchy of Saxe-Coburg and Gotha.

O'Neill was rather taken aback at the tone of the note. After a long day, he decided the Duke would have to wait. He would wash, and dine, before he attended to the Royal visitor.

Half an hour later he was eating alone in the Old Bear, when the door of the parlour burst open. A man entered, with a woman.

'I am the Duke of the Duchy of Saxe-Coburg and Gotha,' said the very drunken man, in a strong German accent.

O'Neill recognised him immediately. He was a younger version of Prince Albert, with dark hair and a smooth handsome face. He was dressed in very expensive clothes.

In contrast, the woman was dressed in a cheap, gaudy outfit. It was obvious to O'Neill what her profession was.

'You are the Earl of Wexford. I presume?' he addressed the Irish lord. 'I see you got my note.' He glanced at the table where O'Neill had left it. 'When I issue an order I expect it to be carried out!' he barked.

O'Neill was stunned. Before he could answer the drunken Duke, the woman started to cackle.

'Freddy,' she flirted, hanging onto the Duke's arm. 'Get me a drink. There's a darling.'

She staggered to the door.

'I need to piss, deary.' The woman staggered to the parlour door, colliding with the landlady, a god-fearing woman who had witnessed many drunken disturbances.

'I am not having the likes of her in my establishment.' The landlady quickly confronted the young woman, barring her way.

The Duke rolled his eyes.

'My good woman. I am the Duke of the Duchy of Saxe-Coburg and Gotha. You can't tell me what to do.'

'I dun't care if tha the King of England, I am not having *her*, in here.' The Barnsley landlady crossed her arms, standing firm.

The Duke started to laugh, too loud for the small room.

'One day, I may be the King of England.' He slumped into a chair. 'Throw the trollop out if you so desire, but get me a whisky. I need a drink.'

The landlady of the Old Bear spared no time in shoving the woman of the night out onto the street. She poured the Duke a whisky, but frowned with contempt as she slammed it down on the table in front of him.

O'Neill had been very apprehensive about meeting the Duke. He had got the impression from the Queen that he would be rather heavy work. His worst fears were now confirmed. He had enough to deal with without having to contend with a Royal 'loose cannon'. O'Neill was shocked by the Duke's behaviour, but he remained composed. He had not yet spoken a word to the Duke. He calmly finished his meal, while the Duke drank his whisky. The Duke mumbled to himself, more German than English coming from his lips.

'I am to assist you, in your duties, Mr O'Neill. When do I start with you?' The Duke now slurred his words badly.

'You will report here Sir, at six o'clock tomorrow morning. That is when we start.' O'Neill said.

'Six in the morning? Six o'clock?' The Duke rudely interrupted. 'What an ungodly hour!'

'We start at six o'clock, and if you do not attend, the good Queen and your brother, the Prince Consort, have instructed me to make a report about your behaviour. I can assure you it will not be in your favour.' O'Neill answered.

His abrupt reply seemed to register. The Duke rose to his feet unsteadily and politely nodded to the Earl.

'I shall be in attendance on the morrow, my dear fellow,' he said. The Duke staggered out of the building.

CHAPTER FORTY FIVE
Lady of the Day

Dorothy Shaw stood outside the Royal Hotel.

She was normally a 'woman of the night', but the hand of necessity had forced her to ply her wares by day. She needed to feed her two little children. She'd persuaded her landlady to look after them. Dorothy didn't know the father of her children – there were so many clients. Barnsley was a boom town in 1840. The migrant workers on the railways came here with money to spend on payday. She needed that money, but there were many other prostitutes fighting for their share.

Like many other women, she had little choice. It was either selling her body, or taking the children to the workhouse. Dorothy knew only too well the harsh conditions that would await her and her children in there.

Although still only twenty, her profession was taking its toll on her looks, making her look prematurely haggard and middle-aged. She covered up the ravages with rouge and paint.

Dot, as everybody called her, was getting desperate. It had been quiet that day in the town.

That Monday afternoon, she had watched as a horse and carriage arrived outside the Royal Hotel. She wondered who this important person was. She watched a gentleman climb down from the carriage, assisted by his manservant. The manservant and the hotel porters then dragged two large trunks into the hotel.

Dorothy took stock of the gentleman. He was young, and there was a foreign cut to his clothes.

'Mannering. Sehen Sie zum Gepäck nehmen Es in das Hotel,' he instructed his servant. The young gentleman was alone, surveying the view of the town.

Dot decided to try her luck. She trotted over to the gentleman.

'Good afternoon, Sir.' She put on her best voice. 'I can give you a good time if you like.'

The man adjusted his monocle, and looked admiringly at her. Before he could speak, a Police Sergeant approached her. She knew Sergeant Stead from her many brushes with the law, but she knew that prostitution was seen as more of a nuisance than a crime.

'Now then, Dot, leave the gentleman alone, there's a good girl. Move along,' he warned her.

'I've got to earn a living ent a? How's a lady supposed to live?' she retorted, unafraid.

Irving Stead was at the end of his shift and did not want to waste time on the prostitute. The Earl of Wexford had warned him about the arrival of the Royal visitor. Not wanting to give a bad impression of the town, he ushered Dot away. He then escorted the Royal Duke into the hotel.

An hour later Dot returned to the side of the hotel. After a while, the foreign gentleman came out, alone. She decided to try her luck again.

'Still after a good time, are you, Sir?'

'Can you give me a good time?' The Duke of the Duchy of Saxe-Coburg and Gotha answered, in a strong accent.

Dot needed no encouragement and linked arms with the gentleman, with no resistance.

'Call me Dot, if you like.' she whispered flirtatiously.

'I need a drink first. I have been travelling all day. Where are your finest taverns?' She led him away from the hotel.

CHAPTER FORTY SIX
A Dark Deed Indeed

Later that night, Dot was with the Duke in his rooms at the Royal Hotel. It had been a good day's work.

Although she had been thrown out of the Old Bear, she had met up with the Duke again. She was now very drunk. The Duke had ushered her into the hotel by a back entrance. He had paid her well but he had been very rough with her.

He was like an animal, and she was very sore. Dot wanted more money for her pains.

She waited until the Duke was asleep. Then she searched his trousers that he had left draped on a chair. She quickly stole his wallet and tip-toed out of the room. Very quietly, she crept downstairs to the outside alley. She thought she had escaped safely.

'You slut, you would rob me, would you?' She recognised the Duke's voice, and froze. He had followed her into the alley.

'Freddy –' she tried to remonstrate, but he hit her across the face. The blow broke her nose. She clutched her face. Then she felt a sharp pain in her stomach.

He had stabbed her. She felt the blood flowing from her wound. She fell to the floor in a pool of her own blood. When she tried to scream, no sound came out of her mouth. Her life blood was pouring from the wound, and she knew she was dying.

The Duke searched her, and found the wallet that she had stashed in her undergarments. Her last thought was about her two baby daughters. Who would raise them now?

The Duke's manservant, George Mannering, was waiting for him. Duke Frederick staggered into his hotel room, his clothes blood-stained, and clutching a knife wet with blood. The woman's blood, Mannering guessed. He quickly appraised the situation.

The Duke slumped into a chair, insensible with drink. Not for the first time, Mannering acted quickly to help his master. He knew that the Duke had been with the whore. He guessed the rest. He stripped him of his clothes, without protest, and washed him as best he could. Mannering put the Duke's nightshirt over his head, and laid Duke Frederick on his bed, where he instantly fell fast asleep.

Gathering up the blood-stained garments, the knife, and the wallet, he lit his folding pocket lantern and left the bedroom.

Mannering had noticed the boiler house, at the rear of the building. He left the hotel by a rear entrance into the courtyard. He then crept into the boiler house door, where a huge cast-iron coal furnace was kept stoked night and day. Mannering opened the furnace door and threw the clothes into the flames.

What to do with the knife and the purse? Mannering walked down the alley, and found the murder scene.

His lantern faintly illuminated the shape of the prostitute, lying in her own blood. This was very bad. If the Duke was implicated in this murder, the scandal would be huge.

The manservant stood for a while, wondering what he could do. He soon found an answer to the problem.

A sigh from further down the alley startled him. He found a tramp, asleep on a pile of old rags in a doorway.

Quickly, Mannering put the wallet and the knife under the tramp's clothes.

Mannering then returned to the hotel, where his master was snoring loudly on the bed.

The body of the prostitute was found early the next morning by a miner on his way to work.

He ran into the Royal Hotel to raise the alarm. Sergeant Stead and his constables were soon on the scene.

Despite Mannering's efforts, the Duke was arrested that morning, on the grounds that he had been seen drinking with the woman that evening and was the last known companion of Dorothy Shaw.

CHAPTER FORTY SEVEN
Behind Bars

Sergeant Susan Priestley was back in Dublin. She continued to avidly follow the events in the diaries of Robert O'Neill.

She had found a significant event, which she copied out in shorthand:

Tuesday September 15th 1840:

We are still at the Mottram Wood Colliery, but events have overshadowed us. The good Sergeant Stead visited me yesterday at the Colliery, and was in a state of vexation. He told me that a prostitute had been murdered in an alleyway in the town.

It was the same woman Duke Frederick had been with on Monday night. I told him that the Duke had not turned up for work this morning. Stead told me that the Duke had been arrested for the murder of the prostitute.

I immediately left my Secretaries in charge and returned to the town to visit the Duke, who was in the Police Cells. He was screaming at the Officers in German. I learnt that a Police Inspector, Richard Gardiner, had been sent for from Wakefield. A dispatch rider has been sent to the Queen, on the Dukes request, for a lawyer.

I feel it most prudent to take cognisance of my position and let wiser counsels prevail.

Susan was elated. Just imagine this happening today, she thought. This was news. A Royal Duke arrested for the murder of a prostitute.

She immediately rang Columbine with the news.

He was pragmatic.

'Good news, Susan, but it's early days yet. I don't remember anything about this murder in the police archives here. I'd remember something like that. Maybe it was covered up. Anyway – keep up the good work.'

CHAPTER FORTY EIGHT
1840
The Peeler Inspector

A constable rode headlong from Barnsley to Wakefield Police station with the news of the murder.

As soon as Police Inspector Richard Gardiner had received the message, he set off for the town on horseback. He was in Barnsley in two hours.

Gardiner was fifty years old. An ex-military man, he had risen to the rank of Lieutenant in the British Army. He had been mentioned in dispatches in the Spanish Peninsula War and had fought at Badajoz, in 1812, where he'd taken a French bullet in his leg.

He had nearly lost his leg as a result of the appalling field hospitals. When he had recovered, instead of being invalided out of the army, he had kept his commission.

He was moved to the Officer corps, and he soon made a name for himself chairing disciplinary and staffing problems. He came to the eye of Arthur Wellesley, who was later to become the Duke of Wellington.

Yorkshire bluntness and a knack for solving problems quickly made him the ideal candidate for Sir Robert Peel's new Police Force, and he had rapidly been promoted to Inspector.

As soon as Gardiner arrived at Barnsley, he was welcomed by Sergeant Irving Stead. He knew him very well: indeed, he had promoted Stead to the rank of Sergeant due to his conscientious and thorough police work.

Gardiner firmly shook Stead's hand, and they talked in Stead's office in the police station.

'Nasty one this, Sir,' Stead briefed the Inspector. 'The Royal gentleman has made us send a dispatch rider to the Queen. The Duke has written a letter to demand that she sends him a lawyer. We have also sent our own report on the murder to the Royal household.'

'Has he admitted to the crime, Sergeant?' the Inspector asked.

'He screams at everybody in German all the time,' Stead answered. 'We managed to get hold of a German woman, to translate. He just rants and raves at her, saying he is of Royal descent, and wants judging by his peers.'

CHAPTER FORTY NINE
No Amusement for the Queen

Queen Victoria was not amused.

1840 had been a tumultuous year for her. She had married her darling Prince Albert on the 10th February, but in June, a madman had made an attempt on her life with two pistol shots. Albert had acted bravely, which had endeared him to her subjects.

By September, she was heavily pregnant with her first child, and she felt hot and uncomfortable. The news of the murder in Barnsley had shocked her and her beloved husband into silence.

Victoria was in a state of despair. A military dispatch rider had arrived at the palace with urgent letters from the police and Duke Frederick. Reading the circumstances of the murder the police had described, and perusing Frederick's letter, she concluded that Frederick required the best lawyer in the land. From the tone of Frederick's letter, she feared that he was not telling the full story.

She sent for the Prime Minister and close confidante, Lord Melbourne. He sat in front of her, on a red velvet armchair.

'William,' Prince Albert addressed the Prime Minister by his first name. 'Tell us. Could this be some kind of plot to discredit us?'

Lord Melbourne considered the facts the Queen had told him.

'Do you think Frederick could be guilty?' he asked her a question. 'The murdered lady was seen drinking with Lord Frederick around the town on the night of the murder. That's pretty damning evidence, your highness.'

'At least the newspapers haven't picked up the story yet,' Queen Victoria sighed. 'But it's only a matter of time.'

A gory, sensationalist murder. She couldn't possibly allow Frederick to be linked to this incident. There would be an unimaginable scandal. She imagined the political cartoons in the newspapers with the heading: "*The Duke and the Murdered Harlot*".

Prince Albert studied the letter that Frederick had sent.

'He admits to being in the public houses with the woman but not to the murder, my sweet.' He tried to back his brother's corner.

'The man is a disgrace,' the Queen said. 'What was he doing with a common trollop?'

'We must send a lawyer, as he has requested.' Albert stated.

The Queen nodded reluctantly.

'It was a mistake to let a monster like him loose on our subjects.' She betrayed her contempt for Albert's brother.

'William. Do you know a lawyer who understands German?'

The Prime Minister pondered for a minute.

'Your Majesty. This situation is very delicate. I cannot be seen to be implicated in all of this. I trust in your respect and silence, in the matter.'

Both the Queen and her husband nodded. Lord Melbourne had helped the young Queen with the difficult decisions of her reign so far. His help would be most appreciated at this embarrassing time.

'I am here to protect you, the country, and the establishment at large,' Lord Melbourne continued. 'I know the very person you require. His name is James Rawlins Johnson. He was a military man, and he speaks fluent foreign languages including German. He was

Wellington's attaché to Blucher, at Waterloo, and he is an expert on criminal law. I believe he is from the Northern Counties, so that may help.'

'He sounds like the man we need,' the Queen agreed.

'You must take cognisance that his fee cannot be paid for out of the public purse,' Melbourne warned. 'We cannot let our enemies know who is paying for the lawyer of a man who is on trial for murder. The Duke is, after all, on a capital charge.'

'Prime Minister,' the Queen answered. 'You will give our equerry Mr Johnson's particulars.'

CHAPTER FIFTY
The Queen's Counsel

James Rawlins Johnson was surprised by his urgent invitation to attend the Queen at Buckingham Palace.

He met the Royal couple and received his brief. It was a worrying situation. The Prince Consort had only just been accepted by the British people, and a scandal involving his dissolute younger brother would be disastrous. The young Queen and her husband were understandably distraught.

Johnson was a Queen's Counsel. But he had been born the son of a Bolton shoemaker. In the Napoleonic wars, he had risen to the rank of Colour Sergeant, as he had been decisive and quick to learn and adapt. After the war, he had entered the legal profession, and had studied law, defying his social class to become a barrister. He was fifty years old.

He travelled north on the new railway to Rotherham, and across to Barnsley, marvelling at the rapid changes the Industrial Revolution had wrought on the country's landscape and society within his lifetime.

At Barnsley Police Station, Johnson was ushered into the cells, where he met the Royal prisoner, who was dishevelled and red-faced. The Police allowed Johnson half an hour with his client.

He quickly introduced himself to the Duke in fluent German. He came straight to the point.

'My Lord, I need to know. Did you murder the woman?'

At this, the Duke broke down into inconsolable tears.

'Mr Johnson, upon my oath, it was not me that did the murder.'

This immediately threw Johnson. He was an expert barrister and had studied in great depth the new art of character and personality reading. Either the Duke was a brilliant actor, or he was innocent. He tried a different tack.

'You were out with the woman and you took her back to your hotel room. Did you not? I believe the Police have witnesses to these facts.'

'That is true, but she robbed me when she left me. I was very drunk,' the Duke sobbed. 'Have you interviewed my manservant yet?' Frederick asked. 'He will confirm the events.'

Johnson nodded. He would interview him later.

The thirty minutes passed very quickly, with further questioning. The police Sergeant entered the cell.

'Mr Johnson, I am to inform you that your time is up. The Inspector needs to question the prisoner,' he stated.

'You do as I say, and only speak when I tell you,' Johnson instructed the Duke.

Sergeant Stead led Johnson and the Duke to a small office. A uniformed man with a military bearing rose slowly to greet the lawyer.

'This is Chief Inspector Gardiner,' Stead said. But Gardiner and Johnson had already recognised each other.

'Goodness me, Richard! It's certainly good to see you after all these years!' Johnson exclaimed. The two men heartily shook hands.

'We were together in the army,' Inspector Gardiner explained to Stead. 'In fact, I trained Mr Johnson. I must say, you've made impressive progress in your career since then. A Queen's Counsel, no less!'

'If only we weren't meeting under such distressing circumstances,' Johnson responded.

The Chief Inspector got down to business. The Duke and Johnson sat down. A young clerk entered the room carrying a ledger and sat down behind the desk.

'This gentleman will be taking shorthand minutes of the proceedings, Mr Johnson, which you can verify afterwards.' Inspector Gardiner had resumed a much more formal tone.

Johnson nodded in approval.

'Chief Inspector,' the barrister stated. 'I have interviewed my client, albeit for a short time, and will come straight to the point. He says he is innocent of this heinous crime. In your eyes, because he was seen with the woman, and appears to have availed himself of her services, it is a case of in *flagrante delicto*. However, the Duke claims that she robbed him. A woman of the night carrying a large sum of money would have been vulnerable to thieves herself. There is no proof that the Duke committed the murder. Was any evidence found in his hotel room?'

Gardiner was about to answer when there was a knock on the door. A constable opened the door, ashen-faced. He motioned for Gardiner and Stead to come outside.

'Adjourn this interview for ten minutes, gentlemen,' Gardiner said. The two police officers left the room. Two constables entered the room, to guard the prisoner.

Johnson wondered why they had been disturbed. The Duke sat in silence.

After ten minutes, Gardiner and Stead returned.

'Gentlemen, we have made another arrest in connection with the murder,' Gardiner stated.

Stead was holding a metal tray, with an expensive leather wallet, almost empty of coins, and a long knife.

'Is this your purse?' Gardiner asked.

The Duke nodded. 'Yes – that is my initials. See –' The monogram "F.S.C.S." was embossed on the burgundy leather.

'And the knife?'

The dagger was almost a foot long, thin and tapering, with an ornate handle. The Duke recognised his ceremonial dagger, widening his eyes in surprise.

'It is mine, but how it came here, I...'

'I will explain,' Gardiner said. 'A man on the tramp has been spending excessive amounts of money in the town. He has been arrested for stabbing a woman in a public house with this dagger.'

CHAPTER FIFTY ONE
A Resolution

Susan turned to the diary entry marked Wednesday 16th September 1840:

I was summoned to the Police Station, where I met the Chief Inspector, Richard Gardiner. He questioned me at great length as to my knowledge of the events leading to the murder of the unfortunate woman. Truth to tell, I could only make verification of the disturbance in the Old Bear tavern.

I later spoke to the Queens Counsel, James Rawlins Johnson. He told me that he has studied the art of character and personality reading. He has interviewed the Duke. He told me confidentially that he fears the Duke has some sort of identity crisis, and seems to switch from one personality to another. One identity does not remember what the other has done. He denies murdering the woman.

I have of course remained in correspondence with the Queen and the Prince Consort.

Susan skipped O'Neill's mundane accounts of the Commission's work on the next few pages, and turned to the next entry, for Monday September 21st 1840:

There appears to be a resolution of the matters. A man of unsavoury character, who was on the tramp, seems to have been apprehended with the murder weapon. He has spent a lot of the stolen money in the town. He stabbed a woman with the Duke's dagger. This seems most fortuitous for the Duke. It alleviates the position of our Sovereign Lady, and the Prince Consort.

Susan paused while she deciphered the Victorian language. 'On the tramp,' she murmured. 'That must be what we call a tramp today.'

Making her notes, the Sergeant underlined the reference to the identity crisis of the Duke by the QC,

Johnson. 'I will remember that,' she muttered, under her breath. She was reminded of Dr Jekyll and Mr Hyde by Robert Louis Stephenson. It was a sinister thought.

How had the tramp gained possession of the Duke's weapon? The Duke may have sincerely believed in his own innocence, but perhaps he did not remember what he had done.

CHAPTER FIFTY TWO
Nelson's Hero

Geordie Jack had been in the wrong alley, on the wrong night, in the wrong town, that night in Barnsley.

He was drunk when the Peelers arrested him. He was now sober in the Police Cell, but he could not remember how he had got there.

He was born in Newcastle, in the year 1788, and had never known his parents. Jack had been left on a convent doorstep. His unfortunate mother neither wanted, nor could afford to keep him. His early life had been a torment. Hampered by a cleft pallet, his words never came out properly. His speech impediment had hampered his rudimentary education. The orphanage schoolmarm had been impatient, with little time or inclination to help him.

He was also very deaf, which did not help his predicament.

To make matters worse, he always shouted, as he was not able to hear himself speak.

The Naval press gang had arrived in Newcastle in 1804. At the age of 16, Jack had found himself on a Royal Navy ship, in the Mediterranean.

This was the happiest time of his life. He was an equal with the other sailors, many of whom were from similar backgrounds. The lowest of the low; the British Empire's underclass, recruited from the streets of the port towns.

The cruel life of the navy, like his early convent days, was all he had been used to.

He had one vice. Drink. It was the Navy that had introduced him to rum. Every time the ship docked in port, he would be arrested for being drunk. Jack was as well known in Gibraltar as the famous Lord, Horatio Nelson.

He suffered beatings and lashings in his Navy days, but he became an integral part of the English war machine.

Jack's finest hour came at the Battle of Trafalgar, in 1805. He was a rigger on *The Royal Sovereign*, commanded by Sir Henry Collingwood. He'd witnessed the cannons firing broadsides, splintering the hull of the mighty Spanish ship, *The Santa Anna*.

From his lofty perch in the riggings, Geordie Jack had revelled in a bird's eye view of the battle.

He saw *The Santa Anna* list over, before disappearing forever. He waved and cheered with the other sailors, as the enemy ship sank in a massive plume of smoke and fire.

At the end of the Napoleonic wars, he had left the Navy, and he had been on the tramp ever since.

He had awoken that September morning, as usual, at about 6am. And as usual, he had a violent headache and a raging thirst. He was an alcoholic, and could not live without a drink. At fifty two, he would not live much longer anyway.

The abdominal pains he'd been getting were excruciating. He felt better once he was drunk, but that seemed to make it worse in the long-run. Jack didn't know it but liver cirrhosis was eating him away.

Jack had ended up in Yorkshire, and he was known as a likeable rogue. He had forgotten how many times he had been arrested for vagrancy. He always got fed whilst in custody, so it did not concern him much.

He yawned and slowly came to his senses. When he tried to get up, something cut into his leg. It was a dagger. But where had that come from? His Navy experience told him that it was a military dagger, but he still could not imagine how it had appeared in his makeshift bed. He rose and wrapped a rag around the superficial cut to stop the blood. As he got up, a bulging wallet dropped on the floor.

He carefully put the wallet and dagger in his sack, and scuttled down the alley as quickly as he could, without looking back. Jack knew many lurkers who would gladly slit his throat for the purse and dagger.

He tried to gather his senses. If he did the right thing, and handed it in the Police, he would be suspected of theft.

The hand of fate then took a hand.

'Jack, wharra you doing today?' A woman's voice echoed across the alley. 'Fancy a drink to tickle the hair of the dog?' It was 'Dancing Nancy', another old vagrant.

Jack had been to most of the Navy ports and docks, and he had seen all the brothels. But he had never seen anybody as distasteful as Nancy. She was the ugliest woman he had ever seen.

She was nicknamed 'Dancing Nancy', because as soon as liquor touched her lips, she wanted to dance with everybody. She came over to him, drinking from a green bottle that she offered to him. It smelled rank. It was some kind of foul concoction and his stomach hurt just thinking about the contents.

'No, Nancy,' he answered. 'I'm thinking of waiting 'til the Pelham opens.' His cleft palate made the words come out in one note, making a repetitive popping sound.

At ten o'clock, the pair of them were drinking in the roughest ale house in the town, a tumble-down building, with broken windows stuffed with rags. A notorious place, where all the down-and-outs went. It was so sordid that the locals joked that 'even the crows fly around the Pelham Tavern.'

At five o'clock, the constables arrived at the Pelham. A disturbance had broken out in the establishment, and although loath to do it, the landlord had sent for the law.

'Geordie Jack' had stabbed 'Dancing Nancy'.

CHAPTER FIFTY THREE
The QC is at Hand

By four o'clock, Jack and Nancy were both out of their minds with drink. Jack had been spending money from the Duke's wallet, and Nancy was doing her dance routine.

Things were getting out of hand.

Nancy had drunk up.

'Gerrus another drink, Jack?' she slurred, very drunk. Jack was slumped with his elbows on the half-barrel that served as a table, too drunk to answer her.

She snatched at the wallet, but the coins rolled out into the spittoons on the stone-flagged floor. The Pelham Tavern was in uproar as the customers fought to lay their hands on the small fortune lying in the spittoon bowls.

'You bleeding stupid bitch!' Jack shouted, but it came out as something different. His cleft palate was doing its job. 'This is for you, you drunken tart.' He pulled out the Duke's knife, and slashed at her. The sharp knife cut her leg, and blood started to flow. Nancy swooned.

The landlord was used to trouble, but this was the worst fight he'd ever had, as the low-lives snatched the coins from each other. He saw the leather wallet, held aloft in Jack's grimy hand, as he slashed into the air with the dagger with his other hand to fend off would-be assailants. The landlord shouted, but the tumult was too great to hear him. Jack would kill someone if nothing was done.

The landlord of the Pelham ran into the street.

'Send for the Peelers!' he shouted. 'Murder!'

Susan turned to the next day's entry:
Tuesday 22nd September 1840.

I have been paid a visit by James Rawlins Johnson, QC. He is a most agreeable fellow, and is in the pay of the Sovereign. Originally from a labouring class background, he is in touch with the upper end of the land-owning aristocracy. I have nothing but admiration for him.

He is an outsider, like me. He is the son of a Northern shoemaker, but is now employed by the monarch. I am Irish and a Catholic. We have both managed to penetrate the dark and secret ways of the British Ruling Class.

The matters have reached a conclusion. It seems the tramp has stabbed a woman of dubious character in a tavern, with the Duke's ceremonial dagger. It was a drunken brawl that ended with the Peelers being called. Although the woman's wound is superficial, the QC quoted a Latin phrase 'Alea iacta est'. My schoolboy Latin translates the phrase as: 'the die is cast'.

If the truth is known, I am not of the same opinion as the QC. My own source is my Secretary, John Fulwood. He is of local stock, and claims the tramp is a largely harmless and likeable fellow.

I await the outcome in anticipation. Sergeant Stead has informed me that the trial is set at Wakefield Assizes, for October 26th. I have received the Court Summons, and I have to attend as a material witness. I am at a loss as to why I have to appear. It would appear that all the cannon that can be mustered will be aimed at the poor tramp.

As for the Duke, he is out of custody, on a large sum of bail. I trust that will conduct his person in the manner of Royalty, as would be expected of him.

Susan read between the lines, absorbed in the events of the past. O'Neill is sceptical, she thought. The trial is going to be a whitewash, with a convenient scapegoat.

CHAPTER FIFTY FOUR
On Trial with Jack

On the 26th October, the QC, James Rawlins Johnson, sat in the public gallery at the Wakefield Assizes.

Normally he would have been on the front benches, but today he was with his client, the Royal Duke Frederick.

Johnson was very ill at ease with himself. He looked at the prisoner with hidden compassion. He knew what was happening, and he shuffled in his seat uncomfortably. He nodded in acknowledgement at the Judge, whom he knew only too well.

The Right Honourable, Judge Nathanial Sowerby, was not quite the 'Hanging Judge', but he was known in the legal profession as the 'Penal Judge' He must be in the pay of the British Colonial Office, thought Johnson, as all his convicted prisoners were sent to serve in the colonies.

Even Johnson had difficulty differentiating between the prosecution and defence barristers in this trial. Both sides showed their contempt for the prisoner, and derided him at every chance.

He pondered on the whole contradiction of it all. He had been prepared to defend the Duke on the principle of *in flagrante delicto*. What a travesty, he thought. Where was the proof that the tramp had murdered the prostitute? There was no body of evidence, other than the knife and the wallet. The police hadn't even proved that the same knife was used to kill the prostitute.

The only facts that condemned Geordie Jack were that he had attacked a woman in a drunken brawl, with another man's knife. The prosecution had no burden of proof, and had presented no prima facie evidence, and therefore there was no case to be answered.

It was indeed strange, thought Johnson. His client, Duke Frederick, had not even been called to give evidence yet.

Something else troubled Johnson. He had wanted to interview Frederick's manservant, Mannering, but he had returned to London. Johnson had questioned the Duke about the missing manservant, but he simply said that the Queen had requested his valet's return.

From the public gallery, Johnson watched the proceedings with avid interest. It was like a play unfolding. The prisoner could not help himself. His speech impediment was taunted by the Prosecution Barrister. His poor health, and lack of education, made easy meat for his tormentors. Even the woman he had stabbed was never called to the bar. Sidelong, Johnson also watched the Duke, watching for his reaction to the trial.

The Duke seemed aloof, as if the events described below had no connection to his actions. Yet many people had seen Duke Frederick with Dorothy Shaw that night. The whole trial was being held for the benefit of the Duke, to avoid scandal. Johnson remained convinced that the Duke suffered from some kind of divergent identity crisis.

CHAPTER FIFTY FIVE
O'Neill on Trial

Susan came to the next diary entry, for Thursday 29th October 1840. The diaries took her inside the Wakefield Assizes, over one hundred years earlier. She was fascinated. O'Neill gave his account:

I have been at the Wakefield Assizes since yesterday, Wednesday. The day is long, and I have brought my work to Wakefield to pass the time. I was kept in a room with the other witnesses, including the woman 'Dancing Nancy'.

The Constable, who is with us, is very quiet. I have no knowledge of the proceedings that are in session. The woman is a constant nuisance, and I have asked the Constable if he will move me to another room. The stench from this woman is quite unbearable, and her language would even put the military to shame. The underclass of the nation is an embarrassment to any Civilized Society.

Susan smiled at the Earl's comments. She read on:

In the afternoon, the silence was broken by screams from the aforementioned Nancy. I later learnt from the Constable that they have had to lock her up in the Cells. She had been drinking from a bottle and was quite inebriated, and acting in a most inappropriate, unladylike manner.

I was called to the Court today in the forenoon at 11 am.

Susan continued to read O'Neill's entry for Friday 30th October 1840:

I have been put through an ordeal today, the like of which I never want repeated. I felt as if it was me who was on trial. I swore the oath on the Bible. I was taken aback when the Judge asked me if I required a Catholic Bible. He had obviously aimed his question to expose my denomination to the Grand Jury.

I politely answered that as an MP, and an upstanding citizen, although of Irish descent, I abide by the rules and laws of this great country. The defence barrister enquired at length about my work with the Royal Commission of Mines.

Before I could explain, the Judge commented sarcastically that an Irish Earl should never have been put in charge of a commission that questions the 'modus operandi' of English Industry.

I was rather taken aback at his questions, but made no comment. The prosecuting counsellor made great play on the activities in the Old Bear Inn, when the Duke arrived with the woman. He was implying that I had invited the pair of them to my lodgings. I answered that they were there under their own volition, and that I could not see the thrust of his point. The defence barrister made no objections to what I felt were attacks on me.

Susan felt for O'Neill. But why were the judiciary grilling him? The only thing that she could think of was that they were deflecting attention from the Royal Duke. Could there have been some kind of plot to discredit O'Neill, and his work on the Royal Commission? There would still have been an anti-Irish feeling in the country. The truth would surely become apparent later.

Susan remembered something. In the Police archives, she had come across the name of Richard Gardiner, the Police Inspector of the time. She broke off her work to go the telephone.

She managed to get through to Wakefield Crown Court, and she was soon speaking to the Archives Department. She wanted more information on Judge Sowerby and the Court Transcript. Within two hours, they telephoned Susan with the information that she required.

'Bingo!' Susan exclaimed loudly to Garda O'Rourke, who jumped, startled.

The Garda had been biding her time minding Susan in the archive library by knitting a jacket for her baby nephew, and she almost dropped her stitches.

'What's all the excitement?' Eileen asked. She was still puzzled about Susan's fascination with a pile of old documents.

'The Judge, the barristers, and the Grand Jury were all mine owners – or were closely connected to them, Susan said, very slowly and quietly. 'They had obviously been briefed to go easy on the Duke, but they could not resist having a dig at O'Neill.'

The evidence, such as it was, had been presented to the Grand Jury. The judge was ready to pass the sentence.

'Guilty,' Judge Sowerby pronounced.

No one in the jury expressed surprise, but the assembled throng in the public gallery gasped and shuffled uncomfortably on their wooden benches. The packed public gallery gasped at the verdict, sending the court into uproar.

Duke Frederick leaned forward with detached interest, to see a twisted and perverted justice delivered to the tramp who had been found guilty of killing the prostitute who had stolen his belongings.

Judge Sowerby donned the black cap. The court fell silent again.

The Judge cleared his throat.

'John Prendergast, otherwise known as Geordie Jack, you are sentenced to be taken hence to the prison, in which you were last confined, and from there to a place of execution, where you will be hanged by the neck until dead, and thereafter your body buried within the precincts of the prison and may the Lord have mercy upon your soul.'

Chief Inspector Gardiner whispered to James Rawlins Johnson.

'The tramp is a dying man,' he said. 'Sowerby has put him out of his misery.'

A week later Geordie Jack was blindfolded and he felt the rope around his neck.

He knew the rope only too well. The last thing he remembered was his days on The Royal Sovereign. The rope that would end his days was identical to the cable line on the mainsail. It was Bridport, three quarters hemp.

Jack remembered that the hanging rope was nicknamed *The Bridport Dagger*.

He was pushed off the scaffold. His neck was broken instantly.

CHAPTER FIFTY SIX
English Lessons

Susan returned to O'Neill's diary, and studied the entry for Friday 30th October 1840:

After the trial, I spoke with Duke Frederick. He was with his QC, Johnson, and the Police Officers Gardiner and Stead. Although the outcome of the proceedings was congenial to them, I have written to the Queen.

Although I cannot express my distaste fully, I hope the Royals will arrive at the same conclusion as me. The whole affair has been totally embarrassing, and unnecessary.

Susan spent the next few days following O'Neill's work with the Royal Commission.

All through November 1840, O'Neill visited Collieries. Most of them no longer existed in 1952, as they had been replaced by large nationalised mines. But she knew the places well. O'Neill mentioned pits at Swaithe, Darley, Lundill and the Oaks. Susan knew that twenty six years after the Royal Commission's visit to the Oaks, a terrible explosion had killed over three hundred miners.

O'Neill's accounts of the inspections were a treasure-trove, and Susan knew that this information would be priceless to social historians.

But she didn't forget that she was on a mission: to find the person who had committed the murders in the railway tunnels, over one hundred years after they had been committed.

The next date of interest to her was a month later, the 28th November 1840:

The Duke Frederick appears to be learning his lesson. Since the trial, he has not been drinking, and seems to have shown interest in our work here. I have delegated one of my Secretaries,

John Fulwood, to his welfare. Fulwood is a local man and an expert in the new Pitman's shorthand. Apparently the Duke has been working on his English as well.

Fulwood's wife is a school teacher, here in town. She has been giving the Duke evening lessons in the English language. She travels to his hotel every night. It is only a short distance and the Duke pays handsomely for his tuition.

Fulwood has told me he is very happy with the arrangement. He has two charming young daughters and they seem much attached to the Royal visitor. He bestows gifts on the two girls, and it seems he is very close to the family. It may be that family life is what the Duke has been missing.

I have watched the Duke at work with Fulwood at first hand. Today at the Thorncliffe Mines at Chapletown, which border on Sheffield, he dealt with an obstinate Mine Owner very professionally. He does not use his Royal patronage as a weapon, but it is obvious that these rascally entrepreneurs are aware of his identity.

It was surprising to note how the Duke, notwithstanding his Upper Class breeding, has taken to the plight of these young wretches, who are in bondage to avarice and profit.

I have just heard back from Prince Albert, who is happy at this development, but he added at the end of his letter to keep up my vigilance. Indeed, such a strange remark that I do not know which way to take it.

CHAPTER FIFTY SEVEN
Romance in the Air

Susan was now obsessed by the diaries. They had completely taken over her life. She returned to her hotel every night, and after her evening meal, she wrote up her notes.

Her thoughts were in the 1840s, and in the mind of the Earl of Wexford. She knew the diaries must have taken hours of work to compile, but what about the man himself, O'Neill? There were many pages covering the Royal Commission's work, but there was very little in regards to his private life. There were various clues there in the journals. She knew that he was an Irish MP and he was a Catholic, and it was apparent that he did not like the cruel times that he was living in.

He was twenty seven in 1840 and he was single, but what was he like as a man? He was obviously very intelligent and conscientious, but the diaries told little of his private side.

One incident in the diaries revealed clues of a romantic nature. She read the entry for Monday 7th December 1840:

Joseph Locke has been to see me. I have visited his house in town, and am well acquainted with his family. He has passed to me an invitation from a fellow MP, the Lord of Wharncliffe, to attend a Christmas ball at his Wortley House.

I have decided to attend because the Royal Duke has been invited as well. I have been instructed to monitor him, albeit in an informal manner.

Susan found herself wondering if O'Neill would enjoy the ball. For a few moments, her mind was caught up with thoughts of full floor-sweeping silk gowns and tiny corseted waists. She eagerly read the entry for Tuesday 15th December 1840:

On Saturday last, I was in attendance at the Wortley ball, and must say it was quite an experience. The Lord, of course is in charge of the new railway, and he and Locke had plenty to talk about.

I was introduced to Charles Vignoles, who is also a principle engineer on the railway. From the outset, I took an instant dislike to him. Like me, he is Irish but he is a most conceited fellow, who is full of his own arrogance. Locke insists Vignoles is a brilliant engineer, but he questions his use of the labour force and in particular, his choices of supervisors and managers.

I met Richard Ward, a young engineer, who seems to be learning the trade, and is constantly at the side of Lord Wharncliffe.

I am pleased to record that the Duke Frederick seems to have maintained his abstinence from drink. He spent most of the night conversing with Ward. His English has improved a lot, thanks to the work of Secretary Fulwood's wife.

I was introduced to Wharncliffe's daughter Sarah. She is a most congenial lady, and we conversed for some two hours about my work and my dealings with the Queen. I found her company refreshing after the dreary talk of railways and suchlike.

Wharncliffe has a large family and he is a larger-than-life character. He has speculated heavily in the new railways, after an illustrious army career.

After spending the night at Wortley Hall, I continued my delightful conversation with the Lady Sarah at breakfast. We had a walk in the beautiful gardens at the hall.

There is a magnificent view of the countryside. The view is spoiled by the Coal Mining, and indeed the Lord owns several Collieries which can be seen from the Hall. My Secretaries have already visited these Collieries in their work, and I am pleased to *say that the lessons of the Huskar have been learned. Female and child labour have been withdrawn from the Wharncliffe mines.*

The Lady Sarah is very much a modern girl, intelligent and interested in politics and literature. Her main pastime is horse riding and we spoke at length on the subject. Back in Ireland, my father owned race horses, and Lady Sarah asked me to accompany her.

We spent the afternoon riding in the nearby countryside, and after a pleasant repose in a local hostelry, we returned to the Hall for a luncheon. All the guests had now gone and the Duke was awaiting my return.

I asked Lady Sarah if I could see her again, and she readily agreed, with her father's consent of course. I approached Lord Wharncliffe and he and his wife seem quite keen on me seeing their daughter again.

Susan smiled to herself. 'Is there romance in the air for Robert O'Neill?' she thought aloud. She continued to read the journals to find out. The entry for Saturday 19th December 1840 read tantalisingly:

I have today been riding with Lady Sarah and if the truth is known, I am besotted by her. I do so miss her when she is not with me. I have never been in love. Could I be in love?

Susan wrote up her notes in the Shelbourne Hotel.

'Yes, Mr O'Neill. That is your problem. You are in love,' she answered him. She was fascinated by the language and prose of Victorian England, but she had to read between the lines to get inside the Earl's mind. There were more clues to follow.

CHAPTER FIFTY EIGHT
Lady Sarah
1840

Lady Sarah Elizabeth Jane Wharncliffe was the eldest daughter of Lord Wharncliffe. She was twenty three and was the first of seven sisters. She had attended a boarding school for young ladies, and had led a rather secluded life.

Sarah was feeling a strange sensation that she had never felt before. She was in love.

As part of the upper land-owning classes, her parents had tried to bring her up as a perfect paragon. Her birth had been a disappointment to her parents, who had wanted a boy to carry on the male line. The birth of all her sisters had also disappointed her parents, but her father, ever the pragmatist, always said that something would turn up.

Sarah was well versed in Literature and played the piano competently. She loved horses, and when she was able, she would ride for hours in the Yorkshire countryside.

What made Lady Sarah different to other young ladies of her age and status was her independent and questioning mind. She was a secret rebel, who challenged the social order of the day.

The tragedy at the nearby Huskar mine had shocked her and she could see the poverty and deprivation all around her in her father's coal mines. His new railway enterprise was no better.

Her contact with the working classes however, was very limited. She had heard about the Royal Commission visiting the area, and knew about the important guests who had been invited to her home for the Christmas Ball.

Her life changed at the Christmas ball. She was introduced to the guests from the Royal Commission as they entered her home at Wortley.

She felt very shy when the Royal Duke Frederick was introduced to her. He looked so tall and imposing in his red uniform trimmed with gold that she was frightened to say something out of turn to him. But the man standing next to her smiled, with a twinkle in his blue eyes.

'I am Robert O'Neill, Earl of Wexford,' he said, in a soft Irish accent. 'I am honoured to meet you, Lady Sarah.' He bowed, and kissed her hand.

Lady Sarah felt a strange sensation as soon as he spoke. She felt rooted to the spot and could think of nothing to say. She was intrigued by O'Neill's boyishly tousled brown hair, and sapphire-blue eyes. His healthy complexion spoke of a man who enjoyed spending time outdoors. She hoped he enjoyed horse riding.

'My Lady,' O'Neill broke the silence. 'Your father informs me that you study politics, and that you are familiar with the work I am carrying out on the Queen's Commission.'

Sarah realised she would have to say something.

'How did an Irish Lord get into the House of Commons?' she blurted without thinking. She realised what she had said and felt her face flush with embarrassment.

O'Neill was used to bigotry, but he recognised Lady Sarah's discomfort.

'I would be all night explaining it to you, my Lady,' he joked.

'Sir Robert, my father has told me all about you,' Lady Sarah took the initiative. 'I would like to know more about the Queen's Commission from your own lips. I have a thousand questions for you. I have studied Irish politics and would like to learn about your work at our coal mines. Will you sit with me and explain all?'

'Lady Sarah, although it may take some time, it would make a change from the subject of stocks and share prices,' the Earl answered. He did not need much persuasion.

They walked into a quiet side room. He liked what he saw in this delightful young woman with her modern thinking.

The ice was now broken, and for two hours, the two of them were locked in discussion on subjects ranging from Roman Catholicism to Social Reform. At the end of the night, Lady Sarah retired to bed, but she could not sleep. The Earl's voice was still ringing in her ears. His soft Irish tones had captivated her.

The conversation continued the next morning as they walked together in the gardens of the great hall in the bright December sunshine.

'I would love to attend a Catholic Church service. Would you take me?' Lady Sarah asked boldly.

'My lady,' he answered, smiling at her. 'What interest could you possibly have in a Catholic Church?'

'It has always intrigued me,' she replied. 'The richness and finery of it all. Our religion is plain and simple.'

The Earl was rather taken aback by her forwardness.

'I know you are a modern woman, but I shall have to get permission from your father to take you out.'

Lady Sarah nodded, but she knew her father liked and trusted the Irish Earl. It would be no problem.

By the time they parted in the afternoon, she knew Robert O'Neill was the man for her. With her father's consent, she would accompany the Earl on a visit to a Catholic Church in the New Year.

CHAPTER FIFTY NINE
The Catholic Church
1952

Susan noticed that O'Neill had stayed in Yorkshire during Christmas 1840. Could it have been his new found love, or the fact that he had nothing to return to Ireland for? Perhaps his work had kept him in the North of England?

It could have been a combination of all three factors.

Susan concentrated on an important date in the New Year: Wednesday 20th January 1841:

Lady Sarah is Protestant but she insisted on accompanying me to church on Sunday. I escorted her to Mass, at the Holyrood church in Barnsley. I met her outside the church and she was a picture to behold.

She resembled an angel in her elegant coat and gloves and she linked her arm with mine as we entered the church. A strange sensation came over me. It felt as if fate had brought us together and although the congregation was sparse, the two of us were in our own world. I have never been very religious, but it was in the house of God that I realised my feelings towards Lady Sarah.

'My Lord,' murmured Susan. 'You are in love. You have revealed your true feelings. What is going to happen next?'

She would soon find out. The diary entry had a dramatic twist:

A most strange occurrence then took place. A messenger entered the Church, and told me to follow him to Fulwood's home immediately. There had been a terrible accident.

CHAPTER SIXTY
1841
The Ice Incident

John Fulwood was reading his newspaper in the kitchen, frequently checking on the mutton joint roasting in the oven.

The weather had been cold now for a month, and his daughters Cassandra and Katherine were outside, playing in the snow.

Today they had an honoured guest. Duke Frederick was sitting in the parlour. He could hear his wife Louise giving him an English lesson, conjugating verbs, with the Duke repeating what she said in his strong accent. Meeting Duke Frederick had been a stroke of luck.

Fulwood was in good heart that cold January morning. Life had been good to him of late.

Aged thirty five, he had been married to his childhood sweetheart, Louise for twelve years now. Their twin girls were ten years of age. Before she had married, his wife had been a schoolmistress, an intelligent and forward-thinking woman who loved learning.

John Fulwood had been the wages clerk at the Oaks Colliery. During their courtship, they had both learned the new Pitman's shorthand and had used it to write their love letters.

They had inherited the house from Louise's parents, who had sadly passed away while the girls were young. It was on the outskirts of the town and had a garden, with room for flower beds, a substantial vegetable plot and a small, round pond, which was the head of an old mine shaft. John had warned his daughters that the pond was deep and dangerous and that the sheet of thin ice covering the water would not bear their weight.

Fulwood was proud of his new post as a Secretary to the Royal Commission, working under the Earl of Wexford. As a local man, he could understand the endemic local dialects.

Working closely with the Duke Frederick, the two men had become friendly, and he had invited the Duke to meet his family. Louise had offered to teach him English.

In return, the Duke showered money on them, and he had become very attached to Fulwood's daughters Cassandra and Katherine. The Duke seemed lonely and appreciated being invited into their home, although it was humble. It was an honour to be the host of such an esteemed guest.

Fulwood's contentment was shattered by awful screams. He rushed outside. Louise and the Duke followed. Fulwood saw Katherine, struggling in the icy water of the pond. John grabbed her and managed to pull her out. But Cassandra was nowhere to be seen. Fulwood couldn't swim. He clung to his soaking wet daughter. Louise screamed hysterically.

'Where is she?' he cried.

'We thought the ice was strong enough, father,' Katherine sobbed. 'I'm sorry...'

The Duke quickly took off his jacket, and kicked off his elegant leather shoes. He plunged into the water.

CHAPTER SIXTY ONE
A Local Hero

Susan continued to read O'Neill's account of that fateful day:

We heard the news as we left the Church and hurried down to Fulwood's house, which is a mile away. Apparently his two daughters had fallen in a pond. One was safe, but the other had been under the water for a long time. Plenty of the good townsfolk also followed us to see if they could render any assistance.

Secretary Fulwood greeted me at his house in a state of shock. He told us about the events. The Duke had made several attempts to swim underwater to reach Fulwood's daughter, but each time he had failed. Thankfully, after a short time, he managed to drag Cassandra out of the water. She was unconscious, but the Duke practised his life-saving techniques on the child, and had brought her back to a conscious state.

Although thoroughly wet, and chilled to the bone, the child had been saved by the Royal Duke. A surgeon has been sent for, and the Duke has told the Fulwoods he will foot the bill.

Lady Sarah assisted in changing the girls into dry clothing and I was very impressed with her natural maternal instincts. She and Fulwood's wife seem to get along very well. The English class system does not seem to affect Lady Sarah. She treats everyone as her equal. We spent the rest of the day assisting the Fulwoods, and Sarah seemed quite at home nursing the girls.

All the family are now fully recovered, except the Duke, who was very ill after the accident. I told Fulwood to keep the Duke at his house until he was well again. He suffered from hypothermia due to his exposure to the freezing water and his refusal to change out of his wet clothing until he was certain that Fulwood's daughters had been treated. Thanks to Fulwood and his wife, the Duke is now on the road to a full recovery.

It seems I have now some good news to send to their Majesties. The Duke is the hero of the hour, and the provincial newspapers have all carried the story of his brave deeds.

CHAPTER SIXTY TWO
Engagement

Susan was excited to read O'Neill's diary entry for Monday 15th March 1841. The characters of the 1840s were becoming so real to her as she became caught up in their dramas:

The Royal Commission's work is coming to an end, apart from visits to a few of the smaller mines.

The work has been obstructed by some of the mine owners, who will stop at nothing to impede our work. The stories that we have gathered are horrific. There is evidence of children being molested sexually by men and older children. They are forced to work in barbaric conditions underground.

I saw Lord Ashley last week. He is rather pleased with our findings. He stated that the facts will surely shock the moral fabric of any civilised society.

I have seen Lady Sarah frequently of late. Indeed her father, Lord Wharncliffe, has sent for me on the matter. The Lord and I have a congenial relationship, and we have many common interests.

I have now asked for his daughter's hand in marriage, and both Lord and Lady Wharncliffe are very keen for our union. The only matter of concern is religion, and the only stipulation seems to be their wish that any heirs should be raised as Protestants. I am happy to comply with this. In my opinion, religion is not as important as matters such as democracy and welfare reforms.

So now I am engaged to be married. Sarah wants to be married next year, so after lengthy discussions, we have set the date: Saturday 20th August, 1842.

THE WOODHEAD DIARIES
PART TWO

THE TUNNEL OF HELL

"If you prick us, do we not bleed? If you tickle us, do we not laugh? If you poison us, do we not die? And if you wrong us, shall we not revenge?"

William Shakespeare, *The Merchant of Venice* (Act 111, Scene 1)

CHAPTER ONE
1952
The Ex-Bomber Pilot

In 1952, the Pennine hills were alive again with the sound of industry. Men, machines, and eleven hundred men were building another tunnel through the Woodhead hills.

Complete with a cinema, clubs, and a post office, the construction workers' village for a thousand men and their families had a proper sanitation system as well.

The lure of high wages had brought men from all over the UK to drive the tunnels and electrify the railway system. This was not the pick and shovel enterprise witnessed a hundred years earlier. It was a new generation of construction, forward thinking, with equipment that would cut timescales and costs. Or so everyone thought.

Like their Victorian predecessors, the men digging the new Woodhead tunnel were having difficulties. Costs had risen due to the problems of the rock strata and difficult geological conditions.

Water was also a big problem. It was everywhere. The moorland was saturated by constant rain.

"Big Jim" Ryan was typical of these new navvies, with technical and engineering skills, rather than just brawn. Ryan was a foreman who had worked on open-cast coal sites and construction projects following the war. On this project, Jim did not have to travel far to work. From Tintwhistle, he only lived half an hour away from the site. It was a welcome change to return home after a day's work. He had always been overseas, either in the war, or on large construction sites.

In the war, he had been a bomber pilot, and had flown many missions over Germany. He had witnessed first-hand the destruction of the German nation. Jim had remained in the air force after being demobbed, and had used his flying skills in the Berlin airlift.

Flying the giant American C-54 Skymaster planes, he had helped to bring in food and materials over the Russian blockade into the besieged city. It had been far more rewarding than dropping bombs.

Big Jim was in charge of a hundred men at the Dunford Bridge end of the tunnel. As part of a specialised firm, he had been brought in by the main contractor, Balfour Beatty, to make a pumping station.

It was September 1952, and the weather was still very good. From experience, he knew that moorland winters were very bitter and the workers could suffer from frostbite caused by the severe cold, even if they wore protective clothing. Even now, in September, Jim was wrapped up in waterproof oilskins.

He watched as the Euclid R24 Dump Truck dug down to construct a large sump. This would collect the water that was being pumped out of the workings. They were working at the side of the old Victorian Number One shaft, about half a mile from Dunford Bridge. It was a large tip from the 1840s and was full of old rubbish. This had to be excavated to install the new sump foundations.

The men had found all sorts of material from the earlier workings. An old sack full of letters had been salvaged, and they had found lumps of metal that might be of value, and wooden props and broken old shovels, as well as rubble, which was being moved by the Dump Truck.

Most of the tip had been removed. They were now getting close to the original ground level.

Jim and his team had attended site meetings. They had been told about the skeletons that had already been discovered. They had also been warned to be vigilant in their work, as the Victorians had disposed of everything on these old tips. Unused dynamite was a big concern. Stark warnings had also been issued by the police that they expected more bodies to be found.

Jim had also been told about the old Number One boiler house, close to the old shaft top. It had been in a ravine and had been covered over by rubble when the second tunnel was constructed in 1845.

His experienced ears heard it first – a distinct clanging sound. The giant American earth-moving machine had hit something. He waved the driver to stop as he climbed down towards the machine's blades.

CHAPTER TWO
The Brick Wall

It was a brick construction of some kind. It caught Jim by surprise. In normal times, he would have let the digger continue and smash up the wall, but with all the warnings, he thought he had better play it safe, and report the find.

He ordered his men to take a break and he walked down to the mobile cabins that served as the company's site offices at Dunford Bridge.

'Judy?' he asked the receptionist. 'I need to speak to Mr Laidlow, as soon as possible. We've hit something.'

Barry Laidlow, the site manager, was at the site of the dig in twenty minutes. He was taking no chances after the recent skeleton finds.

'Right, Jim,' Laidlow issued his instructions. 'Get the digger out of the way. Handball, from now on. Picks and shovels. Let's see what we have. I suspect it's the pump boiler house, from the old Number One shaft. We need to box clever with this one.'

Big Jim and his men used their hand tools to excavate the dig until the top of the building had been exposed and excavated. When the work was done, Laidlow telephoned his superiors, and arranged a site meeting for nine o'clock the next morning. The surveyor, Brian Totty, was called.

Laidlow spread a copy of the old plans out on the now redundant digger.

He pointed to where the elevations of the building were marked out on the original drawings.

'I will say this for Joseph Locke,' Brian Totty said. 'The drawings are very accurate.' He stood back to admire the brick building. 'It is most definitely the old boiler house.

See the round Victorian window and the chimney at the top?' Totty compared it to the plans. 'It's beautiful brickwork. They were craftsmen in those days.'

On the top of the gable was a monumental stone, carved with the inscription:

W and J Galloway
Knotts Mill
Hulme
Manchester 1839.

Totty and Laidlow left Ryan's men to carry on with their work.

It took three days to clear the rubble from around the old boiler house. It looked very imposing. Apart from the rusting iron door, it was in perfect condition.

Laidlow returned to inspect the building. In normal circumstances, they would have destroyed the building, but work was now suspended. The macabre body finds in the tunnels were making the company cautious.

'Barry. I wonder if the boiler is still there. We might get a few bob for it if we weigh it in at the scrap yard.' Jim Ryan was always the pragmatist.

Laidlow laughed.

'How do we get inside? Any ideas, Jim?'

'John Jo,' Big Jim called his burner and welder. 'Get the burning tackle and see if we can get through this lock.'

The gas bottle and burning gear were brought up from the site cabins. Welder John Jo Blackwell was soon burning through the rusted lock that hadn't been opened since 1845.

The door was solid, and still would not move when the lock had been burnt off. It took more heat around the frame and a lot of leverage from jemmy bars to pry the door open. Inch-by-inch, the massive door opened. 'Big Jim' was the first man inside, closely followed by Laidlow.

'Bloody hell,' shouted Jim, as he walked inside. 'What a stink.'

He shone his light at the end of the building, where the boiler would have been. 'The boiler's gone!' he exclaimed. His dreams of a 'weigh in' were dashed.

'Never mind the boiler,' Laidlow gasped. ' Look at this lot!' He shone his torch on something as remarkable as it was gruesome.

In the gloom, they could see bodies. The two men huddled together as the torchlight illuminated the corpses.

'They look like they were put here yesterday. Seven of them,' Jim whispered.

'This place is a tomb,' Laidlow murmured.

The two men emerged from the boiler house, shaken. But the other men were keen to see the bodies, and crowded into the old building in macabre fascination.

The bodies clearly dated from the 1840s. The clothes they had died in were well-preserved. Their skin was dried and stretched over their bones like parchment. Bizarrely, they were all seated, with their eyes closed. Someone must have arranged them in those positions. They looked like waxwork dummies. They were all women, except for one.

The men viewed them in silence. Most of them had seen terrible things in the war, but this was one of the strangest sights they had ever seen.

'Look at this bloke? It's a soldier,' John Jo, the welder, noticed first. He crept closer to the body and shone a torch in the face of the dead man. 'His eyes are open. He's completely cock-eyed.'

The construction workers saw that the corpse's eyes had been strangely preserved, looking in opposite directions.

CHAPTER THREE
The Marriage Certificate

Sergeant Susan Priestley was not that far from Dunford Bridge when the gruesome bodies were found that morning.

She was actually only eight miles away, in the vicarage of Wortley Church, talking to the vicar in his study. They were checking an old marriage register, which confirmed Robert O'Neill's marriage to Sarah Wharncliffe, in 1842.

It was all there in the church archives. The marriage register dates tallied exactly with her cross-references from the Dublin diaries.

O'Neill's signature was in the same beautiful handwriting style as his journals. He had signed his occupation as 'Member of Parliament'. Lady Sarah had signed her occupation as 'Nobility'.

The vicarage telephone rang, and the vicar's housekeeper answered it.

'It's for Sergeant Priestley,' she said, rather bemused.

'I gave the Station the number of the vicarage – in case anyone needed to get hold of me,' Susan explained. She took the receiver in the hallway.

It was the Wakefield Control Room. She was told to ring DI Monroe, who had already set off for Dunford Bridge. More bodies had been found. Susan dialled the number for the site office.

Luckily, Monroe had just arrived. He explained that he was being briefed by the site manager in the Portakabin.

'How many bodies are there?' she asked, her heart thudding.

'Seven.' Monroe answered.

'Wow.' Susan gasped.

'I'm sending for the pathologist straight away. From what the construction team are saying, I don't think even Ned Lawson has seen anything like this before.'

Give me an hour to get there,' Susan said. 'I'm at Wortley.' She replaced the telephone on its receiver. When she returned to the study, the vicar stared at her curiously. She wondered how much he had overheard of her conversation with the DI.

'Is Dunford Bridge in your parish?' she asked.

The vicar shook his head.

'No Sergeant. Not these days. It might have been, back then.' He pointed at the date on the marriage register.

As Susan drove to the construction site, she wondered if Robert O'Neill's diaries could shed any light on these new finds.

CHAPTER FOUR
The Mausoleum

Within an hour, Susan had arrived at the site office at Dunford Bridge. She signed the visitor's log at the site cabin offices and put on protective overalls. She was taken up to the crime scene in a Land Rover.

The crime scene officers were hard at work, putting a cordon around the site. DI Monroe was already standing outside the building. He was talking to the workmen who had made the macabre find.

'You can't keep away from here, can you, Susan?' he joked, as she approached. 'It makes a change from those dusty old diaries in Dublin.'

'Those diaries are the key to the whole investigation,' Susan protested. 'I know I'll find the answers in there.'

'Wait until you see this lot,' the DI said. 'It's unbelievable.' He introduced Susan to the gang of workmen.

Susan admired the boiler house, completely intact after over a hundred years of being buried under the moors.

'It's a remarkable old building, Sir.'

'It was built to serve as a boiler house, not as a mausoleum,' Jim Ryan joked grimly. 'Get ready for a shock, Sergeant.'

'The strangest thing,' said the welder. 'Get a proper look at the soldier.'

Ned Lawson was already standing inside the building with a powerful torch, and a crime scene officer was rigging up a set of lights driven by a diesel generator.

A feeling of trepidation washed over Susan as she entered the boiler house. The seven bodies looked like something out of a waxwork museum. She felt a cold prickle down the back of her neck and she shivered.

The bodies were sitting on the stone shelf that went all the way round the building, their faces contorted, but their eyes closed, as if they were having hellish dreams. The soldier was the exception. His eyes were wide open, but they were abnormal. They appeared to be looking in opposite directions.

As Susan's eyes adjusted to the gloom, she spotted a frame on the wall.

She wiped the dusty glass with the sleeve of her overall.

Inside it was a piece of the same parchment that had been found with the first two skeleton finds.

On the parchment were the words:

"One two three in quick time.
All the children go with us.
Little Danny is next in line, and is running past us.
Bend down, stretch up, turn around,
Clap four times, Stamp your feet, round and round."

Susan opened her notebook, and copied the words.

'We shall have to stop meeting like this, Sergeant,' Lawson said, interrupting her thoughts. He smiled at her, seemingly unperturbed by his grisly task.

DI Monroe entered the boiler house.

'I need to get cracking with these bodies, as soon as possible, Andy,' Lawson told him. 'The air will start to decompose them. Leave me to carry on here – we need to document the crime scene and take the bodies back to Sheffield. I need to freeze them. I just need you to clear it with Christopher Columbus.'

'Right, Ned. We'll leave you to it.'

Monroe turned to Susan.

'We need to take statements from everyone,' he said. 'The press will get wind of this soon. We all need to be singing from the same hymn sheet.'

'Let's phone the chief first,' Susan said.

CHAPTER FIVE
The Press Scrum

The four construction workers, plus site manager Barry Laidlow and foreman Jim Ryan, had almost finished giving their statements to the police officers. They gulped mugs of strong, sugary tea in the site office.

'I couldn't get over that cock-eyed soldier,' Jim Ryan said what they were all thinking. 'It was if his eyes were looking at me – following me around. It was unreal.'

'How come the bodies haven't decomposed? They looked so lifelike.' DI Monroe sipped at his tea.

'I think I can answer that,' Susan said. 'The navvies dug peat to use as fuel in their huts. The peat causes some kind of chemical reaction and slows the bacterial process down.'

'Yes, Sergeant,' nodded Ryan. 'When we cleared away the rubble, we found evidence of peat bogs near to the boiler house. My old Irish granddad used to tell us tales that the old folk would be buried in the peat bogs. It preserved their skin and clothes. It was a way of mummifying the bodies.'

'It's certainly freezing up here in the winter,' Barry Laidlow said. 'The cold might have helped to preserve them as well.'

The site office receptionist, Judy, stepped into the cabin. She looked flustered.

'There are a lot of people outside,' she said. 'Newspaper people.'

Laidlow sighed.

'How did the press get hold of this so soon? Will you deal with it, Detective Inspector?'

'Mr Laidlow. I need to tell the Chief Inspector. May I use your telephone?'

The site manager nodded and Monroe dialled the number.

After a long conversation with Columbine, Monroe and Susan were both fully briefed. They walked together to the barrier gate. They were surprised to see a lot more reporters than last time. The guard on the gate was having difficulty controlling them.

It was quite a gathering. There were newspaper people and a newsreel crew, carrying heavy equipment. Susan wondered who had tipped them off. The press must have found out about the bodies at about the same time she had received the call at the vicarage.

Susan knew Columbine's tactic. He knew it was going to be a long, drawn-out investigation, and he wanted to give his subordinates a chance to deal with the press. He would have his say when more facts were known. He had briefed them on what to mention, and what to stay silent about.

Susan was the centre of attention. A young attractive woman always sold papers, and she dealt with them in a very professional manner. DI Monroe gave them a brief account of the new body finds. He kept it simple and said the remains of six women and a man had been discovered in the boiler house.

The *Pathé* newsreel interviewer was the first out of the starting traps.

'Seven bodies have been discovered today. One was found in the summer.' The interviewer slowly added up the tally. 'There was the first woman, with the baby. That's ten bodies to date. How many more are you expecting to find?'

'We're trying to find out how many people went missing here in the 1840s,' Monroe answered. 'It's very difficult to ascertain the exact figure. The records of the day are vague. The original railway company did not keep accurate figures of their employees. Thousands of men were working on the railway sites. These men –'

'Roger Thompson, *Manchester Guardian*,' a reporter interrupted. Susan recognised him as the man who had helped her with the microfiche in the Manchester Guardian offices. 'DI Monroe? With respect, it is more women than men you are finding. I make it eight females and two males that have been discovered. The two males are the baby boy and the man who has been found today.'

Roger Thompson turned to Susan. 'Why is Sergeant Priestley spending all her time in Dublin?' He stunned the other reporters with his revelation. 'I've also heard that the man found today was a soldier. Can you confirm that?'

Roger Thompson had given Susan the Dublin diary lead. He was obviously fishing for more details.

Monroe was visibly taken aback. How did he know all that? One of the workers could have told him about the soldier. He had forgotten Susan's visit to the Manchester Guardian, and the visits to Dublin were supposed to be top-secret.

Columbine had told Monroe to be vague about the latest finds, and only a few people knew about the Dublin connection.

The DI decided to terminate the press meeting.

'That is all we have to say at this point. We will call a press meeting when we know more. Thank you.' Monroe started to walk away from the press scrum as they shouted questions at him.

CHAPTER SIX
World Headlines

The nation was gripped by the macabre finds in the boiler house and the unsolved Victorian murders. The story was spreading around the world.

Chief Inspector Christopher Columbine was not a happy man. The investigative team were meeting in the Sheffield pathology lab to find out what Ned Lawson could tell them about the bodies. It was the morning after the mummies had been found.

'Jack the Ripper only killed five. We've got ten bodies. But how the hell did they know this, Susan?' Columbine showed her the newspaper headlines.

The *Manchester Guardian* read:
'DUBLIN CONNECTION IN VICTORIAN MOOR MURDER MYSTERY'

And the *Daily Herald*:
'IRISH CONNECTION IN MACABRE RIPPER-STYLE MURDERS'

'I need answers, Susan! I am expecting the MI5 here any time. They will be crawling all over us. Things are very sensitive with the Irish problem. How do they know about Dublin? What else do they know?' Columbine tore into her.

Susan was ready for him and she faced him calmly.

'Sir, not even my family know where I have been. My mother knows I have been out of the country, but she doesn't know where. The only people who know what I've been doing are in this room.'

She shrugged and looked around at DI Monroe, Chief Superintendent Columbine, and pathologist Ned Lawson.

'Well, it's damage limitation now,' Columbine said. 'At least they don't know about the diaries in the Castle. That's dynamite stuff. I trust our friends in Ireland are keeping quiet?' He raised an eyebrow at Susan.

'The soldier thing, now that's different,' Columbine continued. 'One of the workers will have told the reporter about the bodies. Thompson - is that his name, this reporter?'

'His name is Roger Thompson, Sir. He's a historian, as well as a reporter. He gave me the Dublin Castle lead himself, when I visited the *Manchester Guardian* archives,' Susan explained.

'If he gave you the Dublin lead about the diaries, why did he bring it up in the questions?' Columbine asked. 'Why would he want it broadcasting?'

The Chief Inspector pondered. He would say nothing to his people here. He would ring MI5, in the interest of national security. He had been in intelligence in the First World War, and he knew the importance and gravity of this present problem. He turned to the pathologist.

'Ned - what can you tell us about these bodies?'

Lawson opened his briefcase and pulled out an envelope of photographs. He carefully laid them out on the table.

'We've already started transporting the bodies here to Sheffield. I want to preserve them before they start to decompose.' Lawson said.

'Ned. Sorry to stop you,' Columbine interrupted, 'but tell us more about the preservation issues. Why are the bodies in such a perfect state?'

'The boiler house was built on peat bogs,' Lawson explained. 'And peat is a remarkable preservative. It's the acid - and there's no air. They've found bodies in peat bogs in Europe – perfectly preserved. They seem to be ritual sacrifices. They're called bog bodies – fascinating to study.'

Columbine nodded. 'Would the murderer have known this when he put the bodies in the boiler house?'

'I doubt that Sir,' DI Monroe answered. 'But he must have known they were going to bury and seal the boiler house. He wouldn't want the bodies discovering. No murderer wants that.'

'I agree, Andy,' the Chief said. 'Why was the boiler house buried? Does anybody know?'

'I asked the site manager the same question.' Susan joined the discussion. 'They said it was built on lower ground than the rest of the moor.'

There was a blackboard in the lab. Susan started to draw a diagram of the boiler house, sitting in a dip in the land.

'The boiler house housed the steam engine for the 1839 Number One shaft. They decided to dig the shaft there as it would be shallower, and therefore cheaper to construct.'

She drew the shaft on the board.

'In 1845, they started on a second tunnel,' she continued. 'The first shaft was then filled in. If you remember, we found the first bodies at the bottom of that shaft. The waste from the second tunnel was then dumped in the ravine, where the boiler house was. Again, it was done like this, to save costs. It saved having to transport the rubble away.'

'What about the soldier, then, Sergeant?' The Chief was impressed by Susan's research.

The Sergeant opened up her notebook. 'I am almost certain that he is Private Elias Randall, of the Manchester and Salford Yeomanry.'

CHAPTER SEVEN
Private Randall

Chief Inspector Columbine felt better about the situation. He had arrived at the meeting that morning very worried about the press leaks, but things could have been a lot worse.

'How can you be certain that the soldier is this Private Randall?' the Chief asked Susan.

'I have just been talking to a man in Manchester,' Susan explained. 'He is an expert on nineteenth century military uniforms. I sent him a photograph of the jacket that the soldier was wearing by courier, first thing this morning. I called him before this meeting, and he confirmed my suspicions. He described the colours, and insignias perfectly to me.'

Susan looked at her notes. 'It is a blue jacket with a white sash, white trousers, with a braided sash down each side. Hussar's cap, with a feather, and a curved sword. It is definitely the uniform of the Manchester and Salford Yeomanry. Another interesting point – it has blood soaked into it.'

DI Monroe looked thoughtful.

'What were soldiers doing at the tunnel site?' he asked.

'They were there in force to uphold the peace,' she explained. 'There was a lot of trouble when the navvies were locked out, in 1844. Civil disturbances followed. It's all in the diaries. And there are more clues. The soldier's uniform has a number on it.1413. Elias Randall went AWOL in 1845. The military expert gave me another clue. He had a nickname. "Cock eyed Eli".'

'The proper name for it is strabismus. It's very unusual to have it to that degree. And I must research the remarkable preservation of his eyes,' Lawson said.

'He scared me when I first saw him,' said DI Monroe. All the others nodded in agreement.

'What about the rhyme in the wooden case?' Columbine asked, changing the subject. 'At first, I thought it was the old boiler schedule. A diagram of the valves and pipes.'

'It was originally,' Susan explained. 'But that must have gone. It went with the boiler, when it was moved. They left the wooden case on the wall. Then the rhyme was put in it. It's in the same Gothic script as the other two pieces of parchment.'

The Chief shook his head, puzzled. 'But it's certainly not Milton, or Shakespeare. It's more like a nursery rhyme that my daughters used to skip to,' Columbine said. He read from Susan's notes:

"One two three in quick time.
All the children go with us.
Little Danny is next in line, and is running past us.
Bend down, stretch up, turn around,
Clap four times, Stamp your feet, round and round."

'That's exactly what it is,' Susan explained. 'It's an old German nursery rhyme.'

'Who is this Little Danny, Sergeant?' he asked her.

'My guess is as good as yours, Sir,' Susan tried to explain. 'Obviously it's a child called Danny who is being sung to. The name could be altered to another child when it's their turn.'

Monroe turned to the pathologist.

'Ned, what about the causes of death?'

Lawson turned to his notes. 'It's early days yet, Andy. I need the bodies back here to examine them more carefully. There are no obvious signs of physical attack, such as bullet or knife wounds. At this time, I can only hazard a guess, so don't quote me. I would say they were poisoned.'

'So,' Columbine said. 'Whoever put the bodies in the boiler house must have known that it would be filled in. He must have worked at the site to know when it would be covered over. The boiler had gone.' Columbine turned to the DI. 'But what about the boiler chimney? The flue? Was that open?'

'No Sir, it was sealed with an airtight damper plate,' Monroe said. 'The iron door was the same. The building was airtight. In normal conditions when the boiler was working, the damper plate would have been open. It was closed when they removed the boiler.'

'We found surgical instruments and broken chloroform bottles on the floor,' Lawson said, showing them the photograph.

'It was a makeshift infirmary. It's mentioned in the diaries,' Susan said. 'The chimney would have been closed to keep the patients warm. It seems that the Victorian engineers had unwittingly sealed up the building after they had salvaged the very expensive boiler. That's how the bodies were preserved.'

CHAPTER EIGHT
O'Neill is Married

The following week, Susan was back in Dublin, to continue the job of perusing the Earl of Wexford's journals.

Her note books were bulging with information, but she did not have many answers yet. She was still convinced that all the answers would be in the diaries.

First, she cross-referenced the dates, to find out when the Coal Mines Royal Commission's work had become law. That was Thursday August 4th 1842. She knew that O'Neill had married Lady Sarah on August 20th 1842.

She read the diary entry from Thursday 29th September 1842:

We have now settled into Wortley House. We have our own wing of the great building. I would like our own house one day, but Sarah is worried about her father's state of health. He has been frequently unwell of late. Sarah blames it on the railway, which is not going at all well. It is beset by problems, including a cholera outbreak, and industrial relations issues.

Since the passing of the Coal Mines Act in August, and the wedding, I have been kept very busy. The work of the Commission had prevented me returning to my constituency in Wexford this last year. I took Sarah to Ireland as part of a holiday, and honeymoon, to see my constituents.

She liked Ireland very much but truth to tell it was looking run-down. My estates are in a sorry state, and I am afraid I must make a decision of what to do with them.

We visited Dublin, and spent a very refreshing few days there, before our return to Liverpool by the ferry.

Friday 7th October 1842:

I am back in London, and have taken up my seat in the house. I was summoned this afternoon to attend the Queen and the Prince Consort, in Buckingham Palace. I was rather perplexed at the invitation, as our work is complete in the mining communities. I was also surprised to see the Prince Consort's Brother, Frederick, with the Royal couple.

CHAPTER NINE
1842
Another Task

Queen Victoria welcomed the Earl of Wexford in her private apartments that afternoon, in October 1842. She greeted him warmly and made him feel at home.

The two Royal Dukes were also in attendance. They both shook his hand vigorously.

The Queen motioned for O'Neill to sit down on a chaise longue.

'We have heard from Prince Frederick about your recent wedding,' the Queen said. 'And we do hope that you enjoyed our little present.'

The Royal couple had sent the newlyweds a canteen of silver cutlery, which O'Neill's wife, Sarah, was very much delighted with. It was engraved with their initials, along with the Royal crest on the box.

The Queen waved O'Neill away when he tried thanking her.

'We can never thank you enough for your work with the Mines Commission, and we are eternally grateful in helping our Lord Frederick with his education and familiarity with our ways.' She smiled.

O'Neill wondered if she had a hidden reason for thanking her.

'We have special gratitude to the Yorkshire family who have guided our Lord Frederick. The Prince Consort is going to surprise the Fulwood family with a special present. He is one of your secretaries, I believe?'

'Yes, your Grace,' O'Neill nodded. 'If you recall, I sent you the account of the Royal Duke saving the life of

Fulwood's daughter. She had nearly drowned in the icy pond.'

'We do indeed remember. It was a pleasant surprise to hear something positive about our brother.' The Queen nodded to her brother in law.

O'Neill was rather taken aback with the Queen's friendly manner towards him. He could not help thinking that she wanted something else from him.

The Queen ordered tea from a footman who had been waiting discretely in the room.

'I will come straight to the point, Mr O'Neill,' the Queen continued, in a more formal manner. 'There is a lot of unrest in my kingdom. I am most concerned with the events at these new railway sites. Striking workers – navigators I believe they are called, were narrowly prevented from rioting in Manchester. Very disturbing. It is a miracle there were no injuries. The last thing we need is another repetition of the 1819 riots. We have ordered your father-in-law Lord Wharncliffe, to report these incidents to you. Lord Wharncliffe visited us last week. His health is suffering as a consequence of these matters.'

'Indeed. Lady Sarah is very distressed about his health, Your Majesty,' O'Neill said.

'Lord Wharncliffe also told us about the cholera epidemic. We take cognisance that the Lord is the director of the private railway company and we cannot interfere with his business. The loss of life at these construction sites does however grieve me.'

The Queen passed a letter to the Earl.

'I received correspondence from our late Lord Lieutenant of Ireland, Viscount Wellesley. The Lord passed away last month. He was of course the brother of the Duke of Wellington. Before he died he wrote to me about the worrying numbers of workers who never return home after leaving to work on the railways. They are either missing, or dead. Apparently there are thousands of these Irish navigators, at work on our railways. Men and women are not being accounted for. We need answers, Mr O'Neill, and we need them quickly.'

CHAPTER TEN
Impartiality

O'Neill listened to the Queen with interest.

'In short, we need you to take charge of a new Royal Commission. We want you to investigate the problems at this Woodhead site. We realise Lord Wharncliffe is your father in law. It may be difficult. But we require an unbiased report regarding the problems. In our opinion, you are well suited for this inquiry. Your findings will be passed on to the House of Commons Select Committee. Lord Wharncliffe has already indicated some of the problems in his report. Would this new work cause a strain in relations?'

'I would certainly have to discuss it with Lord Wharncliffe,' The Earl answered. 'I would not wish a conflict of interest. It is not my place to be making judgements on his railway company. Also, there is the question of impartiality. I am, after all, his son in law.'

'We spoke to him last week, my Lord. It was his idea to appoint you for this task,' the Queen replied.

This took O'Neill by surprise.

'The last thing we want is friction in your new family,' the Queen continued. 'What are your thoughts, Mr O'Neill, on the matter?'

The Earl thought for a few seconds.

'Your Majesty, Lord Wharncliffe never discusses his business with me. I am, however, well acquainted with one of his engineers, Joseph Locke. Indeed he was my best man at the wedding, and he is very talented. He would know a lot more on the matter than I.'

'Well, my Lord. The matter is closed.' Queen Victoria smiled as the dainty tea set arrived. 'We need you and the

Lord Frederick to carry on with the excellent work you are doing for us.'

The Earl turned to the Prince Consort and his brother Duke Frederick.

'It seems you are stuck with me for a little longer, my Lord,' Frederick said, in his much-improved English.

The Queen nodded. 'The Prime Minister has promised me his full cooperation in these matters. The Irish problems are very pressing. He will give you all the help that you need. This is what we want you to do.'

Susan read O'Neill's diary entry for Friday 21st October 1842:

I have seen the Queen, and she has given me a new task. I had to ask Lord Wharncliffe's permission before I could accept it. Apparently it was his idea to put me in charge of this new inquiry.

There is to be a new Royal Commission into the disturbances at Woodhead, and I have been put in charge of it. I have specifically asked to have my Secretaries back with me on this new Commission, as there will be many people to interview.

I have returned to Wortley House and I have told Sarah of this new appointment. She welcomes it gladly, as I will be about to stay at home with her as the Commission progresses. I sent for Secretary Fulwood today and he seems well satisfied, as it keeps him in full employment.

Lord Wharncliffe has instigated my appointment, and he has arranged a visit to the workings for me this coming Monday. I shall be under the supervision of Joseph Locke.

Lord Wharncliffe has also given the Royal Duke a room at Wortley House, which I am sure he will be more than recompensed for.

My instructions are not to interfere with the railway works. I am to fact find on the appalling loss of life at these earth moving sites.

I have already met Lord Wharncliffe's surveyor Richard Ward, whom I will interview for the Select Committee.

The summer cholera epidemic and military involvement in Manchester have caused particular concern and will be part of my remit.

CHAPTER ELEVEN
1952
The Reporter

Sergeant Susan Priestley was fully engrossed by the diaries. She was trying to unlock the mind of Robert O'Neill.

She had been back in Dublin for a week now. Two weeks had passed since the seven bodies had been found in the boiler house. She felt like she was getting closer to solving the murder mysteries, using the clues in the diaries.

Susan reported her findings to Columbine nearly every night. She was also under instructions to keep her work secret. Although the headlines and press interest had died away, security was still tight. The Irish Garda, Eileen O'Rourke, had been replaced. She knew too much of Susan's work and she had a wagging tongue.

Jean Flanagan, who was in charge of the archives, had also been questioned. But she had been cleared of any breach of the Irish Official Secrets Act.

Susan now had a new minder from the Irish Garda. They had sent a middle aged woman called Eve Fieldsend. She was very quiet and reminded Susan of her mathematics teacher at the Barnsley Girls' High School.

Garda Fieldsend shadowed Susan everywhere, even when she was off duty, and it rather unnerved her. This made Susan more suspicious. Why did the diaries need to have all this security? Somebody knew something. It must be top-secret material.

A woman from the Irish Special Branch had also arrived. She was called Linda Gill. Susan asked Chief Columbine about the new security, but he told her "it had all come from above". He said that they were there just for Susan's security. They had no input in her detective work.

With two minders watching over her, Susan felt like a character in a spy film. Columbine told Susan to ignore them and just carry on with her work.

She returned to her hotel every night for a meal. Then she always went for a walk, to clear her head. It was her only chance to be alone. It was rather a strain being shadowed by two women who were not very sociable.

By now, she knew the city of Dublin very well. One evening, she decided to have a cup of tea in Bewley's, a Grafton Street café, and sat by the window.

A man approached her at her table.

'I would have thought that a Barnsley lass would be supping something stronger than tea.' She recognized his Mancunian accent. It was the *Manchester Guardian* reporter, Roger Thompson.

'Mr. Thompson, I hope that you have not been following me,' Susan snapped. 'I am under strict instructions not to speak to anyone, especially to you press people. You have caused me a lot of trouble with your innuendos. I don't want to sound rude, but I cannot tell you anything.'

She got up to leave, and started to walk out of the cafe. The reporter followed her.

'I was wrong to mention Dublin when I came to the Dunford Bridge site. I didn't realise the embarrassment and the implications it would cause. Your bosses have already warned our newspaper of some security breach.'

'Mr. Thompson, please leave me alone,' she rebuked.

'Sergeant – I have a job to do,' he quickly answered. 'The readers back home are fascinated by this murder mystery. It's better than any Agatha Christie novel.'

'I'll have to report you to my superiors for this intrusion on my privacy. I can't tell you anything,' she said.

'I gave you this Dublin lead in the first place. You owe me a big favour.' He smiled, hopefully. 'And you've never asked me how I knew about the diaries. Can I at least buy you a drink? I will promise not to mention the murders?'

Susan ignored the reporter and she returned to her hotel. She immediately telephoned Chief Columbine. He had given her his home number for emergencies.

'You have done the right thing to tell me, Susan,' he said. 'We cannot stop the man doing his job. And he is quite right. He gave us the lead in the first place and he has still not mentioned the diaries in his reports. He does seem to know a lot about it all. Meet him and find out just what he does know. Just be careful what you tell him.'

Susan knew the Chief Inspector was right. The reporter, Thompson, knew something that she wanted to know about the Earl of Wexford in the 1840s. She hoped it would help her to solve the mystery.

CHAPTER TWELVE
The Drinks Are On Me

O'Neill's diary, Friday 28th October 1842:
We have now completed a week on our new mission. Joseph Locke has kindly given us an office at the new Penistone Railway Station. It will apparently be a ticket office when the station is complete. It is ideal for our work, and even has a coal fire to keep us warm. Locke has warned me not to expect much friendliness from his managers and workers, who on the whole regard us as troublemakers.

We made our first visit to the infamous Woodhead tunnel on Monday.

Susan took up O'Neill's account the next morning. She sat between the dour-faced Eve Fieldsend, busy doing the *Irish Times* crossword, and the Irish Secret Service woman Linda Gill, who was busily knitting an olive green pullover.

But as soon as Susan started reading the diaries, her minders, and the small office, faded away. She was in O'Neill's world again, totally fascinated by his descriptions of his first visit to Woodhead.

She particularly wanted to know what had happened to Billy Birkenshaw, the lad who had escaped the Huskar tragedy, and who had been attacked in Dog Lane, in Barnsley. She wondered what had happened to him in the two intervening years since Joseph Locke had found him a job at the tunnel.

She soon got her answer, as she continued reading the entry for Friday October 28th 1842:

My party of six left Penistone by foot, and we walked alongside the new railway bed westwards, toward the tunnel. The surveyor Richard Ward led the way. It is a very industrious place, with parties of navvies working hard on the embankments and bridges.

Some of the fellows doffed their caps at us. Most carried on with their task, under the watchful eyes of their overseers.

We met Billy Birkenshaw, whom Locke had employed. He was walking back home to Thurlstone after his night shift, and he bade me a hearty welcome. We conversed for some ten minutes about his livelihood.

He is now an official of the navvies' trade union and he was involved in helping with the recent cholera epidemic and the events in Manchester. He is a very likeable fellow, and I wished him all the best in his employment. I need to interview him at the first opportunity.

The journey was quite pleasant, and it took us about an hour to reach the Dunford Bridge end of the tunnel.

My first observation of the giant earthworks was quite something to behold. Secretary Fulwood said it was like a giant ant hill, with hundreds of ants on it. The navvy's shanty town was on the hill, over the tunnel entrance. The first sense to be alerted was sight, but then, unfortunately, came the sense of smell. It was wretched, a mixture of human excrement, wood and coal fires.

Smoke was belching from a building behind the navvy camp. The scene cannot be much different to Dante's Inferno.

Duke Frederick was as fascinated as I at the spectacle of so much activity. He made the comment 'My sister-in-law would make much of this sight', in his much-improved English.

Dunford Bridge is in a valley, with the small River Don running through it. There is a trail from Penistone, which the railway company has been using for their supplies.

There is a slight curve where the new line will go into the eastern portal of the tunnel. We rounded the curve to find that work has already started on a new railway station.

Locke has told me there are some fifteen hundred men at work in the tunnel, in twelve separate workings.

I ignored the works offices and decided to visit the navvy camp on the hill. The shop which the navvies call the "Tommy shop" is just up the incline. A makeshift public house called "The Angel" is next door.

There is mud everywhere, and a small open sewer runs down from the camp. This finally goes into the river some twenty yards away. The stench is so unbearable that Duke Frederick covered his face with a handkerchief.

CHAPTER THIRTEEN
The Five-Fingered Twins

'I wonder if hell stinks like this?' Lord Frederick asked, in his mixed German and Yorkshire accent. He held his lace handkerchief to his nose.

O'Neill's party walked past the Angel pub on a bright autumn morning in 1842. Even though it was only ten o'clock, a party of navvies were sitting outside the pub, drinking, and smoking their pipes.

'Would you save that pretty handkerchief for me, your Royal Highness? You can leave your royal snot on it.' A woman shouted to them, as they passed the pub. She was about twenty, O'Neill guessed. She was sitting on a beer barrel.

It was obvious that the navvies knew who they were. The company officials, like the mining companies before them, would have warned the workers not to say anything incriminating. They would be threatened with their livelihood. The visit of Lord Frederick would also have set the rumour machines to work.

The Earl turned to notice that there were actually two women. They were identical twins. He guessed their dialect as Western Irish.

'For that pretty handkerchief, Molly and Marie would give you all week.' A well-built navvy, with a Cockney accent, shouted over to the Royal party.

The Cockney held up Molly's left hand. 'See the five fingers on their hands. They are the mark of the devil. They will skin you alive, these Riley twins. The Galway witches.'

Lord Frederick then did a strange thing. He stopped, and walked up to the women.

'The Duke of Saxe-Coburg-Saalfeld gives you this as a present.' He knelt on one knee and presented it to one of the women.

He then pulled another handkerchief from his inside pocket, and gave that to the other twin. It took O'Neill by surprise. He wanted to be cordial with the navvies, but most of all, he wanted information from them for the Commission.

O'Neill was wary, remembering the Duke's involvement with the murdered prostitute in Barnsley, two years before.

Before the Earl could say anything, the Duke addressed the gathering crowd.

'Who is the master of this house? You will all have a drink on me.'

'I am George Whitfield, the master of this Woodhead mansion,' joked the landlord, a burly Yorkshireman. 'I do hope that your credit is good, Sir.'

'Mr Whitfield,' the Duke answered, slamming a heavy leather purse of coins on the table. 'That is a King's ransom. Who knows? One day I may be the King!'

The navvies all gave a loud cheer, which only served to gather more attention. Soon, there was a large crowd around the pub, all drinking the free beer.

'A fool and his money are soon parted, my Lord,' John Fulwood sighed.

'But is he a fool?' O'Neill answered.

He thought it wise to leave the Duke with his new friends for now. It might make the Commission more popular with the navvies. O'Neill continued to walk up the incline to the boiler house, and motioned to his secretaries to follow him.

Susan continued to read O'Neill's narrative for Friday 28th October 1842. It contained a description of the boiler house at Dunford Bridge when it was in use:

I left the Duke in the company of the Riley twins, who have five fingers on their left hands. My superstitious priest back in Ireland would surely call it the mark of Satan himself. They are Galway women, and perhaps twenty years old.

My mother always said that it had been Anne Boleyn who had bewitched the English King, Henry VIII, and forced him to break away from the Roman Catholic Church.

The Devil had given her five fingers on her right hand and a mole on her neck. She was a witch, who was following his evil wishes to split God's church.

The Duke was fascinated by the twins and I let him carry on drinking with them. However, I am sure their morals are in tune with this cesspit of the human underclass.

We saw the motley collection of makeshift houses that the navvies live in at close hand. I had read reports of the cholera outbreak in great detail. But I was not prepared for the sights and smells of the place.

Secretary Fulwood passed comment that his pigs and hens live in better accommodation than the navvies.

There was a queue of people around the boiler house. They were waiting to see the surgeon, whom I have read about in the reports of the cholera epidemic. The boiler house is the only building that is constructed properly. It is purpose-made for the steam boiler. It appears that there has been no expense spared for this building. But the poor unfortunate wretches who are ill do not have anywhere to recover, except in a noisy industrial building.

I left my party outside and went into the boiler house to introduce myself to the surgeon. He is Henry Pomfret. The navvies pay him to tend their wounds, and illnesses. He spoke to me while he was tending a young man's wounded leg, which was bleeding profusely. Wounded men were lying all around the makeshift infirmary. I have no doubt it is the only warm place on the moors.

Most of the men were coughing. I understand this is caused by the dust and dynamite in the tunnel.

Two men were shovelling coal into the furnace. This drives the pumps from the nearby shaft. The noise of the pumps was a pulsating rhythm of incessant noise. How Pomfret works in this environment is a miracle in itself. I will broach the matter with the railway directors, but I fear that the 'seed will fall on stony ground'.

Pomfret has another surgeon with him, Harold Thompson. Two makeshift nurses were in attendance. One is called Mary Maloney. The other is a woman with a wooden leg, called 'Peg Leg Peg'.

I thought it prudent to leave the surgeons and their assistants to carry on with their work. I have made arrangements to interview Pomfret later. We left the boiler house to continue with our preliminary visit.

CHAPTER FOURTEEN
The Twins Disappear

Sergeant Susan Priestley read the diary with avid interest. She felt like she was getting closer to solving the mystery.

Monday 31st October 1842:

We returned to Dunford Bridge this morning, to start our work. I was surprised to see my old acquaintance Sergeant Stead at the tunnel. He gave me a hearty handshake, and I told him of our new work that has been commissioned by the Queen.

A strange happening has occurred. He was there to investigate the disappearance of the two Riley twins. Apparently the girls disappeared on Friday Night. Another 'tally woman' had alerted the police.

'It happens all the time' Sergeant Stead said to O'Neill. 'Nothing to get excited about. They will have gone to another camp with richer pickings.'

He bade the Earl a good day, and left the camp.

O'Neill nodded to the Duke and spoke to him outside their office, making sure they weren't overheard.

'Where did you go on Friday night?' O'Neill asked, directly. 'We left you here, in the Angel, with those two women. You did not arrive back at Wortley Hall until Saturday morning.'

'I must confess, Robert.' He now called O'Neill by his Christian name. 'I was very drunk, and I spent the night in the boiler house.'

'You did what?' O'Neill was shocked by his answer. 'It would be a scandal. A drunken Royal Duke spending the night in a boiler house with people who have cholera, and all kinds of ailments. It is to be hoped that this does not go any further. Does anyone else know?'

The Duke looked very remorseful. 'I left early, before anyone saw me. I trust in your silence, Robert? It will never happen again.'

Susan continued reading the entry for Monday 31st October 1842:

The Duke has placed me in a very uncomfortable position. I thought he had cured his drinking problem. I am worried about the outcome of it all.

However, Sergeant Stead has told me the twins' sudden disappearance is nothing to become concerned about. If the Duke gave them money, they may have decided to try their luck at another camp.

O'Neill was now criticising the Royal Duke. Obviously the Earl was perturbed by Duke Frederick's behaviour. The Duke's involvement, in similar circumstances, in the murder of prostitute Dorothy Shaw, had embarrassed and distressed the Queen, but the hanging of Geordie Jack had prevented the Duke from facing the law. Here he was again, drinking with prostitutes.

Her thoughts were interrupted by the Office Keeper entering the archive office.

'Your Chief Inspector wants you on the phone,' Jean Flanagan said.

CHAPTER FIFTEEN
1952
The Ash Tip

The Euclid R24 Dumper Truck was now twenty yards away from the boiler house, digging a diversionary trench.

The boiler house had been cordoned off with police tape, and two policemen were on guard, keeping away any unwanted predators who might come sniffing around the building for macabre souvenirs.

It was two weeks since the bodies had been found. 'Big Jim' Ryan and his team were removing an old slag tip. It was where the ashes from the coal boiler house would have been tipped in the 1840s. The R24 came to a halt, and the driver shouted to Jim. They had all been instructed to be very wary, and they had to examine anything that looked suspicious.

'It's old hessian coal sacks, Jim. Nowt to worry about,' the driver shouted. He started to get back in his cab.

'Whoa there!' Jim's senses were alerted. 'Let me have a look.' He climbed into the trench and opened one of the sacks.

'Hey lads get your bosses back here! We've found more skeletons.' He shouted at the two policemen, running towards them.

Susan picked up the telephone in the Office Keeper's office.

'Chief Inspector Columbine? Susan here,' she said, a little out of breath from running.

'Ah, Sergeant Priestley,' he addressed her formally. There were some muffled voices in the background and it sounded to Susan as if he might have company in his office. 'We have found two more skeletons under a slag tip, twenty yards from the old boiler house. Andy Monroe and the pathologist Ned Lawson are on site. There's not much for you to do here.'

'Any clues, Inspector? Has Ned found anything?' Susan shivered. She was intrigued, but not particularly surprised by Columbine's news.

'The bodies were found in hessian sacks. They are definitely women, and there's one strange thing. Both the skeletons have a remarkable deformity,' Columbine continued.

'Let me guess, Sir?' Susan interrupted him. 'They both have five fingers on their left hand?'

In his Wakefield office, Columbine froze, staring transfixed at the phone.

'How did you know that?' he finally asked. He was in an important meeting with his superiors and they were now staring at him as if he was a fool.

Sergeant Priestley knew she had surprised him, and smiled to herself. The diaries really did hold the clues.

'I will shock you even more. I can even give you their names. They are Molly and Marie Riley. They are twins, and are roughly twenty years old. They came from Galway, on the west coast of Ireland.' Susan checked her notebook. 'They disappeared on Friday 28th October 1842.'

CHAPTER SIXTEEN
1842
One Two Three

Duke Frederick was drunk. He had been drinking all day at The Angel. It was a public house, or what passed for a public house at Dunford Bridge.

He had been drinking beer, and gin, with the young Irish twins, and he had let the drink take over his senses. O'Neill had left long ago with his party, and it was now the early hours of Saturday morning, the 29th October.

Was he seeing double with these two Irish girls? They were identical in every way. They were both very pretty, but both had a remarkable feature. They had five fingers on their left hands.

The girls sat together on his knee, but he had long since forgotten their names. They had matched him with the drinks, but now he was getting tired. It had been a long time since he had been drunk like this. The drink had tasted foul, and his head was spinning.

The Angel was now empty and the landlord, George Whitfield, was getting ready to close his pub. It was Molly who made the move.

'Let's take the Duke home with us, Marie. We will look after him, will we not?' she said. She spoke in a mixture of Gaelic and richly accented English, as she winked at her twin sister.

It was not his body she had her eye on. It was his wallet, tied to the inside of his expensive waistcoat, that she fancied.

The navvy camp was now quiet, except for the interminable sound of the steam pump boiler. Men were either at work in the deep recesses of the tunnels, or fast asleep in their huts, with their women.

The two twins linked arms, either side of the Duke, as they set off up the hill, towards the boiler house.

'Our palace is not far away, my Royal Duke,' Marie whispered in his ear. The five fingers of her left hand started to roam. As they staggered up the incline, the Duke started to sing an old German song.

'Eins zwei drei im Sauseschritt, gehen alle Kinder mit!'

He then sang it in English:

'One two three in quick time, All the children go with us.'

He had taught John Fulwood's daughters, Katherine, and Cassandra the song in German. Their mother had then translated it into English, for him to learn.

'Shush, shush, my Lord,' Molly whispered. 'You will wake everybody up.' She didn't want anybody to witness the robbery.

She let go of the Duke and squatted down. 'I must take a piss,' she said, and lifted her dress. But she had deliberately stopped by a pile of rocks, and she selected a heavy, sharp-edged one.

Lord Frederick was fascinated by Molly's coarseness. Marie felt his hard arousal as his leg brushed against her. She distracted the Duke, caressing his thigh in his tight breeches.

Molly picked up the rock with both hands and tried to hit Frederick on the head. The rock missed. It caught Marie on her roving, five-fingered hand. She cried out in pain and let go of Duke Frederick's arm.

Molly made a desperate grab for his purse.

Frederick reacted fast. He drew his German pocket revolver and fired a bullet at each of the twins. The loud noise of the pistol shots synchronised with the steam pump. The sleeping navvies heard nothing.

The Duke was a crack marksman. The bullets hit the twins in their foreheads. They both dropped to the ground. Their short lives were over instantly.

Frederick now had a problem. How to dispose of the bodies? The answer was yards away.

There was a tip at the back of the boiler house. The cold ash from the coal boiler was emptied on this tip. The problem was solved. He crept into the boiler house, where the patients were sleeping. He found two large empty hessian coal sacks. He quickly put the bodies in the sacks, and dragged them to the tip. He found some wheelbarrows full of ash and emptied them over the bodies.

The murderous deed was done, but Duke Frederick's drunken tiredness quickly returned. Creeping back into the boiler house, he wrapped another large sack around himself. He lay on the stone shelf, next to a man who was in awful pain from an injury.

The cries and moans from the poor wretch did not bother the Duke. Within a minute, he was in a coma-like sleep. Neither the noise of the boiler or the poor sick men, who were coughing all night around him, nor the devil himself, would have awakened him.

The light broke through the high, round window at seven o'clock. The Royal Duke awoke, aching from sleeping on the hard stone bench, with a raging headache. He forced himself to move. He had to leave the hell of the boiler house before anyone saw him. At first, he didn't know how he had ended up there. He could hear the sound of the navvies at work in the cutting below.

Duke Frederick realised that his clothes were filthy, streaked with coal dust from the sack he'd wrapped himself in. There was no one awake in the boiler house yet, and he stole out of the building. As he set off down the path, he glanced over at the spoil tip. The events of last night came back to him in a series of ghastly pictures. He patted his jacket for his revolver. It hung heavily in his pocket. He had his wallet too, rather depleted of coins after his drinking spree.

His heart thudded as he remembered what he had done to the Riley twins. They had been buried well enough. In fact, more ash had already been emptied from the greedy coal boiler. And who would miss them? They were just common harlots and thieves. They all were.

The Duke walked along the trail of the new railway, to Wortley Hall. His clothes were so dirty that at first glance, he would have been mistaken for a navvy returning from the night shift.

By nine o'clock, he had sneaked into the house by a back door. After a quick wash, he bundled up his filthy clothes and hid them under the downy mattress of his luxurious bed. He was soon fast asleep. He slept until the late afternoon. He disposed of the dirty clothes later in the furnace that kept Lord Wharncliffe's glass-house warm.

CHAPTER SEVENTEEN
1952
The Woodhead Surgeon

It had been quite a day for Susan Priestley. She meticulously deciphered the mysteries of the 1840s murders using cross-references from the Victorian diaries and modern-day detective work.

That night, she sat in Bewley's cafe. Her notes were spread out on the table. For a change, she was alone. Her watchers had eased off. They were no longer following her around the clock, and they spent most of the time at the hotel.

'Sergeant Priestley, don't you ever wind down?' A familiar voice broke into her thoughts.

It was the reporter, Roger Thompson. She quickly covered her files from his gaze. But this time, she had decided to be cordial with him, and to try to pick his brains. He knew something about the diaries which had led her this far.

'I can't wind down, Mr Thompson,' she answered. 'I could ask you the same question. How come your newspaper pays for you to follow me here?'

'May I?' he asked, indicating the empty chair opposite hers. Susan did not reply, but he sat down anyway.

'I am a freelance reporter, and I get paid by the highest bidder,' Roger Thompson explained. 'Like you, I am fascinated by this story. And I have a special interest in it. My Great-Grandfather was a surgeon at Woodhead. Unlike you, I cannot go and read the diaries. I'd have to be granted special permission.'

It suddenly dawned on Susan who he was talking about. She referred to her notes and quickly turned the pages.

'Was he Harold Thompson, the assistant surgeon at the tunnel?' she asked him.

'That's right,' Thompson nodded. 'He went on to have an illustrious career. He became famous for his work in the Crimean War and wrote books about various diseases and remedies.'

'It sounds like his experience with the navvies was useful,' Susan said.

'It was,' Thompson replied. 'He lived until a ripe old age – ninety years old. Not bad, considering he was born in 1822. Queen Victoria knighted him in 1875, for his work in medical science. He was a favourite of hers.'

Thompson produced a large, leather-bound book from his satchel. He showed it to Susan. The title was **COMMON AILMENTS and CURES IN THE MODERN AGE**. It had a photographic plate of a bearded Doctor at the front, protected by a sheet of tissue paper. It had been printed in 1870.

'He mentions the Woodhead tunnel a lot,' said the reporter. 'He was an expert on cholera, and venereal diseases. He was a pioneer in the study of congenital syphilis – that is, babies who are born with the disease. It was very common in the nineteenth century, when there was no cure.'

Susan tried not to show it, but she was ecstatic at this news. Here was another cross-reference to her work.

'Mr Thompson,' she began. 'Would it be at all possible for you to either lend me that book, or tell me where I can get another copy?'

'Call me Roger. If I can call you Susan.' He smiled. She nodded her consent.

'It's out of print. You will not get another anywhere. This is a family heirloom that's been handed down. But I will allow you to take notes from it. My father remembers Dr Thompson telling him something strange. His Grandfather told him about the murders at Woodhead – and a Royal connection. All very mysterious.'

CHAPTER EIGHTEEN
The Reporter Knows

Susan was taken aback.

'What do you know about a Royal connection?' she asked Roger.

'Well,' the reporter said. 'Apparently, Great-Grandfather said that there was a Jack the Ripper murderer, about fifty years before the London one. And he didn't just kill prostitutes. He spoke of Prince Albert's brother, Frederick, visiting the workings.'

He had the Sergeant's full attention now. She studied Roger intently, and she was fascinated by what she saw.

He was about her age, in his mid-twenties. But he was very professional in his mannerisms and had a lovely speaking voice that was pleasant on the ear. He was obviously very well educated, but he had a dry humour that amused her. She found herself staring into his intense blue eyes.

'You can buy me that drink you promised me,' Susan smiled at him. 'And then you can tell me more about this ancestor of yours.'

Roger grinned at her. After a short wait, he came back from the bar with two halves of Guinness.

'When in Rome, and all that,' he joked at her.

'Roger, what else do you know about your Great-Granddad?' She addressed him by his Christian name for the first time.

'Well,' Roger replied, sipping at his drink. 'He mentioned Robert O'Neill, the Earl of Wexford, who conducted an inquiry into the deaths at the tunnel. My Great-Granddad had to attend the Parliamentary Inquiry in 1846. He also met the Royal Duke, who had a strange habit. He was always singing a German nursery rhyme.'

Susan flinched as he spoke. She thought fast, trying to piece all the dates together. In her notes, she had made a chronological chart. But she was only up to 1842. She decided to reveal some information to her new journalist friend.

'To be honest, Roger,' she replied, already halfway down her drink. 'There were a lot of strange things happening in 1842. Women going missing – and a cholera epidemic.'

'Like the twins, who had five fingers on their left hands? They suddenly disappeared. Nobody saw them again.' Roger interrupted.

CHAPTER NINETEEN
Five Fingers Again

'How the hell do you know about that?' Susan was taken aback by his revelation. She stared at him with her mouth open. The news of the twins' bodies had been kept secret, and the press had certainly never been told.

'It's all in this book.' Roger patted his great grandfather's book affectionately. 'I just need to find it.'

Like Susan, he had made notes about the book. He found an index card with the correct page number.

'Here we are,' he said. He read out aloud from the medical text: '*A strange phenomenon occurred at Woodhead one day in 1842, when two "tally women" completely disappeared overnight. I knew the two prostitutes, known as the Riley twins, who had the rare disfigurement of having five fingers on their left hand. They were well known in the navvy camp, and were regular visitors to the infirmary in the boiler house. They had very sociable characters and were identical in every way. They were sadly missed by many men in the village.*'

Roger paused.

'Is this the same boiler house, Susan, where they have just unearthed the six bodies?'

Susan nodded. 'It is, but those murders must have been committed three years after 1842. I can't explain it all to you, but the six bodies found in there were killed in 1845, when the first tunnel was opened.'

Roger continued with his narrative: '*They had all the signs of secondary syphilis. No matter what we advised them, they carried on spreading the vile disease, for which there was no cure. The twins were very pleasing to look upon, but still plied their trade in a wanton manner. More than half the women in the camp suffered from the disease.*'

'Horrible, isn't it?' Susan shuddered.

Roger sipped his Guinness, and then continued: '*The disappearance of the twins could not be explained in a rational manner. As high earners in their profession at Woodhead, to say they had gone to another site for more money was not a logical explanation.*'

Susan was silent. She stared outside at the busy street. Roger looked at her patiently, until she had finished with her thoughts. They were getting along very well. She had a sharp, active mind, as well as a natural attractiveness. A no-nonsense Yorkshire lass with brains.

She focused her brown eyes on him. He smiled, and pulled a penny out of his pocket.

'The usual price?' he asked. 'You have gone all quiet on me.'

'I couldn't possibly tell you any more, Roger,' she explained. 'But it's all falling into place.'

Susan was relieved. Roger knew about the missing twins, but he had obviously not linked them to the recent body finds. There was something else she wanted to ask him.

'You've never told me why you're here. Is the Manchester Guardian paying for your stay here?'

'No, Susan,' he said. 'I'm doing some research into the never-ending Irish problem. Freelance research.'

Susan glanced at her watch.

'Time to go, I'm afraid. Garda Fieldsend would be waiting at the hotel, wondering where she had been. Susan didn't want to give her any cause for alarm. She needed to complete her research, especially now she had reached this crucial stage.

'It's been very illuminating, Mr Reporter Man.' Susan held out her hand, for Roger to shake.

'Miss Sergeant,' he answered, with a smile. She felt a slight shock go through her body as he took her hand.

'Well. What now? Can I see you again?'

'Yes,' Susan said, without hesitation. 'Same time. Same place. Tomorrow. Is that okay?'

'It sounds good to me,' he replied.

Back in her hotel room, she turned to her notes, using the diagnostic table of events which she had devised herself.

But her mind was elsewhere. She was back in the cafe, with the Mancunian reporter, listening to his pleasant voice.

CHAPTER TWENTY
Hansard

Susan was back at her usual place in the Dublin Castle archives. She continued to read O'Neill's diary, sifting through them for anything that might be relevant to the murder investigation.

Friday 4th November 1842:

I was back at Dunford Bridge on Tuesday. I interviewed the Surgeon, Henry Pomfret. Mr Fulwood was taking minutes and the account was recorded for the Commons Select Committee. I will not repeat his comments here. He did however, express his opinions, and castigated the railway company in a derogatory manner.

He is most sorrowful that he cannot save more lives. I met a priest and an undertaker who were at work with a corpse. There will always be plenty for them to do in this squalid place, he told me.

He mentioned a McNamara family, from Limerick, who lost four brothers in the recent cholera outbreak. I have noted the name. It seems they are buried in unmarked graves at St James' church, at Woodhead.

Pomfret has given me the name of the McNamara 'tally woman.' She is called Mary Maloney, from Cork. I wish to interview her. This woman assists the surgeons in the infirmary.

Tuesday 8th November 1842:

I had arranged to interview Charles Vignoles, but I am informed that he has been removed from his office. The word on everyone's lips is that he has not paid his calls from the company, and has been declared bankrupt.

Lord Wharncliffe is back in his sick bed, and made the comment to me that 'what he has sown, let him reap'. I know there is no love lost between the two men. The Lord blames Vignoles for most of the troubles on the railway.

Tuesday November 29th 1842:

I have today interviewed the manager, Wellington Purdon, and a most disagreeable fellow he is. I have no doubts the Commons Select Committee will castigate his comments. He values the company more than the poor navvies' suffering. I will let wiser counsels make their own judgements.

Susan wondered what O'Neill meant. She put down the diary, and went to see the Archive Director.

Jean Flanagan found Susan a copy of Hansard for 1846, and Susan cross-checked for the findings of the Commons Select Committee.

Purdon had been questioned on the deaths caused by stemming dynamite with iron fuses. Copper fuses should have been used, to prevent sparking which ignited the dynamite.

Hansard, House of Commons Select Committee minutes, 1846:

Purdon was asked about the stemming fuses and he replied that the safer fuses 'caused a lot of time wasted'. He confirmed that iron fuses may have contributed to twenty six deaths, but he had 'a great aversion to Government officials meddling in engineers' business.'

In other words, the detective thought, it was nothing to do with them how many got killed.

'I bet he was a charming man,' she spoke aloud.

Susan trawled through the diaries, from November 1842 until July 1843. She was searching for a special interview, the one with Harold Thompson, the great grandfather of Roger, her new found friend.

She found it in July 1843.

Monday 3rd July 1843:

Today, I interviewed another surgeon, Harold Thompson. He is twenty one years of age, and is a new kind of Doctor. He is researching certain maladies. In particular, he is researching cholera, and venereal disease. He told me of congenital syphilis, which is common on the site.

As far as I know, these diseases have no cure, but this man seems to be an expert on them. I predict that he will go far in the medical world.

'You are right there, Mr O'Neill' Susan spoke out loud again. Eve Fieldsend, who was still doing her Irish Times crossword, stared at Susan over her glasses.

'Just thinking aloud. Sorry,' Susan apologised.

CHAPTER TWENTY ONE
Tears

Susan and Roger were back at their usual table at Bewley's, drinking tea. They had arranged to meet again, and she had made a special effort to dress up. He was quite shocked when she came in the cafe.

'Wow, Miss Sergeant. You look well,' he exclaimed He had only ever seen her in the everyday blouses and skirts she wore for work, smart but plain.

Susan was wearing a summery floral swing skirt. She wore high heels, and elegant gloves. She had let her hair down, and slight touches of makeup brought out the best in her features. The transformation was amazing, and he just could not help staring at her.

'Bit of something for you,' he said, as he produced a bouquet of flowers.

Susan then did something she rarely did. She blushed. She had never had a boyfriend, just platonic working relationships with her male colleagues. She had always put her career first. She had, however, made a special effort for her new friend.

She took the flowers from him. 'They're lovely,' she said. She had a sudden urge to kiss Roger, but perhaps that was far too formal.

'I'll put them in a jar until you leave,' the café waitress offered, saving Susan from embarrassment.

Susan sat next to Roger and got her notebook from her handbag.

'I have made some notes from the diaries about your famous great grandfather, and what he did at the Woodhead tunnel in 1843,' Susan said. 'The Earl of Wexford predicted he would go far. He was right.'

'I have been reading his book again,' Roger explained. 'Did you know that he was in the front line of the lockout and strike in 1844. The soldiers were there as well.'

Susan checked her notes. 'Really? I haven't got that far yet. I'm up to 1843. The Earl met your great grandfather in July of that year,' she answered.

She could still picture the soldier, Private Randall, in the boiler house. But she could not tell Roger about it. What he didn't know, he couldn't tell. Could he?

She decided to change the subject, and do something she had never done before. Ask a boy out.

'I've been thinking of going to the pictures tomorrow night,' she said. 'Singing in the Rain is on. I love Gene Kelly.' She started to hum the tune. 'Do you fancy going?'

Roger went quiet. He sighed heavily.

'Susan. I would love to go with you, but I have got to go back home. *The Manchester Guardian* wants me to go to Malaya. I have to cover for one of the war correspondents.'

Susan was rather taken aback at this news. She was looking forward to spending some more time with Roger. He was really good company, and he made a welcome change from reading the diaries. She had become quite fond of him. Unexpectedly, she broke down in tears.

Roger then did something that he had never done before.

He put his arms around her, and held her tight. He nudged her face up to his, and he wiped her sudden tears away. He then gave her the most wonderful kiss anybody had ever given her.

'Don't say anything you may regret later,' he said, mocking the arrest code. 'It's only for a week or two. I am not going to fight the MNLA.' He was referring to the insurgent Malayan National Liberation Army. 'When I get back home I'll come and see you. I am only an hour from you by road. Or I can come by train.'

He kissed her again. 'Is it safe to come through that Woodhead tunnel?' he joked.

The two of them spent another hour together, until the restaurant closed, and then he walked her back to her hotel. The 1840s were forgotten while they chatted about their own lives.

After a long embrace outside her hotel, Susan had to fight the tears away.

'Please write to me, Roger. Let me know when you're coming home.' She could hardly get the words out. Her cold Sergeant's persona now had melted. She was a love-stricken girl. He stroked her hair. Being a perfect gentleman, he bade her farewell.

'You need sleep and I must go. I am up early in the morning.'

That night Susan did not sleep much. Her thoughts were swimming with the murder puzzles of the past and fears for Roger in Malaya.

CHAPTER TWENTY TWO
1844
Pardon and Purdon

1843 had turned into 1844, and the Woodhead tunnel was behind schedule. The shareholders were getting restless, and the costs were soaring.

To make matters worse, Joseph Locke had been summoned to Paris. One of his railway viaducts had collapsed. Wellington Purdon and Henry Nicholson had been put in temporary charge.

Richard Ward had just finished speaking at a shareholder's meeting. He was answering questions about the tunnel.

'The original surveys were worked out correctly,' he said. 'I am confident that all the twelve headings are in line.'

'Why is it taking so long to complete the tunnel drive from Number one shaft, Mr Ward?' one of the shareholders asked.

This was just the question Ward had been waiting for, and he was ready with his answer. There had been a seventy foot fall that had killed five men. Purdon had refused to shore it and make it safe before advancing. The men had worked under unsupported ground, which is dangerous in any mining operation.

'You will have to ask Mr Purdon that question. He is the site manager, now that Mr Locke has gone.'

Wellington Purdon was now the object of the shareholders' displeasure. Purdon, the bully, was at home when he was talking down to the navvies. These shareholders, however, were a different kettle of fish. He dreaded the questions they were bound to ask.

Another shareholder stood up. Purdon looked at him nervously.

'I beg your pardon, Mr Purdon, and pardon my impertinence, but why the delay?' The shareholder was purposefully making fun of him.

The meeting gave way to a crescendo of laughter. The chairman banged his gavel down.

'We will have order. This is not the time for levity. Let Mr Purdon speak,' shouted Samuel Jewson.

Chairman Jewson was having trouble with this meeting. Times were bad for the Sheffield, Ashton-under Lyne, and Manchester Railway Company. It was like the proverbial rats leaving the sinking ship. Times had been better under Lord Wharncliffe, but he was in his sick bed, at his home in Yorkshire. Charles Vignoles had been declared bankrupt. He had not paid his calls of £80,000. Even the illustrious Joseph Locke had left them, and his reputation was now in question.

The engineers that they had left behind were no match for the fifty six shareholders. They were baying for blood, wanting returns on their capital.

Purdon had a hard act to follow after the comedian.

'The ground is too soft,' he started to explain. 'We are having trouble timbering it. It was the navvies' own fault they got killed. We need more money in order to finish the tunnel. It is as simple as that.' Purdon spoke from the notes he had prepared for the meeting, but his words were falling on deaf ears.

Ward shook his head in exasperation. He knew that Purdon was lying. He was trying to blame the navvies for his own misdemeanours.

'Purdon? We have doubled the expenditure in the last year, but you keep asking us for more.' A large beer-bellied

Yorkshire man heckled him. 'It looks like gross mismanagement from where we are sitting.'

A loud shout of 'Hear, hear,' came from the other shareholders.

The Yorkshire shareholder raised his hands for silence.

'I move a motion that if in a month's time things have not improved,' he said, pointing at the two hapless engineers. 'We will find somebody else to finish the tunnel.'

'Right – you have heard the motion?' Samuel Jewson seized on this. 'What say you? Are you in favour?'

The shareholders' hands went up in unison. Wellington Purdon and Henry Nicholson had been given a month's notice.

Down came the gavel for the last time.

'This meeting is closed. The next meeting is at the same time, and at the same place, in a month's time. We shall then deliberate on these matters.' Chairman Jewson closed the meeting.

CHAPTER TWENTY THREE
1952
Purdon Plots and Plans

Sergeant Susan Priestley read about the events of 1844 in the Dublin Castle archive rooms. She wondered what had caused the lockout and strikes that Roger had mentioned. The diary soon gave her the answer.

Wednesday 13th March 1844:
We have been urgently summoned back to Woodhead. There have been five fatalities in a roof fall. I have interviewed witnesses, and the reports will go to the Commons Select Committee. I am most concerned about the flippant attitude of Mr Purdon. His account conflicts with that of the navvies. They maintain that he has forced them to work under unsupported ground.

Only one of the men, Peter Meredith, would give a statement. It appears they are fearful of reprisals if they give a statement.

Richard Ward has informed Lord Wharncliffe of the events at the shareholders meeting. It seems Purdon and Nicholson are on notice to improve the expenditure situation.

It is no wonder that the trade unions have gained a foothold here. The obstinacy of the Company beggars any credibility.

At home, there has been a slight improvement in my father-in-law's health. Sarah walked her father around the grounds, but she soon had to bring him back indoors due to the cold March winds.

'Well? Now what?'

Henry Nicholson shook his pipe into the coal grate at the Woodhead site office. 'This roof fall is taking some timbering, Wellington. You just could not wait could you? Now we have five navvies killed, and they were all top men. Too bloody hasty, you are. The chasm above is seventy feet high, and the roof is still coming in. We have been stood now nearly a month. At this rate, we will be still here in six months. It is choking all the systems. Locke would have finished you, if he had still been here.'

'Locke! Bloody Locke! I am sick of hearing his name.' Purdon's temper was on the boil. He was ready to explode. 'I'll tell you how good he is. The bloody viaduct he built in Paris has collapsed. That's how good he is.'

'That's as may be, but how do you propose we get out of this mess that you have caused?' Nicholson retorted.

Purdon warmed his hands on the coal fire, and thought for some time.

'I know a way to save money,' he said suddenly. 'We will hold the navvies' money back, on the next pay day.'

Nicholson shook his head vehemently.

'Oh yes, and what's that going to do? It will cause a strike, and then what?'

'Let them go on strike,' Purdon was quick to reply. We will lock them out. We will kill two birds with one stone.'

'What two birds are you talking about?' Nicholson asked.

'We get shut of this militant lot and we will get cheaper labour in, off the tramp. Work is very thin elsewhere. We are bound to get plenty of labour,' Purdon explained.

'But what about the roof fall at the Number One tunnel? Who will finish repairing that?' Nicholson tried to reason logically with Purdon.

'I know them,' Purdon said, with a contemptuous smile. 'They are not all in the union. Some will work, and it will buy us time. They have given us a month's notice. The shareholders will blame the navvies, and the union people. Mark my words, we will set the trap.'

He gritted his teeth, and stroked his jaw, remembering his painful altercation with Billy in the infirmary that had turned the Yorkshire lad into the militant leader of the navvies. Purdon wanted revenge.

'And Billy Birk, and his bloody union, will drop straight into it.'

CHAPTER TWENTY FOUR
The Return of the Duke

What had triggered the strike? Susan turned the pages of the diary and read the account, as described by O'Neill.

Friday 29th March 1844:

I have today witnessed the utmost folly of men. The navvies have not been paid for some thirteen weeks. They are most grievous, and angry.

The surveyor, Richard Ward, had advised us there would be trouble. But I wanted to see it first-hand. I brought Lord Frederick with me, and John Fulwood, to give a report on the proceedings.

'Ah,' thought Susan. 'Lord Frederick is back. Where has he been for the last year?' The diary soon solved the mystery:

Lord Frederick has returned from Germany. He has been on state business, but he has reported back to me.

He left after his drunken antics in October 1842. He is in time to witness a new civil unrest.

As she read between the lines, Susan thought that the Earl of Wexford was showing his exasperation with the Duke.

O'Neill was inferring that he had something to do with the disappearance of the five-fingered twins. The Duke had been one of the last people to see them alive. Had he been sent to Germany to get him out of the way? O'Neill had suspected something was wrong, but Susan doubted he had told the Queen of the Duke's involvement in their murders.

O'Neill hadn't even known that the twins were dead. The bodies had only just been discovered in 1952. Everybody thought that they had just left the site. Susan continued to read:

Friday 29th March 1844:

It got to nine o' clock, but still no work had begun. We made our way through the throng of navvies at the site entrance. The gates of the site were closed. However, the policemen on duty let us through. Ward was in the meeting.

The two officers of the trade union, Billy Birkenshaw and Peter Meredith, were in a meeting with the company Managers, Wellington Purdon and Henry Nicholson.

Their meeting was over after an hour. The navvies were very quiet, but were discontented. Wages were due to them. The two union officials came out first, and Birkenshaw addressed the waiting crowd.

The transformation of the man is really something to behold. I first met him in the Silkstone Churchyard, almost four years ago, but now his speeches are better than any Parliamentary orator I have ever witnessed. He has metamorphosed from a simple lad, to become a natural leader of men.

CHAPTER TWENTY FIVE
Lockout

The fledgling union was unprepared for its first major battle.

The Railway Workers and Boiler Men, or RWBM, was a conglomerate of skilled, and unskilled, labourers. It had been formed on the backs of vicious government acts, and the unscrupulous company owners who wanted to repress the workers' rights.

Billy Birkenshaw and Peter Meredith were the local representatives of the union. They had been elected after the march on Manchester in 1842. They had held their posts for two years. There was, however, one problem.

Only about a third of the Woodhead workforces were members of the union. There were about fifteen hundred workers on site in 1844. But the general apathy and rapid turnover of men on the tunnel site did little to help the workers' struggle.

Birkenshaw and Meredith were on one side of the table, sitting opposite their old adversaries, Wellington Purdon and Henry Nicholson. Richard Ward was present as Chairman, but in a non-speaking capacity.

Birkenshaw and Meredith had been mandated by the workforce to ask why the wages had not been paid for thirteen weeks. They had refused to work that Friday morning in March 1844. For over half an hour, they listened to Purdon, as he gave excuses for the late wages.

'We have had trouble with the banks, and payments coming from shares. Other items have taken priority over the wages.' Purdon read from a paper. He had anticipated their questions and he had rehearsed his answers in order to antagonise the union men.

Richard Ward listened to him in disbelief. He knew that Purdon was playing a very dangerous game. These were poor excuses.

'So when can the men expect to get their pay?' Meredith asked. 'It is now thirteen weeks since the last pay day.'

'Well that remains to be seen.' Nicholson spoke for the first time.

'What remains to be seen?' Birkenshaw questioned him.

'It depends on certain circumstances,' evaded Nicholson.

'And what circumstances might they be?' Meredith asked.

'For a start, when you get your rabble to go back to work,' Purdon said, inclining his head towards the army of navvies outside.

'With respect, Mr Purdon, they have stopped working because you have refused to pay them. You have even stopped the Tommy shop giving them credit. Is it your intention to starve them back to work with no wages?' Meredith was not going to be fobbed off.

'We have nothing more to add,' Purdon said, with a surly shake of his head.

'I've got one question,' Meredith said. 'If they return to work, when will they get paid?'

'I will consider that if, and when, they go back to their place of employment. Mr Meredith. I repeat, we have nothing more to add. If you do not instruct the workforce to go into work, I shall be forced to lock you out. We can only have men on the site who wish to work. This meeting is at an end.' He got up from his chair and the two managers retired to another room.

Richard Ward was left with the two trade union officials.

Billy shook his head. 'So that was their plan all along. They mean to lock us out, and get blackleg labour in. He wants a war.'

'Have you no input on the matters, Mr Ward?' Peter Meredith looked at the surveyor.

'Much to my chagrin, Mr Meredith,' Ward shook his head. 'I cannot possibly comment.' He too, retired from the meeting.

Birkenshaw and Meredith left the office. The assembled navvies waited in anticipation.

Billy Birkenshaw stood on a cart so that the navvies could all see him. The noise of the crowd died down to an eerie silence as he began to speak.

'We have had talks with the managers,' he started. 'They will not say when you will be getting your money. They have issued a lock-out ultimatum. Anybody who does not go back to work will be locked out.'

The men were silent for a few moments while they digested what he had just said.

'What about the Tommy shops, Billy?' a Liverpool accent rang out. 'They have stopped giving us credit. How will we live?'

'On bloody grass, and stagnant piss,' an Irish voice answered him.

'The company will not move until you return to work,' concluded Billy Birkenshaw.

Friday 29th March 1844:

We listened to Birkenshaw from the hill inside the gates. Richard Ward joined us, shaking his head. He made no comment. Duke Frederick, who had been silent, commented that he mistrusted Purdon. The Duke astounded us with a quote from the scriptures. He recited it in perfect English. It was from Proverbs 14, verses 7 to 9.

'Leave the presence of a fool, for there you do not meet words of knowledge.'

In 1952, Susan read it again. The Duke Frederick was quoting the Bible in English. Perhaps he had learnt it from his teacher, Fulwood's wife. Perhaps he had been learning Milton, and Shakespeare. Perhaps he had been learning children's nursery rhymes?

With Billy's words, the 1844 strike had started.

'But even if we return to work, who's to say we will get our pay. I, for one, am not going to work,' a man with a Scottish accent muttered.

'Nor me,' another voice said.

An almighty roar went up, and the crowd started to cheer. Billy Birkenshaw waited while the noise died down.

'Right. Man the picket lines. We are on strike until we get our money.'

Wellington Purdon gave a smile, as he listened from the inner office. His plan had worked.

'I do hope you are ready for this war, Wellington. It may get nasty.' Henry Nicholson commented.

'Let the battle commence. I am ready' Purdon said confidently.

CHAPTER TWENTY SIX
1844
Enter the Cavalry

Susan followed the strike in the diary of the Irish Earl:
Thursday 4th April 1844:
The navvies' strike appears to be holding and only a handful of men are at work. Richard Ward told me that the men who have broken the strike have not the proper skills to carry out the repairs to the roof fall in the tunnel. There has been sporadic violence on the picket lines, and I have witnessed it at first hand. I am in no danger from the strikers. Now they are being kept away from work, we have conducted many more interviews with them for the Commission.

I have got to be impartial in my work, but I feel privately that the navvies have been forced into this situation by Purdon and Nicholson. The burden of culpability lies heavily on their heads.

Captain Hugh Gregory, of the Manchester and Salford Yeomanry, was trying to argue his point, but he was being overruled. He listened again as the Manchester magistrate addressed him.

'Captain Gregory, I will repeat my instructions. You are to attend the railway site at Woodhead. You are to keep the Queen's peace, and prevent riots and sedition. The railway company has issued the complaint. Legitimate workers are being prevented from entering the site by these strikers. Company property is being damaged, and we cannot allow this in our locality. I am invoking the 1838 Act, *Keeping the Peace Near Public Works*.'

It was the same magistrate with whom he had dealt two years earlier, in 1842, when the navvies had marched to Manchester.

Gregory had, however, researched the law, and he had an answer ready to plead his case.

'Your honour, I fully understand your instructions. However, I have to question the principle and substance behind them. I command a military unit. This strike should be dealt with by the Civil Authority, and they should use the regular County Police force. The 1838 Act specifically deals with the Payment of Constables. With respect, this relates to ordinary citizens being made temporary Constables.'

'Captain. Enough.' The magistrate held up his right hand. He was getting tired of this Yeomanry Captain telling him how to do his job. He was the magistrate, and he had a special interest in this case.

The magistrate had invested heavily in the railway. But there was something else that he was not telling Gregory. Wellington Purdon had given him a handsome purse to send the military to the Woodhead site.

'Captain, what you think, or indeed, what I think, is neither here nor there. The orders have been given ex parte. You will follow them to the letter of the law.' The Manchester magistrate repeated.

The Captain knew he was wasting his time complaining. He knew what was expected of his soldiers. They were to do the dirty work for the railway company. He vividly remembered the navvies' Manchester march two years previously, and the Peterloo massacre of 1819.

Susan followed the events in the diary with avid interest.

Monday 8th April 1844:

The army has arrived in force at the tunnel. They are the Manchester and Salford Yeomanry, and are billeted in the villages around Penistone. We have counted some fifty military personal, and I suspect Mr Purdon has something up his sleeve.

Wednesday 10th April 1844:

I have today acquainted myself with the Captain of the Yeomanry, Hugh Gregory, but he refused to comment on the situation. He has told me that he will confide to me in private, and I look forward to seeing him again. Apparently the Captain was at the Manchester March in 1842. He did say that the Yeomanry had been sent to Woodhead by a Manchester magistrate to deal with disturbances, under the 'Keeping the Peace near Public Works Act'.

Thus the 1838 Act has been invoked. I remember this Act going through the House. I wonder if the shareholders are aware that they will have to foot the bill for the military presence.

Later, I was interviewing the two surgeons, Henry Pomfret and Harold Thompson, in the Number One boiler house. Suddenly a cry came from outside. Secretary Fulwood was with me notating the shorthand, when a navvy with an injured arm, came into the makeshift infirmary. He was shouting 'The blacklegs are coming'.

'Blackleg' is a term used for a strike breaker. Apparently Mr Purdon has got some more labour from another railway site that has just finished, and also workers 'off the tramp'.

We set off down to the gate of the site to witness the arrival of the new labour force. The Yeomanry were escorting the newcomers into the site.

CHAPTER TWENTY SEVEN
The King of the Blacklegs

Captain Hugh Gregory did not like the task at all. He had escorted the new labour force from a special train at Penistone.

The railway now went as far as the town, and the men had been brought in cattle trucks. Most of the new men were Irish, and he fully expected trouble. They marched the blacklegs into the Dunford Bridge yard from Penistone. All the way, on the six mile journey, they were booed by the strikers.

The leader of the new workforce was a red-haired monster of a man, nicknamed "Red Rab" Macgregor.

Captain Gregory met Macgregor at Penistone as he had left the train. He asked him if he was happy to continue on his way to the site.

'There will be trouble at the workings when you arrive,' he explained. 'The navvies have been on strike for nearly two weeks, and feelings are running high.' he warned Red Rab.

Wellington Purdon was also there to greet the newcomers. Gregory had met Purdon before, when the navvies had marched on Manchester. He remembered arresting him in the shareholders' meeting. Purdon hadn't forgiven him for this. It had been humiliating for Purdon and he had been difficult with the Captain ever since the Hussars had arrived, two days before.

Purdon had overheard the Captain speaking to Macgregor.

'Captain Gregory, it is not in your remit to ask Mr Macgregor if he is happy, or unhappy. Your task is to escort these people to their place of work,' Purdon sneered.

The Captain reluctantly carried on, and gave orders to his soldiers to protect the new workforce.

However, there was one in his company who was in his element undertaking this kind of duty. He was Private Elias Randall, known as "Cock-eyed Eli".

The reception for the new workers at the Dunford Bridge gates was particularly nasty. A tremendous barrage of noise greeted them.

'Scabs and blacklegs!' the striking navvies shouted, as Macgregor and his men crossed the picket line.

Susan read the diary, as the Earl of Wexford gave his eyewitness account of the strike.

Wednesday 10th April 1844:

We saw the new labour-force march through the gates, and it was not a pretty sight. Bricks, bottles, and rocks were hurled at the newcomers. The most unsavoury names were also hurled at Purdon and the leader of the insurgent work force.

The leader of the strike-breakers is the largest and most ferocious man I have ever set my eyes upon. He has a flaming red beard, wild long hair, and a surly countenance. He is well over six feet in height and he would make the natural vanguard of any army. His name had arrived before him, since he is well known for his strike-breaking activities at railway sites around the country.

This giant of a man is called Red Rab Macgregor, and I suspect Purdon has chosen him to incur the strikers' wrath.

I pointed out this ogre to the Duke, and suggested that he would make a good king: a warlike chieftain.

The Duke replied. 'Uneasy lies the head that wears the crown'.

Susan felt inclined to agree with O'Neill. It was obvious that Macgregor had been brought in to break the strike.

She also noted how the Duke had quoted Shakespeare, from *Henry the Fourth Part II*. Susan continued to read the diary:

Macgregor is a Scotsman, and is the object of the strikers' anger. Even when the new workers were safe within the gates, I could still hear the shouts of 'Scabs and blacklegs'.

Things got worse when I heard Macgregor ask Purdon where they would sleep. Purdon pointed to the navvy huts, and told him to take his pick of them. He said Captain Gregory and his men would help them settle in. He then told Macgregor, and his men, to report to him at six o'clock the next morning.

With that, Purdon jumped on his horse, and galloped back through the picket line. The strikers shouted more abuse at him as he left.

Duke Frederick tried to remonstrate with the Captain but he could do nothing.

My party then witnessed a most sorrowful sight. The striking navvies were turned out of their homes, which are really just hovels, to make way for the new labour-force. It was a brutish act, and women and children were screaming. It seems this railway company has a lot to answer for.

CHAPTER TWENTY EIGHT
Mary, Mary

Mary Maloney was assisting the two surgeons as the trouble started.

At the age of nineteen, she had already suffered in the cruel world of the 1840s. She had originally come to Woodhead with Danny McNamara. He had died in the cholera epidemic, two years earlier, along with his three brothers.

She had loved Danny, and his loss had been devastating. But she did not have much choice. There was nothing in Cork for her to return to. She made the decision to stay at Woodhead.

She rented out her hut to the navvies, and assisted the Surgeons in the boiler house infirmary. She was now nineteen, and although her face was disfigured by a scar from a knife wound, she was still a handsome young woman. She had not been with another man since her Danny had died. To make matters worse, she had found herself pregnant just after the funeral.

Surgeon Harold Thompson had brought her son into the world. It had been a difficult birth, and he had told her that she could never have any more children.

At first, it had been touch and go with young Danny. He was a very sick child and Thompson was close to sending for the priest for both the mother and the baby. After a few weeks, both Mary and her child improved. However, the Surgeon knew that the child did not have much hope in the world he had been born into.

Mary had a stark choice. Either she carried on at Woodhead or she would have to give up her son to the workhouse.

That afternoon, little Danny was asleep in the boiler house. Mary was assisting Harold Thompson with a navvy who had been badly injured in the roof fall, at the Number One tunnel. She made a natural nurse, as gruesome sights did not bother her. Since the strike had started, the surgery was very quiet, apart from the men injured by the rock fall. Many men had left for other sites, or were on picket duty with the union.

The large iron door of the boiler house suddenly swung open.

A giant of a man with a flaming red beard entered, with a blue-coated soldier. It was Red Rab Macgregor, the leader of the strike-breakers, with a private of the Yeomanry. The soldier was Private Elias Randall. He was helping the Scotsman with the unsavoury business of clearing the camp for the new workforce.

As he entered the building, the soldier made a mental note of the layout of the makeshift infirmary. He noticed bottles of port in a cabinet. The surgeons used it to treat cholera victims.

'Who is in charge here?' The red-bearded man spoke, in a rough Scottish accent.

Harold Thompson did not answer. He was in the middle of a delicate operation. He had just amputated the navvy's leg, and the blood would not stop haemorrhaging.

'He wants to know. Who is in charge here? I can see a lot of blood, but is it from your tongues? Have you all had them cut out?' This time the soldier spoke. He had a commanding Mancunian accent, but Mary noticed that his eyes were pointing in different directions.

The soldier prodded the surgeon with his rifle butt, and caused the scalpel to slip from his hand. This made the blood pour even more from the leg of the poor navvy. The navvy screamed in pain. This awoke the baby, who in turn, started to cry.

'Now look what you have done,' Mary said. She turned to the two men, hands on her hips. 'I hope that you are both satisfied?'

Red Rab Macgregor was not used to being spoken to like that, especially by a woman. The taunts of being called a scab and a blackleg had been ringing in his ears ever since he had come to this infernal place. He grabbed a hank of Mary's hair and twisted hard, making her gasp with pain. He pushed her to the floor of the makeshift infirmary. She started to scream and fight back.

'Who are you, his Irish bitch?' Macgregor glared at the surgeon who was helpless to assist her, as he was struggling to staunch the blood of his patient.

'Is this your bastard?' The Scotsman shoved the rough wickerwork cradle, and the child wailed even more pitifully. 'You have five minutes to get your belongings out of your hovel.'

Macgregor's shovel-like hands roughly fondled her breasts. 'I might make you my tally-woman,' he leered.

Mary Maloney squirmed free of his grip, and she crawled to the door.

Weeping and bruised, she lay on the grass outside the door. The soldier followed her. He grabbed her, pinning her by the shoulders. He had taken notice of her fighting spirit and flaming eyes as she had resisted Macgregor. That had aroused him.

'I'm going to have you as my Irish bitch instead.' She shuddered as his tongue flicked into her ear. At close-quarters, his crossed eyes looked grotesque, and his breath stank of drink.

Mary could hear her little Danny screaming for her. She tried to struggle away from the Bluecoat's advances. She lashed out, aiming for his eyes. Her nails dug into his face. The soldier yelped with pain. Blood oozed from the scratches. He shoved his rifle butt into her chest, knocking her against the boiler house wall. She heard Macgregor laugh from the doorway.

Private Randall wiped the blood off his face with the sleeve of his uniform.

'You will bleed, and scream, when Elias Randall has his wicked way with you. My Irish trollop.' He was aroused just thinking about it.

Suddenly, Randall flinched. He could suddenly feel a cold metal blade against his throat, almost crushing his windpipe.

'Unhand that woman, both of you, or you will meet your maker,' said a strong foreign voice; the person holding the knife.

The foreigner then aimed a small pistol at Macgregor's head.

CHAPTER TWENTY NINE
The Duke Comes to the Rescue

Randall dropped his rifle, and his assailant took the knife from his throat.

He turned around. He stared into the faces of the Duke of Saxe-Coburg and Gotha, and his own Yeomanry Captain, Hugh Gregory. They had heard the woman's screams, and had witnessed Randall's attack on the woman. The Private realised he had gone too far this time.

The Captain fired his pistol into the air. The camp fell quiet. The only sound was the chugging of the steam boiler.

'Lieutenant!' he shouted, at a burley officer coming down the hill on horseback. 'Take this man away. I'll see him Court Marshalled for this!'

Private Randall's face was bloody from the scratches where Mary had defended herself. He cursed under his breath as the Lieutenant bound his hands and instructed him to walk behind his horse. There was pure hatred in his misaligned eyes.

'You are a disgrace to this regiment,' Captain Gregory said, as Private Randall was being led away.

The Yeomanry Captain then turned to the red-haired blackleg king.

'And you, Mr Macgregor,' he said, unable to hide his revulsion for the man. 'You will conduct yourself in the manner of a gentleman. My soldiers will supervise the movement of the people who want to leave. Any woman or child, who wishes to stay in their home, will not be evicted.'

There was a crowd of the new navvies around the boiler house, curious about the disturbance. Captain Gregory turned to address them.

'I will remind everybody that this site is under my jurisdiction, subject to the authority of the 1838 Act, Keeping the Peace Near Public Works.'

The giant Scotsman stood silently, his fists clenched by his sides.

'Mr Macgregor,' Captain Gregory continued. 'I am giving you fair warning. If any of your men fall out of line, they will be arrested and they will never return here. Do you understand, Mr Macgregor?'

The king of the blacklegs, although seething inside, felt totally humiliated in front of his own men. He was already regretting coming here. There were far easier pickings at other sites.

'I understand.' He was forced to answer.

Captain Gregory had taken control of the situation, but he was appalled at the state of the navvy camp. He was shocked at the situation in the makeshift infirmary. It was as bad as any field hospital he had witnessed.

The Surgeon, Harold Thompson, had continued working on the injured navvy throughout the disturbance, to prevent the loss of the poor man's life.

The Captain issued an order to his troops, who had appeared at the scene.

'Bring our Surgeon up here to assist in this infirmary.'

'It is barbaric,' the Duke remonstrated, 'how these unfortunate people are being treated.'

Gregory shrugged his shoulders.

'I am just here to keep the peace. I have issued my orders, and will do my best. You will have to take up the matter with the railway people.'

The Duke helped Mary Maloney to her feet, and took her back into the boiler house. He lifted young Danny from his cradle and passed him to his mother.

The young surgeon was still desperately trying to stop the navvy bleeding.

'Mary, please help with this tourniquet,' he cried out. The Duke held out his arms for the child, and Mary returned to her work.

The Duke softly sung to Danny and the child stopped crying. He took his pocket watch from his waistcoat and dangled it in front of him. Danny was fascinated by the gold gleam of the watch, and he smiled at his new Royal friend, making a grab for the watch.

Susan read about the lock-out in O'Neill's diary as she continued to read his account of Wednesday 10th April 1844. She was fascinated by the drama of the situation, but solving the murders also felt tantalising close:

The newcomers had been turning the hapless wretches from their huts. It was a pitiful sight, and Captain Gregory was trying to maintain the peace. There was a deplorable incident in the boiler house. The leader of the strike-breakers, Macgregor, and a Private soldier, Elias Randall, had assaulted one of the nurses, Mary Maloney. We had been observing the eviction when the unfortunate incident had occurred, but witnessed its aftermath.

Captain Gregory took charge of the situation admirably. The behaviour of his Private was appalling, and I hope that justice prevails when he is court marshalled. The soldier Randall looks such a demonic figure with his slanted eyes.

Today, I have nothing but admiration for the Duke. He is a complex character indeed, and only a wise man could make any sense of him. Although he is Royalty, and has all the trappings of wealth, he takes an interest in the underprivileged of this world.

His compassion for Fulwood's daughters, and now this poor woman who has lost everything, is indeed a joy to behold.

I left the Duke with Mary Maloney in the infirmary. He was holding her baby son. It was very touching. He was singing to the child: a German nursery rhyme, and he had given the boy a gold watch to play with.

These were big clues in solving the murder mysteries, Susan realised. She read the paragraph twice, to be sure. There had been three references to a German nursery rhyme now.

The rhyme she had found herself, in the boiler house with the seven bodies; another when Roger had read from his great grandfather's book, and now the third, in O'Neill's diary. Now a gold watch had been mentioned.

Could this be the same gold watch that was discovered with the first skeletons?

Susan had made a startling discovery. Could the skeletons discovered at the bottom of the shaft be Mary Maloney and her child Danny?

CHAPTER THIRTY
The Virgin Mary

Duke Frederick, of Saxe-Coburg and Gotha, was fascinated by his new found friend, Mary Maloney.

They were from diametrically opposite corners of the Victorian establishment. He was a wealthy Duke with all the fine trappings of wealth. She was from a Cork laundryhouse, with a child born out of wedlock. She did not live in a palace. Mary lived in a stone hut on the most desolate and isolated moorland in England.

Mary worked hard, following the surgeon's instructions until they had staunched the bleeding of the navvy's leg, and laid him on a makeshift bed to rest. She was a gentle and steady-handed nurse, despite her latest ordeal.

Later, the Duke accompanied Mary to her hut, still carrying Danny. The Duke kept singing the old German nursery rhyme to him.

Mary boiled a kettle on a peat fire, to make tea.

The Duke sang softly:

'One two three in quick time. All the children go with us.

Little Danny is next in line, and is running past us.

Bend down, stretch up, turn around,

Clap four times, Stamp your feet, round and round.'

Mary had spoken very little since her ordeal with the soldier. She was very shy of her Royal visitor, but she was fascinated by the tender way that he held her son and sung to him. Danny held the gold watch in his tiny hands, mesmerised by its mechanism.

'This is for you, little one,' the Duke said. He took his watch chain from his waistcoat, and hooked it on the child's small coat. He sang the song again.

'What's that song that you're singing?' she asked.

'An old nursery rhyme that my mother used to sing to me,' he answered.

'You'll have to speak slower, my Lord, so I can understand you,' she said.

'Please call me Frederick. I am learning English, and I think we should learn each other how to speak it properly. You Irish people are worse than me with the English language,' he joked.

For the first time, she smiled at him. He noticed that her scar disappeared when her lips moved.

He had been wondering why Mary seemed familiar to him. Her smile made him realise who it was. His mother had died when he was a boy, but he remembered her taking him to a big church to see a statue of the Virgin Mary nursing the baby Jesus. The serenity and beauty of this Irish woman reminded him of the statue.

Frederick had not been raised as a Catholic. In fact he was not religious at all, but he just stared at her. He was transfixed by Mary, and he could not help what he did next.

He was still holding the child, Danny. As Mary knelt to give Duke Frederick a tin mug of tea, he bent his head close to her.

'I am here to protect you,' he said, in very slow, clear English. 'No harm shall ever come to you or your child.' Mary understood every word, and she believed him.

CHAPTER THIRTY ONE
The Blackleg Leader

Red Rab Macgregor was a proper bastard.

He had been called a bastard for all of his twenty eight years, and they were still calling him a bastard now. He could hear the cries of "bastard" as he drank the sour beer in the Angel public house at Dunford Bridge. It was the union pickets that he could hear, but he carried on drinking.

His flaming red beard dripped with beer and breadcrumbs, as his left hand lifted up the pint tankard. His right hand squeezed a tally woman's breast. He'd found a woman who was more amenable than the Irish slut who had resisted his advances.

The tally woman grabbed the tankard and drank from it.

'They never stop shouting, do they?' she commented. 'Does it not bother you?'

'Sally, it's better to be a rich blackleg than to be a poor union man,' he roared, in his loud Glaswegian accent. 'Sticks and stones and all that.' He fumbled inside the low bodice of her dress, until her breasts were virtually exposed. Befuddled by drink, Sally seemed not to care.

Macgregor had been raised in a Glasgow Poorhouse and he had no idea who his mother was, or who had put him there. Somebody had once told him that his father had been in the Highland regiment and fought at Waterloo, and his mother had been a prostitute on the Clyde docks. But he never really knew, and he never really cared.

Due to the overcrowded conditions in the workhouse, Macgregor had slept on a staircase. The Director had marked his place of residence as "on the step".

The only record of his early life was a copy of the page from the poorhouse records, given to him by the Poorhouse Provost Director in 1830, when he had left, aged fourteen, and determined to make his own way in the world. He kept the only proof of his existence in his jacket pocket. He thought that one day it might come in handy.

He'd had little education and lived on his wits, muscle, and brawn.

Soon after he left the poorhouse, Macgregor had visited a travelling fair. He had learnt a bit of boxing from another boy and he was fascinated by the prize fighters. Having nothing to lose, he entered a fight. He surprised himself when he knocked out the fair's reigning champion at the end of the first round.

The fairground owner, Billy Donnelly, immediately signed Macgregor up as the new champion. For five years, Macgregor toured Scotland and Northern England, as 'Red Rab, the Glasgow Boxing King'.

Donnelly worked on Macgregor's physique and fitness, and taught him the skills of fairground boxing. These skills were not always based on the principles of fairness.

Rab spent five years as the unbeatable champion, and he was the boxing giant of the travelling fairs. Donnelly had always warned him of two deadly vices: women and drink. Advice which for once in his life, he took heed of.

In 1835, Macgregor was nineteen and he was in spectacular shape. He was physically fit, a colossal man, with a lethal right hook.

Then fate dealt a hand. He had an admirer. The Gypsy fortune teller had a sixteen year old daughter called Esmeralda, who dazzled her eyes at him. Soon she was in his bed. It had not gone unnoticed by the ever-watchful eyes of Donnelly.

Macgregor, the prize fighter, was the prize catch for the travelling females. Soon, he was sowing his wild oats in other places, and he started to drink heavily. Esmeralda was racked by jealousy and the Gypsy part of her wanted revenge.

She tried all the curses she knew but to no avail. She then devised a plan with her Gypsy mother. It was just before a big fight at Penrith. Macgregor had never lost a fight, and Donnelly raked the money in, with his illegal betting on the fights. It was a big event. Thousands attended to witness the nomad champion. Hundreds of pounds were at stake.

The two Gypsies staked all their money on an unknown local boy. The odds were very high on the "no-hoper". Esmeralda visited Macgregor just before the fight, but he declined her advances. He was being monitored closely by Donnelly. But not closely enough. She managed to spike his glass of water.

Macgregor lost the fight to the local lad. The gypsies made a fortune. Esmeralda had her revenge. The champion was no more.

Donnelly finished him. He had served his purpose for five good years, but Macgregor's prize fighting days were over.

However, it did not take him long to find employment. His strong physique gave him a big advantage in getting work on the new railway construction sites.

He drifted all over Britain, chasing the money at each site. He was well known by the new police force, and he narrowly escaped a murder charge in Carlisle. Macgregor then avoided a brutal rape charge in Liverpool by a hair's breath.

His name went before him wherever he went. He had no principles, or scruples, and he would do anything for money. He was a very hard worker but he had three vices. Women, beer, and gambling.

Macgregor had first met Wellington Purdon while he was working on the Bermondsey and Deptford railway, in 1836, the first big railway project in London, and Purdon had kept in touch with him, in case he needed a strike-breaker.

Purdon had written to Macgregor in his lodgings in London, where he had been working on London Bridge station. The job was coming to an end, so this job at Woodhead was lucky timing. Semi-literate, he had slowly read the letter. Purdon wanted two hundred men to break a strike, and he was expecting trouble. For this, Macgregor would be handsomely paid in cash. The price was 100 guineas.

Red Rab's luck had been mixed so far at Woodhead. His two hundred blackleg navvies had been whittled down to about half, but he had expected that to happen. The abuse from the strikers, the fear of not getting paid, and the harsh conditions of the tunnel, had caused many men to desert.

Two more men had also been killed, and three more badly injured, in a fall at Number One Shaft. This was due to the roof not being supported. Even someone as reckless as Macgregor knew that unsafe working practices had lost these men.

He had been drinking since the end of his shift at six o'clock, and it had now turned midnight. Macgregor worked hard, and played hard.

'Sheffield Sally,' he leered, squeezing the woman's buttocks. 'Let's go and make a little Macgregor bastard.'

CHAPTER THIRTY TWO
The Union Meeting

The RWBN committee meeting in St John's Church Hall at Penistone had been in session for about half an hour.

The Secretary, Peter Meredith, was speaking.

He was summing up the progress of the strike. They had been on strike for ten days. He highlighted the positive facts first.

'Just a few of our old workforce have crossed the picket line to go into work, but they are mostly unskilled men. They cannot do the dangerous tunnel work.'

'Since the strike-breakers arrived, two have already been killed, and five more badly maimed, by the rash insistence of Mr Purdon that they work in unsupported ground.'

'We have persuaded another hundred men, brought in by Purdon, not to cross our picket line.' This comment caused smiles and nods around the committee.

'Mr Secretary,' John Black, a committee member, formally addressed him. 'We all know the company will not speak to us while we're still off work. We will not go back to work until we get paid. So it is deadlocked. How long do you think we can hold out for, and what can we do to break them?'

'We were coming to that shortly,' Meredith answered. 'It's the next item on the agenda. Billy here wants to say a few things.' He pointed to the President of the union, Billy Birkenshaw.

'Fellow committee members,' Billy began. 'Make no bones about it. We are at war. The point is though, who are we at war with? Is it the company we are fighting? Or is it Mr Wellington Purdon and Mr Henry Nicholson?'

Billy Birk was a strategist, a back-street fighter, and he had spent days planning how the union would win this strike. He had developed since his Huskar pit days, and had learned how to liaise with people, and think things through logically. He was a natural-born leader of men.

'These two managers, Purdon and Nicholson, are acting without a mandate.' Billy paused to explain. 'They were not instructed by the company to start this strike. All the shareholders want is the tunnel completed, at minimal cost, so they can get returns on their money. The longer we hold out, the weaker these two managers become. Did you know that the company will have to foot the bill for the soldiers being on the site?'

'The blackleg, Macgregor, is the problem, I think,' another member interrupted.

Billy shook his head. 'Macgregor is just Purdon's puppet. But we cannot wait until the blacklegs desert the ship, or wait until the company intervenes. We have to put a few holes in the ship, and sink it altogether.'

By now he had the meeting's complete attention.

'So what is your plan, Billy?' a member asked.

'I have a plan, but it must not leave this room.' They all nodded, as he continued. 'We will take Macgregor out first, and then completely close the lot down.'

The committee members murmured in approval around the table.

'How do we take him out?' another member asked. 'He's as strong as an ox.'

'There is an old saying, *knoweth thine enemies*,' Billy replied. 'What is this Macgregor's weakness? I will tell you. Women, beer, and gambling. That's what they are.'

'We all know that,' John Black said. 'But how do we get to him? We can't get into the site.'

'Leave it to me, Johnny boy, I've already got somebody on the inside working on it.' Billy smiled at them all.

CHAPTER THIRTY THREE
Altercation

While the union meeting was in progress, Duke Frederick of Saxe-Coburg and Gotha, was drinking at the best table in the Angel public house. He was accompanied by his new friend, Mary Maloney.

They looked completely out of character with the rest of the surroundings. Duke Frederick was dressed in an exquisite velvet frock coat, with a dazzling white shirt and bow tie. A dress sword hung by his side.

He sported a monocle in his left eye, to assist him with his card game.

Mary Maloney could have also passed for a member of the aristocracy. She was totally unrecognisable as the tally woman from the shanty town.

Earlier that day, the Duke had taken Mary and her child to Manchester by carriage, which he had borrowed from Wortley Hall. They had hatched a plan together. They had booked into an expensive hotel for the day. Frederick had told Mary to ignore the stares from the hotel staff, and the other guests.

Frederick had waited in the hotel's lounge until Mary had bathed, ready for her new appearance.

He had already sent Mary's measurements to the most elegant dress-makers and tailors in the city, Benjamin Hyam, in St Marys Gate. He'd bought Mary a very expensive gown, and baby Danny a waistcoat.

When Mary met him downstairs, she looked stunning, almost unrecognisable in her transformation from her ragged working clothes.

The Duke had pinned his gold watch, and chain, to Danny's waistcoat.

He had given Mary a gold ring. It had belonged to his mother, and he had inherited it when she had died.

Mary cried when he gave it to her. Nobody had ever given her anything like that.

'I wish you to have it, Mary' he had told her. He slipped it on her finger. 'Wear it always,' he said, tenderly.

As they played cards, the Duke stared at her. He could not believe how beautiful she looked in her long blue gown, which had a plunging neckline that showed off her small breasts.

A few of the blackleg navvies, and a couple of off-duty soldiers, were in the public house. They gave the Duke and Mary curious glances, but left them alone.

Red Rab Macgregor entered the public house, caked in mud and dirt from his shift in the tunnel.

Men always shied away from Rab. He swaggered to the bar and they all made way for him.

He was ready for a drink. His mouth was full of tunnel dust. The barman knew what his drink was, and within a minute, the first pint of crude beer had been drunk by the 'blackleg king'.

His thirst slaked, he wiped his lips. He heard a giggle from the corner of the room.

'My dear,' the Duke proclaimed, as he shuffled the cards. 'You always seem to win me.'

Macgregor turned and saw the Royal Duke, who had threatened to shoot him when he had first arrived at the camp.

The Duke had prevented Private Randall from ravishing the Irish tally woman. Macgregor realised that the woman sitting with the Duke was the very same tally woman, dressed as a Duchess, in all her finery.

He remembered how this woman had spurned and embarrassed him. And then the foppish Duke had threatened him. They had both stung his pride, and his vanity.

'Good evening, your Royal Highness. Still here, are you? Shouldn't you be at your palace with your Duchess?' Macgregor mocked, standing in front of the seated couple.

'No, my good fellow, we thought that we would have a little game of cards in this fine establishment. Did we not, Lady Mary?' the Duke said, mimicking an upper class English accent. 'But she always beats me in your English games.'

The other navvies and the two Bluecoats laughed at the Duke's remark. He was obviously goading Macgregor, who was close to losing his temper. The Duke was challenging him.

'You think you are clever, Mr Duke, don't you, with all your perfume and finery?'

Macgregor was almost spitting with anger. He loomed over the Duke and Mary, and pulled a tattered piece of paper out of the inside pocket of his coat.

It was the same piece of paper that had been given to him by the Provost Director of the Glasgow Poorhouse.

'See this, Your Highness?' He waved the paper in the Duke's face. 'Do you see what it says?' The Duke stared at him, blankly.

'On the step. That's what it says. On the step. I am the Duke of the step.' Macgregor waved the paper at the rest of the navvies. 'The step of the poorhouse. That's where I grew up, on a bloody step. But I'll tell you all something. I am sure the Duchess here would fancy Duke Rabbie Macgregor, the Duke of the Glasgow step, better than any jumped up piece of foreign shite like you.'

The trap was sprung. The Duke jumped to his feet. Picking up his kid gloves from the table, he swiped the Scotsman across his face, cutting his lip.

'You will choose your weapons,' Frederick commanded him. 'We fight for the honour of the lady.'

CHAPTER THIRTY FOUR
The Card Game

Macgregor was taken aback by the Duke's challenge. He was not expecting a gentlemen's duel.

This would mean fighting on unfamiliar territory. He was a Gypsy boxer but Frederick was a trained military man. His pride and reputation demanded action and his only hope was a fist fight. Guns, or swords, were obviously in the Duke's favour.

Macgregor's brow furrowed as his internal dilemma played out. He lowered his arm as he heard a voice speak up from behind.

'Gentlemen.'

Macgregor span around to see Captain Hugh Gregory, an unexpected visitor at the Angel, looking serious and purposeful.

'I will remind you that duelling is forbidden in military establishments. As these public works are under military jurisdiction, I will have you both arrested if you resort to arms.'

Captain Gregory wanted to avoid bloodshed, while he was in charge. He was not at all happy about the military being involved in an industrial dispute.

The last thing he wanted to deal with was a death. Perhaps it might be a Royal death. An enquiry would be called along with the Police, and it would probably be the end of his career.

Macgregor sighed internally. This was salvation. He was thinking fast and he saw the answer on the table.

'I see you are playing cards, Mr Duke. Perhaps your honour would be served by a game of brag? The winner takes all, including the Duchess.' Macgregor's swagger was back as he drooled and leered at his final words.

The crowd in the pub laughed together as their hero was back, goading the gentleman.

The Royal Duke nodded, and Macgregor sat down at the table. Mary pushed back her chair, retreating further into the corner. The Duke gathered up the cards and shuffled them.

The cards were old and had been through a thousand pairs of hands. Blood and fortunes had been lost on their turn. They were important to Frederick, and he was grateful when he'd anted up and laid the first card.

The two men began the game of Three Card Brag. A working class version of poker, based on bluff and using only three cards. The highest hand was three of a kind: sevens were the best, and the low hand, one of a high card. Straights, runs, flushes and pairs made up the remainder of the hands.

Frederick had seen the game being played by the navvies and he was vaguely familiar with the rules. However, it was not the civilised game of bridge or whist that he was used to.

Macgregor started to quickly down his ale, and he wiped his mouth and grimy beard each time he put his glass down. He wiped the blood from his bleeding lip with his sleeve. Droplets of blood were caked in his red beard, giving him a demonic appearance.

He stared and sweated profusely, due to the layers of clothing he was wearing: a rough work jacket over a cotton shirt. The heat from the alcohol, the coal fire, and the people now watching the game did not help either. The Duke only sipped at his drink. Temperance was a large part of his plan, and he remained calm.

Word of the game had travelled fast through the community. There was now a large crowd in the public house to witness this game of high stakes. The onlookers' eyes veered between the card-players, and Mary, in her unaccustomed finery. Mary didn't take her eyes off the Duke and Macgregor as she nervously twisted her new shawl in her hands.

The Duke and Macgregor had placed coins and notes into the middle of the table: the pot.

This was a small fortune for the patrons of the Angel, and Sally, the Sheffield prostitute, looked on jealously, working out the amount of men she would have to sleep with for the same amount. No one spoke, save the two players, and no one dared to interrupt and join the game.

Macgregor turned his three cards carefully from the table so that no one could see. They were all black, all spades, a high card: a queen. This was a high flush and he smiled internally. Brag required total confidence, but he remained calm. The Duke was new to the game and Macgregor could tell.

Every hand the Duke had played so far was over-done and he had only shown low pairs. Macgregor gauged the Duke as naïve and believing that the pairs were good. His flush was better, and he wondered how to raise the stakes.

'Three guineas,' slurred the Scotsman, and he threw in three golden coins.

The crowd gasped. This was a month's work in the hellish tunnel.

The Duke looked up at the black-leg and asked, 'Good hand, eh Macgregor? First one tonight?'

Frederick knew his pair of sevens was probably beaten but he had to play out the hand.

'See you,' he replied, and threw in the equal amount.

The pot was at seven guineas and again, avaricious and eager eyes stared on.

The Scotsman turned over the flush and Frederick his pair, to delighted squeals from the onlookers. Macgregor raked in the money over to his side of the table.

'I like those pairs, Mr Duke, but not good enough today.'

His gaze fixed on Mary and the remaining money left by the Duke. A lascivious tongue traced along his lips.

'Not looking good, Duchess?' he drawled. 'Hope you don't mind it rough tonight.'

Cackling laughter filled the room.

'The game of cards, Macgregor, as in life, is not over until the final hand has been played,' retorted the Duke.

Macgregor looked at the Duke, raised his beer glass and finished the pint in one.

'Life and talk is cheap, Duke. You got any more money on you? You're going to need it.'

The Scotsman picked up a gold coin and tossed it over to the barman, George Whitfield.

'Get a round in,' he shouted, to the loudest cheer of the night.

A pint of ale was brought over for the hero.

The next hand was dealt by the Duke. 'Are you playing or talking?' he asked.

The Duke looked down at his dealt cards, focussing on the detail of a rubbed corner on one and a small cut on the back of another. Inside he sighed contentedly.

Both players placed a shilling in the pot to start and the game began. Macgregor had been using the tactic of going 'blind', which meant that he only had to pay half the stakes on each round of betting. But he had no idea what his hand was, because the cards remained face down.

The Duke had shied away from this tactic, and had been looking at his cards at the first opportunity.

The Scotsman carefully picked up his cards and he made a smile, 'Not looking good, Mr Duke,' he sneered and he threw in a guinea to start. He shot a look over at Mary and winked. Mary looked away in disgust and contempt.

Frederick went to pick up his cards but then stopped and returned his hand to his money. The move was slow and deliberate but had the desired effect of showing hesitation. He paused, picked up a coin and announced, 'A guinea blind.'

Macgregor looked amused by the actions and words.

'Are you sure about that, Mr Duke?' he asked. 'Doesn't look like you know what you're doing to me. Do you want to ask the Captain's advice at all?'

Macgregor gestured over to Captain Gregory who was engrossed in the spectacle. He gave a small shake of the head and pursed his lips. This was clearly something that he did not wish any involvement in.

'It's two guineas to you, Macgregor. Are you in, or out?' Frederick said stonily.

Macgregor picked up his glass, stalling for time, drank half, and slammed it on the table. Froth spilled over the glass, but not on the cards or money.

'Alright, rich boy, like that is it? Looks like this is the end for you.'

Macgregor was bluffing, thought Frederick. He hoped he had some sort of a hand and would keep betting. The Scotsman threw in a five pound note, 'I'll raise you blind, man.'

Frederick had learnt through the night that the person going blind could not be turned or seen by the other betting person, so he knew that he had Macgregor.

The game continued until Fredrick had spent the remaining money left on the table. Macgregor still had around five pounds and there was about thirty in the pot. This was where the game was going to finish, one way or another.

The Scotsman looked on smugly and a hole appeared in his crimson-stained beard.

'No money left, your highness? If you haven't any family silver to throw in, you'll have to pack.'

Frederick had heard the phrase and thought whimsically about setting off on a *journey*, but Macgregor meant that he would have to fold. The Duke had no intention of doing that, and he stared again at the markings on the reverse of the two cards which he had noticed earlier in his game with Mary.

The Duke then took out a wallet from the inside of the jacket and pulled out a number of pieces of folded paper, to more gasps from the crowd. He counted out half of what the blackleg was holding, and placed it in the pot.

'You sure about that, your highness? There's always a spot for you in the tunnel when that's gone.' Macgregor hissed confidently.

The Scotsman looked smug at first, but he then realised that the last of his money was needed to match the bet.

'Looks like the bank of Macgregor has dried up. Not too much to say now, Scotsman? Lost your will, have you?' the Duke asked.

Macgregor looked at his cards again carefully. He knew his hand and was confident, but he still needed to be sure. His eyes were glazed from the alcohol as he looked at the cards and he saw the two kings staring back at him. 'A high pair,' he thought. 'The Duke hasn't even seen his hand yet, I've got the smarmy fucker.'

Macgregor threw in the last of his money, knowing that he had to keep going and he could not see the Duke, who was still blind.

The pot looked massive. There was more than a year's worth of wages in there and the amassed crowd salivated at the sight of it, urging the blackleg to win.

Frederick knew it was time to pick up his cards. He slowly and carefully picked up the three cards as a hush descended on the pub. He split the cards and saw the two cards he had expected: Aces.

The cards had been identified earlier, and the plan was almost complete. He just had to hope that Macgregor had a lesser hand. Frederick looked over at Mary, smiled, and prayed internally.

The Duke drew a breath and counted out the remainder of his money. He needed to draw out the same amount that he knew the blackleg was carrying, but he did not have enough money with him.

Frederick knew something about Macgregor. He had one hundred guineas on him. He glanced at Mary.

'My Lady. I need to borrow your ring, just for a few minutes. She slid the ring from her finger and passed it to the Duke.

He looked up at the Captain.

'Captain, would you please vouch for this? Is it worth one hundred guineas? '

Frederick passed him his mother's old ring. The Captain took the ring. He eyed the workings and the Latin inscription. He read out the words and translated them: *Amor est vitae essential: Love is the essence of life.*

'The ring is priceless, but let's make that a round hundred guineas to you, Scotsman.'

The Captain nodded, and placed the ring in the centre of the table, on top of the money.

Macgregor froze in a state of mental numbness.

The tension hung in the air and all eyes rested on Macgregor. This would leave a pot of over 250 guineas, enough to pay for a substantial house, something unimaginable to the amassed patrons.

Macgregor's eyes widened and he was forced from his stupor. He looked from the money and the ring to the Duke a number of times. The Scotsman considered his situation. He concluded that the Duke must be bluffing, and had nothing. Even if he did have a hand, would he have a pair? A low pair, he hoped. Macgregor had Kings. He considered the amount as well: A hundred guineas. How did the Duke know about that?

The crowd were startled. They craned their necks to watch the expression of the giant Scotsman. They started to murmur. A hundred guineas? Where had the Duke got that figure from?

Macgregor's brain raced. The Duke must have found out that Purdon had given him money to break the strike. But how? A hundred guineas exactly. This small fortune was inside a secret pocket sewn inside Macgregor's shirt. The stakes were high indeed.

If he said that he did not have the money, the Duke would come out with the truth, and it would look bad for Macgregor. While he'd been paid handsomely, his men had received nothing to break the strike.

'What's wrong Macgregor, cat got your tongue? You have the money. Let's see it.' The German aristocrat spoke slowly, in fluent English.

The crowd gasped again. Macgregor had been holding out on wages and it had been rumoured that he had the money with him.

The Scotsman was in a corner. His only choice was to expose the hidden money, or lose the hand.

The dilemma was quickly resolved by greed. He pictured himself wearing the glinting ring as he defiled the former whore.

On the next table was a discarded plate with the remains of some half-eaten and disgusting tavern food. Macgregor deftly reached for the knife and held it up in one swift movement, his face serious.

'Macgregor!' shouted an excited Captain Gregory. 'No weapons.'

The Scotsman smiled broadly, and then with two slashes at his own chest, with the precision of a surgeon, he exposed the lining of his cotton shirt. The ugly cuts showed the edge of a strip of cloth, which he then pulled from the lining.

The strip of cloth was then unfolded, to show gleaming coins discretely hidden inside the material. One hundred guineas.

Shouts rang out from the crowd, 'What the hell is that, Macgregor? That's our pay, you Scots bastard!'

'Shut it,' shouted the big Scotsman as he stood up. 'You'll get your money after the game. If anyone has a problem with that, let me know now.'

The 6 foot 5 inches frame of the Scotsman seemed to fill the whole public house. He clenched his fists and jaw, and searched around the room, looking for a challenger. He had been in many fights like this and knew that it was all brass balls and he just had to pick off the first one to say anything. No-one did.

Macgregor picked up the material strip and poured the guineas into the pot.

'Alright. I'll see you.'

The words were simple and definite. This was the end of the game. The only decision that was left was to see who would take away the money, and the woman.

Macgregor was confident. He picked up his cards and said 'You've got fuck all, Duke' He displayed a pair of Kings to the watching crowd.

The cards fell onto the table and showed the two members of royalty.

The pub erupted in cheers. The hand was a good one and would normally win in such a situation. People danced up and down and a prostitute raised both her arms in the air, greedily eying up the Scotsman.

Frederick waited for the noise to wane. His inaction intensified, as the pub had expected him to throw in his hand, but his cards just stayed on the table and he remained motionless. Excitement turned back to tension as the Duke sat impassively.

'Good hand, Macgregor,' the Duke finally said.

His hand then moved to the face-down cards and he slowly picked them up, enjoying the moment and the now silent establishment.

'But not good enough.'

Frederick turned over the hand to reveal the two Aces.

'You fucking German bastard,' shouted the Scotsman, enraged.

Pandemonium erupted as he went to tip up the table, but was stopped mid-action, by the deafening noise of a musket going off. Ceiling plaster trickled to the floor of the Angel and silence resumed.

'The next person to move will be shot,' exclaimed the Captain, as six of his men came into the pub. 'Better leave it Macgregor. And the rest of you can all leave. I am closing this establishment.'

The barman, George Whitfield, looked on, more in relief than anything.

Macgregor eyed up the scene, staring at the cards, the Captain, the soldiers, and the Duke. Finally he gazed at Mary. 'Next time, my lady,' he said disconsolately.

He staggered to his feet, defeated, spat on the floor and left the pub.

The Duke now played to the public gallery. In a theatrical stance, he bowed to Mary, and removed her shawl. He then scooped up the winnings and wrapped them up very carefully in the garment.

'For you, my Duchess,' he told her, with a smile. 'I am away to my residence. I bid you fine people a fine Good evening – or *Guten Abend*.'

CHAPTER THIRTY FIVE
Red Rab Returns

Mary Maloney was asleep with her baby Danny, back in her stone hut. She was dreaming of her childhood in Cork.

She was awakened by a rough hand across her mouth.

'One bleeding word, you Irish bitch, and you and your bastard are dead,' a stinking, beer-drenched voice whispered. 'I want that purse back and then I will have you.'

It was Red Rab Macgregor.

Mary tried to scream but he pressed his hand tighter, while his other hand pressed a knife to her throat.

Suddenly, a rifle bayonet pressed against Macgregor's back.

'Put down that knife. You are under arrest for attempted rape and robbery.' It was Captain Hugh Gregory. The Duke had warned the Captain that he suspected Macgregor would try to attack Mary, and they had waited in the darkness for the Scotsman to attempt to retrieve his money.

'That's the last we shall see of him,' the Captain said, as his men led the Scotsman away, his wrists bound. Macgregor struggled as they pushed him through the low doorway, but he knew that he was beaten.

The Duke comforted Mary, helping her to light the fire and make tea.

'Your Grace,' Captain Gregory said, from the doorway. 'Pardon my boldness. How you did you know that Macgregor was wearing that purse?'

The Duke winked in the firelight.

'Captain, it was easy. The tally woman, Sheffield Sally, was with him the other night. She was in my pay. He was talking, in his drunken sleep, about his ill-gotten gains. And she'd felt a lump in his shirt when she was with him. He wouldn't take his shirt off. Where else could he leave a large sum of money in a place like this?'

'Very shrewd, your Grace.' Captain Gregory nodded.

'One thing puzzles me, Captain. How did you know there would be trouble here?' The Duke asked. 'I was surprised to see you in the Angel.'

The Captain laughed.

'The Hougoumont gunnery sergeant, Meredith, warned me that there might be trouble,' Gregory said, leaving the hut. 'He advised me to bring six of my men and we would be suitably rewarded from the winnings. Old soldiers and all that,' he added, with a sly wink.

The next morning the RWBN trade union held an emergency committee meeting at St John's Church Hall at Penistone.

There were only two items on the agenda: a return to work, and what to do with the one hundred and forty guineas that had suddenly come their way. They were only in session for half an hour. They agreed unanimously to return to work later that day, and a treasurer was elected to divide the money into two funds. One would reimburse the navvies who had been on strike, and a welfare scheme would be set up for widows and severely disabled workmen.

To the sound of great laughter, Billy Birk summed it all up.

'Certain remunerations have already been paid to anonymous parties who helped us through our difficult times.'

CHAPTER THIRTY SIX
Return to Work

Susan cross referenced her notes. She wanted to find out when the lockout and strike had finished.

She found the answer at the date Monday 6th May 1844:

All the men have returned to work, and they have a satisfactory resolution. The company has removed Wellington Purdon and Henry Nicholson from the managers' roles, and has promised to pay the navvies the monies that are owed to them.

Richard Ward is to be, henceforth, in charge of the project, and for once common sense has prevailed. He is a very capable fellow and is popular with both the men, and shareholders.

The strike-breakers have all left the site, and the weekend has seen much merriment. The Tommy shop has reopened, and credit is back, so at least the navvies can stock up, albeit at outrageous prices.

The strike-breaking Macgregor has been arrested for attempted robbery and rape and will appear at Manchester Magistrates Court in July.

The railway company is going to hold their own independent inquiry into the events, but no doubt they will try to cover themselves from public disgrace.

I have filed all the statements for the Select Committee. In my opinion, the strike was provoked by gross mismanagement, and lessons should be learnt.

I have sent the Queen a report on the conduct of Duke Frederick. He is the hero of the people, and he can do nothing wrong.

I felt it prudent to omit any mention of the tally woman, Mary Maloney. I am not sure that the Queen would approve of his friendship with the lady.

Richard Ward was now in charge of the tunnel. His energy and forward thinking had injected a new dimension into the project.

His first task was to form a workers' committee, a revolutionary new practice.

'These men have all the skills and experience that I need,' he explained, to O'Neill and Duke Frederick. 'We need them to complete this tunnel.'

Ward listened to the ideas of Peter Meredith and Billy Birk. The first problem was how to overcome the seventy foot roof fall that had been the downfall of Wellington Purdon.

They came up with the idea of making a steel shield, which would be slowly advanced, and would protect the men clearing the roof fall. Behind these front men, an army of bricklayers and joiners would shutter the walls of the tunnel.

It was a spectacular success. The bad ground was left behind, and in two months, the tunnel was well under way.

CHAPTER THIRTY SEVEN
1952
The Fairy Queen

Susan Priestley was putting up the Christmas decorations at her mother's house in Cawthorne, a pleasant village to the east Of Barnsley.

'I saw Mommy kissing Santa Claus,' Jimmy Boyd's voice rang out, for the umpteenth time, from the wind-up gramophone.

Her mother had just bought the 78 RPM record. 'Mam, you'll wear that needle out,' Susan shouted. 'Put Mario Lanza on for a change.'

Her mother was in the kitchen. She was in her own world, singing the song out of tune, and out of time, with the record. She took no notice of her daughter.

At Christmas time, Susan always thought about her Dad. She missed him, especially at this time of year. It was nearly eleven years since he'd died, on January 2nd 1942.

She had been fifteen then. She had helped him put up the decorations, that last Christmas, before he had died. Susan was standing now on the same wooden step ladders that they had used then. Her hands touched the step where she had scratched both their names in the wood while he was putting the fairy on top of the tree. Susan held the same fairy in her hand, fighting to hold back the tears.

'Dad and Sue 1942' the carving said.

The police had awoken her mother at two thirty that January morning, to tell her about the accident. Susan knew well enough what the families had gone through at Woodhead in the 1840s, bereaved by rock falls, sickness, and explosions. Susan had been through it as well.

Spending Christmas at home was a welcome distraction from her work in Dublin. Her thoughts were distracted from the hundred-year-old murder mystery. She couldn't stop thinking about Roger Thompson. How would he be spending Christmas?

At first, the journalist had written to her regularly from Malaya, but the letters had suddenly stopped. After several weeks of worry, Susan had contacted the *Manchester Guardian*. When she'd explained who she was, the receptionist had put her through to the editor. He explained that Roger was in hospital, in Kuala Lumpur, and he was very ill.

He had contracted a tropical disease, he had told Susan.

Susan had even driven across to see Roger's family in Glossop. She had written to them and they had invited her for Sunday lunch. Roger had also stopped sending letters to his parents, and they were concerned for his safety.

Roger's father, an ex-military man, had tried to explain why his letters weren't getting through.

'They will be censored. Don't forget, Malaya is on a war footing.'

Susan had got on very well with Roger's sister Eileen. They had talked about Harold Thompson, their great grandfather, the surgeon at Woodhead.

'I'm sure there's some stuff up in the attic,' Eileen had told her. 'This house has been in the family for a hundred years. Do you remember, Dad? You once showed us some papers? I remember seeing some old photos of him – and some of his medical notes.'

Mr Thompson had taken a real shine to the Yorkshire girl.

'We'll have a look later. I'm sure I put it somewhere safe up there. We'll give it to Roger when he gets back from Malaya,' he said.

As she drove back home, past Woodhead, along the moorland road, Susan thought about Roger, and hoped that he was safe.

'I saw Mommy kissing Santa Claus, underneath the mistletoe last night...' the song went on. Susan struggled to put the fairy on to the top of the tree.

There was a knock on the front door.

'Get the door Mam? It'll be Aunty Florrie.' Her mother's sister visited, like clockwork, every afternoon at three thirty.

She heard the parlour door open.

'Aunty Florrie, what do you reckon to the tree?' she shouted over the music.

There was no answer, but she heard a man's voice singing, in time with the music.

'She didn't hear me creep, down the stairs to peep,' the voice sang.

Susan looked down from the top of the step ladders. Roger Thompson stood in the doorway, leaning on a pair of crutches. She got down quickly from the steps and rushed across the room to greet him.

'Do I need this?' he asked, picking up a sprig of mistletoe from the sideboard. Ignoring the presence of her mother, Susan pulled him close and smothered him in kisses.

'Where have you been, and what's all this?' she asked, pointing at his crutches.

Susan's mother turned off the gramophone, and made an excuse.

'I'll make a pot of tea,' she said.

CHAPTER THIRTY EIGHT
The Loft Notes

'I was injured by a couple of stray bullets,' Roger explained to Susan, 'when I was with a British patrol. It's a long story.'

Susan held him tightly. 'I thought you were dead,' she said. 'We couldn't get any news of you. Never leave me again.'

She cried tears of joy. Susan suddenly realised that she loved Roger.

Susan's mother brought a tray of tea and biscuits into the parlour.

'The newspaper said you had an illness. We were all very worried,' she said. She squeezed his hand. 'You've lost weight as well.'

Roger helped himself to a plate of chocolate biscuits.

'Yes,' replied Roger. 'It's all hush-hush, and all that. I was unconscious for a week, and the Malayan food didn't agree with me. I'll tell you all about it later.'

He smiled, and got something out of the bag he'd brought with him.

'I've got a present for you, from Eileen. She found it in the loft.'

Roger handed her an old wooden box. It was full of papers.

'She told me that you'd been over to Glossop. My Great Grandad's papers might help to solve some of your riddles.'

Susan carefully laid the notes on the parlour table. Her mother politely disappeared to the kitchen, to prepare supper.

'Before we start, I want to tell you something. I have missed you so much.' Susan looked into Roger's eyes, and then kissed him again. 'I thought that I had lost you.'

He blushed.

'I couldn't stop thinking about you while I was in that hospital.'

Susan held Roger's hand.

'Can we start at the 1844 strike?' she said, excited by the secrets that they might contain.

He quickly found his ancestor's notes, and she read from them.

At Woodhead, in 1844, I was in attendance when the strike and lockout took place. I had never witnessed a more depressing and sorrowful place. There, I experienced the full depth of human misery. It was only a few miles from my home in Glossop, but to me, it was hell on earth.

Later, in the Crimean War at Balaclava and Sevastopol, the conditions were bad, but I would swear that place on the Pennine Moors was much worse. The navvies that built the railway were disregarded in the rush for profit.

The injuries, caused by explosions and rock-falls, were as horrific as those on any battlefield I have known. We were working with much cruder and more basic equipment. Amputations of limbs and the treatment of cholera were difficult in that God-forsaken place. Even the simpler maladies of dry coughs were difficult to cure there.

It was at Woodhead that I first became interested in congenital syphilis. My research on the subject is well documented but it was there that my interest really began. On the lonely moors, I discovered certain clues of the dreadful signs that are apparent in babies.

There were about one hundred women in the camps, and over half of them suffered from syphilis. It was therefore apparent that their offspring were always at risk of contracting the medical disorder.

The disease is basically secondary and the baby is born with it, having contracted it from the infected mother. The symptoms include damage to the teeth, bones, eyes, and brain, along with hepatosplenomegaly, anaemia, and jaundice.

Our nurse, Mary Maloney, was to become the object of my studies. She was very friendly with the Royal Duke Frederick, who was the brother of Prince Albert. Not many days would go by when he would not visit her. It was a remarkable relationship. They were from diametrically opposite ends of the class system. He was of Royal blood and she was a former tally woman, from the bottom end of the social structure. Duke Frederick idolised both the woman and her child.

I had brought the child into the world and he was very weak. I put this down to the diet, and had grave fears he would not survive. The infant mortality rate at Woodhead was extremely high.

The Royal visitor even asked for me to examine the child, and added that money would be no object. He even offered to pay for medicine or a special diet.

I subjected the child to a close examination and found he had infectious sores and rashes. He was jaundiced and Mary told me that he sometimes suffered from seizures.

The baby's teeth were the most obvious sign of the disease. The incisors were notched. These are now known as 'Hutchinson teeth'.

I then examined the mother, and she told me her history, in confidence. My suspicions were confirmed. She had advanced syphilis, and it had been passed to the baby.

CHAPTER THIRTY NINE
April 1845
Thompson Diagnoses the Problem

'Surgeon Thompson, is there nothing that you can do, or prescribe?' Duke Frederick desperately asked. 'I could even take them to the Royal physicians, on Harley Street.'

The two men stood outside the makeshift boiler room infirmary, in the April sunshine.

'Your Grace, I'm afraid that all the money in the world could never heal them. The disease is too far advanced.' Thompson tried his best to be diplomatic, without revealing what they were actually suffering from. There was silence except for the incessant steam boiler.

'Your Grace, there is something very personal that I must ask,' the Surgeon said.

The Duke nodded.

'You are very close to the nurse, and her child, are you not?' Thompson asked.

'Of course,' the Duke gave his assent.

'As a physician, and in complete confidence, I have to ask you.' Thompson paused, while he chose his words carefully. 'Have you had carnal relations with the lady?'

The Duke hesitated. 'No Sir, not with Mary,' he said.

'Thank God,' the physician sighed. 'You must never touch her in that way.'

Duke Frederick nodded again. Dr Thompson was relieved that the Duke did not seem surprised by these extremely personal questions.

'I wish you to examine me as well, Doctor. I keep losing a sense of things, and forget what I have done. I have memory lapses.'

Susan and Roger read Harold Thompson's notes with interest:

I examined the Duke at great length and found certain lesions on his arms, and in his ears. I conversed with him in detail for some two hours and I have never encountered a patient quite like him.

It is not so much his physical appearance, which on first examination gives the impression of a normal, strong male. It is his mental state that is quite remarkable.

'I wonder what he means by mental state, Roger?' she asked. 'Robert O'Neill had some doubts about the soundness of his mind.'

He shrugged his shoulders.

'I don't know. We should read on. We may find out.'

The Duke has a split personality. From memory, he can recite events and passages of poems, in German and English. His main persona is of a warm and very humorous nature. He is quite logical and very intelligent but he has confided in me that his aggression is exacerbated by drink. He then reverts to a different character, belligerent and aggressive.

He undoubtedly has a split, twin personality, and switches from one to the other. The change takes just a few seconds.

When the Duke is his other self, he is in a dark, depressive world, and I believe he is capable of dark deeds.

He has a dissociative identity disorder. This is normally as a result of severe trauma from childhood. Extreme repetitive physical, sexual, or emotional abuse are the usual roots of the disorder.

'This is dynamite, Roger! And these notes were in your attic all this time?'

'They were in an old chest that belonged to my grandfather. He died in the First World War, at the Battle of the Somme,' Roger explained. 'My dad knew they were there, but the papers were of no interest to him. He always told me that his granddad was a famous doctor. When I was studying journalism, I took more interest in him. I read his medical book, and was captivated by his time at Woodhead. I suppose this extra material would have been too hot for his famous medical book. He was careful what he wrote. He wouldn't have wanted to upset the medical establishment of the day.'

Susan checked her notes from Woodhead. She found O'Neill's notes from the trial at Wakefield Assizes in 1840 for the murder of Dorothy Shaw, and read out the relevant passage:

'I later spoke to the Queens Counsel, James Rawlins Johnson. He told me he has studied the art of character and personality reading. He has interviewed the Duke. He told me confidentially that he fears the Duke has some sort of identity crisis, and seems to switch from one personality to another.'

'So, Susan, the two of them reached the same conclusion with regards to the Duke. My Great Grandad, and this Queens Counsel.' Roger said. He was as intrigued as she was.

'It would have never got past the Victorian censors,' she said. Susan carried on reading from Thompson's notes:

Without a doubt, the Royal Duke suffers from congenital syphilis, so the fact remains that it was contracted from his mother. It follows that he is the younger brother of Prince Albert and so the question must be asked of the Prince Consort's health. Was the same sickness the cause of his death?

The remarkable paradox is that Duke Frederick has the same disease as the tally woman and her child, whom he had befriended.

I took the decision not to tell the Duke of my findings but stressed the serious natures of his friend Mary, and her child's health. *I held back from telling him that they were both terminally ill.*

Roger quickly summed it up: 'These notes were written in 1870, some nine years after Prince Albert's death in 1861. He is inferring that Albert had the same disease. You are right Susan. This is explosive.'

CHAPTER FORTY
The Top Brass Deliberate

Chief Inspector Christopher Columbine, of the West Riding Constabulary, gripped his pipe tightly between his teeth. Five senior Police officers, Columbine's superiors, listened intently to Sergeant Priestly as she presented her findings.

The meeting had now been in progress for two hours. Susan had almost finished describing her progress with the diaries, and the vital evidence she had found in Thompson's notes. Susan had her audience riveted to their seats in Columbine's Wakefield office.

'Blimey,' Columbine exclaimed, when Susan had finished speaking. 'So Thompson's notes and the Earl's diaries point to the same thing.' The Chief Inspector looked at the senior officers. 'The Queens Counsel spotted his symptoms first.'

He packed his pipe with tobacco and lit it, while he deliberated, creating a cloud of smoke around him. Susan stifled a cough.

'So the Royal Duke was some kind of nutcase, running about killing everybody. Is it any wonder the diaries have been locked up for all this time?' Columbine announced.

'That is not quite correct,' Susan said. Columbine looked at her with surprise. 'He didn't carry out all of the murders. Somebody else was involved. The clues are in the 1845 diary and Thompson's notes.'

'That may be the case, Susan, but without a doubt, the Duke did commit some of the murders.' Columbine frowned.

'The Riley twins and the murdered prostitute in Barnsley were certainly killed by the Duke. All the circumstantial evidence points in that direction,' Susan explained.

Columbine looked at the other Police officers. He had brought them in for advice. This case was a hot potato and now implicated the top echelons of the British crown.

'What do we do? Has anybody got any ideas? I think we should take this further and warn our political masters.' Columbine stared around the room expectantly.

'We should inform the Home Secretary and set up a meeting with the Prime Minister,' the Chief Superintendent said.

The senior officers all nodded in agreement.

'That seems to be the only solution,' the Chief Constable added. 'We must refer these matters to the top and let wiser counsels prevail.'

CHAPTER FORTY ONE
1845
Eli Returns

In December 1845, the railway tunnel was preparing for its grand opening.

Chief Engineer Joseph Locke had returned from rebuilding the viaduct in France.

Most of the difficult work had been completed, but the navvies were still labouring, laying sleepers, and ballasting the railway lines.

The news had been released by the railway company that another tunnel was to be built alongside the existing one. The new tunnel would increase the capacity, and enable more coal to be transported from the Yorkshire mines to the growing industries in Lancashire.

A new railway from Penistone to Doncaster was also under construction. The railways were revolutionising the country, and conditions for the men building them were slowly improving.

The two surgeons, Henry Pomfret and Harold Thompson, were still working in the Number One boiler house. They were as busy as ever with the navvies' ailments and injuries. But the steam boiler had already been removed from its mounting and taken to another site, ready for the construction of the new tunnel.

The infirmary was moving half a mile away, to a purpose-built building which would help the surgeons to control infections and make the patients more comfortable. Richard Ward had promised the surgeons that he would build them a new infirmary, and unlike Charles Vignoles, Ward kept his promises.

Locke and Ward were preparing to fill in the number one shaft, as it was causing the air in the tunnel to short circuit, preventing proper ventilation. If the tunnel was not sealed, smoke and steam from the locomotives would have trouble clearing when the trains travelled through the tunnel. The combustion from the engines would be unpleasant and dangerous for the drivers and passengers.

There was jubilation among the navvies as this meant more work for them while they were waiting for work on the new tunnel to start. Some of the navvies had settled permanently in the district and had married local girls.

But not all the navvies would be retained for the new tunnel. Richard Ward and Joseph Locke were expecting trouble.

The Royal Commission into the navvies' conditions was nearing completion, and the Earl of Wexford continued to document events at the tunnel in his diary:

Monday 15th December 1845:

I visited the site today to interview Joseph Locke, who has recently returned from Rouen.

Duke Frederick accompanied me, to visit his friend Mary Maloney. He spent all the day with her, and her young son.

I was surprised to see the Hussars at the site. I asked Mr Locke why he had asked for them. He stated that just four soldiers will be in attendance, until the new tunnel work is started. Not as many workers will be required. Although he is not expecting any trouble, he has decided to deploy the Hussars as a precautionary measure. They will also give colour when the first train arrives.

I noticed that Private Randall is back and I broached the matter with the illustrious Captain Gregory, who is in charge of this patrol of soldiers. He replied that as part of Randall's penance, he was to be posted 'on this lonely moorland', as he described it to me. I asked Gregory if he was fearful of retribution from Randall, but he answered that it would be foolish if he tried anything. Gregory added that following the Private's time behind bars, any misdemeanours on his part would lead to transportation to the colonies.

Friday 19th December was a sad day in the history of the Woodhead Tunnel. O'Neill noted the events in his diary:

Today Lord Wharncliffe passed away and there has been much grief in the household. Sarah and her mother were with him when he died. He will be mourned by us all.

He has missed the opening of his beloved railway by a few days. On Saturday 27th December, the railway will officially open.

Both his engineers, Richard Ward and Joseph Locke, visited him last week, but he was very ill and they were unable to talk for long. The vicar of Wortley visited today and spoke to Sarah. The funeral is to be next Friday. Friday 26th December. That is to say, the day before the railway opens.

CHAPTER FORTY TWO
Cock-Eyed Eli

Private Elias Randall of the Manchester and Salford Yeomanry was shivering in the bitter cold of the Pennines.

He'd been put on sentry duty in the most godforsaken place in the world. He started to plot his revenge on the people who had put him here.

He could not get them out of his thoughts. Captain Gregory, his cocky superior, represented everything he hated about his military past.

The fanciful Duke Frederick and his Irish tally woman slut, he hated with a vengeance. They were all to blame for his jail sentence. To rub the salt in more, he had been posted back to Woodhead, where his tormentors were.

His wooden guard hut was little use against the icy wind that was constantly blowing off the moors. His only company were the rats and rabbits that scavenged on the filth and litter from the camp.

After he had been arrested for attacking Mary, Randall had served twelve months in the Savoy military prison in London where he had been beaten and sodomised by the other inmates.

It was the second time he had served time in the Savoy. He had been imprisoned there in 1819, after Peterloo. As Randall stared into the miserly coal brazier, he thought about his life. The cavalry had been his life, but he had never fitted in anywhere.

Randall had been born in the Salford slums. But the real cause of his unhappy childhood was the squint eye he'd been afflicted with since birth. Because of it, he had been bullied and picked on by his own father, and his brothers and sisters.

The neighbourhood children soon picked up on his eye disorder. Their taunts were unbearable. They nicknamed him "Cock-eyed Eli". This name had stuck with him for the rest of his life.

Their cruelty affected his early life. He played truant from school. He hated the daytime, when people could see him, and the only time he felt safe was at night, creeping around the dimly-lit streets and alleyways of Salford, which were his natural habitat.

The hand of fate came to his rescue one evening, when he was fourteen. Sitting on a street corner, he saw a dray-man struggling with his horse. Elias loved horses, and found he had a way with them. He soon calmed the horse down and the dray-man recognised his potential. He employed Elias, delivering barrels of beer and spirits to the city's public houses and drinking establishments.

Elias got around his eye disorder by staring at the floor, and he avoided conversation when he was in company. He did this to avoid eye contact.

At the age of sixteen, he had his first brush with the law. After a night of heavy drinking, he met a prostitute and ended up in her filthy abode. The woman had a young daughter and after his session with the mother, he had tried his advances on the young girl. A drunken, brutal, argument ensued and he was arrested for attempted rape and immoral behaviour.

The judge took note of his job with horses, and in his leniency, gave him a choice. It was either prison, or joining the cavalry. Elias opted for the cavalry.

His first commission was with the celebrated Scots Greys regiment as a groom. The Napoleonic wars, in Portugal and Spain, had resulted in many cavalry casualties. A chronic shortage of upper class public school boys found Elias in the saddle at Waterloo in 1815, on active service. He had cut down the retreating French Old Guard. Randall had only been eighteen at the time.

Despite his skill with horses, Randall was despised by the rest of the regiment for his lower class background. Many of them had attended public school. But the streets of Salford were not quite the Eton fields.

Elias was constantly picked on and his nickname of "Cock-eyed Eli" never went away.

When the Napoleonic wars were over, Elias was transferred to the Manchester and Salford Yeomanry. At the infamous St Peters Square massacre in 1819, named in a mockery of the Waterloo battle, Randall had scythed down women and children. Some of the other soldiers had felt squeamish that day in 1819, but not Private Elias Randall. He had loved it. It had given him a sense of power. He was someone to be feared.

Peterloo had been the best, and then the worst day of his life.

He had revelled in the charge at the rioters in the Manchester square, but he went a step too far. He killed two defenceless women and their babies with his sabre.

A prominent politician had witnessed his attack from the wooden platform where the speeches had been made.

Randall was immediately arrested and put on trial for murder. He was sentenced to die by hanging and was sent to the Savoy military prison in London. He was the only member of the regiment to be arrested.

After a year of imprisonment, where he was beaten and lashed, the initial murder charge was reduced to culpable homicide.

The legal profession had rescued him. The cavalry charge on the masses had provoked outrage throughout

England. But the verdict implied that Randall had not intended to kill, which whitewashed the whole affair.

All the charges were finally dropped in 1820, after the furore had died down. It was too much of an embarrassment for the judges who had issued the Riot Act. If Randall had been found guilty of murder, the judges could have also been implicated in the crime. The wheels of justice did not turn fully round for the families of the deceased. They wanted someone to pay for the outrage, but the judges wanted a way out of the impasse.

Their fellow members of the judiciary had got them off the hook.

Randall had nearly died by hanging. The establishment wanted to forget it. He returned to his regiment.

"Cock-eyed Eli" did not die, but he never forgot what had happened.

CHAPTER FORTY THREE
Randall's Revenge

The old infirmary in the Number One shaft boiler house had almost closed.

Susan pieced together the evidence carefully from Surgeon Harold Thompson's notes. He recalled this time in detail.

By the end of 1845, the first tunnel was almost complete. I had the task of emptying the Number One boiler house. The boiler had been removed, and with the help of my two nurses Mary Maloney and Rachel Foulkes, all the equipment had been transferred. Just a few patients were left.

Rachel Foulkes had recently arrived to help with the nursing. She had a wooden leg, the result of an injury sustained in the St Peters Square massacre in 1819, in her youth. She was a social reformer, a trained nurse, who had heard of the plight of the workforce and wanted to help. We always needed assistance with nursing so we welcomed her readily in the infirmary. The navvies nicknamed her 'Peg Leg Peg'.

Sadly, the health of Mary had deteriorated, and she was a lot weaker. The Duke visited her on most days and took care of the child Danny, singing his German nursery rhyme to him.

He wrote the song out in English, and pinned inside a wooden case with a glass door where the boiler's diagrams had been displayed.

Both Mary and the other nurse were great friends, and she had been staying with Mary in her hut.

As the work on the tunnel neared completion, the four soldiers were billeted in two regulation army tents, at the side of the new Dunford Bridge railway station, under the watchful eye of Sergeant Coltrane.

Coltrane was an elderly soldier, nearing his retirement age. Like Randall, the other two soldiers had served time in military prisons, but for less serious offences.

The Sergeant had posted Randall on the midnight watch, knowing that it was the worst duty. The incessant noise of the work in the day prevented much sleep. To make matters worse, supply trains were now coming to the site, with their noisy locomotives.

Randall's only escape was in the Angel public house in the afternoons. He was the perfect customer and he kept himself to himself. But he was listening and watching all the movements in the navvy camp.

All through the month of December, his daily ritual continued. He would do his night duty, and then he would snatch a fitful few hours of sleep in his tent. Spending the afternoons drinking, he would grab another short sleep, before the sequence started all over again.

Randall's behaviour appeared normal, and the ever-watchful Sergeant Coltrane started to take his eye off him. He too would be glad when this duty was finished.

One night in early December 1845, rain lashed down. Private Randall was bored. At three o'clock in the morning, he left his post, and he walked into the railway tunnel. Using his lantern, he walked to the bottom of the Number One shaft, where the tunnel had first started. Six years had passed since work had begun, in 1839.

The tunnel was deserted as he walked along the single line of tracks to the shaft bottom. He had overheard the navvies saying that the shaft was going to be filled in to prevent the air short-circuiting.

A connecting tunnel joined the shaft to the main tunnel. It was twenty yards long and it was being prepared to be sealed off. Large building stones had already been built up to make a blocking wall.

Randall had seen enough. He returned to his post, where nobody had missed him. A plan had formed in the mind of "Cock eyed Eli".

CHAPTER FORTY FOUR
1838
The Young Cork Girl

It was Christmas Eve 1845. Mary Maloney was in her hut, lying on her straw mattress. Her baby Danny was sound asleep in his cot. The hut was quiet compared with the days when it had been full with snoring navvies.

These days, it seemed empty. But she had the company of nurse Rachel Foulkes, who was asleep in another bed. She had been kind to Mary.

Mary could not sleep. She stared into the embers of the peat fire. The only light in the hut came from the red glow of the dying flames.

She had been traumatised in a most cruel way and her young life had seen more misery than anybody could imagine. She had only seen glimpses of happiness. Nowadays, she felt almost too weak to carry out the work she loved, looking after the injured navvies.

Mary had lost her man Danny to cholera and the baby he had given her was very ill. She wanted to give him the best life possible, but the grave looks on the faces of the surgeons and her beloved friend Duke Frederick warned her that little Danny may not survive infancy.

Where did it all go wrong she asked herself? She was still only twenty, but she had been to hell and back.

Her mother already had thirteen children when she was born and after rudimentary schooling in the local village, she was sent to work as a servant girl in a nearby grand house.

It was 1838, and at thirteen, Mary was already a very pretty girl. Although thin, she had long black hair and a pleasing smile.

The house belonged to a wealthy Cork landowner called Thomas Monroe. A strict Presbyterian family, the Monroes had ruled the area since Oliver Cromwell had planted Ireland with Scottish landlords in the seventeenth century.

The Catholics had been driven from the land. Ireland had remained fairly peaceful since the dictator's time but political events were simmering under the surface. Daniel O'Connell and the Whig party had politicized the Irish public in a new wave of nationalism.

Monroe Castle had been built in the style of an English stately home in Cromwellian times, and many servants and labourers were employed by the family.

Mary started her service as a housemaid. Her duties involved cleaning, scrubbing, and polishing silver. The servants were housed in quarters away from the great house, and Mary shared a small bedroom with another housemaid. She was paid a pittance for her wages, and she worked fifteen hours a day to earn a few coppers to give to her mother. Mary visited her family weekly, on Saturday afternoons, when she was free for a few hours.

Her day started at five o'clock in the morning. She was under the auspices of a huge Irish upper-housemaid called Margaret Murphy. Mary's mother had helped her to get the job, as Margaret was an old friend.

She was strict but fair with the young girls in her charge, castigating the housemaids when they did not clean the giant house properly, but noting good work.

At first, Mary had missed her overcrowded home, but at least she had a job. Soon, she learned how to pace herself in her new role. She was a shy girl who kept herself to herself and only answered when she was spoken to. The mansion had many servants, but there wasn't much chance to make friends.

Mary's lodging mate was another Cork girl, Theresa McManus. The two girls soon became close friends. Theresa had lost her parents at a young age and she had already been in service for a few years. An only child, she'd had a better education than Mary, but the tragic deaths of her parents had changed her life. One of her aunts had placed her in service. It was either that or the workhouse.

Theresa helped Mary to improve her reading skills. The girls were allowed old books that had been discarded from the library, and at night, they read by candle-light, learning about the world outside. They loved to read poetry from the old books. Although work as a housemaid was hard, it was a happy time in Mary's life.

The servants had no contact with the upstairs family, apart from fleeting glimpses of one another in the corridors. Despite providing the Monroe family with all the comforts they needed, the servants lived in another world from them.

The Monroe family was indeed a world apart from the Cork underclass that Mary came from. Thomas Monroe was the head of a family that had been showered with wealth and privilege. He was the fourth generation of a strict Presbyterian family, ruling ruthlessly over the lands that he owned.

Monroe was in his fifties and was a widower. He had lost his wife ten years previously to consumption, and he had never remarried. He had two sons and one daughter, so the family line was protected. But he was becoming worried by events affecting his position and lifestyle.

Rural Ireland was changing for the worse for his elite class and the Irish Catholic peasantry had started leaving, for the promise of life in England or the new colonies. When they found work abroad, they sent for their relatives. The landowners' hold on the Catholic poor was starting to weaken.

One night in the spring of 1838, the Monroe family were sitting at dinner. Thomas Monroe sat at the head of the table, studying his offspring.

His eldest son and heir Edward was a huge disappointment to him. He was a gambler, and a womaniser. Now at the age of twenty two, he was basically a loser in life. If he wasn't kept in check, he would be in danger of ruining the family fortune.

Sitting next to Edward, Monroe's younger son James could not be more different. Aged twenty, he was studying the sciences at the Trinity College in Dublin. He was industrious, and had a particular interest in engineering. Well-mannered and polite, he came across as a perfect English gentleman.

On the opposite side of the table, his daughter Anne reminded him so much of his departed wife. At nineteen, she had taken over his wife's duties in the household. He was much closer to Anne than his two sons.

'Father. The situation is becoming serious,' Anne broke the silence, speaking with authority. 'Everybody seems to be deserting us. Two more families have left today.'

'Let them leave. They are just heathen peasants that wallow in their own pig swill,' Edward commented.

'That is quite enough.' Thomas Monroe reprimanded him. 'The labourers on these estates are paying for your disgusting habits, heathen or not.' Monroe did not like his son's gambling and wasteful pastimes.

Thomas Monroe motioned with a regal air of pompous grace for the house butler to refill his wine glass, which he did.

'But this O'Connell fellow has stirred things up, giving the Catholics rights,' he grumbled. 'Too many of them are leaving.'

'We live in a time of great change,' James joined the conversation. 'The old order may be over. Machines and mechanisation are paving the way in all the great industries. We had a lecture the other day on the revolutionary machines in Northern England.'

'That's where our labourers are going – to become trouble-makers over there,' Edward ranted. 'Striking and marching around, getting ideas above their station.'

'That's as maybe, Edward, but they are only fighting for their jobs and it is giving rise to the trade unions that represent them,' James was quick with his reply. He had come to see the unfairness in society, and the advances in humanity that the new technology would eventually bring.

'They should be hung, or sent back here to work our land. I would show them a thing or two.' Edward showed his contempt for anybody below his class.

'I shall need a new lady's maid, Papa,' Anne said, swiftly changing the subject. She did not like arguments at meal times. 'My maid is leaving with her family for America. We may have to advertise the post.'

'Anne, I am sure that you will fill the position with a lower servant from the household,' her father said, wiping his lips with a napkin. 'We too have to be frugal in these times, and I'm sure you can find someone suitable.

'Thank you, Papa. I will start looking for my new maid in the morning.'

Thomas Monroe nodded his assent as he noted how different his children were.

CHAPTER FORTY FIVE
The Lady's Maid

The next morning, at six o'clock, Mary Maloney was dusting the dining room in Monroe Castle.

In her starched white maid's uniform, she looked older than her thirteen years. She was certainly a good worker. She kept to a tight schedule. She had to be out of the room before any of the family rose from their beds.

Mary had lit the coal fire in the massive grate. When she finished dusting, she started cleaning the silver cutlery on the giant dinner table.

Out of the corner of her eye, she saw Margaret Murphy enter the room. Pausing to glance at the neatly laid fire with approval, the upper-housemaid approached Mary, who bobbed a curtsey to the senior servant.

'Mary, are you happy in your work?' Murphy asked her. 'I saw your Mammy last night and she was asking about you.'

'I am, Mrs Murphy. I am very happy working here. Please tell Mammy that I am well.' Mary answered quietly, and went back to cleaning the cutlery.

Margaret Murphy nodded. 'Well Mary, I have some good news for you. The Lady Anne is requiring a new lady's maid and I have put your name forward. You will see her at ten o'clock if you will. I will allow you half an hour before that time to make yourself presentable. Does that please you?'

Mary dutifully curtsied and she carried on, cleaning but her mind was on the interview with Lady Anne.

At ten o'clock, Mary found herself knocking on the door of Lady Anne's bed-chamber. Margaret Murphy had escorted her, and on hearing the Lady answer, she left Mary to her own devices.

Mary was very nervous at first.

'Sit down, Mary,' Lady Anne said, in a gentle English voice. She pointed at an upholstered chair opposite herself. Mary lowered herself into it nervously. She had never sat in a chair like that before. She had only dusted them.

'Are you happy in our employment, Mary?' Anne asked.

'Very happy, My Lady,' Mary smiled and answered in her soft Cork accent.

'Tell me about yourself. How old are you?' Anne asked.

'I am thirteen, my Lady,' Mary said.

'You look older than that. Tell me about your interests in your free time.' her employer enquired.

'In the evenings, I love to read. My friend Theresa has learned me to read and we read poetry every night,' Mary answered.

Lady Anne was very impressed with this young girl who had come from a Cork hovel, but had learned to read poetry. The girl's long dark hair curled out of her maid's cap. But what Lady Anne really liked about Mary was her smile and polite manners. Her mind was made up very quickly.

'Well, Anne. I would like you to become my new maid. What say you?'

'My Lady. You will have to be patient with me, for I know nothing of the duties and requirements of a maid.' Mary was honest with this aristocratic lady.

'We shall learn together, Mary,' Anne said. 'You will return here at three o'clock.'

That afternoon, Mary started her new position as a lady's maid in Monroe House.

CHAPTER FORTY SIX
1839
The Return of the Prodigal Son

For the first time in her life, Mary Maloney was happy.

She got on very well with Lady Anne, who treated her with kindness and dignity. Lady Anne was a modern woman. She had been to a boarding school, rather than being taught by a governess. The young lady was intelligent and forward thinking. She did not agree with the necessity of treating servants as slaves.

Lady Anne needed her maid to be more of a friend than a mere tool, to be used when necessary.

Overcoming her initial shyness, Mary soon got used to life upstairs. She learned to only speak when being spoken to and not to gossip about her employers. There was one part of the day she really looked forward to. In the afternoons, she would accompany her mistress, out walking, or travelling in her carriage to visit nearby Cork city.

In the first month, Mary only had contact with Lady Anne or her father. He spent most of his time in another part of the house, attending to the affairs of his estate. Both of Anne's brothers were away. James was at Dublin University and Edward was in London.

The months passed by quickly for Mary, and she got to know Lady Anne very well. Rather than mistress and servant, the two became very friendly.

One September day, they were walking in the grounds of the castle, discussing poetry. Anne's favourite poem was The Deserted Village by Oliver Goldsmith.

Anne told her that Goldsmith was Irish. She had Mary fascinated by the hidden meanings in his poem. They both sat on a bench at the side of the castle lake. Suddenly, they were rudely interrupted by a man on a horse, galloping towards them.

'Anne!' shouted the man. 'What is the meaning of this?' He waved a letter at her. It was her oldest brother, Edward.

Anne knew only too well the contents of the letter. He had written to her father asking for money. No doubt to feed his gambling debts. Monroe had discussed the matter with Anne and had flatly refused his son's request.

'Edward, calm down will you?' Anne said. 'You will have to take up the matter with father. It is really not my concern.'

Her brother shook his head and dismounted from his horse. He was obviously drunk, and he was very unsteady on his feet. He fell to the ground. Both women tried to help him to his feet. He managed to sit on the bench. He stared at Mary.

'You are a pretty thing. I shall have to get to know you better,' he leered.

'You are a disgrace.' Anne stamped her feet. 'You will keep your hands off my maid. And you had better sober yourself up before you see father.'

Anne took Mary's hand and they ran off down the path, leaving Edward sitting slumped on the bench, his horse cropping the grass peacefully.

'What's your name?' He called after Mary. 'I will see you later.'

As they walked away, Anne shook her head.

'That was outrageous. I must apologise for my brother's behaviour. I will tell father. He will deal with him.'

CHAPTER FORTY SEVEN
The Curraghbinny Woods

An hour later, Mary was back in the servants' quarters. She was completely unaware of the argument raging in the upstairs dining room.

Thomas Monroe was berating his eldest son. He pulled no punches.

'You are a disgrace to the family. You have squandered a fortune on God knows what. I am at a loss as to what to do with you. It's a good job your mother is not here to see how you have turned out.' He paused while he collected his thoughts. 'Let me sleep on it. Get out of my sight.'

Edward had been silent throughout his father's tirade, and now he rose and left the room. His tail was certainly between his legs. He could not answer his father.

He had been in London for six months, to conduct his father's banking affairs. Edward had conducted his affairs alright. He had invested heavily in a foolish venture. He had bought stocks in a worthless gold mine in America. He had also lost a great deal of money on gambling, drinking, and women.

'It could not happen at a worse time.' Thomas Monroe turned to his daughter. 'What are we to do, Anne? Edward will be the ruin of us.'

Anne could only nod her head.

The next day, Mary was attending on Anne in her room. It was a Saturday morning, and Mary was brushing Anne's hair.

Mary looked forward to Saturdays, as she would visit her family for a few hours in the afternoon. The two of them were chatting as usual, when suddenly the door burst open. It was Anne's brother Edward. He strode arrogantly across the room towards them.

'Edward, this is my room and you will knock before you enter,' Lady Anne said.

'In my house, I will do what I want. Where is Father?' he snapped at her.

Anne did not answer.

'Did you hear me?' Edward barked. 'Damn you all. I am going for a ride.'

As he left the room, he stared at Mary with undisguised lust.

Shortly afterwards, Mary left her mistress and walked across the Cork countryside to her mother's house, which was about six miles away.

It was September, and she enjoyed the walk in the sunshine. After a pleasant day with her family, she started walking back to the Castle at around five o'clock. Mary wanted to return before nightfall.

In contrast, Edward Monroe had spent the afternoon drinking in a Cork public house. As usual, he'd become very drunk. He set off at about six o'clock. His way home was southwest of the city, through dense woodland known as the Curraghbinny.

Edward Monroe was in a foul mood. Since his return from England, his father had cut off his allowance. After spending what money he had on his person, the tavern owner had refused him credit. To add insult to injury, another two of his so-called friends had denied him credit as well. Even a high-class prostitute had denied his advances that day.

As he rode home in the faltering September light, he spotted a young girl in front of him. He recognised her immediately. It was his sister's maid. He soon caught up with her.

'Whoa. My pretty little thing, slow down. Let me accompany you home to my Castle,' he said. He dismounted from his horse.

Mary was shocked at his advances and very frightened of him.

'My Lord, I will make my own way home. My Lady is awaiting me,' she said.

Monroe took hold of her hand. He was fascinated by this lovely Irish girl. He was used to getting his own way with women and he did not like being spurned.

'You will do as I say. You will accompany me home. Jump up in the saddle with me.' He was now getting aroused by her.

'My Lord. My mistress is expecting me,' Mary could only say.

'My sister can wait.' Monroe took hold of both her hands. 'I want you first.'

Mary shook her head.

Edward Monroe grabbed her roughly around her waist and kissed her on the lips. His lips were wet and his breath stunk of beer. The hair of his moustache was coarse and painful against her skin.

Mary pulled her hands out of his grasp and tried to get away from him. Monroe swiped her across the face, hard, still wearing his riding gloves. Mary, a born fighter, lashed out with both hands and scratched his face, her long nails gouging his skin. Blood oozed from the scratches.

'You little hussy,' he screamed.

Mary broke free from him and managed to run away. She screamed for help, but the woodland was isolated and nobody heard her.

Edward Monroe mounted his horse and bolted after her.

Mary left the trail. She ran into a field. In the dusk, she didn't see the rocks littering the field. Mary fell headlong, her ankle badly sprained. She tried to limp away, but Monroe caught up with her.

He dismounted from his horse and pushed her to the ground. He lay on top of her and tried to kiss her again. The alcohol on his breath sickened her, and his cheeks were bleeding.

The poor girl tried to push him away from her. As Mary tried to escape, he pulled a dagger from his belt. In one swift movement, he slashed her across her lip. The blood spurted from the cruel wound and the girl passed out of consciousness in great pain.

The bullying lord then violated the virgin girl and left her lying in the field.

CHAPTER FORTY EIGHT
Aftermath

The unfortunate girl was found the next morning by two male servants who worked at the castle.

They were on their way to work and saw her lying in the field in the early morning light. Mary was still unconscious from her ordeal. One of the servants ran to the castle for assistance. He alerted the butler, who immediately went upstairs and awoke Lady Anne.

Anne quickly dressed herself and ordered a horse and carriage to fetch Mary. She sent for the family's surgeon, who lived in the next village. Realising the gravity of the situation, she also sent for a Constable.

Lady Anne waited anxiously on the castle steps for the coachman to return with Mary. She was brought into the house in his arms, still unconscious. She looked tiny and fragile, like a broken doll. Her wounded lip was still bleeding and her clothes were muddy and ripped. Mary was taken upstairs, to a bedroom in the castle.

Lady Anne was shocked by the state of Mary. It was obvious that she had been attacked violently by a man. As she waited for the surgeon to arrive, she held Mary tightly.

'Who did it Mary? Tell me who it was,' Anne pleaded, but Mary couldn't answer. She was unconscious, breathing with a slow, shallow pulse.

The door opened. It was Anne's father, Thomas Monroe. He studied the unfortunate girl and knitted his eyebrows together. He retreated without saying a word. He had strong suspicious about what had happened.

A few minutes later, he returned.

'Your brother Edward violated your maid,' Thomas Monroe said gravely. 'There is blood on his clothes and he has scratches on his face as if has been in a struggle. He is still asleep, drunk.'

'Father! It can't be true.' Lady Anne recoiled, replaying the events of two days ago when Edward had arrived at the castle and had tried to make advances towards Mary.

She knew in her heart that Edward was responsible for this crime. Anne took a deep breath. 'He is despicable. This poor girl will be disfigured for the rest of her days.'

'The constables will deal with it all, I am sure' Monroe said, resigning Edward to his fate. He had washed his hands of his errant son.

It took three days for Mary to regain full consciousness. Her mistress watched over her day and night. Mary's friend, Theresa McManus, also took on the role of nurse, gently binding Mary's wounded lip and bathing her.

Edward was arrested and he was being detained, pending trial on a charge of rape and aggravated assault. The police needed to speak to Mary, and they had instructed Anne to let them know as soon as her maid regained consciousness.

Thomas Monroe entered Mary's room quietly.

'I take it she has not stirred?' Monroe stared at the girl lying motionless on the bed, her face as pale as alabaster, marred by the bandage around her upper lip. 'I would like to speak to her before the constables see her. I need to find out if the girl had encouraged his advances.'

'Father! Mary was brutally attacked and left for dead. There was obviously a struggle. And he has ruined her forever.' she told him.

'Nevertheless,' Monroe said. 'Could she have been a party to it?'

'Party to what?' she interrupted him. 'She was obviously a maiden. There is no question of her being complicit. I know her. She is a quiet, respectable girl.'

Monroe moved towards the doorway.

'Edward has ruined us.' He turned back to face Anne. 'I have sent word for James to return home from university. He may assist us in this sad affair.'

The next day Mary started to stir. As the poor girl tried to speak, Anne gave her some water.

'I am sorry, my Lady,' were her first words.

'Mary, hush now. You need your strength back,' Anne reassured her.

It was a full week before Mary was able to leave her bed. Her strength began to return, and she was able to start eating. The family surgeon visited her every day. He confided in Anne.

'She lost a lot of blood from the knife wound, and being left outside overnight in that state could have killed her. But it is the other damage I am concerned with,' the physician explained.

'Other damage? What do you mean?' Anne was curious.

'Well,' the doctor was reluctant to tell her. 'There are all sorts of implications. Time will only tell.'

The doctor had said enough.

James returned from university, and met Anne at Mary's bedside.

'She is a pretty little thing,' James told Anne later. 'Edward is a brute.'

Anne nodded. 'She was a pretty little thing. That wound has ruined her looks.' She sighed. 'The trial date has been set. It will be in two months' time at Cork Magistrates' Court.'

James had spent an hour with his sister and her maid, and was moved by the plight of the servant girl.

'I can easily believe that Edward could commit such a crime, but he was exceedingly foolish to do such a thing so close to home. Mary did not deserve this.'

'Will you visit Edward? I cannot face him. He has brought disgrace to the family.' Anne was adamant.

'I suppose I shall have to visit him in prison,' James continued 'Father agrees. He has disowned Edward.'

After six weeks, Mary was able to walk in the gardens with her mistress. She was slowly recovering. One morning, she was very quiet and subdued. Lady Anne noticed her mood.

'What is wrong Mary?' she asked.

Mary broke down in inconsolable tears.

'My Lady,' the maid sobbed. 'I have missed my time of month.'

Anne held her maid tightly.

'You may miss a month. It is normal sometimes,' she replied. But in her heart she knew the truth. Her maid was carrying her brother's child.

CHAPTER FORTY NINE
The Trial

The local newspaper 'The Cork Advertiser' carried the headline:
MONROE ON TRIAL TODAY

The citizens of Cork talked about nothing else. The injustice of the class system had been exposed, and people clamoured for a place in the public gallery at court.

The Catholic Cork residents were suspicious of the English court with its Protestant ways and open bias for the establishment. The judge had travelled from England and everyone expected a whitewash.

Judge Jerimiah Lyndhurst had never set foot in Ireland before. He was unknown in the colony. In the packed courtroom, the question on everyone's lips was: would Edward Monroe be found guilty? And what sentence would he be given?

Thomas Monroe and his youngest son and daughter were in the court to hear the verdict. Edward Monroe had shown no remorse for his crime. He felt as if he was bulletproof, and he fully expected some sort of leniency from the court. After all, he was part of the elite class of Ireland. Surely he was untouchable by the law? But as the trial started, his composure started to crumble.

Thomas despised Ireland and was only at home in London with his friends, in their world of gaming houses and high class brothels. He looked around the court, but there were no friendly faces. His family stared at him from the public gallery with no sympathy. And where were his high class friends now?

Public opinion was against him in this highly charged trial. The facts were undeniable. An upper-class landowner's son had raped a peasant girl, slit her face, and left her for dead. The chattering classes had somehow found out that he had impregnated the girl when he had raped her.

Edward had been advised to plead guilty to the charge and hope for a merciful outcome. He looked at the courtroom in desperation. Surely the judge, an English advocate of justice would help him to escape punishment?

The Right Honourable Judge Lyndhurst swept into the courtroom in his dark robes. He carried a large black, leather-bound tome.

'Be upstanding in court for the Right Honourable Judge Lyndhurst.' The usher prepared the court for the drama that was to be expected.

Lyndhurst had been sent to this Godforsaken place to pontificate on this highly charged case. He opened the law book at a page he had marked and then he stared at the prisoner.

'Mr Monroe,' he announced, speaking with a deliberate slow English drawl. 'I have been studying this case at great length.' He deliberately paused. 'The two fundamentals of a crime are known as *actus reus* and *mens rea*. The first Latin term means 'guilty act'. The second is 'guilty mind' – the intent to commit the crime. In simple terms, the question is this? Did you understand your moral culpability in what you were doing? Did you know that it was wrong?'

The courtroom was very quiet as the crowd in the public gallery listened to every word the judge said.

They listened, but apart from the two barristers, few people understood what he had said. It was too much for the semi-illiterate residents of Cork city to take in.

Where was the judge going with this? Edward Monroe clutched the handrail in the dock and waited until Lyndhurst spoke again. The judge's moment had come.

'So, Mr Monroe. The question is simple. Did you understand that in raping and assaulting the poor girl, you were doing wrong?' He surprised everyone with his obvious sympathy for Mary.

Judge Lyndhurst paused while he surveyed the court. He turned to Monroe.

'I put it to you that you knew exactly what you were doing. Furthermore I put it to you that you knew it was wrong. Finally, I put it to you that you thought that you would get away with the crime.'

The judge scanned the courtroom before turning back to the prisoner.

'You are a disgrace to your fellow man. It appears you think you can do what you want in this colony of our sovereign queen.' He paused, staring at Edward Monroe. 'It also appears that the landowning classes of this country are quite simply out of control.'

The courtroom, which had been silent, gave a ripple of approval.

'Silence in court,' barked the usher.

'It is common knowledge that the unfortunate victim is now carrying your child,' the judge continued.

The crowd in the public gallery, who had only heard gossip of Mary's pregnancy, now became more vocal as Lyndhurst confirmed the rumour.

The judge did not need the usher. He glared at the public gallery and waited until the noise had died down.

'Mr Monroe. I have studied your conduct throughout this trial and you have shown no feelings or contrition for the poor girl that you have violated.'

Lyndhurst turned to the defence barrister.

'The victim of this crime was the maid of the prisoner's sister, I believe. Am I correct?'

The barrister stood up.

'My Lord, Mary Maloney was indeed Anne Monroe's lady's maid.' It was the only time the barrister spoke throughout the whole proceedings.

The judge addressed Edward Monroe. 'The poor girl was employed by your family. Did you think that because you employed her, you could do what you wanted with her?'

The court was getting noisier with gossip. All eyes turned to the father of the prisoner and his youngest son and daughter in the public gallery. Thomas Monroe avoided their gaze, staring at the rail of the public gallery. It seemed as if the judge had put his entire family on trial.

'Mr Monroe,' the judge thundered. 'What do you intend to do about remuneration for the unfortunate lady?'

Edward Monroe was stunned by the judge's question. He could not answer. He was speechless.

'Answer me.' The judge was playing to the gallery. Monroe still did not answer.

'Well, Mr Monroe.' Judge Lyndhurst had rehearsed his judgement. 'You have not answered my question. I will answer it for you. You will pay for the baby's upkeep and welfare. For a man of your wealthy background, I estimate that a payment of two hundred guineas would support the mother and child.'

The courtroom gasped. It was a princely sum. With his gambling debts, Edward Monroe would not have that kind of money. It would fall on his father to foot the bill.

'Furthermore,' Judge Jerimiah shouted. He had still not finished his judgement. But the noise in the court was getting louder.

'Order, order!' the usher had to shout.

'Furthermore,' the judge continued his tirade at the prisoner. 'I am going to make an example of you. While I have been in Ireland, I have been doing some research. I have in front of me a number of sentences that have been recently given by this court.' He glanced at his notes, shuffling his papers in a slow, dramatic manner. 'A felon by the name of Seamus Patterson was sentenced to one year's penal servitude for stealing a loaf of bread. Hannah Devlin was sentenced to death by hanging for the murder of her two children. Niall Grogan was sentenced to ten years' hard labour for violating a woman.'

The judge nodded to the prisoner. He had mentioned a comparable case. He put down his notes and delivered his verdict.

'In normal circumstances, this case would now go to the Crown Court. I am now going to save time and tax payers' money.' The judge then circumvented procedure and delivered his verdict. 'Edward Monroe. I sentence you to life imprisonment in her majesty's colonies. Take the prisoner away.'

'Upstanding in court,' the usher shouted, as the judge left the courtroom. The place was in uproar. Thomas Monroe, James, and Anne Monroe sat in the gallery stony-faced, as the courtroom emptied.

CHAPTER FIFTY
The Fire

As the Monroe family entered their carriage outside the courtroom, the crowd vented their anger on them. The Cork populace had sensed a change in the justice system. Reason had prevailed.

Cries of 'Rapist' and 'Murderers' were heard from the crowd.

James Monroe was first to break the silence as the three of them returned to the Castle.

'He has disgraced us,' he said.

'What are we to do, father?' Anne despaired.

Thomas Monroe shook his head.

'We have been made an example of by the judge. I suspect that he was sent from England by his political masters. All the years of hard work have now been ruined.'

Monroe was not far from the truth in his understanding of the judgement. The Whig government was in crisis. The last thing they wanted was trouble in their own backyard in Ireland. The Prime Minister Lord Melbourne had suffered enough with demands for Irish emancipation and had generously allowed a lot of reforms to take place.

There would have been riots if Monroe had been allowed to walk free. The Home Secretary, the Right Honourable Lord John Russell had been given clear instructions on how the trial should be deliberated.

Later that evening, the Monroe family were sitting around the fire, deciding what to do about the situation. Thomas looked at his daughter.

'Anne, what are your plans for your maid?'

'We cannot abandon her,' Anne replied. 'She will stay here, at least until the child is born. We at least owe her that much.'

'It is the question of the money that worries me,' her brother James said. 'How will we pay her?'

'Let her have her child first. We will deal with it later,' Thomas answered.

As winter approached, Mary grew larger with child. On a snowy morning in December, she started having pains. When Mary started losing blood, Lady Anne immediately sent for the family surgeon. After a quick examination, the doctor decided to move Mary to the nearby convent, adjacent to the Castle.

'The nuns are used to women's problems,' the doctor explained to Mary. But he feared the worst.

Mary miscarried that same afternoon, and the doctor told Lady Anne some more bad news.

'She is infected as well. When I spoke to her before, I feared this would happen.' The physician came straight to the point. 'She has syphilis.'

Anne was devastated by this news.

'My brother is vile. He desecrated this poor girl and now has effectively killed her. Should I tell her the truth?'

'She has had enough bad news. You may want to wait until she recovers from the miscarriage,' the doctor replied.

'I would trust in your silence on the matter,' Anne said.

'My Lady. I have sworn the Hippocratic Oath. I am only telling you because the poor girl will not bear this truth alone. And unfortunately, your brother must be the source of infection.'

Anne told her father the news later that day.

'Can it get any worse than this?' she cried. 'I could feel the bitterness toward me when I left the abbey. We are hated in our own country.'

'At least she will not be expecting money for the upkeep of her child. It may be a small mercy,' her father remarked.

But things did get worse. The family were singled out for the worst treatment of all.

Nobody knew who started the fire. Some said it was a rebel Republican group, and some said it was the wind that had blown the embers of a coal fire from a grate onto a carpet, setting it alight.

The fire spread rapidly in the middle of the night. The old wood-panelled building was highly inflammable. Thomas Monroe and his daughter Anne perished in the fire. Their bodies were incinerated. The servants' quarters were spared as they were separate from the main castle building. The servants fought to put out the fire with buckets of water, but the castle was a smoking ruin.

When the charred bodies of Anne and Thomas Monroe were recovered from the shell of the castle, they were not recognisable. James Monroe was at Dublin University. He was spared.

The Mother Superior broke the news to Mary the next morning. She took Mary to an upstairs window, where they could see the smoking remains of the castle, stark against the snow.

Mary was devastated by the news. With Anne dead, she had lost her best friend. Her employment had now disappeared. She had been violated, disfigured, and had now lost her baby.

'Lady Mother, what is to happen to me?' Mary asked.

The mother superior shook her head and made the sign of the cross. '*Permissum senior dues indulge penurious insons insontis,*' she softly said in Latin, and touched Mary on her head.

Mary knew enough Latin from Mass, to know she had said something about God and the innocents. She felt a little comforted. Surely she would be looked after, amongst these women of God?

The next day, James Monroe visited Mary at the abbey. He took her outside to see the still smouldering ruins of the great castle.

'It is sad, Mary.' He fought back tears. 'Like you, I have lost everything. My family is gone and with it, our fortune.'

'What do you intend to do, my Lord?' Mary asked James.

'I will go to England. I have some relatives in London. I will have to earn a living somewhere.' He turned to Mary. 'I have been speaking to the Mother Superior. I have paid her enough money to nurse you until you are well. She has promised me you will be well looked after.'

With that, James left her and Mary was on her own.

CHAPTER FIFTY ONE
The Magdalena Laundry House

On New Year's Day 1840, Mary was sent to the Cork Magdalen laundry house. The Mother Superior had kept the money that James Monroe had given her for Mary's welfare.

The laundry house was the Irish way of dealing with "fallen women", girls who had become pregnant outside marriage. Prostitutes and criminals were sent there, but also innocent girls like Mary, who had already been through a terrible ordeal.

It was nothing short of a prison run by the nuns. They ruled the inmates with physical punishments and enforced silence. The girls worked long days scrubbing, bleaching, and ironing for the whole of Cork. Institutions such as hotels, hospitals, and schools paid to have their laundry done by the women. The nuns kept the money, but the girls never saw so much as a penny piece.

The girls worked for long hours in hot temperatures, lifting heavy weights, and blistering their hands with bleach and starch.

Every window was barred and every door was locked.

Mary was locked in a cell every night at nine o'clock with three other women. By March 1840, she was in a terrible state. Her face and her hands were burnt by the bleach, and the wound that had been inflicted by James Monroe was badly infected.

The food in the laundry house was unfit for humans.

Mary decided that she would escape.

She hid in a hamper of laundry bound for a hotel on a bright March morning. As soon as the cart was unattended, she ran away and hid, wrapping herself in a shawl that she had stolen. Escaping was the easy part.

It was what to do afterwards that Mary would have trouble with. Mary started walking north towards Dublin. She had little choice. There was nothing left in Cork for her. Her mother had a large family and could not look after her. The Monroe castle that had been her home was now in ruins.

On the first night, Mary slept in a crude barn that gave little shelter to the freezing wind. At dawn, she set off again and finished off the crusts of bread she had saved from the laundry house and tucked inside her clothes. She got a lift part of the way on a farmer's cart bound for market, hiding her face in her shawl.

Mary entered Dublin as the light was fading. As she approached the dock area, she was faint with hunger. She spotted a church, and entered, finding an empty pew at the back. It was a Saturday, and the mass was just finishing. As the congregation left, a priest approached her. He recognised her laundry house uniform and guessed her dilemma.

'A lost girl from our Sister's house,' he said kindly to her. 'You are hungry. Are you not?'

Mary just nodded. She liked the priest's friendly voice. He led her into a vestry and offered her bread with some cold porridge which she stuffed into her mouth.

When she had finished her meal, the door opened. Two stern-looking nuns entered.

'We will deal with her now, Father,' one of the nuns said. She grabbed Mary by her arm. The priest had betrayed her.

Mary was too quick for her. She ran out of the church.

'Have you no compassion?' she shouted as she ran.

Mary ran down to the docks. She felt very tired. It had been two days since she had slept properly. As she passed an alleyway, she could see people settling down for the night. She knew they were homeless, but she had little choice in the matter.

In the dim light, Mary saw a young woman with a small baby. Thinking it to be the safest option, she sat next to the woman and soon she was fast asleep.

She awoke to the sound of the baby crying.

'I'm sorry she has woken you up, but it's time you moved,' the mother said. 'The night watch will be here soon to clear the streets.'

'Thank you,' Mary said.

'You look like you need help,' the woman said. 'The laundry house would take you in.'

Mary shook her head and showed the woman the brown dress and apron under her shawl. 'I have just escaped from the Cork laundry house. I cannot go back.'

'I understand. You had better come with me.' The woman rose, her baby clinging to her.

Mary had very little choice but to follow the woman. She led Mary through the Dublin streets to a very squalid part of the city.

'At least we will get something to eat here,' the woman said. She pointed to a soup kitchen at the side of a church. Mary shrunk back, but her companion explained that it was run by Quakers. Both women joined the long queue to be fed.

They sat in a large bare hall full of homeless people to eat their thin soup and bread. The woman introduced herself as Colleen Calaquan.

'I am a fallen woman,' she said, staring frankly at Mary. 'I had the baby last month. I fear I must give her up.' As she breastfed the baby, she gazed at it with love.

A rough-looking man approached her.

'Colleen. My little angel. When are you coming back to us?'

Colleen tried to ignore the man. He looked closely at Mary. She instinctively tied to cover the wound on her lip.

'That's a nasty looking cut you have there,' he said. 'Still, it will be hard to see in the dark. Pity. I bet you were attractive before. You could still earn a lot of money.'

Mary tried to figure out who this man was.

He pulled a coin out of his pocket. It was a two shilling piece. 'You can have this tonight if you come with me.' He put the coin back in his pocket. 'I'll be seeing you later.' He disappeared as fast as he had arrived.

'Eamon Brannon. He's my Fostaitheoir,' Colleen muttered.

Mary knew her Gaelic. Colleen was referring to her pimp.

CHAPTER FIFTY TWO
Danny Boy

Mary slept in the alley with Colleen for the next two nights.

By the next time Eamon Brannon appeared at the Quakers' soup kitchen, she had decided to give way to his advances. Mary was getting desperate. She had suffered dreadfully since Edward Monroe had raped her. Mary had lost everything, and the streets of Dublin were no refuge from danger. She now had to sell the last remaining thing that she possessed. Her body.

Brannon promised her a room in a squalid tenement building. He told her that the first week's rent would be free, and then he would call on her weekly for the money. The room just contained a bed, covered with filthy clothes instead of blankets. Mary's first time was with the pimp. He lay on top of her. All she could think of was the millions of bugs that must be in the bed.

It was all over in minutes. Brannon left her in the room. Mary was now a prostitute, and she would have to fend for herself. She solicited another client that night outside a public house. He was a drunken man who could hardly perform. He kept dropping to sleep. It was easy money.

The next morning, she threw the clothes off the bed and disposed of them on the street. She then completely scrubbed the room. Her training as a maid had taught her to adapt. With her ill-gotten gains, Mary bought second-hand blankets. She disposed of her laundry house attire and bought some cheap and rather gaudy clothes.

The most difficult task was the wound on her lip which had disfigured her. She overcame this by applying cheap rouge to the wound, and she started to paint her lips. It improved her looks and quite soon she was used to her new life. She started getting regular customers.

Dublin City was a thoroughfare, with all kinds of passengers and sailors passing through the port. She plied her trade in the Monto district where she lived, a warren of streets and dilapidated tenements.

The British army barracks were near to Mary's patch. She did a roaring trade, along with the many other prostitutes who worked the area. The soldiers had plenty of money, and Mary grew used to surviving by selling her body. Her former life as a lady's maid seemed like a distant dream.

Mary discovered that prostitution was ignored by the authorities most of the time. She was arrested twice for prostitution, and she managed to get off with a small fine. It was a token gesture.

But the times started changing. There were more Peelers in the city and they were starting to clamp down on the city's prostitutes.

CHAPTER FIFTY THREE
The Street Woman

The Tories were elected into power in 1841. They were determined to clamp down on prostitution in Ireland. The order came from London to make the sentences for the prostitutes harsher as a deterrent and to set an example. Also their clients would be made an example of. Their names would be published in the local newspapers, which would cause much embarrassment to their families.

When Mary was arrested for a third time, the judge warned her that she would be transported if she was caught again. She was in a dilemma. She needed the money, and feared the workhouse.

By May 1842, life was much harder for Dublin prostitutes. The weather was still cold, and the wind howled through the dockside streets.

Although it was Friday night, which was normally the busiest night of the week, it was very quiet on the streets. They were crawling with the police. The Tory government seemed to be making their anti-vice policy work.

Mary was working her patch in the Monto district, but apart from a group of young men who had mingled outside a pub, the street was deserted. Other prostitutes were waiting on the street, but Mary liked to work alone.

Suddenly she heard a shrill whistle. It meant only one thing. The Peelers!

The bitter cold had slowed her reactions down. Two policemen held her tightly.

'We've got one here. Take her to the Castle,' said one burly Peeler. Mary shuddered. They were going to lock her up!

'Rosie –where the hell have you been?' A young man broke away from the group outside the pub and ran across the street. 'I've been waiting an hour for you.' He turned to the policemen. 'This is my girl you have here, officer. I am taking her to England with me for a new life.'

The policemen looked rather surprised at the man, but they didn't want to get into an argument. There were much easier fish to land in their net.

'She shouldn't be on the streets dressed like that,' one of them said. 'Certainly not with her face painted. She looks like a whore.'

'Sorry, officer.' The man took Mary's hand. 'It will not happen again. Come on Rosie. We are late.'

The policemen let Mary go, and the man took her across the street and out of the way of the snatch squads.

'I'm Daniel McNamara,' the man quickly introduced himself. 'I'm from Limerick. I was watching you from outside that pub. You were very lucky. You could have been arrested.'

'Aye, and transported,' Mary answered. 'I am already on a warning from the magistrates. The next time I am caught, I will be sent abroad to Australia.'

'Jesus,' Danny said. 'Would you believe that? Transported to Australia? Not many come back from there. It sounds as if the English are getting desperate. Sending you girls there. Holy Mother. What would you do there? What is your name?'

'I am called Mary Maloney,' she explained. 'I am from Cork. I was forced into this life.'

She had tried to hide the knife wound on her lips, but now she pulled away the shawl she had wrapped around her mouth, and showed it to Danny.

'See this?' she said. 'I was attacked and left for dead.'

'Will you look at that?' Danny exclaimed, shocked. 'Come on. Let me buy you a drink, Mary from Cork.'

CHAPTER FIFTY FOUR
The Fostaitheoir

'I have come from Limerick in search of work,' Danny explained, as they sat down in the dark pub. 'There is nothing at home. People are leaving in droves. These lads are from all over Ireland,' he explained, indicating the men he had been with when Mary was being arrested. 'Some are from Sligo and Mayo. Times are hard, and there are better opportunities abroad.'

Mary was beginning to like this fresh-faced young boy.

'So do you think you will find work here in Dublin, Daniel?' she asked.

'I might have to go to England' he answered 'Or America. Have you a place here, Mary? I could do with a place to lay my head for a couple of days.'

'I have,' she answered. 'But it is rented from my Fostaitheoir.' It did not sound as bad to say it in Gaelic. 'He is not a nice man. I have made no money tonight with all the Peelers about.'

As they sat in the pub, they could still hear the police whistles.

'I am very grateful to you for saving me tonight,' she said softly. 'I will sneak you back to my room, but you must be very quiet. The pimp knows everything that happens.'

Danny looked at her and felt really sorry for her. She was reduced to a life on the streets. She was really pretty, and although disfigured by her wound, she had a lovely soft nature. He knew then that he would like to know her better.

They sneaked into her room. He did not make any advances towards Mary. He slept on the floor, and Mary lent him a blanket.

They were rudely awoken in the early hours. A man suddenly entered the room, carrying a lantern. Daniel guessed who he was. The Fostaitheoir.

'Ah. I see you have a client, Mary. The Peelers have kept most of the girls in. A lot have been arrested. I will be back in the morning for the rent.'

Danny took an instant dislike to the pimp, but he said nothing to Mary until the morning. They were walking the Dublin streets together.

'Have you got to do this?' he asked. 'You deserve better, Mary Maloney.'

Mary just smiled. 'There is nothing else. I have nowhere to go.'

He noticed how her face brightened with the smile. He suddenly kissed her on the lips.

'I am away now. I've got to look for work – but can I see you later?' he asked. Mary nodded, and wondered if he would keep his word. The city was full of people leaving in droves, or going nowhere.

Later that week, Mary was sitting in her room. The Peelers had been out in force again, and the city was very quiet. She had returned home without a client and she was getting worried. It had been two weeks since she had paid Brannon the rent for the room.

Suddenly the door burst open and Brannon stood in her doorway. His face said it all.

'My rent. Where is my rent? You have now missed two weeks. It is not a charity that I am running.'

'Eamon,' Mary tried to explain. 'The Peelers have been out all week. There is no work.'

Before she could say any more, he punched her on the face. As she recoiled, he hit her again. She smarted with the pain, and she fell on the bed, sobbing.

'I shall be back in the morning,' the pimp shouted. 'If there is no money you will leave. It's the streets for you.'

CHAPTER FIFTY FIVE
Mary and Danny

Daniel McNamara had been busy that day, but he still had nowhere to stay. He decided to visit Mary again.

It was nearly midnight as he knocked on her door. It took her a while to answer, and he was shocked when he saw her condition.

She had a bruised eye, and a swollen cheek where Brannon had hit her.

'Was it the Fostaitheoir?' he asked.

She nodded. Feeling sorry for Mary, he put his arms around her.

'Come here,' he said, gently lifting her onto the bed. 'I am going to take you away from all of this.'

He kissed her on the lips. They both felt desire for each other. They lay on the bed together.

Danny was very gentle with her. It was the first time that Mary had known that love making could be special, not just a brutal, short act. They took their time, and they embraced each other tenderly, eventually drifting off to sleep in the safety of each other's arms.

The next morning, Mary was the first to wake up.

'You will have to leave before Brannon comes. There has been enough trouble,' she said. She ran her fingers through his hair.

'Don't you worry about him,' Danny replied confidently. He kissed her. Within minutes, they both fell asleep again.

'I hope this is a client, Mary Maloney.' A loud voice woke them. 'And not your lover boy. I have come for your rent. You have had your warning.' It was Brannon. He had entered the room without knocking.

Danny fumbled in his trouser pocket. 'How much is the rent?' he asked the pimp.

'Oh the tuathanach is paying, is he? Have you had to sell a pig, then?' Brannon said, dismissing Danny as a peasant. 'It's two shillings Lady Mary owes.'

Danny paid him the money and waited until Brannon left. He got out of bed quickly and followed the pimp downstairs.

The pimp whistled as he strode down the dockside street. It was quiet, and still early. Brannon was happy. He had made his first money of the day. Now he would visit some other unfortunate girl who was in arrears with his lewd racket.

Suddenly, a man grabbed him from behind and dragged him into a dark, narrow gap between two warehouses.

'The money. Give me back my money' It was Danny.

'Oh. The pig farmer is it?' the pimp recognised his voice. 'You will have to do better than that. I will have my lads on you.'

Brennon had misjudged Danny. The Limerick lad had been a street fighter all his life. He was very strong. Danny spun Brennon round and punched him in his face. The pimp fell backwards and Danny grabbed his purse that was tied to his belt. As he started to count the money, Danny took his eye off Brennon.

The pimp got to his feet. Although his nose was bleeding heavily, he withdrew a stiletto blade from his belt and swung it at Danny.

Danny swerved and grappled with the pimp, grabbing the blade. In one movement, he stabbed Brennon. He fell to the ground in a pool of blood.

The Limerick boy grabbed the purse and walked back to Mary's room.

'Come on, Mary. We are away. He will trouble you no more,' he said, entering her room. Mary was already dressed and she did not need telling twice. She started to pack some things.

'Leave all that. You will not need anything where we are going,' Danny said, but she insisted on packing some blankets.

As they left the squalid room for the last time, Danny started to explain. 'Yesterday I was at the Eden Quay. There was a man who was advertising jobs in England. They want lads to build a railway in the North. The ferry leaves this afternoon. I asked about you. They want women as well, to see to the workers.'

Mary had very little choice in the matter. Her life had taken another dramatic twist. She had to put her trust in Danny. She had only known him for a few days but she knew that he was the man for her.

The body of Eamon Brennon was discovered later that day by a worker from the warehouse. The Peelers were soon on the scene. A Sergeant summed it up instantly.

'He was a known pimp and must have made many enemies.'

The Sergeant knew that there would not be a lengthy investigation. He watched as the coroner gave his judgement: 'Death by an assailant or assailants unknown'.

It was one less criminal on the streets, he thought.

CHAPTER FIFTY SIX
1842
Woodhead

The Englishman at the Eden Quay was taking the names of the new workers. He worked for the Sheffield, Ashton-under Lyne, and Manchester Railway Company and they were desperately short of workers.

His instructions were clear and he knew them off by heart.

'Look for able bodied men. No cripples or disease-ridden individuals. Be vague when you tell them of the wages. Mention the free ticket to England, but avoid telling them that it's just one way. Don't tell them that it's tunnel work. Just get them to England. We will sort them out when they get here.'

'This is my wife,' Daniel McNamara told the man, as they got on the ferry. 'She is coming as well.'

The man just nodded as he filled in the register.

'What are your names?' he asked.

Danny was quick with his answer. He gave false names.

'Daniel and Mary Shanahan,' he said. They walked up the gang way. Neither of them had been on a boat as big as this before, and even though it was only carrying them over the Irish Sea, Mary felt apprehensive.

Danny wondered when the body of Eamon Brennon was going to be found, and if anyone had notice him, but he pushed away his fears and tried to appear light-hearted.

'Shanahan. Why did you pick that name?' Mary asked.

'It's where my mother was born,' Danny said, laughing.

They need not have worried. The boats leaving Ireland were full of families trying to escape a life of poverty. The inquiry into the murdered pimp was just another statistic in a city of sin and depravity.

The ferry was a paddle steamer and the railway company had booked the afternoon sailing from Eden Quay, with two hundred navvies on board. The young couple stared at the sea in wonder, and tried not to feel sick at the motion of the boat on the waves.

They talked and wondered what was in store for them as the steamer approached Liverpool. At first light the next morning, a large city appeared in view. It looked similar to Dublin in many ways, with its docks full of sailing boats, large smoke-blackened buildings, and tall warehouses.

They disembarked from the ferry. After the long journey by sea, the ground seemed to sway. The Englishman gathered them together to explain where they were going.

'You are going to Woodhead on the other side of Manchester. You will travel by train to where the lines terminate. Then it is a walk to the tunnel that is under construction. It is the longest tunnel in the world and will be three miles long.'

The Irish workforce set off with what goods they had brought with them to the new Crown Street Railway Station in the centre of Liverpool. Most of them had never travelled by railway before.

The immigrant workers were herded into open-top carriages for the trip to Manchester. Both Mary and Danny were fascinated by the journey, which didn't seem to take long, travelling at amazing speed. They passed houses, countryside, factories, and mills.

The Irish arrivals marched across the city to the new terminus of the Sheffield, Ashton-under Lyne, and Manchester Railway Company.

This was to be called London Road Station and was still being constructed. The new navvies were then put in some more open top wagons. The journey took them a short distance, to a place called Dinting where a viaduct was being constructed. From there, they followed the company agent on foot, following the new railway bed to Woodhead on the western side of the new tunnel.

They passed through the navvy camp on the hill, behind the portals of the tunnel. The sight and smell was awful.

'More coffin fillers,' an Irish voice shouted at them.

The navvies watched the new arrivals as they passed by. Mary saw a mixture of pity and envy on their faces. As she walked through the camp, she felt a growing sense of misgiving.

Passing the trail, they could see the shafts that had been sunk down to the tunnel. All kinds of materials were being lugged up the hill to supply the camp.

It was twilight as they approached the east side of the tunnel. The company man spoke to them again.

'This is the Dunford Bridge end where you will be working. The manager will speak to you soon. They had stopped outside a building. Mary noticed people waiting to go inside. Her curiosity got the better of her and she asked a woman in the queue what it was.

'It is the Number One boiler house. It's used as an infirmary. Are you a new tally woman?' the woman asked.

Mary nodded. She knew the term already.

'I'm here with my man Danny,' she said.

The woman pointed towards the navvy huts. 'There's an empty hut over there. The navvies have left who had it before. They have gone to another site. I should fumigate it if I were you,' she said. Mary thanked her for her kindness.

She wanted to talk for longer, but two men wearing top hats had come to address the new navvies.

'My name is Wellington Purdon and I am the manager of Dunford Bridge,' the man announced. Mary took an instant dislike to the manager. He was small and wore a shirt and a tie with an embroidered waistcoat. The manager pointed to his companion. 'This is my colleague Henry Nicholson. You will assemble at five o'clock in the morning, at the tunnel entrance. The tommy shop is still open, where you will get your dockets for food. I suggest you find a hut and get some sleep. Are there any questions?'

'How will we know it's time to get up? We may lay too long,' one of the navvies asked. A ripple of laughter went around the band of new navvies.

Wellington Purdon had little time for levity. 'You will know when it is time to get up. We have a giant clock that makes a noise.' He was referring to the steam whistle that went off at four forty every morning.

Mary and Danny found the empty hut the woman had told her about. It smelled of stale food and peat, but Mary was happy. 'I will clean it in the morning when you are at work.' Danny softly kissed her. Their new life had begun.

CHAPTER FIFTY SEVEN
1845
Retribution

Mary thought about the three and a half years that she had been at Woodhead. Had it been that long since she had left Ireland?

Her man Danny was now dead, and the Duke had entered her life. He had been very good to her, but she did not love him in the way she had loved Danny. Mary always missed her Limerick lad this time of year. She wished he could be here to see his son growing up.

As she stared into the dying peat fire, Mary wondered what was coming next in her turbulent life. The tunnel was now complete and she was helping in the infirmary. The surgeons said that she was becoming a fine nurse. A new tunnel was being started. The income she got from putting up the navvies would be safe for a few years.

Mary slowly drifted off to sleep. Little did she know that it was to be her last sleep.

A man with vengeance on his mind was thinking about Mary that winter's night. Elias Randall had plenty of time to plan his revenge in his lonely sentry post. It was now or never.

The orders had come through from the regiment. On Christmas Day, the troops were to stand down. Then the full regiment would arrive at Dunford Bridge, as part of the official opening ceremony. The first train was planned to go through the tunnel on Saturday 27th December. The regiment would then return to headquarters.

The railway station had already been decorated with trimmings and bunting. A make-shift band stand had been erected in readiness for all the dignitaries.

On Christmas Eve, Randall had started drinking in the Angel at ten o' clock in the morning. He became violent when he had drunk too much. By midnight, revenge was uppermost in his mind.

As he resumed his duty, his head was swimming. The tally woman was going to be the first to suffer. He had been locked away because of her, and the beatings and humiliation had taken its toll on him.

As the beer went in, Eli's brains were slowly draining out. His mind was fixed on revenge, and he was going to have it that night.

By the early hours of the morning, he had not seen a living soul as he put his plan into motion. Leaving his post, he climbed up to the navvy huts. He silently approached Mary Maloney's cabin, and without making a sound, he opened the crude door of the hut. In the gloom, he could just make out a woman in one bed and a young child in a cot. Putting his hand over her mouth, he stabbed her in her stomach with his dagger. With a small groan, she was dead.

Moving away, Elias caught something. It fell on the floor with a thud.

To his horror, he realised what it was. A wooden leg. He felt down the woman's leg where the blood was dripping from the fatal wound. He realised he had killed the wrong woman. It was Peg Leg Peg, the nurse friend of Mary Maloney.

'Margaret, is that you?' A soft voice broke the silence. Mary had been awoken by the noise of the falling wooden leg. Still crazed by drink, Elias swiftly rushed to her bed and slit Mary's throat. Her arterial blood sprayed in his face. It hastened his adrenalin. He had been trained to kill French soldiers in this way, swiftly and silently

The young boy started to cry. Feeling no remorse, Randall's only concern was to quieten him.

'Join your mother in hell, you little bastard,' he said, as he slit the child's throat.

He now had to get rid of the bodies. He knew where he would put them. He had hatched a plan for this, but just in case they were discovered, he needed somebody to take the blame. There was a piece of parchment on the crude table, where the Duke had been showing Mary his English. He tore it in half and stuffed a strip of parchment in each of the dead women's mouths.

It had started to pour with rain, hissing against the thatched roof of the hut. Randall draped Mary's frail body over his shoulders and carried the dead child in his arms. In the pitch darkness, he walked to the tunnel entrance. Randall had left a lantern there, already lit. He picked it up and walked into the tunnel. He placed the bodies at the bottom of the five hundred foot shaft. He heaved some railway sleepers over the bodies, and arranged rubbish so that the bodies were out of sight.

He quickly returned to the navvy hut. He stuffed the other body, and the wooden leg, into a hessian sack. Carrying the body into the tunnel, he hurried along to the slit tunnel. He dumped the sack on the side of the slit and covered it with a large rock.

CHAPTER FIFTY EIGHT
The Boiler House Party

Private Elias Randall was convinced he had got away with the murders. The camp was still deathly quiet as he came out of the tunnel.

Certain no one had seen him, he decided that he would return home to Manchester. Although this would be desertion, he would have a few days' freedom to celebrate what he had done. After all, he was used to being in trouble with the army.

The foul weather changed his mind. His head, which had sobered up while he had been committing his foul deeds, was now banging with pain. He needed a drink, but where would he get one? "The hair of the dog", as it was called by the soldiers.

He remembered his visit to the boiler house that day when he had been arrested. He'd seen bottles of port in a cupboard.

Randall set off to the boiler house, and opened the large steel door. There was just one candle burning.

He could just about make out figures, asleep, on the makeshift straw beds. Staggering over to the cupboard, he found a bottle that was nearly full. With one swig, he half-emptied it down his parched throat. The liquid tasted vile, but he quickly finished off the bottle. As Randall belched loudly, he heard one of the sleeping women patients stirring.

Randall was as high as a kite, and wet through with rain and sweat.

He found another bottle; full. He smashed the top off on the corner of a stone shelf.

'Let's have a party,' he slurred. 'Here drink this.' He forced some liquid down the woman's throat.

He then sat the woman up. Lighting another candle, he did the same to all the other poor patients. They were all women, and all very ill. One by one, he made them drink the liquid. He suddenly felt very tired. Unable to stand, he sat down on the shelf that ran around the building. In the dim light, he could see the red blood on his blue uniform. It was from the three victims that he had just murdered.

He had got his revenge on Mary. As he passed out in a coma, he saw spectres of French soldiers at Waterloo. This hallucination gave way to the women and children he had scythed down at Peterloo.

As his life ebbed away, he saw Mary's baby boy asleep, for eternity, at the bottom of the Woodhead shaft.

CHAPTER FIFTY NINE
1952
Elias Goes to Hell

It was Christmas 1952, but Susan and Roger were reading about the events of Christmas 1845, one hundred and seven years previously.

Mrs Priestley's carpet was covered in notes about the period, as Susan and Roger tried to piece together the final chapter of the complex murder mysteries.

Susan's mother sat in her late husband's favourite armchair. Fascinated, she watched and listened to the two of them working the murder mysteries out. She had taken an instant liking to this Glossop lad with his lovely manners and friendly ways.

The two were totally engrossed in the notes as Susan read aloud from the notes of Harold Thompson:

I have for years lived with the memory of that morning at Dunford Bridge, on Boxing Day 1845.

I had arrived at the camp as the dawn was breaking, from my home in Glossop. The ground was sodden with rain, and mud was everywhere. I had been charged with moving out the six remaining patients from the old infirmary in the boiler house to a new site. I had arranged for the two nurses to assist me with the task.

I encountered Duke Frederick at the Dunford Bridge Station, and we exchanged pleasantries. The station was trimmed with bunting and decorations, ready for the arrival of the first train.

To my surprise, the boiler room was in darkness and the two nurses were not there. They were always punctual, and I had expected them to be looking after the patients. The Duke entered the building but it was difficult to see in the morning gloom. He called out their names but to no avail. We both left and walked the short distance to the navvy camp.

The door to Mary Maloney's hut was partly ajar so after knocking, with no answer, we entered.

The place was empty but there was blood everywhere. It was obvious that some dark deed had been done. I deduced the blood had been caused by arterial spray. The Duke was beside himself as we then ran back to the makeshift infirmary.

We lit candles and saw to our dismay the six women patients unnaturally arranged in sitting positions on the stone shelf. They were lifeless. There was also a soldier sitting there. It was Private Randall, the soldier who had assaulted Mary Maloney during the strike.

His blue Hussar's uniform was red with blood, which had soaked into the raiment.

Bile and blood had dripped from his mouth. His eyes were still open.

'What have you done with the women, you bastard, Randall?' The Duke shook the soldier. There was no response.

'I think he's dead,' Doctor Thompson took Randall's pulse and checked for vital signs.

'Look at the blood,' the Duke cried. 'He has murdered Mary!'

There was a chloroform bottle on the shelf next to the dead soldier, almost empty. Doctor Thompson smelled the dregs and nodded gravely.

'He will go to Hell for what he's done.' The Duke groaned. 'My Mary.'

CHAPTER SIXTY
Struck Off

Susan and Roger continued to read the Surgeon's notes:

Randall still held the bottle in his hand. I examined him for a pulse. He was dead, and I had a problem.

I had been experimenting with Chloroform, which was a mixture of acetone and ethanol. I would give it to the navvies to ease the pain, whilst carrying out amputations. It was obvious what had happened. The empty bottles were on the floor, and there was a lot of broken glass. He had died from drinking the Chloroform, thinking it was the port. He had also administered it to the six women. He had inadvertently put them out of their misery.

The Duke was beside himself with grief so I administered a sedative to him, and he quietened down very quickly. I deliberated what to do for the best. Never in my life did I have a more difficult decision to make. If I had reported the matter to the authorities, there would have been a lot of awkward questions to be answered. My biggest fear was about the Chloroform. It should never have been left there unattended, mixed in old port bottles.

In short, if there had been an inquiry I would have been struck off the medical register. I was a young surgeon and it would have been devastating for my career. Also the poor women were more or less dead anyway. The soldier had put them out of their suffering, and then he had taken his own life.

I have had many a nightmare about my actions that day. Even the sights I saw in the Crimea were not as bad as that day at Dunford Bridge.

I had very little choice in the matter. My mind was made up as a manager knocked on the steel door of the infirmary. I went outside to speak to him. He was in charge of a team of navvies, who were waiting for me to empty the boiler house. They were ready to fill in the ravine, and bury the boiler house. They were desperately short of tipping space for the new tunnel.

I decided to entomb the bodies for eternity. I had been entrusted with the key of the old boiler house and I informed the manager that the building had already been emptied. He then returned to his men at the top of the ravine. I ushered the Duke out of the building and locked the door of the place of death. The Duke was very groggy so I took him to the new infirmary, where he fell asleep on a straw bed.

I then returned to Mary's hut and set fire to it. This was the normal practice to fumigate a navvy hut.

By the end of the day, the navvies had started to cover the ravine where the boiler house had been. In a week, there was no sign of it at all.

I have often wondered where Randall had put the bodies of the two women and the child. Another concern was the seven other people in the boiler house. Would they be missed? The six women were more or less dead anyway. Their men had either died or deserted them for other sites, and left them to fend for themselves. The harsh conditions, accidents and poor food, contributed to hundreds of deaths. It was very common at that awful place. There were no records kept of women at the sites.

Another fear was the soldier, Randall. He would be the subject of a Court of Inquiry, for going missing whilst on duty.

CHAPTER SIXTY ONE
See the Conquering Hero Comes

'The diary follows up the story,' Susan explained to Roger.

The Earl of Wexford's diaries, Friday 26th December 1845:

I arrived in the forenoon and I met the Surgeon, Harold Thompson, and enquired as to the whereabouts of the Royal Duke. Thompson was in the new infirmary, which is a better place than the old one, and the Duke lay asleep on one of the beds.

Thompson informed me that the two nurses had left the site. Already the huts, where they had lived, had been emptied. All the contents and straw beds had been burnt. He went on to say that the Duke was very upset, when he learned they had left, and he had been required to calm him down.

'He had destroyed any evidence,' Roger said. 'And he sedated the Duke.'

'That is what it looks like,' Susan agreed. 'It was a quick fix to save any lengthy inquiry. But you could tell by his notes that he questioned his own actions for the rest of his life.'

'Come on, you two,' Susan's mother took over. 'Let's have some dinner. I hope Yorkshire food suits you, my lad?'

After dinner, they continued to read the Earl of Wexford's diary for the 26th December:

We attended the funeral of Lord Wharncliffe today. It was in the afternoon, at the Wortley church. Several dignitaries were there and the congregation was swelled by visitors, who have come for the railway opening tomorrow.

His official title of Colonel James Archibald Stuart-Wortley-Mackenzie, 1st Baron Wharncliffe was used in church, and the wake was held at Wortley Hall.

Being Catholic, and used to longer funeral services I was surprised that the proceedings were over in an hour. Some of the dignitaries then came back to the Hall.

Saturday 27th December 1845:

What a magnificent sight it was to see the first train go through the tunnel today. It was hauled by two brand-new locomotives that had arrived from Sheffield. The twenty carriages were full of people who wanted to travel on the new line.

The train stopped at Dunford Bridge for half an hour. It was bitterly cold and snow was underfoot, but it made a splendid view. The company directors, various mayors, and dignitaries alighted from the train.

A band played 'Hail the conquering hero' above the sound of the giant locomotives. Prayers were then said, including 'Non Nobis Nomine,' a short Latin hymn, used as an expression of thanksgiving.

Speeches were then given and Joseph Locke and Richard Ward were praised for their valiant efforts in building the tunnel. It did seem hypocritical that thanks were also said for Superintendents Purdon and Nicholson, but not for the hundreds who had died in building the railway.

The trade union officers William Birkenshaw, and Peter Meredith, were also at the ceremony.

I witnessed the sight with the two surgeons Pomfret and Thomson, who I have the utmost admiration for.

Duke Frederick was not at the tunnel opening, but a full regiment of Yeomanry were in attendance, on horseback, in their blue and white uniforms.

I spoke briefly with Captain Gregory, and he told me some interesting news. He informed me that Private Randall has gone AWOL.

I returned home to Wortley Hall in the late afternoon, to find that the Duke had been brought back from Woodhead. He has been very ill.

It appears the surgeon had sedated him after hearing that the tally woman, and her child, had left the site. He is very subdued and obviously missing his Irish friend. I tried to broach the subject with him but he would not discuss the matter.

My wife, Sarah, has tried speaking with him, but he would not respond to her either. She reported that he was staring into space, singing a nursery rhyme. We have decided to leave him to deal with his grief.

'What did the military court of inquiry conclude about Randall going AWOL?' Roger wondered. 'My great grandfather must have been worried about that.'

Susan searched the police archives and borrowed copies of the *Police Gazette* from the mid-1840s. It didn't take her long to find what she was looking for.

'Here it is,' she said. 'It looks like a wanted poster and it even mentions his nickname, which soldiers would know him by.'

She showed Roger the newspaper:

The Manchester and Salford Hussars

1413. Elias Randall. Private, Commonly known as "Cock-eyed Eli".

Missing from his post at Dunford Bridge, Yorkshire, December 24th, 1845.

A charge of desertion is issued against this man.

CHAPTER SIXTY TWO
1952
Piece it All Together

'So let's just put all this into context Sue,' Chief Inspector Columbine asked her. 'Randall killed Mary Maloney, and the baby?'

She was back in Columbine's Wakefield office with DI Andy Monroe. The excitement of investigating the murders at Christmas with Roger was over, and she had now returned to official police duty.

'Yes, Sir,' Susan answered. 'She was wearing the ring that the Duke had given her. The child had the Duke's gold watch, and chain, on his expensive waistcoat. It appears that the Duke sincerely cared for Mary. But it was Randall who slit their throats and put the parchment in Mary's mouth. He put their bodies at the bottom of the Number One Shaft. He appears to have murdered Mary as revenge for being sent to the military prison. Randall also killed the woman with the wooden leg. She was Rachel Foulkes, commonly known as Peg Leg Peg. He put her body in the slit tunnel and stuffed the other piece of parchment in her mouth. He then poisoned himself and the six women in the old boiler house.'

'Perhaps the Chloroform helped to preserve the bodies,' Monroe mused.

'But you said that the Duke killed the five-fingered twins?' Columbine asked, scratching his head.

Susan nodded.

'The Duke killed them with his pistol. He had been drinking with them all day. I'm not sure what his motive was. Perhaps they tried to rob him. I suspect he had lost his mind with alcohol. He put their bodies in the ash tip behind the boiler house,' Susan explained.

'Do you think he was like Doctor Jekyll and Mr Hyde, with his split personality?' Monroe suggested.

'Well, DI, it's funny you should say that,' she said, as she checked her notes. 'Did you know that Harold Thompson actually treated Robert Louis Stevenson in Bournemouth, in 1866? It was just before he started to write his book, The Strange case of Doctor Jekyll and Mr Hyde.'

'And the Duke murdered the prostitute in Barnsley too?' Columbine asked.

'Yes Sir,' explained Susan. 'His manservant planted his knife on the tramp, Geordie Jack. He got the blame, and they hung him for it.'

'So what became of the Dramatis Personae in this case, Susan?' Columbine asked.

Susan looked at DI Monroe, who did not understand the phrase. She smiled.

'The cast of players, or actors,' she explained. 'They led interesting lives. Robert O'Neill, the Earl of Wexford, took over the estate at Wortley following the death of Lord Wharncliffe. He lived a long life and died at the age of eighty, in 1893. He had three children to his wife Sarah, who died in 1890. Harold Thompson, the surgeon, lived until the age of ninety. He died in 1912. Queen Victoria knighted him, and he was a leading expert on diseases.'

'Another question, Sergeant,' asked Monroe. 'We all know the Coal Mines Commission resulted in children being banned from being employed in the mines. But what was the outcome of the other Commission that the Earl was in charge of, the investigation of the railway company?'

Susan searched through her notes for the details of the Parliamentary papers from 1846. She read from her records:

'O'Neill was conscientious in his duty. The report was composed of two hundred and two pages. The minutes of the evidence had an index of fifty four pages. The report was formally received by the House of Commons Select Committee.'

Susan paused, and looked at Columbine.

'But nothing was done about it. It was not even debated. This is what O'Neill thought about the conclusion of his Commission.'

Susan read her notes from O'Neill's diary to Monroe and Columbine:

'So my report had taken four years to compile, and it was never debated. I have reported back to the Queen. She, like me, is most dejected. We both thought that at the very least there would have been a public outcry.

The Queen has informed me that she had been doing her own investigations. 'It is a great pity, My Lord. But what is to be expected of a House of Commons where one railway is said to have eighty members in its pocket? They are all shareholders,' she told me with a sigh.'

Monroe shook his head. 'Profit and greed,' he said.

'What about the Royal Duke Frederick? Put us out of our misery. What happened to him?' Columbine asked.

'He just disappeared for a long time,' Susan answered. 'Perhaps he returned home to Saxony. There is no other reference to him for years. Of course, his brother Albert died, in 1861, at the young age of forty three. To my knowledge, Frederick did not attend the funeral.'

Susan was enjoying the drama of wrapping up her case.

'I traced the history of his family, and suddenly, there's a reference of him visiting Britain in 1888.'

'Did he visit Yorkshire again?' Monroe enquired.

'No. He was in London. There's a reference to him as an advisor to a mission for fallen women.' Susan paused. 'In Whitechapel, in East London.'

Columbine gasped. Susan had dropped a bombshell.

'Whitechapel...where Jack the Ripper carried out his murders,' Columbine mused.

CHAPTER SIXTY THREE
1953
Churchill Revisited

Susan and Columbine had returned to Number Ten Downing Street to meet the Prime Minister. He welcomed them warmly into his private office. Susan's report was on his desk.

'The Irish government know nothing of Harold Thompson's notes? Am I correct?' Churchill quickly opened the meeting.

'That's right, Prime Minister,' Susan said. 'A descendent of the surgeon found the vital notes in his attic.'

'How curious,' Churchill laughed. 'The case becomes even more mysterious.' Churchill pondered for a moment, trimming his cigar. 'So our Irish friends have only got part of the story from this Irish Earl, in his infamous diaries?'

Susan nodded.

'Queen Elizabeth must be protected,' the Prime Minister said. 'She must never know what her ancestor was up to.' Churchill stared at Susan's report. 'I need Sergeant Priestley with me for the next few days. Chief Inspector Columbine, I would remind you, this is all top-secret. You are still under the remit of the Official Secrets Act.'

Columbine nodded his assent. Susan wondered what the old man was planning.

'Did you know that I have never met Mr Éamon de Valera, the Taoiseach of Ireland?' Churchill mused. 'However, he has been a thorn in my side on many issues. Well, all that is about to change. Tomorrow we shall have a secret meeting. You, my pretty young Yorkshire Sergeant, will be my right-hand man.'

Churchill chuckled at her. He leaned back in his leather armchair as he lit his cigar, mischief twinkling in his eyes. Susan was amazed.

The next day, Sergeant Susan Priestley was part of a secret special delegation.

She travelled by train, with the Prime Minister, his trusted aides and security guards, in a private First Class carriage. They were escorted onto a ferry to Belfast.

At the port, a shining black chauffeur-driven Bentley was there to meet them, and they journeyed to the border of the republic with a police escort. At times, Susan felt completely overwhelmed by the situation. She had been very nervous about travelling with the Prime Minister, but he was good company and the journey passed very quickly. He shared a common interest in her love of English Literature, and her young brain quite fascinated him.

'I was intrigued by your story of the Pennine railway tunnel at Woodhead' he told her. 'When I was the MP for Oldham, I used to regularly use that route, but I never knew the history behind it all. It is fair to say, in hindsight of course, that it was capitalism at its very worst. The same Irish navvies were sent for in the Crimean War, and they built a railway which supplied our army. We have a lot to thank them for. A very colourful race they are, the Irish.'

Churchill laughed. 'I often refer to Eamon de Valera as Devil Eire,' he explained.

The Prime Minister's delegation sped across the border to a small town, called Clones, in the west of County Monagon. The meeting was to be held in an old courthouse, in top security.

The building was protected by both the Irish Garda, and Churchill's own security guards.

Susan had expected a cool reception when the two leaders met. She was very surprised when it finally happened. It was all very cordial.

A further surprise was that de Valera was accompanied by Linda Gill, the Irish Special Branch officer, who had minded over her at Dublin Castle. Susan remembered how cold the Irish woman had been. She was rather taken aback when Linda Gill gave her a hearty handshake.

CHAPTER SIXTY FOUR
The Taoiseach

'We are agreed, Mr Churchill, that we have only one item on the agenda. That is to say, the contents of the diaries,' the Irish Prime Minister spoke in a quiet tone.

'Indeed, Mr de Valera. I assume that you have read them?' Churchill was fishing. He wanted to know just how much the Taoiseach knew.

'Mr Churchill I found them rather long and boring,' Mr de Valera admitted. 'But Miss Gill here has kept me informed of your Sergeant's remarkable progress with them. I cannot understand why the British crown made the decision to put the hundred year ruling on them in 1845.'

Churchill smiled at Susan.

'I think our young Sergeant here has discovered the answer to that question.'

The Irish Prime Minister tried to remember what he had read in the diaries.

'It appears to me that Robert O'Neill was a great Irishman. He was at the forefront of his country's struggle with the British Crown. He was a reformer, who worked to abolish female and child labour in the coal mines. He exposed the corrupt practices of the railway directors, and profiteers. His diary demonstrates the vital importance of Irish labour to your railways, but at such a sad cost of life.'

Churchill listened with avid interest. He had been fully expecting a lecture by the Irish leader. The annexed six Northern Counties had been always a stumbling block in their relations.

'As you know,' the Irishman continued. 'My aim is for a united Ireland. I will never rest until we achieve that end.

The sovereignty of the British nation is of no concern to me unless it affects the interests of our Irish state. When you spoke of conscription in the North during your war with Germany, it enlisted many of our Catholic subjects. This would have been against their will.'

'Mr de Valera,' Churchill answered. 'We differ in our beliefs on many matters, but I have come here today on this great matter. I do not wish to discuss our other differences. They are not under consideration today.'

'I agree, Mr Churchill. Let us put all other matters to one side and stick to the agenda.' Eamon de Valera consulted his notes. 'The biggest embarrassment, as far as I can see, is this Royal Duke. He was the Prince Regent's brother and the brother in law of Queen Victoria. Was he not?'

Churchill nodded.

'It has taken this young lady months to research the diaries,' he said.

Susan was ready to explain everything to the Irish Taoiseach, but Churchill shot her a warning glance. He realised that de Valera knew that Duke Frederick had been a loose cannon. But did he want the Irish government to know that the Duke, a close ancestor of the Queen, had been a murderer, mentally unbalanced by syphilis? De Valera only had O'Neill's diaries as evidence.

Churchill, ever the strategist, decided that he would not reveal the full truth to Eamon de Valera. He did not want the Irish leader to know all the details. The last thing he wanted was for the Taoiseach to use the information as some sort of blackmailing weapon to gain advantage over the British Crown.

'I am not going to be the one to cause an embarrassment to your new Queen,' de Valera announced, rather surprising Churchill. 'The coronation is in June. Is it not?'

'That's correct,' Churchill agreed.

'As I see it, the only solution is to put the diaries away for another hundred years, and let somebody else deal with it all. I have far more pressing matters.' It was obvious to Churchill that the Irish Taoiseach was looking for something in return.

Churchill breathed a huge sigh of relief, and lit his first Havana cigar of the meeting.

'Do you have brandy in this Godforsaken town, Mr de Valera? I know you are going to ask me for British investment, but what else are your pressing matters?'

'Mr Churchill. It was you who put the 1922 border through this town. So it is your fault it is Godforsaken,' de Valera said, with a wry smile.

'The Irish history is different to the English version. It was Lloyd George who separated the six counties.' Churchill had the last word on the matter. 'Let us put that to one side. Whiskey will suffice.'

CHAPTER SIXTY FIVE
1981
The Last Train

'Is it really the last train, Roger?' Susan asked her husband, as they were driving to Dunford Bridge.

'It sure is, Miss Sergeant,' Roger Thompson answered. It was a July morning, in 1981. 'It's the Harwich ferry train, and it will be coming through the tunnel at dawn.'

Roger and Susan's oldest daughter Samantha accompanied them. She was the same age as Susan had been when she was investigating the murders in the tunnel. She had followed in her parents' footsteps, studying for a doctorate in history at university.

'I always wondered why you called mummy Miss Sergeant,' Samantha said, from the back of the car. 'Is this place really the reason why you met? What were you doing here?'

'We were investigating some murders back in 1952. They had been committed a hundred years before, when the first tunnel was being built,' Susan explained.

They were surprised to see a lot of people waiting at the dilapidated station. Everyone was waiting to see the last train go through the Woodhead tunnel.

Roger got his Eumig Super 8mm cine camera ready to film the event for posterity.

If only people knew the truth about this place, thought Susan. She had not even told her husband everything about the murders. She was still sworn to secrecy under the Official Secrets Act.

Two massive electric locomotives, hauling their ten carriages, came out of the tunnel and roared through the little station. Cameras clicked, and the engine driver waved at the large crowd.

Susan thought of the first train in 1845. She could still recall how the Earl of Wexford had described the event. There was no bunting, decorations, grand speeches, or troops in dashing blue uniforms now. It was the end of an era.

THE END

ABOUT THE AUTHOR

Dave Cherry was born in Barnsley and is proud of his roots. A former miner and electrician, he's developed into a true Renaissance man of Barnsley culture.

He became a household name in Barnsley with his comedy song 'The Stairfoot Rarndabart', which pokes fun at the local bottleneck. This song alone made £20,000 for the Barnsley Hospice.

Dave is rarely out of the pages of the Barnsley Chronicle, 'I'm in more than the mayor," jokes Dave. He's lost count of the times he's appeared on local radio and TV too.

Dave's musical comedy, 'The Old Club Trip', was performed at the Lamproom Theatre in Barnsley for three years in succession. This show raised another £24,500 for the hospice.

In total to date, he has raised over £69,000 for the hospice, as well as money for other charitable organisations.

Another of Dave's passion is the transference of old films to a digital format. Dave learned how to copy old cine films, and as an avid historian, he is fascinated by films showing local places in bygone days.

Dave now has over four hours of archive cine films in his private collection and has donated a lot of films to the new *Experience Barnsley* Museum.

'The Woodhead Diaries' is his first novel, and it reflects his deeply-held values of socialism and equality.

Made in the USA
Charleston, SC
10 November 2014